WELCOME TO

ABYSS

The Abyss line of cutting-edge psychological horror is committed to publishing the best, most innovative works of dark fiction available. ABYSS is horror unlike anything you've ever read before. It's not about haunted houses or evil children or ancient Indian burial grounds. We've all read those books, and we all know their plots by heart.

ABYSS is for the seeker of truth, no matter how disturbing or twisted it may be. It's about people, and the darkness we all carry within us. ABYSS is the new horror from the dark frontier. And in that place, where we come face-to-face with terror, what we find is ourselves.

"Thank you for introducing me to the remarkable line of novels currently being issued under Dell's Abyss imprint. I have given a great many blurbs over the last twelve years or so, but this one marks two firsts: first *unsolicited* blurb (*I* called *you*) and the first time I have blurbed a whole *line* of books. In terms of quality, production, and plain old storytelling reliability (that's the bottom line, isn't it?), Dell's new line is amazingly satisfying . . . a rare and wonderful bargain for readers. I hope to be looking into the Abyss for a long time to come."

—Stephen King

Please turn the page for more extraordinary acclaim . . .

HEART-BEAST

TANITH LEE

A DELL BOOK

"The moon is a mask"
Tanith Lee, *The Book of the Dead*

PART ONE

PART ONE

1

The blinds, which were down, filled the room with the yellow colour of the inside of a peach. Within this globe of yellow the man and woman wove about each other like two naked icons of amber.

It was the height of the day. Outside, above a familiar hubbub, the bodiless voice uncoiled from a minaret, calling the Faithful to prayer.

Marjannah's black hair hung over the side of the bed in three sliding ropes. Her arms, flung backward, clenched the tawny pillows, and her mouth, mulberry in the light, parted on a low scream. Her slender legs locked the back of her partner, and her anklets of thin gold clicked together.

Daniel Vehmund rode her body, making upon it the immemorial stabbing motions of the sexual act. His hips were narrow and hard, smooth—like his back—as ivory, and from his frantic head the hair rained golden as the aura of the room.

Marjannah cried again and arched her pelvis upward.

Disturbed by mysterious carnal currents, or some breath of air through the lattice, little bells rang on a slender chain. And, in a cage, a topaz bird let out a chirp.

"Kill me," said Marjannah.

Her arms poured from the pillows to clutch the assassin's back. She uttered two wild and sobbing shrieks that each pierced all other sound, soared, and sank to nothing. Gasping, Daniel hung above her, then sank on her motionless body.

"Death," said Marjannah. "My beloved."

They lay still for perhaps fifteen seconds, and then Daniel eased away from her and turned on to his spine.

Marjannah sighed.

"For those moments you are mine," she said.

Daniel smiled. For those moments, it seemed to him, he was no one's, not even his own, but possessed solely by the demon of pleasure, a blind spasming thing of fires.

Marjannah stroked Daniel's hair, cheekbones; and the bird in the cage began to trill, fluttering on its perch.

"I shall have the girl fetch us coffee and sweetmeats."

"Not today, Marjannah."

"Can you be this heartless as to leave me so early?"

"There's someone I have to meet."

"You lie to me. You do not wish to stay with me."

That was true. "It would be Paradise on earth to stay with you. But God makes us perform our duty."

"You have no duty."

"Yes. I expect a man with a letter from my mother."

"I do not believe in your mother."

"I have one."

Marjannah rose from the bed and stretched her beautiful body, her hair rippling and her anklets clacking.

Daniel watched her in a silent holy appreciation of her splendour, which in no sort would retain him further that day.

In acknowledgement, the girl put on her embroidered robe, and touching the tassels of the blinds, let them up.

Parched light burst in. Certain shabbinesses of the room were revealed: torn threads, a mouse-hole. The topaz bird had turned to a virtuous white, and it strutted up and down.

Daniel rose. As he dressed himself in his under-linen, shirt and breeches, he glimpsed outside the close-hung roofs which scaled, like counters, to the market of the sukh. Across the sukh, far away, tall slender towers arose with teardrop domes of coloured mosaic.

He was not happy exactly, but the thought of the probable letter excited him. He knew that when he had read it, a descent would come, as if from strong wine. He would be filled with yearnings, rage and hatred. But these he held at bay. He had given way to great anger once before, and that had brought him here, to this strange exotic environment of brilliant dyes and alien sounds, its smells of spice and vice, its ornamental women, and surges of a religion that to the cold churches of his earlier youth was like a blast of burning.

"Shall I see my lord after the sun sets?" asked Marjannah, with what he took for the humility of her false repertoire. Doubtless she would put him from her mind as soon as he was gone.

"No, sweetheart. Not tonight."

"Alas." But she smiled.

Perhaps she would entertain, instead, the rich Turk who courted her. Daniel did not much care. Marjannah was a spirit of the exotic environment.

He took a fruit from a pottery dish and went out of the room. "Farewell," she said. In the corridor he saw the 'girl'—the old servant woman—in her cubicle, preparing thick sweet coffee. She grunted, but did not speak to him.

On the outer stairs, where sometimes the prostitutes brought their customers by night, were broken flowers

and sun, and the tang of urine. He passed the vacant
room of the porter known as the Black Giant.

The great heat had waited.

He passed along an alley of brown shadows, over
which fig trees hung their waxen bulbs. A concertina of
narrow steps ran down between the walls, which almost
touched, overhung by a vase of red roses on a balcony.
High up floated rags to dry, and then the dried sky, which
looked less blue than indigo.

Daniel Vehmund moved out into the sukh, under its
crimson and ochre hangings. Today the market seemed
full of camels. They trod between the stalls at the midst
of an open square, stinking and proud, accoutred like
brides. The man with the letter would not have come
with a caravan from the mountains, but up from the port.
He was to be found where the agent always sent them, at
the French Inn on the edge of the sukh's southmost quarter.

The crowd was, as ever, mostly heavy and idle. Daniel
pushed his way through. There were no women but those
of the lowest sort, beneath modesty, servants or slaves.
Once or twice one saw a carrying-chair borne through, its
veiled entrance strung with beads, smelling of jasmine
and musk.

A man flung five daggers in the air, flashing, catching
them by their hilts. The usual snake-charmer was at the
turning of the booths, by the doll-makers. The serpent
swayed from the pitcher, sinisterly following the motion
of the pipe. Beyond, the dolls were giving a puppet-show,
and Daniel paused to watch a turbaned warrior embat-
tled with a jinn. The warrior whacked with his crescent
sword, and the jinn collapsed in a clashing of copper
discs: the battle of good with evil was always easily solved
in stories. But the crowd cheered and clapped.

Across the layers of the sukh, a wall of the inn was growing visible, its sign of a ship, European and incongruous, above the stars and blades and magical tokens of the market.

Daniel eased through a knot of hagglers and stepped around a gambling party on the ground. He was by now accustomed to the occasional exclamation or pointing of fingers. Fair northern skin was not unknown here, but his blond hair elicited comment, and his eyes had sometimes caused a little trouble. The Evil Eye was feared by ignorant and wise alike, it seemed, and any uncommon thing concerning the eye might denote it. Daniel's eyes were of an odd colour, tawny like washed brass. Hazel, his mother had called them.

A tall man in a dark robe stood in a little space, looking fixedly at Daniel.

Before the man was a board, and on it three earthen cups. A few of the idlers stood about, to see the ancient trick performed, but none willing to bet on where the object, to be hidden beneath one cup, would next appear.

The man had a long and bony face, pockmarked and sallow. His head was wound in a faded white cloth. He beckoned to Daniel peremptorily.

Daniel would have walked on, but a fellow in the crowd, perhaps the man's accomplice, took his arm and urged him suddenly forward, "Come, come."

Daniel shook him off. "No."

The pockmarked man had produced something which shone and flashed, as the knives had done. A jewel of glass most probably. He slipped it under the central cup, and moved the vessels rhythmically about over the table, circling each other, finding new places.

When the cups stopped moving, the idlers laughed. No one would guess where the object now lay, certain that it would not lie where it seemed to, for at this trick, old as antique Greece, the bystander was always wrong.

Daniel shrugged and walked off across the sukh. The fellow did not snatch at him again.

Hungry dogs clustered at the foot of the French Inn and, even as Daniel approached, someone kicked them away, a drunkard come out into the air, who hailed Daniel like a long-lost brother. Daniel manoeuvred by him, and entered the pungent darkness of the tavern.

At once a kind of fear dropped over Daniel. He knew it, and paid it no heed. He reached the counter and addressed the one-eyed man. "A sailor from the *Algerac*? Is he here?"

"Over there, Monsieur. The bearded one in the corner."

Daniel proceeded through the gloom, jostled by rough shoulders now, and the languages of three or four nations. He got to the table, and sat down facing the bearded sailor.

"You have a letter for me?"

"You are to give your name," said the sailor.

"Vehmund."

"I have a letter for Vehmund."

The dirty fingers went into the dirty coat, and came out bearing a sealed paper. Thus it had travelled, this thing from his mother, in God knew what makeshift and filthy resting places, gripped and passed by what foul and feckless paws. A wonder it had reached him.

Daniel held out his hand.

"You are to pay me."

"The letter first."

The sailor grunted, gave up the letter, then took the fistful of sous.

"You aren't generous, Monsieur Vehmund."

"I gave you what you were promised."

How many times this, or like, dialogue?

The sailor slurped his vinegary wine, and turned away to look at the women displayed on the gallery. One, an Arab girl with a fringed shawl and black kohl eyes, drew his attention. He got up sullenly and sidled off.

Daniel broke the seal of the letter. His hands shook and, after all, he did not want to read it, to begin again . . . to go back. But the closely written, educated lincs were already before him. *My dearest* . . . Sometimes the handwriting was altered, girlish and not her own, as if she were too tired and had called another to form the letter for her—but who was there to call on?

A wave of sorrow poured through his body, numbing his limbs. She wrote in so ordinary a way, as if nothing were amiss. News of the farm, which his brother was managing, of the seasons, the winter lambs, a spring storm. As if he must pine for all this, which in any case was not properly known to him. He had come back to her that first time a stranger, as it seemed she had meant him to. He remembered how he had seen her at the doorway of the house, milk-white in her pale gown, and her hair turned grey. A madonna of smoke.

And after the words of the farm, her truths and lies about herself. *'I am quite well these days, and Janet and I have been baking, up to our chins in flour. All the cats have had their kittens, and we are overrun with cats worse than the mice. I let them sleep their sleeps on my bed now, if they want.'* By that message alone assuring him of the vast change which he had wrought, striking off her shackles— and at the thought his heart beat, almost choking him. He pushed memory away, and read of the small things of the farm, and so came to the glimpsed soul of the letter. *'I miss you so, more with every day. But I am content to miss you as long as you prosper. Write to me soon and tell me everything. Is there money enough still, and does your employer grant you a better wage? Is your health good?'* And then, *'I fear you must stay away some months longer, to assure your success.'*

What had it cost her to pen these words? To couch the fact in such general and evasive terms?

Some months . . . It was a year since he had left her; they had known he must be absent at least so long, and much more. For his brother, though a brute, was not quite a fool. But she was safe from the brute, it seemed; she had promised to tell him if otherwise. Would she keep her promise? How many aeons had gone by, his childhood, his years at the city school, when she had hidden everything, and he, conniving, had not seen it.

In the hot and shadowy inn he read her farewells to him, and the letter was over, ended.

A boy glided to his table, knowing infallibly the moment.

"Urak."

The boy slid away, and returned instants later with the misleadingly small jug of spirit and the deceptive little glass.

Daniel Vehmund drank the liquor, and a terrible darkness, deeper, steeper than the shadow of the inn, enclosed him. No longer a creature of sunlight with his pastel tan and golden hair and eyes, but black as night in that corner the sailor had vacated for the quim of the Arab girl.

And the inn drew off and left him in his darker darkness.

When he had finished the jug he turned it, as was traditional here, mouth down on the table, got up and left the tavern. He was steady enough; the drunkenness of the urak had sent him only inwards to the core of an unbearable pain which, at this time, he must always touch in order to resist it.

Remote now the clustering sukh, its notes and smells.

The man in the faded turban had remained at his table. His crowd had drifted off, yet still he moved the vessels over and about each other. Daniel stopped to watch him, and a sourceless fascination held him there. Hypnotically the cups moved, as the snake to the charmer's music. Where was the glass jewel?

The cups ceased their motion. The pockmarked man looked up and met Daniel's gaze with his own black eyes. Daniel shook his head.

The man turned up the cups one by one. Nothing lay under any of them.

The sukh, pressing on every side, seemed distant, a mile off. But this man was close, and the board empty.

Then the pockmarked man opened his lips and out ran his tongue. It was grey and horrible, like the tongue of some lizard. And on the tongue, a water-drop on a diseased petal, rested the jewel of glass. It gave off one huge spark, like lightning. It was pure and cold, more real than anything, the sukh, the sky, the earth or air.

"By Christ, a diamond," Daniel Vehmund said.

The tongue, lizard-like, snapped back, and the jewel vanished.

The man waited, mysteriously.

"What do you want?" Daniel said.

The man, the jewel pent in his mouth, jerked his head and, raising his hand, beckoned Daniel forward, as if he knew him and was his guide.

Daniel reached into his coat, drew out a coin worth more than he had paid for the letter, and tossed it against the empty cups. "A clever trick."

He walked away quickly, through the unreal sukh. The image of the diamond did not leave him. It was printed like a blot of darkness on the day—a blot of white fire within his lids.

Afternoon was spent in the orange grove of Surim Bey's courtyard. At his desk beneath the awning, Daniel copied out, in fair flowery English and fancier French, his employer's letters to various foreign merchants of the region. He was the secretary of Surim Bey, who paid him his wages, the money on which he subsisted. A fat coffee-coloured man of middle years, with bright sloe eyes, Surim Bey was not often in person seen by Daniel.

But, on this afternoon, Surim Bey came swimming down into the courtyard from the pavilion above on the roof. He wore his white house robes, a scarlet cap, and Moorish shoes thickly embroidered. His tread was soft as his voice.

"My young secretary at his work. Turning my ugly words into pretty phrases."

"Sir," said Daniel, shortly. He had refused from the first to offer him the honorific of *Lord*.

"Continue, continue," said Surim Bey, and crossed the shady square beneath the awning, to sit down on a divan. To this a slave presently crawled and tendered sweets and sherbet.

Daniel Vehmund went on writing.

Surim Bey watched him with his deceptively languid, glittering eyes. Daniel intrigued him, and though the infidel was rather too old for Surim Bey's sexual taste, he had drawn out inventiveness. It was the golden-ness of Daniel's youth which attracted his master's attention. Surim Bey had been moved, now and then, on other afternoons, to experiment upon Daniel. Sometimes the ex-

periments were so slight as to go unnoticed. Yet on one
occasion a naked girl, her face veiled, had crossed the
courtyard between the pots of orange trees reflecting in
the fish-tank. And, on another a half-tame cheetah had
sprung down from a window of the first storey. To both
these apparitions, girl and cat, Daniel had given only half
a look. He knew the extent of his master's power, ac-
corded these visions the label of his master's ownership,
and left them alone. The cheetah had indeed come to his
writing table (the girl had not), and Daniel had gone on
with his work. He showed no fear, as he had shown neither lust nor shame at the girl's nudity. Surim Bey had
observed avidly from an upper room, through the lens of
a magnifying emerald. But in its green scope the cheetah
only trotted away and the girl slunk through an arch, and
Daniel was left pristine as a shell upon a shore.

Today the experimenter had another means to hand.

As Daniel finished with the letters, leaving them neatly
stacked, Surim Bey called to him gently.

"Come, sit here. I will reward your labours with a piece
of this divine lacum."

"I don't eat such sweets," said Daniel, standing before
him.

Surim Bey was enchanted by Daniel's beauty, and by
his otherness. If only he had been eleven or twelve, or a
little younger, a slave from the markets. But Daniel was
free, a man, and marked with a cicatrice of darkness.
God in His omniscience knew what it was, this shadow.
On some afternoons it stood black as a demon at his
shoulder. As now.

"No, you must not displease me. Sit here. Let me tell
you something of the nature of this sweet you so de-
spise."

Daniel was the man's servant. He sat, neither close to nor far off from Surim Bey, and waited.

Surim Bey drew a sacred sign in the air, gracefully, and on his fat hand the metal rings smouldered.

"There was a sultan whose favourite had betrayed him. He slew her and her paramour. But then, in his grief, he would eat no food. He faded, growing thinner by the day. The grand vizier brought to the palace courts a sweet-maker of great renown. 'Make a sweet to tempt the mouth of the sultan. If you succeed your fortune is assured. If you fail, it is the axe for you.' The sweet-maker hurried home in terrible fear. That night an angel visited him, and gave to him the skin of a virgin bull written with script of gold. It described the recipe for a sweet never before devised or dreamed of. The sweet-maker set to work, and before the sun rose he had concocted a lacum so lush that he himself trembled. It was borne to the palace and offered to the sultan, who at its smell could not resist. And so delicious was the sweet that the blood came back to his heart and his joy in life returned to him. He grew well and prospered for a hundred years. And this, my dear Daniel Vehmund, is the story of the lacum which you spurn, a delight invented in Paradise."

"He would have done better to have spared the woman," said Daniel, coldly.

"Woman? Which woman?"

"The favourite who preferred another man."

"Oh, hush," said Surim Bey, easily. "You are uncouth, you Europeans. Cruelty, too, has its loveliness. That is not the point of the tale."

Daniel said nothing, then he said, "Your story, sir, doesn't make me want to eat the sweet."

Surim Bey reached out and chose from the platter one

of the tinted sugary pieces of the lacum. He savoured it. At last he swallowed it.

"I have told you a legend, however. Now you must tell me in return some extraordinary thing."

Daniel said, "Today I saw a diamond in the sukh."

"That is indeed extraordinary. It was not a diamond. To find such jewels you must attend the shops behind the Street of Silk. Or is this a riddle? You saw the diamond upon the person of some rich man conducted by his slaves?"

"I saw it on the tongue of a trickster moving three cups about on a board."

Surim Bey brooded. "That is very strange. It cannot then have been a diamond. Would you know a diamond? Have you seen them often?"

"Only in books."

"Glass. It was glass. Or quartz perhaps."

"Not so extraordinary then."

"No, you have interested me. Let me tell you something else about this lacum. Into it are mixed a few flakes of other stuff. It will surprise you."

"Opium."

"Not at all. A hashish so fine it is called *Kindness*."

Daniel said, "What would I gain from eating it?"

"What did you gain from the urak your eyes tell me you have been drinking? To know yourself, perhaps. Or some other thing. Whether or not you saw a diamond."

Daniel took a piece of the lacum. He ate it slowly, indifferently. Surim Bey smiled and watched him. The fat man's sensual pleasure, in this case, came all from looking, observing.

No change, however, appeared to take place in Daniel. He seemed only a little sullen.

From the minarets up in the sky the unhuman voice began to call to prayer.

"I must go in to God," said Surim Bey, standing up in one flowing movement. "And you to your retreat, my lion."

"Shall I come tomorrow?"

"Yes, there will be letters from three cities I will have you read to me."

Daniel nodded. As he rose in turn, the courtyard swelled a little, as if it breathed. There was no other thing.

Outside the walls of Surim Bey's house, beyond its door that had on it in bronze a manticore, a man-headed leopard with a scorpion's tail, the narrow streets were now flecked and flickered by approaching sunset.

Porters hurried with their burdens, beneath prayer as the lowly women were beneath shame. In yards, and spaces about a stone well perhaps, with a single palm tree, others had bowed down.

In the sukh, when he came to it, the devout prayed and the ordinary did not. The sun was a flattened golden blaze behind the distant towers.

Daniel walked to the place where the man had played with the three cups. But he was gone, all trace of him brushed away, for now a dark astrologer's booth was there, set up for the night.

It was the diamond Daniel wanted, to see it again and maybe to touch. A crystal of pain, so clear and hard, a tear of agonized fury pushed from the earth like pus from a wound. Why, Daniel did not know. But for how long his emotions had been mysterious, and ruled him. He gave way to them, controlling only their outer show in order to protect himself from others. There had come that moment, in the cold land he had left, that moment when he had crossed over from reality to sin, and so to feeling. The moment when he had grasped the neck of the man between his hands, and rage had given him the strength to crush the life from him, so that as he crushed he beat the shaggy filthy head against the stone mantel of the fireplace in a sort of searing joy. Then, and since then, in a kind of dream, Daniel Vehmund wandered the world. He saw on his flight and in his hiding these sights which on the normal path he never would have; and he lived in a manner different and unusual. And he was altered. He had relinquished or become himself in a way few creatures can or would desire to. And this also he knew, remotely.

And now, in this marketplace of the alien East where he inhabited, a source of intriguement and appeal for others, he wanted the diamond as a child wants a star, with all the profound need of a man.

It was as if the stone were his. It was as if the stone were animate.

So now he cast about him, turning his head a little.

The sun was slipping away. The sky above darkened and lifted to an incredible height, in which planets and suns hung on their invisible cords.

A boy in rags came from the astrologer's booth to light a torch upon a post.

Daniel turned through the market and away into the side streets that ran down towards the port. The flowers of the hashish called *Kindness* had opened inside his brain. The opening revealed to him his great lust for the diamond which perhaps was glass, and guided him towards it, down into dangerous quarters, the warrens of one-roomed houses plastered together from the mud, like termite mounds.

All true light but that of the tiny white planets and suns overhead died behind him. Now and then a trickle of light that was not light, but murky yellow as oil, spilled from some crack or crevice. Or a window, dull russet like a brick, appeared on the black above in a lattice of bars. The rats scurried. Men scurried from doorway to doorway. In the gutter lay the corpse of a dog vitreous with flies. A great ghostly moth quivered on a wall.

Suddenly, between the dome of sky and the termite mounds, a gap showed the pale blade of the sea, acres below, behind an ancient wall. Against the wall the hovels and cells cluttered, clambering over each other, the slits of doors above the slashes of windows. No light at all was exuded from this place, and no sound but the whine of night insects, and from somewhere a terrible rhythmic clatter like pots smitten on each other.

Daniel felt himself confused and lost. Then the germ of the hashish cleared again a road for him.

A hole stared from the jumble of the hard mud.

He went to it, and atoms fled into the darkness either side. Putting out his hand he felt a wooden door, which at his thrust gave way. Bending his head, he stepped into a cave all full of eyes which watched him, as Marjannah and Surim Bey watched him, crouching for purchase on shelves of the dark air.

Then a lamp was lit at the back of the cave, and he saw the man who had played with the cups in the sukh, sitting there on the ground, behind the lamp, watching him also, and the hundred other eyes took fire.

The room was full of objects piled on each other, old brown parchments and tarnished skins, even perhaps of virgin bulls with golden script . . . There were chests and caskets that winked and blinked. And everywhere mummified cats, stacked in their wound wrappings, gazed down from lapis eyes and eyes of green glass paste.

It was a treasury in the hovel. There were rich things there and awful things.

But the pockmarked man sat behind his lamp, and he beckoned again, as he had in the sukh.

Daniel did not inquire what the man wanted. It was what he, Daniel, wanted, now.

He went across the room and sat down facing the man, so the lamp shone between them.

The man filled two stone cups from a leather bottle. He passed one cup to Daniel, and the flame burned red through his hand above the lamp. "Urak."

"Perhaps you've poisoned it." Daniel thought of his body picked clean; his hair and teeth, his bones, taken away for use; and his flayed skin hung for the making of a book.

"You are my guest. You are welcome to my house. I must treat you as I would treat my son. That is the Law."

"Is there Law here?"

"Everywhere."

"But your Law isn't mine," Daniel said.

"God is forgiving. At the last you have only to tell Him you were mistaken, and to speak His true name, and He will receive you."

Daniel tested the urak on his tongue. It tasted of fire and earth. It seemed innocent, and surely, at this moment, he would know otherwise. He drank the mouthful of spirit down, and something clinked against the inside of the stone cup. He looked into it. The drink shone black, and he could see nothing.

"It is there," said the pockmarked man.

Daniel put his fingers into the cup and something hard and tense was there against them. He drew it out, and it came from the drink's blackness like a white orb from cloud. The lamp struck on it. It flashed. He held the diamond in his hand.

Daniel set down the cup and wiped the jewel on his sleeve.

It was oval in shape, about the largeness of a pigeon's egg. Faceted, it gleamed and glared, holding the lamp within itself over and over. A glimmer of greenness, like a ripple on an English lake, moved through the colourless intensity. And it was faintly flawed: a shadow, in the depths of its brilliance, coming and going. Not real. It was a shape of some special quartz—or some silicate ember carefully cut and burnished to this luminance.

It had imbued the urak he had drunk.

He held the jewel like a lightning bolt.

"A clever toy," he said, as he had complimented the trick in the market.

"No, it is a stone old almost as creation." The man folded his hands. "I shall tell you where I found it."

"Another story," said Daniel.

"I am a robber of tombs," said the man quietly. "I am under the curse of death many times. These curses eat me piece by piece, yet still I live. I fear nothing now, not even fear itself."

"Glass or quartz," said Daniel. He drank more of the urak, and felt the flower of the hashish dying in his brain.

"A diamond forced up from the gut of the earth, discovered in darkness, struck free when your race was young and mine not much older." The man bowed his head. "It was an old tomb, and in it were golden grave goods. A bane was written on the doorway, and I held my breath in case the dust there was venomous. In the inner chamber the corpse lay in his painted box, with the husks of old marigolds upon it. He wore a diadem of pearls, but in his bowel, which had rotted away, yes lodged in the blind worm of his anus, *there* I found it."

"And where was this?" Daniel asked, holding the jewel lightly, carelessly.

"In a land of rocks and carved temples. Perhaps he had been a king."

Inside the jewel the shadow had a form as it came and went. Long and low, something on four legs, some beast.

"If your story were true," said Daniel.

"It is true. More true than life, or Now. The present is never real. Only the past. Sometimes the future."

"Here," Daniel said, and he held out the silicate or quartz or glass for the man to take.

The man said, "It is called The Wolf, for the image some see in it. Do you see it?"

"No."

From the ceiling of the hovel, which seemed disproportionately high, mummified bats depended, and a vulture-thing with a golden head. On a parchment caught by the lamp's glow were the signs of the zodiac over the strand, perhaps, of India.

Daniel pushed the diamond at the pockmarked man. Who turned his hand aside.

"It is yours," the man said.

"I won't buy it."

"Sometimes it is bought—but it is not to be bought. It is yours."

"Then I don't want it."

Daniel put the diamond called Wolf down beside the lamp. The flame in the lamp fluttered, sank, rose again. He felt very sick, chilled and cramped, as if one of the evil fevers of the port were fastening on him.

The man did not look up as Daniel got to his feet.

The room lurched, and all the dead cats watched; and

far off the ghastly rattle of crocks beaten against each other went on and on.

"Take it," said the man, "for the love of God, I entreat you."

Daniel found the door and went out into the dirt streets of the termite hills.

A half moon shone on the scimitar of the sea. Its light pulled on his eyes like thin chains, and, leaning on a corner of a mud house, he vomited fire into the darkness. It was the rattling of the pots which made him sick, if only it would stop. He blundered upon them, a line of broken vessels tied up and cracking together in the wind, amulets against some jinn. He stumbled in circles, and a woman like death plucked on his sleeve. "Come to my house. I will tend you—" And later three skeletal dogs followed him along a lane of rubbish.

Then he saw again on a wall the moth, or another, and, turning out of the alleys of the warren, passed a courtyard with lemon trees and the music of a five-stringed lute.

Daniel climbed up to his lodging and lay down on the bed while the room tipped like a boat.

He saw his mother sitting upright in a chair, with the line of red blood coming from her nostril; and on the table, like a tear of the moon, lay the diamond, pulsing and green, and the beast ran inside it all through the night, lifting its head at the voice from the tower that called to prayer.

The next day, soon after sunrise, Marjannah came with the Black Giant, and bent over him in a ray of light that might only have been the sun. She told Daniel nonsensically that the fortune-teller had revealed his sickness by the tracks of the little snake in the sand. The Black Giant raised Daniel in his arms and carried him in a blanket through the early streets, to the room of saffron blinds.

For two days, and their dark halves of nights, the fever bore Daniel on. He was lucid and raved by turns. Even in his raving he heard his own words, and did not betray himself.

Marjannah had brought in a physician from the tenements, an old man who smelled pleasantly of perfume and anise, who touched him on the brow, heart and testicles, tenderly. Some medicine was prescribed and an incense burnt in a brazier beneath one of the windows. The incense made the bird drunk, and it sang all day and sometimes through the night. Its song seemed sweeter than a nightingale's, or perhaps Daniel imagined this. Marjannah fed him milk soup and bits of fruit.

He was not grateful to Marjannah. He wished she had left him alone.

He dreamed he was suspended in a deep fissure in the ground, and the greenish diamond shone in on him. His body writhed and twisted like water in a channel. He dragged himself out on to the land in moonlight. It was a sandy place, but on the cliffs the tumuli of temples stood. He could not rise to his feet, but ran like a beast over the white sand. He knew, even in the dream, that the dream lied, that this fantasy was a cipher, not even the emblem of a reality. Then he woke each time on Marjannah's bed, and Marjannah lay on the floor on a rug with one cushion under her head.

The first two days and nights the Black Giant, coming in from his portering, had carried Daniel to the latrine like a baby. But on the third day Daniel was a man again. He thanked the porter for his care and gave him some

money. He thanked Marjannah. He would need to buy
her a present.

She begged him not to go. She had sent a messenger to
the house of Surim Bey to explain Daniel's absence. He
must stay and allow her to tend him.

Marjannah was a freed slave. She had belonged only to
one man, who at his death had set her free. Daniel had,
in his early days among these streets, seen her at her
window. Her unveiled smiling face had told him all that
was necessary and he had mounted the steps to her.

There had remained in Marjannah a slavishness. She
longed to be the property again of one man, and tried her
hardest to attach herself to Daniel Vehmund, his golden
foreignness and difference. Then, again, the Turk would
possess her if Daniel did not. The Turk would immure
her inside marble screens and hang her closed apartment
with roses.

Marjannah cajoled Daniel to remain, and next
tempted him to sex. He told her he was not yet fit
enough. She said that if he was not fit enough for con-
gress, he was not fit to go alone to his lodging. The old
woman-girl put down a dish of spicy pastes and black
bread. They ate together, and the voice called from the
towers. Daniel thought of the pots clacking together in
the wind of that windless night. *Kindness* had enabled
him to find the pockmarked man; or had that only been
another dream?

At last he escaped from the room of Marjannah and
went to the house of Surim Bey. The master did not
receive him, only the bespectacled indigenous secretary,
who heard Daniel's reading of the important letters and
wrote on his tablet accordingly.

Daniel wandered to a well in the sukh, and watched
the men watering their camels and mules, and the covert

women who came with pitchers. The fever had left upon him a deep depression. He saw no purpose in existence, the meaningless scrambling on the game-board of Fate.

Daniel's lodging lay east of the sukh. Here reared a crowd of tall yellow houses, packed with humanity: the artisans, musicians and petty shop-keepers of the quarter. There was seldom peace, even by night, squabbling and work being constant, the clink of hammer upon metal or cobbled leather, the gambling, the tuning of instruments, thin warbles of song, and shrill bawling of angry women. Beneath his high window two goats were housed in the courtyard under the vine, and some chickens scratched busily. The cock crew at dawn, and at other times when it decided.

As he approached this place through the slender network of streets, Daniel remembered the farmhouse of his childhood, the sounds of boots on winter mornings, and the tufts of sheep on grey-green hills. With tired astonishment, he felt no call upon him from the past; and yet it was true, as the man had said in the hovel, that only the present was unreal. Not until this place too had gone into the past would it gain credibility. For now it was a mirage.

The sun set as he came into the last street, which turned first a deep red and then an immaterial colour like cinders. Overhead the higher storeys leaned, and the old arch with the great stone jar, battered and riven, set at its foot.

He climbed a stair again and got into the upper half of the house.

Daniel reached his room, to which there was no lock, and went inside. A meager grudging chamber awaited him, well-known now and of no interest ever. He had brought nothing away with him to harbour here. The bed, merely a pallet on the floor, a stool, a jug kept for water by the window . . . and something new. Something unforeseen and peculiar. It sat in the shadow beside the window, before the box with his clothing, under the broken mirror.

Daniel approached. Pockmarked as a moon, the face unseamed from the shadow, and the eyes looking at him. The dirty cloth still wrapped up the head, but from the parted lips a rusty blackness had poured down into the dark garment. There is generally no mistaking the face of death. And Daniel had seen it before.

He knelt beside the dead man and found that his throat had been sliced and his tongue cut out. On the palm of each of the hands, which rested open on the floor, an eye had been drawn in blood.

The corpse was terrifying and also mystical as it sat there by the nightfall of the window.

To Daniel, momentarily stunned, there came a truth.

The robber of tombs had in turn found his lodging and visited here to press on him again the diamond. But a thief had also been deceived by the glint of the jewel, and following, he had come in and slain the man, so taking the gem away with him.

A wild panic assailed Daniel. He fought it down. It was nothing to do with the dead thing, but only with the abduction of the jewel. And the jewel was not his. Even had it been genuine, what would he have cared for it? He did not understand the concept of riches; they meant nothing. Yet it was as if, in stealing the diamond, the thief had stolen also some part of Daniel Vehmund, some insubstantial vital element, nameless, inexplicable, and precious.

Daniel straightened.

The corpse must be removed from this room. Plainly

the drawing on the palms was the sigil of some guild of thieves, claiming the murder for a particular source. It might therefore be possible simply to thrust the body into the alley: The sigil of the eye would send suspicion to the proper area—though there would be no hue and cry. The dead man had no status.

Daniel's mind was empty, though jumbled by fragments of thought.

Night filled the top of the window and in the court the goats shifted, creatures of Satan. Otherwise an odd silence had dropped over the quarter.

Daniel leant once more to the dead man and pulled him up against the slot of the window. It would be awkward but not impossible to throw him out like garbage or excrement, outside the yard and over the wall.

The limp stem of the broken throat swivelled and the dead head rested on Daniel's shoulder. The dead lips twitched as if they would speak. Had he concealed the diamond in his mouth, as in the market—and was this the reason for the brutal act of cutting out the missing tongue? The buried king had swallowed the diamond whole, it had closed his bowel, maybe killing him.

Daniel heaved up the corpse, swung it over, out, and let it go. A black lozenge falling through air, it slid by the vine with only a rustle of leaves, and down beyond the outer wall. Affrighted by its passage, the goats bleated stridently, and ran across the enclosure. Daniel shuddered, and pressed his face a moment against the warm plaster. Then he poured water from the jug and washed his hands.

There would come eventually a complaint, as passagers in the alleyway stumbled on the dead. Perhaps they would not bother with it. Offended by its stench, some-

one on the ground floor would at last deliver it up for
burial.

Daniel paced the room, trying to cast off the spell of
fear that was on him. He had no feeling for the man
whose blood had been spilled in this room. He thought of
the man he had slaughtered with his own hands, the big
bulk lying across the stone hearth. There had been no
blood spilt then, and now no blood had smeared his
room, the trickster's robe had absorbed it.

Daniel knelt on the floor.

"Our Father, which art in heaven."

He prayed frankly, like a child, not understanding the
words but allowing them to calm him with their magic.

Below, the cobbler began to work with nails, and a wife
chanted at her pots. The goats had ceased bleating.
Blackness spread over the court and the alley.

The manticore burned on the door of Surim Bey, for a
lamp was lighted nightly above it.

Daniel stared at the beast as he waited for the porter
to answer his knocks.

"This is not your time," the porter admonished Daniel.

"Let me in."

"He is occupied," said the porter.

"Yes, he is with his boys. Let me in anyway."

The door was unbarred and unlocked, and Daniel
moved into the foyer of the house. Beyond the arches the
lamplit courtyard lay peacefully about its little pool of
golden fish.

A man came, seemed to think some urgent business
had brought Daniel, bowed low, and went above.

Presently Surim Bey stepped down the stair and across
the court. He wore a wide white robe embroidered with
purple iris, and in the wing of either arm came a honey

boy, clean and sweet, both composed and coy before Daniel's gaze.

"I await your command," said Surim Bey, not enraged, only dulcetly perplexed.

"I'm sorry to call on you at night."

"Yes, night is the season of songs. But you are not here to sing."

"To ask your help."

"My help?" Surim Bey enlarged his sloe eyes, about which the kohl made a black ribbon. One of the children giggled. And Surim Bey murmured, "Hush. We are in the presence of Destiny."

Daniel said, "There was death in my room."

Surim Bey opened his arms and the two boys uncoiled from his sleeves. "Away," he said, and they skipped off into the darkness like sprites, laughing, careless as gazelles.

Daniel stood beside the pool. The fish came and went on the rim of his eye, catching the light of the lamps and of the distant stars.

"Death?" said Surim Bey.

"A dead man. The man I told you of, from the sukh."

"The man with the diamond of glass."

"It must have been real. One other thought so."

"Who is that?"

"The thief who followed and killed him under my window."

Surim Bey looked upon the stars.

"And what has become of the body of the dead?"

"It lies in the alley. His hands bear the mark of an eye done in blood. The trademark of some band of cutthroats?"

Surim Bey shook his head slowly, as if beneath water not night.

"No, that is not the mark of the murderer, but a protection set by him. The *eye* is to distract the eyes of those who come to see; that is all."

"There's no reason any should connect the corpse to me."

"I trust not," said Surim Bey. "I should not like you to come to me with the jackals of the guard on your heels. What then do you want of me?"

"The diamond," said Daniel. "Shouldn't you like to look at it?"

"Yes. As much now as I should like to look on the Gardens of Paradise."

"The man had brought the jewel to me, and the thief took it."

"You wish that I should use my powers of influence to locate this thief, subtract from him the jewel, and offer it again to you. But you know that if it is such a wonder as it seems, I shall keep it. It will be *my* prize."

"You won't keep the jewel," said Daniel. "The jewel carries a curse. I know that you avoid such things."

"Why then should I trouble myself?"

"In case I'm mistaken, or I lie. Only when you have the jewel, will you know its properties."

"Has it a name?" said Surim Bey.

"That man called it The Wolf."

"It is unknown to me," said Surim Bey, "but I do not like its name."

"In size it's only a little smaller than a hen's egg, cut and polished, with a greenish aura. There's a flaw in the lower part resembling an animal, a dog or wolf, and so the name."

"Nor do I care for the description. Green as a jealous moon, having a beast trapped in it."

"From the tomb of a king."

"It will have come from Sind."

"Or from space," said Daniel, "like a levin bolt."

"Are you drunk?" asked Surim Bey. He came closer to Daniel and peered into his eyes. "No, this is not urak. Never have you spoken in such a way. The jewel has ensorcelled you."

"Yes," Daniel said.

"Tell me that you do not wish me to find the jewel. That will be better."

"Perhaps I can find it myself. Tell where I can purchase *Kindness*."

Surim Bey laughed scornfully, as if he sang. "That is not for you. I will do my best for you. Go from me now, and never disturb me in such a manner again. Do you understand?"

Daniel nodded. His face was savage as an angel's and Surim Bey watched him cross the court, the unquiet, nervous tread, and made in the air a warding sign. With such steps and faces of angels, men hastened to death or love.

Surim Bey spoke some words of the Law, and doused a lamp which hung above the fish-tank. Then he ascended slowly again into his room of joy, which promised no love but certainly a type of death.

He dreamed he was in a forest, like the thick woods above the farm, but very black, silent. Among the trees he came upon the dead man he himself had killed, and on his breast sat a black wolf, which licked at his neck. Blood began to flow and the wolf lapped it.

Daniel woke. He said aloud: "Something has happened."

Something had happened—to him. But probably it was only the thing that had happened months ago, catching up to him. It had run after him all this way, over earth, over water.

He lay on his back and saw the stars set high up in the window. There were noises in the building, a tapping, creakings, and somewhere the rhythm of a potter's lathe. Dogs howled and were still.

There was another noise he could not place, seemingly above the building, a faint drone of sound that slowly faded even as he distinguished it. Perhaps some strange wind from the mountains, or a semum off the plain.

He moved from the pallet over to the box, lit the candle he kept there, and took out his mother's letters.

Perversely, appropriately, as he looked at them, he heard a woman begin to weep below in the tenements. It was a bitter music; and then the semum rose again, and faded again. And he sat reading the five papers, all that had come to him in his months of exile. And it seemed to him he had no home to which to return, and nowhere he might advance to, that he was lost like a cork bobbing on the sea.

But he recalled the diamond.

Surim Bey was sure to find it, for Surim Bey was cunning and powerful. Surim Bey however would cheat him of the jewel, for it was not cursed, was it—only odd.

Yet, if he should regain the diamond . . .

His brain cleared and he suddenly saw the gem translated into money, coins and notes, and that this bought safety and strength, and these were worth having. Might he not after all go back, if he had money?

Then he thought the diamond was not real.

He put the letters away, blew out the candle and lay down. As he entered sleep, which came surprisingly quickly, he heard the semum swirling above the roof.

* * *

Attended by the Black Giant, and veiled for the streets, Marjannah came again and drew Daniel to her saffron room. She wore a thin red silk, like henna, dappled with brass sequins, her robe of celebration.

There had been, for several days, no work at the house of Surim Bey. The bespectacled secretary had, every afternoon, politely sent him away. Surim Bey, who spoke but could not write the languages Daniel penned, was seldom so slack, and Daniel considered if he were being put off. His night visit to Surim Bey could have given just cause enough, for the fat man might forget but not forgive.

In Marjannah's apartment the old woman served a banquet: portions of roast kid, olives and stuffed figs upon green palm leaves, and forbidden wine.

Daniel had bought a bracelet of glass flowers for Marjannah. She played with it happily.

"Why do we feast?"

"To mark your return," she said, "my lord."

He did not want to eat, but made love to her throughout the afternoon, until the light turned from yellow to bronze on all the walls. They lay in this bronzen exhaustion and he tried to find the means to tell her that he would be going from that place, from the place where she was, where she had been born and rooted like a plant. She could not move, but *he* would leave. A restlessness had grown on him, over the past scatter of days and nights. He wanted now to escape, as if from a prison, a jail of yellow rooms and courts with orange trees. He would give up the diamond to the fat man. He needed only to make some arrangement for letters. There was nothing else to keep him here.

"Tonight is a night of full moon," she said. "A night of lovers."

This was not so. It was the night of the new moon, or
the moon's darkness, which favoured lovers, and thieves.
(The thief of the diamond had not been particular.)

He felt so restless, now that his desire was slaked, he
could hardly bear to remain a moment longer. He told
her the lie that he must work in the house of Surim Bey
since he had been absent during the afternoon. She did
not believe him, but she made no protest. Her sad eyes
were full of the image of the Turk; Daniel could almost
see him there in their black and white ovals.

He wandered the upper streets with their courts and gardens. In some parts beggars sat by the gates, waiting to be
fed according to the Law. He descended to the sukh, and
there the torches were being lit for the sun was down,
although he could not remember its going, only the
bronze walls growing pale, then blue. At the French Inn
he bought urak, but it turned his stomach and he could
not drink, as he had not been able to eat. It seemed to
him the fever had come back on him.

The night was like glass.

He went down into the gut of the metropolis, down to
where the mud houses were. It was suggested to him he
was seeking the hovel of the robber of tombs, but surely
by now it would be scoured empty, anything of value
carted off; only the occupant's personality had kept the
scavengers at bay. There had been no clamour from the
alley beneath the house, but the corpse was no longer
there; Daniel had gone and seen as much. While he had
lain in Marjannah's arms and body, perhaps even then
they had swept it up.

In any event, he could not find the special hovel, recollecting only it had lain against an ancient wall, of which,
now, he discovered no trace.

The glass night was terrible. It pressed on him while keeping all else away. Men passed him like shadows beyond a veil. He wanted to reach out and pluck at them, but the veil came between. Then, from a spot on the fringes of the streets of mud, he saw down to the ocean, and the moon began to rise.

As Marjannah had foretold, it was full. Round and porcelain it came up from the ground or the water, and whitened the world which stared back at it. There were marks on the moon's face, perhaps masses of curious land, or mountains, enormous valleys of white dust.

Daniel gazed on the moon's face.

Dimly, high over the noises of the streets, he heard again the swirling drone of the semum. It was like a wild sheer roaring, not a wind at all, but the noise the moon made as it hung in darkness over the earth.

Something horrible started inside him, a feeling of heat or cold. And he ached in every bone, every pore of his flesh sensitive, so even the touch of his clothing, the air, was unbearable.

It was the fever. It had not gone from him. He turned and went towards his lodging. No one would disturb him now; he might lie there and rave all he wanted and who would trouble with his voice, calling in a foreign tongue that he had slain his father, that great impressive sin, slain him with bare hands and beaten his skull against the stone fireplace, while his mother sat in the room above, with the thread of blood running scarlet to her lips.

There was a wedding in the street. Musicians filled the road, playing pipes and harps, and drums banged. The torches blasted a golden hole in the night, and from the house came cries and shouts.

Daniel forced a way between the people and their

lights, and got at last into his upper room, where he lay down at once on the pallet.

Below, in the window, the torches blazed; there came the throb of voices.

Unseen, the moon moved up the sky. He felt the eye of it piercing through walls, as if the buildings between and beneath had become transparent. Soon he would see it, gouging its flame downward through the roof. The shadows of joists, of apartments, would tilt against it, shapes like those of a forest, against a white round, colder and brighter than the sun.

He was burning with heat. He stretched towards the water jar. He could not control his arm and the jar was upset.

Outside there was a bellow as the bridegroom went into the street, a second thunder as he thrust his fist through the skin of a little drum. Over these sounds the drone of the moon grew louder and more awful as it approached.

Ghastly pains, white hot, began to spear through Daniel's body. Something unprecedented and incredible was occurring. He sensed confusedly that he should summon help, but who would help him? Marjannah, who would have flown to his side, was far away. Besides, what physician could diagnose this ailment—these hurts as if the pectorals and ribs, cranium and spine were being torn from his body. A scream broke from his mouth, and in the street was laughing and singing, and women were shrieking too in some weird festivity of the wedding.

And the scream was choked. His throat had shut as though a huge weight compressed it. He struggled to breathe, to live. A convulsion ran up his body and his back arched from the bed, lifting him on a hoop of iron into the air. In agony he tried to scream again, but hardly any noise left him. His entrails were molten and his eyes blinded by an inner radiation. He tipped from the pallet, arched and sightless, and with his hands he wrenched at the plaster of the wall. But the moon was roaring on the roof. All sound but that was now gone. He felt his body melted in fire and all his bones thrust out as stark as knives, and in a last spasm he was bowled down a tunnel into the dark behind the light.

A servant of the cobbler's wife, the girl was a slave of slaves. She had no rights or pleasures, and time was a chaos to her, for at any moment of it she might be called to some action not of her own will. Even in deep exhausted sleep she might be roused roughly, as now. The goats were restless. She must go out to them. Perhaps a fierce dog was by the wall and troubled them, and she must climb up and throw a stone at it.

The cries of the wedding had died away, and the paid musicians were long gone. Outside, the night held only slight noises of the house and of the neighbouring houses pressed so close. In this bowl the movements of the goats were sharp and angular. They did not bleat but hurried to and fro, rustling the vine.

The girl went to them and softly spoke a prayer over their backs. Responding to her voice, the goats huddled near to her, butting at her body with their smooth noses. She climbed on to the stool, and craned to look over the wall. Nothing was there. Perhaps it was the memory of the murdered man who had lain there, some supernatural filament of the atmosphere which disturbed them.

High above, the full moon stood on a roof-top. The girl looked at it with thoughtless wonder. Like God, the moon could be of small value to such as she. It was no more than a vast lamp lit for others.

But the whiteness of the moon was streaming now into the courtyard.

The eyes of the girl travelled round the familiar surrounding. And saw something unusual. From an upper window, that which belonged to the foreigner, something hung down against the wall.

She could not make it out.

It was dark, and long, and also hairy, for the moonlight picked out layerings of texture upon it. Some rug, or maybe the hide of some animal, for there seemed to be, elongate and tufted, a kind of mask or head to it.

Then it moved. This was not a trick of the moonlight. There came a harsh and urgent scrabbling like pieces of metal scratching on a wall.

The girl crouched between the pressing goats, and the three living things stared upwards at this other, presumably alive creature, which slid over now from the window and began to writhe and scratch its way diagonally along the wall.

The servant girl was terrified, but she did not make a sound, for in her universe assistance was not to be expected. For a similar reason, or through some instinct, the goats continued not to bleat.

The moving thing humped on along the wall. The head was heavy, swinging, questing, but now into the light there crept long sinuous paws, their tendons standing out and their nails gleaming as they retracted, stretched, and struck into crevices of the house.

It had progressed only a few feet when again the creature halted. Fastened there on to the wall like a fly, it raised its heavy head towards the moon.

The girl saw a pointing snout and two eyes that abruptly burned up flat as silver coins. This was enough to convince her that the thing on the wall was real, and she curled herself into a ball, her arms over her head, and saw no more. The goats meanwhile kept immobile, only trembling rapidly, watching from their slotted keyhole eyes.

The creature hung on the side of the house a few seconds more, and then moved on, downwards, until it had reached the wall of the courtyard. Here it poured itself out, and for a moment stood there, a low mass, formless still and made all of dark and moon, and then the head swung again and the cold beam of the eyes passed over the tableau in the court. This did not interest it, or else it did not yet recognize its interests. The moment ended and the thing dropped away from the wall into the alley on its far side—dropped like a sack of vegetables, ungainly and sudden.

Down on the alley floor she heard its claws scrape the baked ground, and then the slow rush of it as it went away.

Night moved through the streets and alleys. Night slipped around corners and ran along walls.

From lit doors and windows they looked into the dark and saw it running. In the dark is always something to be feared; light the lamp and bolt the door. In the blackness there is always the intimation of death, and of the tomb.

To the giant porter, journeying late with some burden, the intimation came, so that he pressed an amulet to his lips. And to the girl Marjannah in her saffron window, so she wept and went to speak to the caged bird for comfort.

And how many score beggars and loiterers turned at a whiff of the Devil, not certain, thankfully not sure.

It was innocent and timid still, unschooled in its powers, and all this place a wonder to it.

Evil sprinted across the shadows, marvelling at its freedom, dangerous—how dangerous—but not fully primed.

And over all beat the white drum of the irresistible moon, changer of waters, dragger of tides, working on the tides of water and blood within all men, upon the wombs of women, and on every sentient animal that breathed on the earth.

In his house, Surim Bey arose from his couch in a chamber redolent of hyacinth, licorice and sex. And at the high window he probed the night with a sense of encirclement. The instincts of Surim Bey were fined. Besides, men of his combed the byways and the wharfs for news of a jewel; he was alert and ready.

And to Surim Bey it seemed the night had taken on a form, and furled about his house, pressing its jaws to his gate, looking up toward the window.

A vague sound came from the unseen, not a cry, almost a single word, whispered.

The boy on the bed ran to Surim Bey and clung to his leg.

"What is that, Papa?"

"Do not be afraid," said Surim Bey, the hair erect on his fleshy neck, on his arms and hands, like the quills of a beast.

"Is it a dog, Papa?"

"Yes, my darling, only a dog."

The sound did not come again.

Surim Bey spoke the words of a charm into the electric air.

But the rat-catcher was an irreligious man, without superstition, and he came back from the upper streets in the full-blown moonlight, down among the hovels, with his pole of trade over his shoulder. From the pole hung the mummified vases of three rats, their heads alone ratlike, with stiff whiskers, and their ratskin tails hanging. Their eyes were glass that winked. These rats, live once, now lived on the pole of their master, advertising the downfall of their kind.

The moon was high but, between, the shadows seeped dark as wounds.

There was an open place with a well, washed white, and the well's shadow like ink; and as the rat-catcher crossed this area like a clock-face, something came out of the dark rim to meet him.

The rat-catcher hesitated, for he was used to little things that darted in and out of shade and light, but this was a large thing, too large to be a dog or perhaps even a man moving on his hands and knees.

It smoked over the light, and was gone into the shadow of the well; and the rat-catcher had stopped, not wanting to go on and meet it there.

There was a great silence, the absolute quiet of the moon upon the termite mounds, the little lives all folded small and hidden.

But the rat-catcher with his pole of trade was out in the white night.

At last he took a step, and nothing moved, and maybe the formless smoke he had glimpsed . . . maybe it had gone away or never been. So he stepped into the edge of the well's black shadow. And the shadow rose up to greet him. Rose until it was the height of him, almost in the shape of a man, but wrong, very wrong; and he saw the head of it, heavy and huge and thick, carved black as ebony, with a sort of mane to it, and tapering length, and two wide eyes that had nothing in them but moonlight.

Then he was opened, in a slight, almost gracious gesture, from chin to crotch. Before he could scream his voice-box had been torn away.

He fell back with his arms outflung, and the pole clattered down. The three mummified rats who had been his prey watched as he was shredded and turned inside out.

Presently there was only a soft and gentle dripping, like a benison of water from the well.

The rats lay still, and something came and sniffed them, and a black paw, longer than the foot of a man, with wide gleaming nails, turned them over and left them there.

The moon was going down behind the heights, among the gardens and the courts, making mirrors of the pools and tables of the flat roofs.

Night closed on the space with the well, the hovels, covering everything.

Sunlight stared in a patch on the floor.

It was late. The noises of the street and house had their sluggish afternoon intensity. Heat burned in the room like a rose.

Daniel sat up on the pallet, and a dreadful giddiness swung inside him, and cleared reluctantly. His body ached and hurt, as if he had been beaten.

He remembered how he had come back here, sick again with the fever. There had been pains in his limbs, his ribcage seeming to erupt . . . But he was whole, cool enough now, only dazed and shaken as if after some terrible experience, his body strained and internally bruised by spasms he had thought would kill him.

There had been dreams too in the moon-stricken darkness . . . He could recall nothing, only a running motion, peculiar images as of the streets and walls seen from abnormal heights and angles.

Daniel got up. He had slept in his clothes, all but the coat, and he had spilled the water from the jug.

As he stood there, a knock came neatly on the door. It was so incongruous he said, without thinking, "Yes, come in."

And in through the door came the bespectacled secretary of Surim Bey, very properly dressed in his white clothes, and smelling of perfume. He poised in the rumpled room, not looking at it, and only at Daniel—as if Daniel were his usual self, washed and combed and reasonable.

"Good-day, Mr. Vehmund. You are to come to the house of Surim Bey."

"Oh," said Daniel, "there are letters, are there?"

"He has some news for you."

The secretary fastened together his plump and manicured hands, and Daniel tensed as a pale note seemed sounded through the room. News of what? There was something he had asked of Surim Bey. It was the diamond. The fat man had discovered it. An absurd terror flashed over Daniel, making him weak in his pain.

"I won't come today," said Daniel. "Give my apologies to him. Tomorrow. I'll come tomorrow."

"You must come today," said the secretary.

"You can be damned, and so can he. I'm not his slave. I'll come tomorrow."

"I am to wait for you," said the secretary calmly.

As if Surim Bey had guessed Daniel's resistance. As if Surim Bey himself were resistant to keeping the news longer than he must. As if he wished to get rid of the news, all taint of the jewel, the jewel itself.

"All right. Wait then, outside."

The secretary went out to stand in the cramped and crooked corridor.

Daniel made himself ready as best he could, his muscles protesting at every movement and his hands shaking.

He combed back his hair, and thought of the golden hair of his mother which had gone grey, and the thought made him heart-sore, like a child.

When he emerged, the secretary bowed, and walked before him as if never previously had Daniel gone to Surim Bey's house, and he must be led there. Of course, the secretary did not want to walk beside an infidel.

They ascended the brown streets to the orange grove of Surim Bey. In the courtyard, the secretary left Daniel; and Surim Bey was seated on the divan beneath the awning. Surim Bey was fresh from bathing, wholesomely ripe like, of all things, a plum.

"Sit," he said, and Daniel sat slowly on the chair where the desk generally stood, and tried to ease his churning muscles. "I have found what you sought," said Surim Bey.

"The jewel."

"The jewel known as The Wolf, for a slight flaw in its heart. It is a stone of ill-repute, as you forewarned me. Nothing is spoken of it, yet signs are made against it. The thief who stole gave up the stone. It has changed hands several times. Now it has passed into the possession of a Frenchman, a pig, a brothel-keeper, who will leave here as soon as he is able. He is ignorant of the jewel, and keeps it with him as a great treasure he will sell in the north."

"You've learned a vast amount."

"Of course."

"What is this man's name?"

"He has no name," said Surim Bey. His eyes looked flat as eyes in a poor painting. "But he will sail aboard the *Cos* in three days time. A small vessel. You should have no trouble in locating him. Have you money for your passage?"

"No," said Daniel.

"I will give you money," said Surim Bey. He clapped his hands and the rings burst sparks. There was a scurry of motion: those who went to do his unspoken bidding.

"Why?" said Daniel. "Why will you give me——"

"Because I wish to be rid of you," said Surim Bey. "I wish to be certain that you go far away. And the jewel also."

The pains in Daniel's body caused him to lose track of what Surim Bey had said. It did not seem curious to him that Surim Bey would fund him, or that he himself would leave to follow the jewel. After all, he had been planning on departure, though not northerly perhaps, for it was from the north he had run away. But then this did not matter.

"And why won't you tell me the name of the Frenchman?" he said randomly.

"I have vowed not to reveal it. It will be simple for you to select him from the others on the ship."

The red shadows of day lay stretched out on the courtyard. The tank of fish cast a shadow which reminded Daniel of some other scene in black and white. But it was probably a dream.

A servant came with a large lacquer coffer, and Surim Bey, unconcerned it seemed, counted out the shining coins, put them into a purse of silk, had the servant bring it to Daniel.

"You have laboured well for me," said Surim Bey. "Do not delay now. Go elsewhere."

"Did you see the diamond?" Daniel said.

"I have looked on one who did."

Daniel said, "What is it you fear?"

"The jewel is cursed. You told me."

"I invented that to put you off."

"You were wise in your invention. I would not touch it. I would not have my servant touch it. I would not have it go by my house. I desire that you, who have touched the jewel, depart immediately."

Daniel got up. The servant had backed away beyond the chair.

"It could be worth a fortune," Daniel said.

"No. It is the lamp of fear."

"If I take it from your Frenchman, I'll be rich."

"Yes. Already its riches come to you. It is meant for you, I think. Or one like you."

"All these riddles," said Daniel. "I'll pay you back your money when I can."

"No. Send me nothing."

"I'll take my leave then."

"Go quickly."

Daniel laughed. As he did so, a tremendous surge coursed through him. The court seemed tiny and the fat man like a figure of paper. The ship was near as fruit to be plucked, and there the diamond shone, a stone of brilliance in the forest of sunlight, space and time.

And Surim Bey murmured some words of prayer. Daniel beheld how he was dreaded, and it made him want to laugh again, but he only left the court with the money in his coat, and walked through the narrow streets in silence, past the doors and walls and gates and towers, already gone from them.

2

On the deck of the *Cos* three passengers stood and watched the drifting of distant land to the port side. The ship was bound westerly with a murky cargo, twelve blue days into her voyage. She would not be putting in anywhere until she reached her goal. Great golden slices of the earth had passed by, but soon the sea would open. Big fish ran through the waters like swords. Incongruously smells of the morning coffee and chocolate still drifted about the deck. The sailors were at their indigenous duties, in dirty clumps of industry. Above, the sails hung like cloud, crowding the ship, shadows and canvas.

By the rail, near to the half deck house, Pierre Faude leaned at his selected station, smoking a cigar. He was thin, dark, and quick of movement, in a sombre coat, and badly shaved. He radiated anxiety, was like an insect guarding something in its belly, smug with achievement, alert for predators. No one who looked at him would not know he had some trophy hidden, probably on his person. He gave himself away, for he had never had such luck before. A jewel had been given him in exchange for a man's honour, and Pierre Faude was content to make the bargain. To his untutored eye the gem was fabulous,

and he had since had it valued, albeit surreptitiously. A
diamond. The worth of it was his motive for coming
away, leaving a lucrative if chancy trade behind to the
management of others.

Although there had been the business, too, of the dead
girl. He had taken a risk with her, even though he had
taken it complacently enough. He was a supplier of
women, after all, and now and then, for a recompensing
fee, he had suffered such women to undergo certain
rigours. They had no one to complain to. He had found
this one among the dross of the waterfront, a girl with
eyes and hair from a Persian miniature, and satin skin.
She went with him in desperation, starving, mad with
hunger and despair. And he fed her, tended her, brought
her up to be the perfect merchandise. Without him, she
would have died in a few days, in pain and misery. Instead, one month later, in a close room, before some
twenty men, she had been tied above a carpet, and kicked
to death for their delectation. A dreadful end, slow even,
for the executioner was versed in his form of torture. But
then she would have perished anyway, and he had given
her—Pierre Faude, who in the vernacular of the op-
pressed she had called her 'Father'—that month of sumptuous life. Everything must be paid for. Yet there might
be a scandal. To come away was not unwise.

He leaned on the rail and watched the outline, like
solid water, of some country he did not wish to see more
closely. And when the date merchant, one of his fellow
travellers, came to speak, Pierre Faude put him off with
quick avid little movements and a reluctant tongue.

The date merchant, who wanted only a man to talk
business with, business being his life, retired, and along
the deck in his place came the Englishman, Vehmund,
the one who had kept to his cabin such a while, perhaps

ill, not even dining in the saloon. The Frenchman did not like the Englishman. Of course their races were traditionally opposed, but it was more than that. Vehmund was very handsome, a thing Faude was unused to in men. It made him uncomfortable, a commodity he could not price. Besides, he felt, the Frenchman, an infallible fear that Vehmund was for some reason interested in him. Even through the shut cabin door he had felt this. Did the English scum know of the jewel?

Daniel Vehmund positioned himself at the rail, not six feet from the Frenchman.

Behind them, across the deck, towered the mainmast like a stalk of cumulus. The wretched sailors scurried up and down on the eternal labour of the ship, like the damned.

"Fine sailing weather," said Daniel Vehmund.

"Just so," said Monsieur Faude in a clipped, repressed voice which meant, *You will leave me alone.*

"Last night," said Daniel, "I saw the moon over the water. A new moon, yet how large she appeared." Faude did not reply. "And the fish in the waters are bizarre, aren't they?" Daniel had altered his vocabulary to speak in French. He spoke it well, and Faude interpreted this gesture as a further intrusion.

"Just so," repeated Faude curtly, in English.

"How are you finding the voyage, Monsieur?"

"A voyage. No less, no more." Faude had lapsed into his mother tongue, despite himself.

"And your cabin? Is it comfortable?"

"Why do you want to know?" demanded Faude, sick of this.

"Mine I find rather cramped. There is the difficulty of where to put things."

"Indeed."

"If one were carrying, for example, something of note, some treasure——"

Faude stared at Daniel, gnawing his swarthy mouth. The scum did know, then. Had someone sent him? Was he perhaps in the pay of those who wished to create a scandal over that slut?

"What do you want?" said Faude.

Daniel looked at him. His eyes were like honey. Such colouring in a woman or a young boy, what it could have been worth.

"I want only your goodwill, Monsieur."

"Then you will reveal your true purpose."

"I have no—*purpose,* Monsieur."

"Yes, you are a hound of the authorities. You try to learn my plans."

"I should be overjoyed to learn your plans, Monsieur. Are you about to confide in me?"

The Frenchman swore and spat over the ship's side.

Daniel waited patiently, deadly as a stone which becomes a snake.

"How much do you require?" said Faude. "To leave me in peace."

"I require nothing."

"You say you're unbuyable?"

"Not at all. You amaze me, Monsieur. Why are you so suspicious? One would think you had a great deal to hide."

A sailor slid from the rigging and scrambled off over the deck like a monkey. Unnerved, Faude fingered his ill-shaved chin. "I will ask you to state your price, or to leave me alone."

"My price," said Daniel. He looked long, with, it seemed, a flirtatious lilt of the eyes. "Possibly you have something in which I have an interest."

Faude said harshly in French: "Understand this. If you enter my cabin, on any pretext, I will shoot you. I have the means. Understand also that there are those who wait for me in the next port at which we shall call. If I fail them, they will search about, and maybe they will find you, *Monsieur*."

"How unfriendly of you," said Daniel. He was mild, like a drunkard who is sweet, and cannot comprehend or take seriously any insult. "What have I done?"

"Do *nothing*, I beg you, Monsieur Vehmund. For your own sake. You will fail."

"If you shoot me," said Daniel, "I presume you will have to answer to someone."

"Don't suppose it. My friends at the port will take care of me."

"So mighty you are," Daniel gazed at Faude. "But you do have something excellent in your possession. If I told you it was mine, would you believe me?"

"Of course I should not."

"Because, Monsieur, it is. Mine. By some law more insistent than religion and more enduring than money."

"You will be wary," said Faude.

"And you, Monsieur, will be nervous. Now you must wait every moment to see if I will come to claim what is mine. You must stay awake all night."

"You're mad," said Pierre Faude, believing what he said, and badly frightened.

"Gentle as a dove," said Daniel.

He turned away, and Faude was struck by something cruel, animal, in his profile.

"Remember," said Faude, "it is not myself alone you must deal with."

"Watch and pray," said Daniel. And walked away along the deck.

* * *

In the ship's saloon at sunset all five passengers of the *Cos* gathered with the captain and his two officers, to dine.

The captain was a cheery villain, lacking his left eye and the two last fingers from his right hand. He was nevertheless armed at all times with cutlass and pistol. His clothes, once of a garish elegance, were stiff with filth. The two officers were lesser images of him, the second officer even having gone so far as to lose a left little finger. All wore earrings.

The passengers were various. Aside from the pretty Englishman and the swart Frenchman, there was the portly, bald date merchant, a portly hairy merchant dealing in olive oil, and a lean and lowly clerk, about twenty years, who kept to himself in a sort of humble aversion.

Daniel Vehmund came into an established society, where the pattern was already set by eleven previous dinners. Here the date and oil merchants held forth on their commercial hopes, and the captain now and then took the floor, telling them that all men were rubbish, and giving much evidence, relating to the ship and the shore. The clerk nibbled his hands and said nothing. The Frenchman grinned and bobbed at appropriate parts, but ventured little that was original.

Daniel, having arrived, sat silent. He watched whoever spoke, and he apparently listened, but offered neither comment nor approval. The captain did not challenge him. To the captain the north-western races were of this turn. He expected nothing of them and had scorn for anything they gave beyond a nod. In this way, he scorned the Frenchman, Faude.

"But will the weather hold to port, captain?" asked the

date merchant, who prided himself besides on his sea-man's stomach.

"It will, it will. God is kind to us. At this season we can expect only the best." He looked at Daniel and beamed. "No storms, no tempests."

Daniel nodded.

Obliged, the captain looked at Pierre Faude, who answered, "Good, good," in French.

In French, the captain said, "You are glad then you pick my ship for your travels, Monsieur?"

Faude frowned, reached a decision. "She's well enough. But I have been threatened by this one," he indicated Daniel. "Indeed, I'm on the verge of asking protection from you, captain."

The captain's one bright eye glittered.

"What is this? A feud?"

"I carry a certain item, on which a claim is already made, in port, you understand. This English says he will relieve me of it."

"May I ask——?"

"Regrettably not, captain. I'm sworn. Or I would tell you."

The date and oil merchants had fallen quiet. The clerk ate his thumb. They gazed with six popping eyes at the Frenchman, then at the Englishman.

The merchant of dates addressed Daniel Vehmund. "What have you to say at this?"

Daniel looked up. "Nothing."

"But Monsieur Faude accuses you——"

"That's his affair."

The captain lifted his hand. In bad English he said directly to Daniel: "You am been marked as threat. What say your words?"

Daniel shrugged. "Monsieur Faude mistrusts me," he

said. "I expressed an interest in a large cut diamond he carries."

There was a long hiatus. The ship creaked, the lamp hung steady above them.

The merchant of oil spoke.

"A diamond?"

Pierre Faude flicked his hands. "It's nothing. An inferior stone. It has personal value to someone in the port where I'm taking it."

"A diamond," repeated the captain. He smacked his lips and looked at Faude consideringly. The First and Second Officers did as he did.

"I am bound on this commission," said Faude. "I am expected."

"I should like to see the jewel," said the merchant of dates.

"Impossible!" declared the Frenchman. He took out his handkerchief and blew his nose as noisily as a trumpet, as if to herald an end to all this.

Daniel observed him. Now Faude could expect attack from any number of quarters, not least that of the benign, one-eyed captain.

Himself, Daniel did not mean to attack Faude. He did not exactly know what he would do. Only that some barriers of air and cloth and skin were between him and the gem he had last seen dredged from a cup of wine. It belonged to him. He who had rejected it now believed in its faithfulness, as if it would of its own come back to him, despite Pierre Faude and all the partitions of avarice and the ship.

He had been unwell when he had come aboard, aching in every limb, shivering, sick. He had crawled to his cabin and waited sickness out. And the disability gradually passed, as the world passed in water. He had noted

Pierre Faude before he spoke to him. As Surim Bey had promised, identification was simple.

Daniel felt light, and sure. As if he was drunk, which on the inferior liquor of the captain's table was not conceivable. He had only to attend.

The conversation veered suddenly, unconvincingly, to tales of shipwrecks, devious and immaterial. Every man at the table, bar Daniel, looked now on Faude as at a being from Mars. And Faude grimaced and squirmed under the microscope, telling lies even by his silence.

Night bloomed over the sea in a huge arc of strangely-lighted black. Stars and moon, trails of phosphorus along the rollers of the waves, combined to give the sombre air a kind of silver aura.

Daniel lay for hours on his back, looking at this phenomenon through the porthole. Then at length his eyes closed against the glowing dark. He slept and dreamed, as he had dreamed on land, of the diamond. It hung inside Marjannah's birdcage, but in a midnight alley above the port. As he approached it he felt a wind blowing from the cage on to his face, and he dropped to his knees and ran on that way, which was easy.

The dream stopped with a sensation of choking.

A sailor, one of the least of the ship's flotsam crew, had slunk into the cabin. Now he kneeled on Daniel's body, leaning forward, his hand across Daniel's mouth and his scarred and bearded face hovering close. The sailor stank in the manner only a human thing can, self-neglected and ill-used, of sweat, the natural functions, and some other thing, some horrid evil gladness in the deed. And the deed was to be murder, for the other hand had a knife in it, clean and unspoilt as the man was not, yet ready to serve him.

Daniel was too unnerved, too astonished to be actually afraid. *Faude has ordered this.* The sailor was in his pay, and doubtless the captain also, to keep him amenable. Daniel could not speak for the vile gag clamped across his lips. He breathed slowly of the night and the man's stench, and met the darting eyes of the sailor with his own. The sailor laughed without noise and showed his rotted teeth. The odour that came from him was unspeakable.

"Die quick," said the sailor, and his knife dived like a bird at Daniel's throat.

In that split second something broke from Daniel's eyes, the only communication he was able to make. He felt it happen—not a plea, not a curse, not wrath, not terror. It was a command. As if to a savage dog, his eyes seared out a cold dominant *No.*

And the sailor hesitated; the knife did not complete its stroke.

It gradually became clear the man was hanging there, as if in a web, enmeshed by some invisible force that bore out of Daniel Vehmund's yellow eyes.

Truly, the man was wilting, withering. His hands fell away and he rocked backwards. His face collapsed and the awful mouth yawned open, whimpering.

"No," Daniel said softly, "you can't, can you? *Can* you?"

"God is great," whined the sailor. "Forgive me." He shook so violently the bunk groaned at it.

"Get off me. Get out. Go and lose your miserable self."

Gibbering, the man obeyed. He backed to the cabin door and crouched there, like a cripple. Saliva dripped from his wobbling mouth. The knife had fallen with a faint clink to the floor. He could not seem to stop looking into Daniel's eyes.

Daniel blinked, slowly, deliberately.

The man dashed from the door of the cabin and was gone up the ladder to the deck.

Daniel let out a sigh. His eyes felt great and burning, full of strength that was not in the rest of him.

He lay back, and touched his throat, and suddenly he laughed. He did not know why. But it was as the sailor had laughed—something to do with the essence of a death not his own.

Daniel Vehmund approached Pierre Faude sometimes on deck.

The Frenchman quivered, but Daniel did not speak to him, only stood at the rail, not six feet away, watching the far-off solid water of the land's shape.

At dinner they did not exchange words.

Faude carried the diamond on his person, in a little suede pouch over the heart. It seemed to burn a hole there. At night, as it lay beneath his pillow (and the pistol next to his hand), he felt it stir and sometimes he seemed to hear from it weird high-pitched noises, very faint and thin, coming up through the pillow into his ear.

The date and oil merchants avoided both Daniel Vehmund and Pierre Faude. The clerk kept to himself and chewed his fingers, eating himself for consolation.

Beneath his sinister jollity, the captain was displeased. The passengers were perhaps dangerous, and there were unsettling rumours now among the junk of his crew.

The moon, slowly night by night, opened over the sea. The ship's wake lay white as snow. Big fish rose to play in

the moonlight and water. The moon drew them up. The
ocean swelled towards the moon, engorged.

It seemed to Daniel that he must shave more frequently.
The hair on his jaw was tougher. He examined his body
in surprise; at his groin, on his arms, the hair appeared
thicker, like coils of golden wire. He was lethargic. He
stared out of the porthole at the tilting moon. His appe-
tite lessened. He was afraid the fever was coming back.
At the same moment, he knew a strange elation. As if he
stood at the brink of great control, a nearly magical ability of some sort, to order and align the random course of
life. He would steal the diamond after all. In the moonlight. Wrench open the man's door—the locks were poor
—and spring in on him. How straightforward it was, in
fact.

Then again, Daniel became clumsy. He reached out for
ordinary things, a comb, a cup, and missed them. He
knocked over the stack of his books in the tiny cabin, so
they paved the floor.

When the moon shone down on the ship, he would
fancy he saw through the masts and rigging, through the
forms of sailors, to the struts of skeletons and smoke of
blood . . .

He wondered if he were now going mad. He did not
feel afraid. He had glimpsed the sailor who had come to
kill him, and the sailor hid himself. *He* feared.

Above, the starry map of sky hung over the sea and the
vessel, in waiting for moonrise. In the saloon the lamp
hung straight as a heavy fruit above the spicy mash and
unleavened bread which, on the ship, passed for a dinner.

"The English does not like my cuisine," the captain

said, for Daniel Vehmund was again absent from the table.

The date merchant chuckled. "A poor sailor."

"But the sea is flat," said the captain.

"I have seen men puke upon a lake."

The oil merchant said, "Monsieur Faude for one is glad to be free of his menaces."

"But surely he does not menace Monsieur?" inquired the jocular captain. "What does he do now?"

The table, as before, stared at Faude. Faude said, uneasily, "There's been no further threat."

"That is good," said the captain.

"But what is the trouble with your men, captain?" asked the date merchant. "They seem afraid of something."

"Nothing. It is nothing."

"I heard two of them speaking of a demon on the ship," said the date merchant. "Only the godless are so superstitious."

"Quite true," said the captain. "They are imbeciles."

Outside, the watch had been set. The ship drifted forward dreamily. The east blued like steel.

Later, the passengers dispersed to their accommodation, and the captain and officers, having made a cursory patrol, to their cabin under the wheel. The moon was up by then, painting everything with a merciless whiteness.

When the loud voices of the captain and his seconds had died away, the ship rested like a materialization on the pane of that hard white light.

Two of the watch had sat down under the mainmast to a game with a pack of greasy cards with greenish, scaly backs like alligators. A third man snored softly in the forecastle. High overhead, like a resting bird, someone or other was suspended in the precarious nest of the look-out. Perhaps he dozed, or scanned the sequins of the sea, seeing now and then from his vast distance the shadows of sails slink along the deck like sentient things which moved there.

Moonlight congealed. Silence but for the slightest stirrings, wood and iron and canvas muttering, the lap of water, soundless twang of stray star upon the strings of masts, the ribs of the ship breathing in the sea.

Up from the ship's centre, from below, something came, heaving off the hatch, which dropped over with a dull thick bang.

From his height the man above looked down. He saw a shadow move, and vanish—which was all he ever saw, apart from men on the deck.

In the forecastle, the sleeper did not twitch.

But by the mast the two game-players looked up and away towards the cabins of the passengers. Who had come out? They waited; no one walked along the deck. They were not comfortable, these men. They got up and peered away under the widenesses of the sails.

On the white deck nothing, nothing.

At the wheel aft, the wheelman held his course, not attentive to the noises of the ship.

A dark form, like that of a man on his hands and knees, appeared on the space below the mizzen-mast.

Holding steady, the wheelman gazed down, expecting incongruously any moment for a man to stand upright. The darkness slid instead to the ladder and folded up it on to the platform.

The wheelman held the wheel. He stared. Not fourteen feet away a lump of black, solid, hunched like an animal, and with the suggestion of a face, a sloping jaw and two spots of moon—yet all darkness and unfashioned.

And then the darkness stood up.

"God is mighty," said one of the card-players. "What was that cry?"

"No cry," said the other, hastily, "no cry."

"Yes. I heard someone call."

Each man bowed slowly and spoke in a whisper to God.

At the stern, the wheel rotated a little, this way, that way. No man kept the helm. Where the moon pinioned the platform, something sat, its huge head raised, more like the visage of a bear than a wolf, yet long-snouted, the jaws open, matted. The cold eyes that had no soul in them mirrored the moon. It sat watching the moon, this thing not a wolf and not really like a wolf, perhaps a deformed and primal wolf, watching with the blood dripping off it, black, on the white planks.

The wheel gave a small moan, and turned again, a degree this way, that.

Under the mast the two men left off praying.

"It was nothing. One went to relieve himself."

They smiled together. "The fat ones go every night to piss." "The clerk hides himself, like a woman."

The moon balanced high on the mainmast, then infinitesimally began to descend.

Aloft, the lazy watcher could not see to the station of the wheel for sail. Could not see the black blot there, and the wheel swinging a degree off, a degree back to its course.

The moon crept down the sky.

The blot beside the wheel had soaked away.

The second card-player lifted his head and saw, over the bowed head of his fellow, the face of Satan standing on the moonlight. The man could not speak. His mouth came open, and in that instant the black claws of the

Devil raked through the body of the other man. There was a snap and gush of blood, and head and body were separated. Out of the deluge came a long paw and, as the living card-player started his scream, hooked out his throat.

The wolf-thing paused above the bodies, touching a black tongue in their blood. It did not drink or feed. It pushed the pieces of them aside and went on along the deck, under the moon-shining forest of rigging.

It stepped like an ape on two feet, two hands, dainty, monstrous, and the large head lumbered to and fro like a noiseless engine. The eyes were blank as the moon left them, greyish perhaps, but nearer black.

It paced up on the ladder to the forecastle, and coming up there, it stopped again and seemed to regard the man who slept. Then it ran lightly, and amazingly fast, to him, and sunk its teeth, each one pointed and like a dagger of bone, into his entire face, tearing it free like a mask. And one taloned foot or hand of it cut off the smothered glottal outcry the ruined thing made as it died.

In the forecastle, in the pond of blood, the beast looked up at the moon again, and parting its daggered mouth it gave off a low soft music of hunger. A hunger food could not appease. It spurned the fourth dead man, and lifted its thick black neck. The eyes burned white on the rigging's top. It loped down once more along the deck, like a weightless thing, and going to the foot of the mast, sniffed it with a grey wrinkling of its jet-black snout. Then it reared, and setting its ape-paws that were also hands, the feet of a wolf, or something other than wolf, into the bracings, it began, without any apparent effort, to climb, to *glide* upwards to the fifth man in his nest above.

He did not know, this man, as the others had not, what came up the night towards him.

He was thinking now of the meal he would get when he came down, as soon as the next watch relieved him, but it was an untidy ship and this might not be for a while.

The slightest sound below caused him to glance over. He might not have bothered.

The creature climbing on the mast was foreshortened. It was a black mass out of which an eager angry mindless head stared up. He saw the dead-white reflective eyes of it and the black tongue between the palisade of fangs, and he shrieked. For God and men and all the world to help him. But none heard, none heeded. One minute after his shrieks commenced, an enormous paw, most now like a hand whose fingers were bright claws, raked in over the side of the eyrie and opened him to let out all that he was.

The blood fell like a rain from the mast-top, staining black the sails, puddling on the deck.

It was this blood the men saw who came up on the next watch, and in the blood on the deck one huge print of some footfall, too wet and smeared to reveal anything.

Before them, darkness had descended the mast with the moon, and gone away down into the place below, in at a half-open door which fell shut behind it. There, in the oblivious gloom under the deck, the cabin of Daniel Vehmund, darkness lay on the floor, motionless like a suit of discarded fur; and its eyes set as the roaring moon set with a howling whistle below the horizon of the sea.

In the first light Pierre Faude opened his small eyes to a hammering on the door.

"What is it?"

He was told by the voice of the Second Officer he must rise, dress himself, and come at once to the saloon.

"Why in God's name?"

"There has been an atrocity."

Pierre Faude sat up and flung off the cover. He said wildly, "The Englishman?" But the Second Officer did not answer, had gone away. There was hammering on another door.

Faude dressed quickly, something he was good at, for there had been emergencies in his past. Was the English ill, or dead? Would suspicion fall upon Faude, who had suborned one of the crew, although to no avail. Faude had heard Daniel Vehmund screaming over and over in the early night. Either the others did not hear or did not choose to. Perhaps Faude's enemy *was* dead, for there had come a silence after the screaming, which went on and on. Lulled by the cries, pleased at Vehmund's suffering, Faude had slept.

Outside, in the narrow way, Faude noted that the Englishman's door was shut; it had been ajar in the night. In closing it, Faude noticed something about his own door. Four long, diagonal scratches, deep, as if made with the point of a knife, ran over it. There was that about them which made him shiver, for in sleep he had not heard this vandalistic act. It flashed upon him that the Englishman had come out in the quiet, after his cries, and done the scratching. He was mad, unsafe—and presumably, after all, alive.

On the deck in the rising light Faude saw that all the crew were gathered, even to the scoundrelly cook. They seemed in a dark unsettled mood, shifting about like dogs that had been given a scare. Beneath the mainmast lay some bundles done up in hemp. There were rusty marks on the deck.

Faude went down to the saloon, and here were the captain and his officers and all the passengers, bar Daniel Vehmund. No sooner was Faude in the room than some of the crew came clattering down and stood craning in at the doorway. The captain did not admonish them.

"Where is the English?" demanded the captain.

Faude said, "How should I know?"

One of the officers said, "I knocked on the door and got his answer. He says he is sick and cannot attend. But he lives."

Faude was sorry, and at the same time a sense of alarm fastened on him, for why should the life of Daniel Vehmund be in question, and what occupied those corpse-shaped bundles on the deck?

The captain spoke again. "I shall not delay for the Englishman. The rest of you will listen. Murders took place during the night. Five of my crew, the watch, the wheelman—praise to God the weather is clear; we have not drifted far. Also the look-out on the mast."

There had been a clamour which now died off. The sailors in the doorway kept still, knowing already. "There is a madman aboard," said the captain. "I believe that he stows somewhere in my ship. We shall search. For your own safety, you passengers will remain here together. Are you armed?" The merchants and the clerk signalled that they were not, and the First Officer handed them out terrible-looking knives.

"In the night," said the date merchant, "I heard a man shouting as if in pain."

"It was the English," said the merchant of oil. "I know such cries. He had taken some drug. That is why he is not here."

"None of you," said the captain, "is suspected of this crime. For which of you, even the English, could climb up a mast? It may be the Devil is among my sailors." A growling came from the men on the ladder. The captain, with no hesitation, drew his pistol, and the growling ceased. "I will find him out. He kills as if possessed by demons. There was much blood."

"It was full moon," said the clerk, unexpectedly. He nibbled at his finger and added, "Blood flows more freely then. Is harder to staunch."

"Remain here," the captain said, as the fat merchants stood anxiously with their knives, and Faude took out his own pistol. The sailors crowded off from the ladder to allow captain and officers passage. Presently orders were barked for the searching of the ship from stem to stern.

"But does the Englishman live?" asked the date merchant.

"Perhaps he is the villain," Faude said. "He's unhinged. On my door below he has made great scratches, like those of some wild animal. Who can say he could not climb the rigging? What's known of him?"

"The same is true of you, Monsieur," said the oil merchant. "What do we know of *you*?"

Faude said, "I am a man of business, like yourselves." He rounded quickly on the clerk. "And you. How do you know so much of blood?"

The clerk did not respond, breakfasting on his own skin, his eyes mournful and clandestine.

The heat of the day came down from the sky and up from the water. The ship glistered. Her deck had been scrubbed clean, and the dead things in their hemp were laid neatly aft. The vessel had been searched. She gave up nothing new: her cargo of illicit goods in the hold, her bolt holes packed with shadows and rats—no more. The captain had harangued his crew. He had ranted and demanded of them, but they gave up no murderer either. Instead the old tale surfaced, of the demon.

To the captain this notion now seemed horribly apposite, for he had seen the cadavers, ripped open and one of them beheaded. He did not berate his men, but exhorted them to pray and to go about in pairs. They must sleep too in relays, for tonight the whole ship should wake, and watch.

Just after midday, the Englishman came up from his cabin. He was white and exhausted, the colour of his hair too bright on him. He stood blinking at the sunlight, and the sailors drew away from him, making signs against the Evil Eye.

The captain crossed the deck and spoke to Daniel Vehmund in strong faulty English.

"You am sick?"

"A recurring fever. Yes. But it will pass."

"Tell me now. How do night go you?"

"I don't know. I remember nothing of it. That's how the fever takes me."

All about them, the sailors gathered in a snarling, cringing circle. From the bracings, faces looked down. Hands gripped knives and pieces of sharpened wood.

"Five my men die."

"I heard of it. Have you got the murderer?"

"No yet," said the captain, staring Daniel Vehmund over, his haggardness and air of being used up. "Am you travel ship before?"

"Yes."

"Up masts you go?"

"No," Daniel smiled. Once his smile had been charming, now it hung there like a wreath. "How could I?"

"In sickness perhaps you am mad. Climb."

"I lay in a stupor. Are you accusing me of the death of your men?"

"One do it."

"Not I."

The captain gazed into the peculiar eyes of the invalid and found there nothing to prove innocence, or guilt.

"You am armed?"

Daniel shook his head, weary of its weight.

The captain did not care to arm Daniel Vehmund.

"Tonight we keep watch on deck."

"If I can," said Daniel. "I'm afraid you may have to excuse me."

"I cannot."

Daniel shrugged. He looked at the man with western hauteur.

The captain thought: *He is only like the rest.*

The day moved over like a brazen shield, and ended in a brief flare of sunset, the blue poppy of a dusk one minute long. Stars sprinkled the sky, and the calm sea was dusted with silver. The night was beautiful and filled by fear.

On the ship, quantities of lamps burned. The round moon would not rise for another hour, and they wanted light.

The passengers sat in the saloon, where they had eaten a hasty, skimpy meal. On the table now before them were the three knives and Faude's pistol. Daniel Vehmund also had a knife, Faude knew, for the sailor who had failed in taking Daniel's life had let drop the weapon in his cabin —this much Faude had learned. Daniel was not in the saloon, had not come there as instructed. The Second Officer reported that the English kept to his bunk, writhing under the blanket. He seemed to have no coordination, for when the officer touched his head to ascertain the fever's strength, Daniel Vehmund struck out at him, and missed him.

"Do we have the plague as well as murder on this ship?" asked the captain. He had gone grimly above with the officers to maintain a watch. Faude knew three men had been sent down to guard the passengers' quarters and the Englishman's door. They were armed with the huge knives, but they had departed reluctantly. The crew feared Daniel Vehmund.

"The sailors say," the date merchant murmured now, "that the Englishman has the Evil Eye."

"He is addicted to some drug," said the oil merchant. "I have seen such things before."

"Is the drug enough to send him insane and make an assassin of him?"

"Certainly. God is mighty, and the gifts of his kingdom are not to be toyed with. These western and northern men do so at their peril."

Faude said, "You think Vehmund is the murderer?"

"Very likely," said the oil merchant. "A mad dog, he will be seen to as such."

The clerk spoke again, unexpectedly. "His strength must be very great. None of the five men was able to resist him, and there were two together who could not master him."

"Yes, he will be strong as five men from the drug," said the merchant of oil, "but tonight the whole ship is alerted. They will take him. He will need to be chained and a purgative administered to rid him of the drug."

Faude checked his pistol for the third time.

"However strong the devil is, he can't withstand a bullet."

"He may not feel even a bullet at first," said the merchant of oil, with a strange smugness. "Has Monsieur never seen the holy men who pass swords through their cheeks and arms without pain or blood?"

Faude said, "I understood that was a trick."

The oil merchant said, "Sometimes."

Faude was very nervous, yet also pleased at the turn events were taking. A witless slavering Daniel Vehmund shot down or hacked to bits did not dismay him. What could be better. (And over Faude's heart the diamond throbbed in its pouch, the price of honour, his treasure trove. None of these others had pried further or tried to discover it. They were ordinary men and might be discounted.) Faude wondered idly how the fat merchants would fare if the madman came at them. He himself would need only one clear shot.

Below, in the area between the passenger cabins, the three sailors of the *Cos* squatted by the walls and played softly with dice, their knives ready at their feet.

Above, out of sight, the round white moon rose from the eastern ocean.

They did not see and yet they sensed it, its invisible pull upon them; the moon, changer of tides, shifting the tides of water in their bodies, and the blood.

"I have thrown the Eye," said one, for it was an antique game they played, passed down from the levels of Egypt into other lands, so through centuries to the congested lanes of wharf-front sties where they had been birthed and haphazardly grown.

The three men craned inward to the dice, and started apart, snatching up their knives. A voice, scarcely human, had screamed behind the cabin door they supposedly watched. They watched it now with wide and reddened stares. Silence. And then the ghastly scream again.

"The fit comes on him," said the man who had cast the Eye.

"The demon possesses him," said another.

They held their knives ready and backed away in the narrow space.

"Oh God—oh God help me—" they heard the voice crying in English. The single word *God* was known to them. The demon was cursing God in its spasms of entry.

There came a rumble of movement, a commotion, and then a scream of agony so awful that it almost deafened them. They heard the sound of a man's body falling back on to the bunk. After that, nothing.

The sailors waited. There was no other way to describe their condition. After some minutes one ventured that he might go up and tell the captain about the cries from the Englishman's cabin. The two others commanded that he stay with them. And *wait*. So they waited.

After some seven or eight minutes more, there was a new sound from the cabin. It was at the door.

The three men braced themselves, their knives held ready.

They anticipated the door smashed open and the blond madman coming out, a tangle of limbs, a blade, a howling and the whites of eyes, for they had, each of them, seen such possessions before.

Instead of the opening of the door, an appalling noise began, which was in fact just what they had expected, the door's opening, but by different means. For the partition was being rent and ripped wide on its inner side, pulled bodily apart.

The men in the passageway let out a concerted shout of consternation. Which in another moment was smothered.

A phenomenon was occurring. Something they had never ever seen before, if *any* man ever had.

Through the wood of the door there stuck four points,

like the spikes of four shining black iron nails. For a second they pulsated there, and then they were drawn down the wood, from top to bottom, slowly and steadily, and the wood tore like paper.

What weapon was this? Not the knife their comrade had left behind when fleeing from Daniel Vehmund's eyes. Something else——

As the first rending was completed, a second began at once, four more spikes thrust through the door and dragged to its foot.

In bemused horror the three sailors watched.

Then a whole panel gave, cracked right out and fell down before them. And through the gap they saw——

The three men spun about and scrambled, whimpering, for the ladder up to the deck.

But the glimpse of Hell they had had was already upon them. The remainder of the door splintered out with a groan and landed sideways in the passage. Darkness came out and across it, and took the third man instantly, slicing him like the door, from neck to thigh. With a mindless shrieking, already dead, he went over, and the dark thing from the cabin reached out and caught the second man as he tried to turn, peeling off half his face and breast and laying bare the heart.

The first sailor, he who had cast the Eye, had succeeded in getting on the ladder, struggling to raise the hatch, and beating on it, yelling and praying. At the last instant he too turned. He saw the face of a thing of the Pit before him, Abbadon of fire and blackness, a black mouth gaping on the points of teeth, and pushed his knife into the muzzle above, pushed to the hilt, and hauled it free with a shout of triumph, to stab again under the round, ignited colourless eye.

Then two hands or paws fastened on him and

wrenched out his entrails, and gagging on death he too toppled down into the sink of the passage.

The knife had done nothing, for the thing which stood up now on the ladder was pristine, and it dripped only with the blood of others. It touched with its snout against the hatch, which began abruptly to move as the men above yanked it away.

There were seven men about the hatch, and others grouped beyond. At the muffled commotion below deck the hatch had become a focal point.

The seven men looked, as the others had looked, into the face of Hell. Two turned and ran off crying. The other five, as the big black shape propelled itself out on them, raised and twisted their arms to stab and slash at it. The knives sank in, as if into a solid softness, like mud—sank in and slid out unmarked. Upon the thing which came from the open hatch the blades made no impression. The men reeled off from it, while others pressed forward to see.

For perhaps one minute the circle of human things gazed at the creature which had come up from the depths of the ship.

It was huge and low, like an enormous dog. Yet not dog-like; as it was not properly wolf-like. The head was too big for its great body. The head was heavy and lurched from side to side, ungainly and yet exactly coordinated. A ruff of black hair filled in the neck and curved about the shoulders or haunches. Its ears lay flat and its eyes were wide, like flat mirrors, reflecting nothing. Then it reared up like an ape and lolloped forward and split a sailor in two pieces as easily as a knife passing through bread. It scratched out his heart and laid it on the deck in the lamplight, glistening. And the circle of men shrilled and gave way and fled.

From the stern of the ship the captain came rushing at the sounds of panic, the screams and squeals of men.

Men ran against him, their stinking fear gushed in his face and their hands grabbed at him like those of babies afraid. He pushed them off, and saw, like a dream from his single eye, a large black thing which bounded up and down and cut through the stems of men. He saw his Second Officer try to shoot at it, and his arm detached and flying through the air, the spout of blood, and then his throat laid open, and the man fallen, and the black beast turning suddenly and the glimmer of its eyes and the blood spraying from its jaws.

The captain raised his pistol. "God is with us," he said, and fired point-blank into the body of the beast he saw and scarcely believed in.

It received the charge with a little jump, like a hiccup, sideways. The bullet had gone into it and left no mark. And then it had a man again, and it stared at the captain who had fired on it, as it unseamed this man like a garment and strewed him on the planks.

There was blood everywhere, lakes and seas of it, blacker than night, scarlet where the lamps found it.

A sailor crept behind the beast, slipping in the blood.

The captain waded forward. He fired again, again point-blank. And now the beast shook itself. Finishing with the man it had undone, it leapt upward, kicking out its back legs and catching the other man who had tried to come behind it. Talons on its feet disembowelled him.

The air was frayed by screaming and noise, growing dimmer.

Men had tried to climb the masts. One hung there in two parts, under the severed sail, his head nodding obscenely to the motion of the ship.

The captain flung his pistol away and seized a lamp

from the deck house. As the beast loped towards him he threw the fire out on it.

But the fire slipped like water down its back and went into the blood on the deck, sizzling out.

The lamp broke in pieces.

Pinned to the wall of the deck house, the captain felt the cold heat of the iron claws, felt them disbelievingly, until the vast jaws snapped together on his throat.

Behind the beast the sail fell with a crash, trapping men under its folds.

As they struggled, white rolling figures like children playing at ghosts, the beast darted through them and red sprang out on the white shrouds, and one by one the mounds of men went down, sodden, and the beast bounded over them.

And there was a last man, the First Officer, in its way, raving, under the moon. Meaningless, a shot was fired. The beast champed him in half, and a silence came. Silence came over the planks littered by blood and broken things. Over the ship.

In the silence the beast flowed up the littered deck. The moon blazed above the sea, and the beast flowed towards the moon. It was gone like a black wave.

The date merchant rose from the table and going to the door, listened.

"It is quiet now."

"They have subdued him," said the oil merchant.

"No one calls to us," said the date merchant.

The merchants had shut the door on hearing the hubbub break out. This had annoyed Faude, who had wanted to see. Now he said sternly, "Let's open up and learn the fate of the bloody Englishman."

The date merchant hesitated, drew back.

"How quiet it is. Would they not shout? Would the English not screech?"

"They've stunned him," said Faude. Hopefully he added, "Or he's dead."

He shouldered past the date merchant and undid the door.

Outside he saw the ship, her deck and masts bright with ascending moonlight. And a long river that shone blackly, with a bit of smoking broken lamp on it. Then he saw sections of bodies strewn about, could not take them in—limbs, offal, a man's arm. Faude retched convulsively and slammed shut the door.

"What is it?" asked the date merchant fearfully.

"He's run amok," said Faude in French. "He's killed them. Got away——"

"Impossible," said the merchant of oil. "There were twenty men or more."

"Look for yourself," said Faude. He wiped his mouth. He was astonished, nearly ashamed.

No one else dared the door.

They sat down at the table and were silent; and, outside, the silence of the deck rang under the moon.

An hour passed, and there were no more noises, beyond the muttering of the ship.

The oil merchant said, "Someone must go and see. Is there a helmsman? What will become of us?"

Faude said, "I have the pistol. You,"—pointing at the clerk—"bring your knife and follow me."

The clerk got up without a word and stood there obediently.

Faude was not brave, only impatient. He thought the captain and men had fired at random (they had heard the shots), and missed through incompetence. Faude trusted his own marksmanship. He did not like to be caged.

As they went up out of the saloon, a memory came to him of the girl with Persian eyes he had sent to her death. She had called him 'Father'. But her curse would be worth nothing. Did even God Himself listen to the poor? One imagined not.

The deck was a desert, bleached white where it was not covered in blood and mortal sections.

"As you said," Faude informed the clerk, "blood flows freely at a full moon. Who told you such a thing?"

"It is alchemical," said the clerk. He did not bite his hands, seemed resigned. Life had always imposed on him.

They crossed the deck, going towards the stern of the ship, and so went by, among other portions, the remains of the captain.

"In Christ's name, what's happened here?" asked Faude.

At the stern of the ship the wheel was unmanned. The wheelman had been torn in ribbons like the rest, and the wheel was black with blood.

"We shall drift," said Faude. "But there is shipping in these waters. Someone will come to our assistance."

They went back along the deck, going by the bodies, under the sails, one of which was ruined, and up to the forecastle.

There were no dead men there. They had either run or been pulled down.

The moon was behind them now, throwing shadows from their bodies.

They stood there, looking out at the unmarked indifference of the sea.

Under them, in the dark beyond the moon, the figure-head, man or woman, some form, was clothed over. As if it coupled with the figurehead, under the bowsprit there,

darkness clung with its claws sunk in the wood. It hung
like a sloth, belly up, listening. It heard the two men, on
the forecastle presumably, breathing and alight with life.
And like a caterpillar now it swung itself off and around,
and began to ease up towards the rail.

"Where is Vehmund?" said Faude. "Can he have flung
himself overboard?"

With pistol drawn, phallus of strength, he went to the
port side and leaned over at the sea, far down and shining. And then something dark was coming up from the
dark under the ship, and Faude stared at it in wonder.
Until two eyes flamed white at him, the moon struck like
a crescent in them twice. Then he fired straight down into
the long encroaching mask, fired faultlessly—and somehow missed. For out of the sea and the dark the vision of
night came on.

Faude shrieked and jumped back, and night came after, off the rail, and launched itself at him. It crouched on
his belly as he cried and voided himself and next it shut
its teeth in his face.

At the crunch of bone, the clerk kneeled down.

Quickly he said, "I have been misguided. There is no
God but God."

The beast killed him with a single blow.

In the saloon, at Faude's shriek, the two merchants
shut the door. They hauled the table, moaning and sweat-
ing, to barricade it, and piled the chairs below and on
top.

After this, in the renewed silence, they bowed themselves and gave themselves over to prayer.

They prayed for half an hour, and then ceased, looking
at each other.

Their homes, pleasant with wives and comforts, were

far away; their lives seemed tiny, as if viewed from high up in the sky.

"No one has come to the door," said the merchant of dates.

"Nor has the Frenchman returned," said the oil merchant. "I think we should not expect any good."

"It is a demon?"

"I fear so."

Then there was a scratching.

They thought death was at the door, and looked that way; but then the floor groaned and they looked at that instead.

When the boards burst they were all eyes. Up through the fragmenting wood came a black and hairy lump, the haunches of something, and after that the head.

The head drew the body up with it out of the hole.

The date merchant prayed as the beast boiled over him. Ignoring his screams, the oil merchant prayed also until four blades sheared through him and a white light like fire burst in his brain.

He woke at dawn, with the rose-gold light streaming through the porthole, soft as a pigeon's breast. The enormous quiet soothed him.

He lay, lazily listening to it, the low creaking of the ship as she moved, the soundlessness empty of shouted orders, the sailors' yammering. Only wood and waves. And smooth rosy light.

Daniel imagined Marjannah coming towards him clad solely in morning, and desire sponged his body. But he was still weak from the bouts of fever. He ached in every muscle. He would not have been of much use to Marjannah, had she been here.

He got off the bunk carefully, wary of vertigo, and

stood up in the cramped cabin. The fever had caught him, as it always seemed to, fully clothed. He went to strip off his shirt, which was screwed and crumpled like a rag, and saw before him the cabin door. What there was left of it.

He had locked the door. It seemed someone had tried to come in at him, for the door was broken up in shards.

Looking more closely, he saw out into the passage. Bodies lay there, which perhaps had fallen down from the opened hatch above the ladder. They were heaped, and very bloody, and now he smelled the odour of them, the blood and guts which had spilled about.

Daniel did not bother with his shirt now. The silence of the ship had grown unique and horrible.

He made his way through the narrow passage and tipped a corpse off the ladder. He climbed up, and came out into the morning sunshine on the deck of the *Cos*.

Death was all around him, proliferate and tangible.

He stared at it, and on his beaten body the sweat broke out in a searing tide.

He began to walk the deck, slowly, looking at the dead. Most he did not recognize. Even if he had been familiar with them, he doubted he would have known them now, their faces daubed by blood and matter, distorted by extraordinary terror. And this was true of all of them, their butchery, their looks of fear beyond fear. Their eyes were all open. He recalled the eyes of the robber of tombs; could not recollect the other eyes, those of his father that he had killed, whether they had stayed bulging open or not. He found the captain by the half-deck house, and the officers.

Everywhere were scattered clean knives, gleaming, and by the captain he found a pistol which had been fired.

In the saloon, through the door which, even in his

weakness, he had desperately tumbled down with its barricade, he saw the bodies of the two merchants. And up
in the forecastle, the clerk, with only his neck broken, not
bloody, and nearby Pierre Faude, identifiable from his
garments but not from his face, which had been destroyed.

Daniel stood over Faude's corpse. Presently Daniel
kneeled down and automatically felt inside the Frenchman's coat. After a moment he brought out a pouch,
black with gore. Daniel loosened its strings and slid out
of it the diamond, smeared with blood.

He held the stone in his palm, kneeling above the dead
man, the sun plashing through its facets, white like surf
and white like lightning, and a pale thin green that trembled.

The ship rocked. There was no one at her helm now.
Her sails, all but one, were up and out to suck the slightest wind. She would move as nature determined, and one
man could have little or no say in it.

Daniel stood up and shut the diamond in his hand.

The massacre on the deck affected him oddly. He was
not much sickened, not puzzled. It was as if he had expected all of it, and the broken door to his cabin, too.
Whoever had done these things had come for him and
had not harmed him. Daniel, alone of all these men,
lived. And he had recovered the jewel.

Daniel lay on his bunk, ill and in a fearsome sort of
deadly peace, and the ship moved as she would, over the
sea.

The thought came and went in Daniel's head, rocked
as though in a cradle.

Only I.

Only he had been spared. And he could remember

nothing of the night. The pain had been on him and he had lost consciousness, as before. Not till the dawn did he know anything. And yet.

And yet, was there a vague memory, the whiteness of the moon, a leaping and stretching of light and shadow and form. A memory like that of the glee of hatred he had felt battering the head of his father on the fireplace stone. That joy. It must have been a dream.

He lay there all day, and when the sun began to go, he was frightened, but nothing happened. The fever did not come back.

The moon rose, a little less than full.

He went up on the deck and gazed about at the reeking carnage. Oddly, no rats had come up to feed.

The sea was rougher and the sails breathed at the wind. There was no land in sight. Water everywhere.

Daniel stood at the rail and he felt the utter abysm of the ship, its human life stolen. It came to him he had not asked himself what could have done such awesome acts, nor tried to arm himself, nor searched, nor feared. Only the possible return of the fever had made him afraid.

What had happened? Why had he been spared?

Daniel turned the diamond in his fingers, and he thought of casting it into the sea. He would not find it again after that.

But he did not cast the diamond away. He grasped it and watched the moving night with a still surprise.

3

Out of the east the storm came like a wing. It covered the sinking sun and drove the seas up before it. The ship was driven with the rest, broomed westward, into the night.

There was nothing Daniel could do. He could not take in sail or secure the hatches. He hung on the rail, with the waves of black agate splitting before his face, stinging him with spray like needles. Did he wish to die? When he began to ask himself this question, he went below. He sat in his cabin (he had removed the dead sailors from the passage), shoved this and that way by the force of the water.

The ship streamed through the gale, balancing herself somehow on the rollers, diving and coming up again. Seas broke on her back and were dashed away.

Before the storm she had wandered days, nights, on the waste of ocean. He could not steer her as he believed she was meant to go, and he left her to drift. He ate from the ship's stores, cold rations the dead cook had abandoned in his galley. In the captain's quarters was a store of dried figs and apricots, and brandy in a keg.

He was sorry for the ship, masterless and lost, with only Daniel Vehmund there who did not know or try to help her. The weakness had gradually left him. His hair had grown very long, and he was thickly bearded, as if he had been sick for weeks, adrift for months, but surely that was not so. Ten, thirteen days had passed, not more.

After he had heard the storm raging for three or four hours, he fell asleep. So he did not see the dim outline of land across the spangled sunrise, the hard edge of the land through the spears of rain and sea.

The ship came in on the rocks like a monument. She beached there, big and curious, not suitable, her spars nearly horizontal and the water pouring over her.

The jolt woke Daniel Vehmund, and sent him up the tilting ladder, up the buckled deck, to see.

There was only so much life left now in the *Cos*. She had gone through too much, and was finished. She had run aground as if to end it.

He got out of her awkwardly, leaving everything behind but the diamond carried in the bloody pouch against his heart.

Beyond the rocks was calm, and in the calm was a bay, and he swam for shore over the quietening sea. The day was hard, the sky a roughened blue, and the land seemed empty, nothing there. There were rocks above the shore, and finally, when he had rested, he tried to climb them, and came up in a sort of natural path, and so up to a plateau. From here he saw a plain below, cupped in the rocks, and a white road leading over it; and another height, up in the air, maybe a mile away.

He was bemused by this, for somehow he had not visualized coming again to land of any sort.

Turning back, he saw the ship far out, leaning on the rocks in the sea. She was being gently washed away by the surf, and the bodies on her deck were already gone; the storm had had them. She looked pure, and dead.

He was in a sort of trance as he went down on to the plain by easy stages. And as he travelled the plain, he looked about in wonderment, as if he had never seen the world before, as if he had come back from elsewhere.

There were orange orchards on the plain, gone wild. Lizards basked on boulders. The road, when he came to it, was dusty, and curled up to the height, a tall hill where stood the remains of a castle, perhaps of the Crusaders.

Daniel saw distant buildings, white walls, red roofs. But no people. He did not want to see them. Part of him wanted to stay here, eating the fruit of the trees, tranced, pointless and without onus in the world.

He ascended to the ruin. There was a courtyard, and vast stone rooms, and flights of stairs that went to nothing in the blue sky. Here and there were carvings: eagles that bore a cross, a lion holding a key in its paw. He sat on a grassy place above the stones, among the darting of lizards, and looked out over the plain. He could see for miles, the earth empty as Eden in the beginning, the sea coiled like a crocodile about the coast. Daniel did not know where he was. What did that matter? It was so silent here he heard the slender passing of the wind, the crickets in the grass, the scrape of a lizard's armour along the stone.

After a time, he took out the diamond, and let the sun play on it.

It was white and brilliant, the facets sharp as blades— and in the core of it the flaw like an animal, maybe a wolf.

The diamond had found him out, and he in turn, losing it, had pursued. How it glittered.

"I," he said. A bird flew across the sky with great dark wings.

He had done it. He had killed the men on the ship. There was no memory, yet there was a certainty. The diamond changed him, gave him vast strengths and awful hungers. The diamond had touched something inside him, bringing it to bloom. A flower of death and savagery.

But he did not hurl the diamond away. He held it clasped in his hand, staring into its brightness until the beast there seemed to run.

When sleep came, he was not aware of it. There passed a succession of curious images: A vault, and in the vault a huge casket, opened, with a skeleton inside, fleshless, and with a collar of golden flowers; then a cave on the ledges of which sat bats with the great green eyes of cats; next a procession with coloured banners, chariots, and women singing. Last there was a little image, tiny: a girl's face painted on ivory, with autumnal hair.

The following vision was of a fire burning, and after he had looked at it some while, he knew that he was awake and it was real.

Daniel sat up.

Across the grassy space the night had fallen complete without a chink. With the night, men had come. They were gathered by the fire about sixty feet away from him, up against the stonework. They ate and drank, and nearby horses moved at their tetherings. The firelight played, showing old jackets, fringing, journey boots and greasy caps of hair. One man had a necklet of coins he played with; two others were arguing. They had perhaps not seen him; certainly they had left him alone.

Daniel turned his head. On a wall nearby someone had written in white chalk the word *Terepha*.

A shadow sat under the wall, waiting for him.

Daniel drew the knife the murderer-sailor had gifted him on the ship.

The shadow said something mildly, in a language Daniel did not understand.

"No," Daniel said. He said experimentally in French, "Why do you watch me?"

The shadow leant forward, and the fire stretched out and described him sidelong. A man that, even seated, was very tall, a thin face of bones with arched and heavy brows gone to grey, and grey hair making a frame. The eyes were dark, clouded. The lips parted on long teeth and the man spoke, in French. "I watch you because you interest me."

"How pleasant for you," said Daniel. He sat watching the man in turn. Daniel knew nothing, the month or season, the hour, the country he was in, the name of the man across from him. "Have I rewarded your study?"

"You slept very deeply, as I've seen the sick or the troubled do. Sleep is an escape."

"But here I am again," said Daniel.

"You can put away your knife," said the man. His French was harshly accented, not in the Arab manner, as if deliberately distorted. "Neither I nor my men will offer you harm unless you give us cause."

Daniel thought of the road below on the plain.

"Why come up here?" he asked.

"The ruin also interests me. Will you share our meal?"

"You're kind."

"Not at all. We are both travellers in the night. My name is Julinus. Yours?"

"Vehmund."

Julinus called softly, and all the men came to attention. One got up and brought some bread and meat and a black bottle to the dark where they sat, and put these things down like a picnic.

The name Julinus was not reassuring. It smacked of gypsy doctors without credentials, readers of stars and cards. Yet the man's clothes were good, not poor, not gaudy.

They ate in silence for some minutes.

"You've been in the sea," said Julinus eventually. "There was the rumour of a shipwreck."

Daniel pondered where the rumour could have come from, if it was founded on truth—someone who had seen the *Cos* far out on the bay. He said nothing. Julinus drank from the bottle, wiped its mouth and passed it to Daniel, who drank in turn. It was wine, old and dark as a half-rotten plum.

"Where are you going?" said Julinus.

"Inland."

"You don't speak the language."

"I shall manage."

"Yes, French is often spoken, as in all places of civilisation. But you have no luggage." Daniel smiled. "How mysterious you are," said Julinus. "I should like to fathom the problem of you. Do you have any money to make your way?"

Daniel said, "The question of a thief."

"It occurs to me you may wish to sell me something. I carry my own funds in a coffer. As you see, I'm well protected from bandits."

"What could I sell you," said Daniel. "The clothes I stand up in?"

"Your long hair perhaps," said Julinus. "It would make a handsome wig for someone less fortunate."

"Neither my clothes nor my hair are for sale. I've never sold my person."

"Oh come now," said Julinus, "all men prostitute themselves, one way or another. We hire ourselves as clerks and secretaries; we speak softly when we should wish to shout."

They drank from the bottle again. The waning moon was rising, through the old walls, down on the plain.

"And some of us," said Julinus, "are enslaved by the lunar disc. She makes us mad. Do you think that you're of that number, Monsieur Vehmund?"

Daniel put his hand into his coat. He had tied it to him as he swam, and it was caked with dried brine, stiff and unfriendly like all the rest of his sea-washed, sun-dried garments. He pulled out the pouch, still stained and damp.

"I have something here," he said, "which I'll sell you, Julinus."

He drew the diamond forth into the night and held it up like a vast crystal of salt. The firelight caught it and it burned up, and two of the men looked over from the fire, but, presumably schooled by Julinus, they stared only for a moment, then looked away.

"Now what is that?" asked Julinus the travelling doctor, astrologer, or charlatan.

"What do you think it might be?"

"It might be a prism of glass."

"Just so," said Daniel. "Do you want it?"

"It sparkles brightly. Not glass, I think. Is it sorcerous?"

"Of course."

"Where did you come by it?"

"I took it from a dead man," Daniel said.

"Such things," said Julinus, "are often come at in such a fashion."

Daniel rested, holding the jewel in his hand. In a second it would be gone. How apt. To fly, to pursue, and now to give away.

At the fire some of the men laughed. They were a universe off.

"I don't believe," said Julinus, "that I could pay you what such a trinket is worth."

"Take it," said Daniel. "It's been bad luck to me."

And what will happen when it's far from me, not as it was when the thieves had it and Surim Bey hunted for it, but acres and oceans away. Then, I'll only be myself. I'll be alone, Daniel, nothing more.

I'm delirious, he thought, *imagining these things. Is the charlatan even here?*

"No, I couldn't take your jewel without a fee paid you." Julinus turned back to the fire, and called again, perhaps a name. The man with the coin necklace got up and went among the horses.

Daniel's eyes moved once more over the word chalked on the wall: *Terepha.* What did it mean? To what was it related? To himself?

"Who wrote that word?" he asked the charlatan.

"That? Who knows."

"One of your men wrote it. Before they came, it wasn't here."

"Why concern yourself?"

The man walked from the horses carrying a box. He brought it to Julinus, and went away.

Julinus took a key from inside his coat and opened up the box. Inside were packets of papers, leather bags of stuff unguessable. In the midst was a second box of black metal. Julinus took it up and pressed at the lid in three swift caresses. The lid rose. And there was the glint of gold.

"Sequins," said Julinus. "I find them serviceable. They're old but worth their weight. I'll make you an exchange."

Daniel grinned.

"Give me what it's worth."

Julinus raised the box and emptied it before Daniel on the ground. (The charlatan would have other coffers.)

The ancient coins glowed like night suns on the turf. Daniel did not try to count them.

"Yes, that's good."

"You're satisfied." Julinus extended his hand, and Daniel placed in it the diamond. In leaving him it seemed to smear some residue behind, a coldness, a warmth, clinging to his fingers. And in the depth of his body a kind of plucking, a muscle stretched too far.

Julinus handed him instead the black bottle, its mouth now unwiped, and Daniel drank deeply of the plum-rotten wine.

He felt no release. He felt nothing, now.

"A sensible choice," Julinus said. "I see it in the cold north-west, on the throats of women, as the candles shine."

"Where," said Daniel Vehmund, "is this place?"

"A hill-top."

"No. What country are we in?"

"You are on the large continent of Europe," said Julinus. "Did the ship drift? I won't tell you anything else. Let it be an adventure for you."

They drank until the bottle was void.

Julinus pointed at the ground. "Gather up the coins."

Daniel moved his hand over them and let them lie.

"Won't you miss them?"

"I have them here," Julinus tapped his coffer. The diamond was gone. "I'll leave you to your sleep now. Tomorrow, you'll think it all a dream."

"Tomorrow I'll be rich."

Julinus' man, Aaron, slowly crossed the stony ground between the ruined walls of the castle. He had been an orphan of the alleys until Julinus took him in, and cared for him. He had grown with no other parent; he was like Julinus' clever dog now, and one that could use its paws.

Standing over Daniel, Aaron hoped the young man would not wake and spoil the perfection of the half-light, the motions of the campment as it uncurled itself and made ready to be off.

The golden Italian sequins lay in a neat mound by the young man's hand. He had not gathered them in, yet in sleep his hand had played over them, as if seeking something else.

Aaron steadied himself and leaned down a little. He shot Daniel Vehmund in the chest.

The men started and cursed at the report, then went on at their business with the horses and the bags.

Julinus sat to one side on his gelding, a tall noble figure, indifferent.

Aaron raked the gold into a cloth. He did not bother with the obliging man he had shot, who lay relaxed, not having woken. His hair, in the emboldening light, was the colour of the coins, but Julinus had not said it should be harvested. Let him keep his hair then, until the crows and falcons, who picked him clean, took it for their nests along the rock.

PART TWO

PART TWO

1

It was a green morning. The trees that covered the top of the rise filtered the spring sky through a green bubble of new leaves. The duck pond, long empty of ducks, was dark as jade among the oaks, on whose trunks the emerald moss was glowing. In the dell of grass tumbled the old cottage, its walls stoled in the dark green ivy which ate them alive. From a chimney in the tilted roof the smoke rose in reluctant boasts. The fire was ill-laid as usual, and, as usual a squabbling came from the main room.

By the window, Laura made out the sulky tones of her sisters, Elfie and Alice, the sullen tremolo of her mother. Then the crash of the father's voice. Of them all Jason Wheelwright did the least. But he was the man, head of the household, this 'covey of women' as he was wont to name it. "Where's my bread? Am I to starve? Four damnable women and can't make a breakfast."

"Laura!" shrilled the mother through the open window. "Come here and fry your father's bread."

Laura went in reluctantly, but a slave. It was impossible not to be obedient.

Kneeling at the hearth where the porridge pot splut-

tered, she fried a plateful of bread in the pan for her
father.

He was a short stout man, red of face from drink and
outdoors, dressed little better than a tinker, which he had
once been. Now he did whatever work came his way and
could not be avoided, and drove a hard deal for it. The
cottage, an inheritance, had brought him to this spot
some years before, and here he set his family: his podgy,
smile-less wife and three daughters. Of the daughters,
Alice and Elfie, fourteen and fifteen years, tended the
cottage as they must—and their rampaging father while
he was by. Fortunately he was often out, loafing about
the countryside, at fairs for bargains—the house was littered by useless items he had got—at his bits of work for
the neighbouring farms, or drinking at the alehouse in
the village. The father and two younger daughters were
much alike in looks; even the mother resembled them,
save the women had whey faces for his flush. They might
all have come from one mould. Yet the eldest daughter,
Laura, was quite dissimilar. Tall and slender, she had a
dark flame of hair, which colour Jason Wheelwright
could recall seeing only in an aunt. Her eyes were black,
and her skin very white and clear. She moved too in a
different way, held herself differently, and spoke unlike
the rest, for she had benefited from her schooling in the
village, which Alice and Elfie had not. Truly, Laura was
an iris on the mire.

Jason was proud of Laura as of a lucky knick-knack he
had picked up for a song. Yet also he was unhappy with
her, for she was plainly too good for him. Alternately he
praised and attempted to crush her down. From the
mother and the two sisters she had, however, constant
dislike.

"Will you be going along to laze at the farm today?" Mrs Wheelwright asked her eldest daughter snappishly.

"Yes, Mother."

Unlike the others, Laura had taken it on herself to get work where she could. At haymaking and at harvest she saw to it she was employed, her fair skin scratched and her back sore from bending. Elsewhere she had milked cows and minded sheep. But also she had come to the attention of a woman at one of the farms: a graceful, gracious woman who, on hearing Laura speak, had asked her if she read well. Laura replied that she did. Thereafter, and for the past seven months, and when the winter ways were passable, Laura was engaged to read to this woman, whose eyes, due to a severe illness, had lost their ability to focus for long on pages of text. For the service Laura was well paid, and though the father drank some of this money away, her mother made use of the rest of it for food and other necessities. Nevertheless, it was Laura's mother who was scathing.

"Her eyes are no better then? But she can see well enough to write letters. And she sends them to foreign parts, I hear." Mrs Wheelwright was a diligent gossip in the village.

"She's once or twice asked me to pen her letters for her," said Laura idly.

"And you never told me," accused the mother. "Do you read for her the letters she has in return?"

"No, never."

Baulked, the woman made more tea for her husband. He, crammed with bread and porridge, now smoked his pipe in silence. Wheelwright was due to work on a distant farm today, and should already have set out. He would be late, and his labour of the botched sort when he got there.

Laura washed the crockery and, having dried the
dishes and put them away, took off her apron. She left
the house to the sounds of her mother's disapproval and
the sisters' scorn—none of them could read more than a
word or two.

Above, on the lane, the green day became blue as the
large sky opened. Laura felt a sensation of liberty at having escaped her family.

The walk was two hours long, but Laura made nothing
of it. She looked around her as she went, at the trees and
hedges, the dark fields with their beginning quickening,
the birds and animals that chanced to be about. Strange
feelings assailed Laura, too, as she walked. There was a
curious excitement in her that had no foundation in fact.
It was perhaps only the effervescence of the spring itself.

After a time, the shoulders of the hills appeared, and
the forest that rode them, dense and old, with the look of
a furry sleeping thing in the thin blue air. The Vehmund
farm, where Laura was bound, lay in the lap of the valley
beneath, and already the hilly pastures she negotiated,
with their rusty dots of cows and sprinkles of sheep, were
Vehmund land.

It was Mrs Vehmund's son who maintained the farm
now, for her husband had died, the victim of a terrible
murder. He was attacked in the farm kitchen at his very
hearth, as it was thought by some gypsy or other
wanderer he had surprised at robbery, for a great amount
of money had reportedly been stolen. His wife, for some
while an invalid, then fell dangerously sick: the illness
that had left her unable to read print. She had been from
the first a lady, and not much concerned in the running of
the house, which was seen to by the woman Rosamunde
Ax. The men of the farm were cloddish, and her son a
kind of human mass that moved and spoke but seemed

barely sensible—this was the opinion Laura had formed. Jenavere Vehmund—Jenavere being the name by which Laura was instructed to call her patron—had been a misfit from the first, and now existed in a sort of fragile parasitism, offering nothing and receiving nothing beyond her bed and board and those comforts, such as Laura, that she herself had acquired. But it was she who brought the wealth on which her dead husband had founded his farm. That had been her use. She was still tolerated because of it.

Laura took the track down into the valley and soon came among the beeches, and then into the orchard that lay before a grey stone house. The sheltered apple and pear trees were still covered in late blossom. Beyond the orchard was Rosamunde's garden of herbs, planted cabbages, and the old tough vine that clung to the wall and produced grapes in July. Some chickens strutted in the yard. The door stood shut.

It was Rosamunde who opened it and admitted Laura to the great kitchen, which had been the site of murder.

She was a small brown wrinkled woman in middle age, who looked at Laura with a stab of hate.

"She's ready. Go up."

In such a way Rosamunde Ax always greeted Laura, whom she resented and feared as she resented but did not fear her sickly mistress. Rosamunde had tended Mr Vehmund while he lived, and now was the servant of his son. She had worked the flesh off her bones for both of them, expecting and getting no thanks, seeing her proper place in such chains. But refinement of any type she abhorred. There had been another son, sent off to a school to learn fool's ways, and had learnt them. Rosamunde had hated him also, but, since he was a man, God's superior creation, she did not show it nor brood on it. That one, any way, was off now to another country, with his tutoring. The mistress had read aloud the letter of his intention, which came over a month after the murder, from some alien place across the sea. It seemed he had gone straight from his studies in the city to this foreign spot, telling no one. Which was itself curious, for he had been anticipated home. Rosamunde recalled this well, for she had been angrily baking at the mistress' order, against his arrival.

Laura had gone through the kitchen and up the back stair to the upper floor. Here she proceeded along a passage and knocked at the door of Jenavere's room. She was admitted by a low sweet voice.

Jenavere sat where habitually she did, in the big bedroom over the kitchen, the Master's Chamber, now solely hers.

The window was thrown open, and from below came the sounds of the chickens and the scent of the orchard.

Jenavere was in her chair, her feet on the footstool, and the book lying ready beside her.

Where Laura was a copper-haired woman of white skin, Jenavere was a silver woman. Her hair was grey, yet so fine and soft still that it shone like platinum. The blue had left her eyes and they were like the winter ocean, as cold, yet not cruel in that way. Cold and gentle. Her complexion was pale, marked with a few deep couth lines. She did not look her years, nor any proper age, lost therefore, and out of time. She wore an old grey gown, and on her breast was a silver pin from which all of her had taken accent.

"Here's my good angel," said Jenavere Vehmund, and smiled at Laura shyly and remotely, as if looking down on one she was fond of out of a cloud.

Laura took her seat and opened the book. They did

not spend time on meaningless inquiries. As she began to read, Laura noticed that a pile of old letters lay on Jenavere's knees. She held them still with one hand, like an animal.

After Laura had been reading for an hour, Jenavere stopped her, as seldom happened. Unusually, Jenavere seemed to want speech more than entertainment.

Laura sipped from the cup of cider Jenavere provided her in order that Rosamunde should not be called on.

"I've been re-reading these letters," Jenavere said, "from my son, Daniel. He's in the East, I've told you. It seems I haven't heard from him for so long. Letters take months across so many miles, and are sometimes lost."

"It must be a worry to you," said Laura. She was sympathetic, for she was pleased by Jenavere, her looks and refinement, not least at being singled out by her.

"I feel our parting," said Jenavere. "My other son and I aren't close. He was his father's. But Daniel was mine." She made no apology; seemed to expect Laura to comprehend, which Laura did. The lump of manhood left at the farm was obviously only accidentally of Jenavere's making. The other son, though Laura had never seen him, must be of this finer material.

"Is there some hope," Laura asked, "that he'll return soon?"

"No. No hope at all," answered Jenavere quickly, almost as if afraid. "There can be nothing for him here."

Laura did not reply that Jenavere was situated there.

"I imagine you know the terrible story . . . of his father's death," said Jenavere. "His father left nothing to Daniel, everything to our eldest boy, Marsall. Daniel must make his way elsewhere. But how I miss him. It cuts like a knife." Jenavere hesitated. She said, "Time doesn't lessen the ache. I feel it worse every day. And since there's been no news, I picture all sorts of calamities. Things without a name. This is the foolishness of mothers."

Laura could think of nothing to say that might be helpful.

On the bed two of the cats awoke and began to wash each other. Jenavere looked at them kindly.

"Such simple, perfect lives," she said, "without a care. And we are animals too, but clutter ourselves with feeling. Laura, will you write a letter for me to my son? My eyes are worse today."

And so Laura, replacing the book with paper, pen and ink, took down the letter. It was uncomplex, mentioning details of the farm, and season, without a reference to Jenavere's own weakness. It concluded: *'Write to me soon, I beg you. I think some letter of yours has not reached me and I am hungry to hear of you.'*

When the letter was done, Laura herself offered to take it, and Jenavere thanked her. The village was far off from the Vehmund farm, and Rosamunde or one of the girls must otherwise be constrained to go.

Another hour passed in random dialogue, but Jenavere was slow and very still. Finally she paid Laura her fee, without show, and so tacitly dismissed her.

Laura felt downcast going out. Jenavere was trapped, as she was. With no arrogance at all, Laura knew herself a swan among the messy household of the cottage. Jenavere, a noble prisoner, occupied her cell like one awaiting execution.

Rosamunde was in her garden, fighting with the weeds. She neither spoke nor looked as Laura went by. But above, in the open window over the yard, the silver figure raised its hand in farewell.

As Laura moved through the orchard, she mused irresistibly on the murder. Her mother had once been full of the tale. The master of the Vehmund farm had been strangled.

Some of the blossom had fallen and carpeted the way, unsuitable corollary to her thoughts.

Two men were riding across the hill. She recognized one immediately. He was the lumpen Marsall Vehmund. The other man was a stranger, and too far away to discern much else.

Laura went on, got through the beech trees and up on to the earth path that ran across the fields above.

As she passed below, she noticed both men glance her way, and thought no more of it.

However, some ten minutes later, as she was walking homeward, the sound of hoofs came to her. She looked back, and found the second man was riding after her along the path.

The way was narrow, and Laura drew up against the hedge to let the rider by.

He was a gentleman and smartly clad. A glimpse of his face and figure pronounced him young, fawn, handsome, and oddly intent upon something. Laura found that he turned his eyes also on her. She prudently looked away.

When he came up, rather than ride on, he drew rein.

"The oaf from the farm says your name is Laura Wheelwright."

"Yes, sir," said Laura, gazing at the ground.

"Well, Miss Wheelwright, what business do you have with such burning hair? I thought the trees were on fire."

Laura indignantly looked up again.

"I haven't any blame for my hair."

"Indeed not. It's all to your credit. And the rest of you to match, I see."

Laura was taken, despite herself. Although she had

long ago been warned against the flattery of men, and especially of men of this class, she was not displeased. She said nothing.

"Well," said the rider, "only let me see your eyes a moment. Are they green or blue?"

Laura lifted her eyes and gave him one long stare. Perhaps she should not have done.

The rider laughed. He said, "Black as jet. Well, what colouring. If I were a painter I should make a canvas of you, Miss Wheelwright. But as I'm not, may I only humbly inquire if I can escort you to your house?"

"No, sir, you can't."

"That's a pity then. A grievous pity. May I ask instead where your house is to be come on?"

"I live with my family, sir."

"Wait. I know the name. Your father does husbandry and carpentry bits, I'm told. Ivy Cottage, isn't it?"

Laura, who had resumed gazing at the ground, made no affirmative move.

"They've warned you," he said, "against characters such as I. My name is Hyperion Worth. I live beyond the next village, *that* way—which to you is somewhere behind the sun." Laura did not argue. Geographically he was right, for she had never been so far as that next village. "Come, won't you let me sit you on this dear calm roan horse and lead you home."

"No, thank you, sir."

"Well then, I'll be off—as you'd doubtless like to tell me to be."

And with a sudden flaunt of reins, hat, and fawn hair, handsome Mr Worth took his leave and galloped away into the pasture, regardless of the grazing sheep, who ran.

* * *

Jenavere spent the afternoon as always, looking from her window, dozing, the afternoon of a very old woman. Now and then one of the cats would leap lightly on to her lap and, after a period of time, off again. She greeted them softly and let them go without remonstrance.

The sun set behind the house, the dusk began, and a firm spring moon rose over the pastures.

Rosamunde's hard knock came on the door.

"Master says will you come down to sup?"

It was not Jenavere's custom to take any of her meals in company with her son. For him to ask her was a summons.

"Very well."

She went down slowly in her grey dress, through the shadows.

In the kitchen the fire blazed and the lamps were lit. Amid the hot light sat her elder son and his companions, his three lieutenants of the farm. No others had the privilege of eating inside the stone kitchen. Marsall slouched at the table. His boots had walked thick mud across the floor; Rosamunde would clean both before she went to her bed. Now she had served them ale, and all four drank deeply.

Jenavere took her place at the opposite end of the table, not speaking.

"Good evening, Mother," said Marsall, in a peculiar exaggerated diction he used only for her. "How are you today?"

"I'm well, thank you."

"Splendid. Lovely. I rejoice. Have you been baking?"

"Rosamunde baked today."

"Then you weren't hale enough to bake?"

Sometimes Jenavere had, formally, carried out certain

domestic tasks, but Rosamunde did not welcome her, and Jenavere had let them go.

Getting no answer, Marsall Vehmund grunted something to his companions, and all four laughed piggishly.

"I've got some news, Mother," said Marsall next, in his pointed voice. "A fine gentleman came. A fine rich gentleman from fifteen miles away. He wants to buy the land, and keep me on as his man. We shall have the house still, and the orchard. What do you think?"

Jenavere knew quite well it did not matter what she thought. What she had thought had been, anyway, absurd. For she was frightened at the idea of Daniel's being left with nothing. But then, all the property, all the coin, her husband's and what she herself had brought him, had passed to Marsall. And anyway, Daniel was a million miles off, and no letters came.

"You must do as you think wise," she said carefully to her elder son.

"It seems to me," said Marsall, "we could do worse than sell. Nothing changes, but if there's bad luck, rich Mr Worth will bear it, not we. And with the cash—why, I could do something with that."

Marsall was of an even thickness from his shoulders to his knees. His feet were large and his head small, thatched with dun hair. He was like his father. Into marriage with that violent ugly man Jenavere had been bullied, for Vehmund fancied her, and her father owed Vehmund money. From the first he had been rough, his love-making less tender than the farmyard, his wrath preposterous and deadly. He had struck her initially on the tenth day after marriage, and went on from there. While she carried the two sons (and the two miscarriages) he had, it was true, not touched her, but instead he smashed things, or vented his rage on the animals that were also his property. Once she had seen him kick a bull between the eyes, and he had broken the necks of kittens he deemed superfluous.

Jenavere's hatred of him was greater than any other hate of that house, much, much more than anything the poisonous Rosamunde could devise, and steady like a low-burning flame. She must have impregnated Daniel with it, although, in her efforts to spare him, she had somehow got him sent away to school in the city. He was always like her in looks, in other ways, and Vehmund had seemed glad to see the back of him. When Daniel reappeared at the farm, educated and like a gentleman, Vehmund prized him as something valuable—since funny. Daniel's wit and knowledge made him laugh, as if at a performing monkey. Daniel ascended to the university, and still Mr Vehmund was amused, grinning at Daniel's tricks, with the other son, Marsall, who was like a second self.

Then came the day that Daniel returned to visit Jenavere, and walked unseen across the field like an itinerant, as if it had been meant. There was a fair at the village, and even Rosamunde was gone, her trays of bread set on the windowsill.

Vehmund had been angry, over what Jenavere could not now recall. But he had begun to berate her in turn, and finally he smote her, as was his way. She had pulled herself up from the floor and into her chair, when the door crashed open and Daniel sprang into the room. He had seen, once, twice, the evidence of blows on her face before. He had seen her sicken, known her nearly always ill, through all the years he had been alive. Never before had he come upon the root of her punishment at its enactment.

Daniel raced at his father, attacked him like a wild

dog, instantly, and the big thick man had slung him off, so Daniel too fell on to the floor with blood on his skin.

In his guttural, bestial voice, the father had reviled the son. He had told Daniel to go down, down to the kitchen, and fetch the strap, which the man had used upon both sons in their childhood. Without a word, Daniel got up and went to the door. There he said, "I'll wait for you," and was gone.

"Tend your face," said Vehmund to Jenavere, and went after.

Then she sat in her chair, the blood on her lip like a thread of boiling ice, her ears quarrelling with sounds, her heart beating in huge pulses.

She heard, below, the strangest noise. A sort of stumbling and grumbling, and then weird blows that shook the room coming up through the chimney breast. At last there was silence, and in the silence, eventually, she heard instead the light steps of Daniel and held herself ready for some shock or terror. He entered her room, white and composed, the blood already dead and dry at the corner of his mouth. He said, "I've killed him."

She had not argued. She had known. They had made plans at once. He took the money from his father's hiding place in the kitchen, and was gone before anyone came. Thereafter he sent the letter from abroad. He had never been suspected. The county reeled to the tale of the gypsy vagabond who had murdered Mr Vehmund while his sickly wife slept in the room above. For half a year people went in horror of this invention, men sleeping with their guns, women turning off tramps with screams of fear.

Stricken, she had not realized how she would miss him, worse than when he had been at the school. She was ill a long while, and, coming back from it, wanted only Daniel, and he was not to be had.

In some potent silly way, Laura reminded Jenavere of her golden son. Laura also was too chiselled for her setting. Laura too was beautiful, and young.

"So," said the pig son who, incredibly, had once lived in her womb, "maybe I'll sell to precious Mr Worth."

Spring opened into summer, and a green flood covered the earth. The trees were heavy with their flags, the fields sprung with grain, and the grass on the hillsides grew as fast as the sheep and cows could crop it. The broad stream which ran above the valley turned shallow and brown. Frogs hopped between the shining stones. The forest greened to black.

Laura was enlisted among the milkmaids of a neighbouring farm and was gone before dawn, while her father lay snoring, or in the summer evening, when he made ready for the ale-house. She did not have the leisure much to make the long walk to and from the Vehmund farm, to be Jenavere's reader.

As the sun westered, Laura paced homeward from her milking. She was drowsy with the summer heat, the gnats that rose from the ponds and the butterflies that skimmed over the flowers. In the fields the early poppies bled under long shadows.

A sad resignation was on her also, as ever, that it was to the ivy cottage she was going, to her mother and father and the two sisters.

When she came down from the lane among the oak trees, Laura saw a roan horse standing tethered by the house.

She could not think whose it might be, but now and

then local officers of the land had come to berate her father. She thought it must be something of that sort.

When she got near the cottage, a gust of wild mad laughter flew out through the window.

It startled her.

She put her hand on the door with some trepidation.

"And here the girl is," exclaimed Laura's father excitedly, as if she was a personage of note.

The wife and daughters sat at the table, and the father in his chair. In the chimney corner sat Hyperion Worth. He rose as she entered, and bowed to her. He was so unsuitable there that all the room seemed awry, as if its very angles were out of joint. The faces of her kindred turned on her avidly.

"You must pardon my intrusion, Miss Wheelwright," said Hyperion Worth. "I called on the chance of seeing you. And your family have made me welcome."

"Welcome you are, sir," cried Jason with enthusiasm.

Laura stood by the table in her working gown, her red hair wound round her head, and her hands limp from milking cows.

"Why," she said, "should you wish to see me, Mr Worth?"

"Come now. Why does any man call on a pretty girl."

Rather than take umbrage, the fluttered family almost applauded, and the two ugly sisters giggled.

"Generally," said Laura sternly, "men mean a pretty girl no kindness."

"Hush, Laur," said Laura's mother. "You'll offend the gentleman. And him coming all this way to see you."

"I'm obliged to him," said Laura. "But he made the journey at his own whim."

"Quite so," cut in Hyperion. "And am amply rewarded

by the sight of Laura, so fresh and fair after her hard day."

"On the contrary, I'm very tired," said Laura.

"Not too tired, I hope, to take a walk with me."

Laura looked about her. Her father grinned and her mother simpered. It was left to Laura to defend herself.

"Yes, sir, too tired. For I've been walking about all day."

"Why, then we'll sit here and enjoy the hospitality of your family," said Hyperion, without a shade of apparent regret.

Laura sat down, and her mother grudgingly poured for her a cup of cold stewed tea.

Hyperion and Jason fell to discussing the land, about which it seemed both knew something despite their indolence.

"Now, when you've finished your cup," murmured Laura's mother, "go up and comb out your hair. You know it looks its best unbound, and it's very maidenly. Then go with the gentleman for a little walk."

"Mother, how can you tell me to do that?" asked Laura in irritation.

"It's plain he's sweet on you," said the mother. "He spoke quite freely of seeing you on the lane and being struck by your looks. And here he is, all of fifteen or sixteen miles out of his way for your sake. And he brought us this tea. He mentioned a horse as being useful to your father."

Laura was not sure if her mother only wished her ill, or if greed motivated her.

"There are nothing but stories," said Laura, "of young peasant girls led off by so-called gentlemen, disgraced and brought low for the rest of their lives."

"Nonsense. It's a commonplace," contrarily said the

mother. She proved that her motive was mostly greed: "He'll do you nothing but good. Think of what he may lavish on us. There's plenty made a like arrangement."

"You would sell me," said Laura, "for a horse and a packet of tea."

"You're too high and mighty, my lass. What do you expect for yourself? You're lucky to have caught his eye, and looking the fright you do. Go up and tidy yourself."

Laura was taken by a sudden fit of fury.

She stood without a word and went up at once to the bedroom she shared with the two sisters. Here she washed herself and put on a better dress, and combed out her fiery smouldering of hair. Presently she came down again, and Hyperion, staring at her, pretended to shield his eyes.

"I'm dazzled," he said.

"Then we'll go walking," said Laura.

She saw her mother sneering at this aboutwardness, and the two girls made faces at her from behind the teapot. Jason got up, and taking Laura's hand, placed it in Mr Worth's. Such a gesture of giving was beyond all bounds of decency and sense, and Laura had anticipated nothing else.

Only when they were outside and alone did she withdraw her hand from Hyperion's.

"My family, as you see, are wretches," said Laura.

"Yes they are. But even so, the high colour of your annoyance suits you and I can only thank them for causing it. I hope you're not at war with *me*?"

"No. You're simply pursuing your adventure as a man will. But *they* . . ." Laura did not bother to conclude.

"Yet you've come out with me."

"I prefer your honest wickedness to their cheat."

"Well," said Hyperion, "I'm not so wicked. What is there in a walk?"

Laura did not respond. In all the tales, several of which she knew to be true, the maiden accompanied the gentleman and he led her into some trackless wood and there had his way with her. Thereafter she was the scorn of everyone, while he went whistling off about his business.

Hyperion Worth, too, doubtless knew the tales and doubtless had careless seduction in his mind. Her family had shown they did not heed, providing they were recompensed. There was only Laura to persuade.

They walked up from the cottage and across the lane on to a path which ran between the fields.

The sun was lower now, and a lavender bloom lay on the edge of things, which otherwise were of a golden greenness. Birds sang. They came into a little wood, too slender to fit the woods of the tales, and here they sat down together on a fallen tree and watched the sparrows and mice searching the undergrowth.

"Well, this isn't so terrible, is it, Laura?"

Laura failed to answer.

Mr Worth pried the earth with the toe of his boot.

"Am I," he inquired, "abhorrent to you?"

"I can scarcely see *you*, sir, for what you are."

"What am I?"

"A man of a higher class than mine."

"Pure accident. There are no titles in my family. Nothing but trusty money."

"With which you always buy what you want."

"What a sharp tongue you have," he commented. "I know I can't buy you."

"My family will try to make you do it," said Laura.

"My thanks for your warning; I foresaw as much. Let

me tell you, Laura, I have a beautiful house with ranks of windows, with balustrades and statues and a lake. Can I induce you to visit there? It's only a dozen miles away."

"Thank you, no."

"Don't believe I have a fearsome father or paragon of a mother who will bolt out at you. I'm quite alone in the world."

"How fortunate," said Laura.

"Yes, fate has given *you* to a den of jackals," remarked Hyperion Worth. "Won't you let me try to lessen that sorrow?"

Laura rose. "I'll go back now, Mr Worth. Sunset has begun."

He followed her from the wood and they retraced their steps through the metallic glow of sunfall.

"Your hair burns into the sky," he said.

But Laura only pressed bravely on towards her dreadful home.

He said nothing more, but delivered her up to the kowtowing family, mounted his horse, and rode away.

Throughout the summer, then, Hyperion Worth paid court to Laura, the eldest daughter of Jason Wheelwright.

He brought to the cottage at various times hampers of food, a clutch of wines, some dresses for the younger daughters, and material and lace for the lazy mother to make others when she was inclined. On no occasion did he bring for Laura anything beyond a bunch of flowers picked along the way. For so much she was glad, but she began at last to fear the time when he grew vexed and left her alone. For then the presents to her grasping tribe would cease, and how they would lament to her.

No doubt they thought she had given in to him and

spread herself beneath him in some copse or nook on their walks, but Laura had done nothing of the kind, nor had he ever asked that she should.

By harvest she had started after all to admire the patience of this attractive and light-hearted man. It would be no vile thing to give way to him. Only custom and the danger of falling into some social abyss put all idea of it from her mind.

Yet he deserved something for his fidelity and airiness, and so she came to repay him by talking with him and by listening to him.

He told her of a lonely childhood brought up by retainers and a trail of cold aunts, the last of whom had fled like frost at his twenty-first birthday. Of age, he had come into riches, and these he enjoyed in an undaunted happy manner, spending for pleasure without either dissolution or guilt. He asked Laura again, and more than once, to visit his mansion. He described its delights, but she would not be swayed.

"You're used to having your way by means of bribes," she said. "Doubtless you bribed the cold old aunts with gifts, to make them like you."

"It's true," he said. "I remember bringing Christmas roses to one of them and grapes from the vine to another. Of course these cost no money, but they cost my time, and I offered them like a cherub. But did those icy women crack? Not they."

"Don't think *I* shall," said Laura.

And he smiled. "I adore your adamance, Laura. You're like Athene. Passionate and serene at once. Who can win a goddess?"

And at the cottage, husband and wife puffed proud, and even the nasty younger daughters stayed their jibes. Although, when they lay in bed with Laura, Elfie and

Alice would sometimes keep her deliberately awake, mimicking the transports of lovers, about which they knew very little.

At the harvest, Laura went to help on the farms, and so earned money which her mother gripped and her father drank away.

She had not seen Jenavere Vehmund for some while, for Jenavere had been ill and listless through the summer, and did not call her to the farm even when Laura's other work permitted it.

Then, as the days shortened and streams of saffron and brown crept up the trees, Jenavere did call for Laura, by means of a note brought by a carter.

Rosamunde Ax was at her baking. From the hot oven she acidly said, "Go up. She's ready."

In the upper room Jenavere sat by the hearth where a fire was kindled. She was wan and listless, not silver today but only grey, and the red of the fire seemed to have drained all the blood from her.

"How glad I am to see you, Laura." But she did not look glad, only sad.

The book was set to one side and not forthcoming. It seemed Jenavere wanted to speak, yet she was silent.

Laura said, "Haven't you had word of Daniel?"

"None," said Jenavere. Her face flattened with grief, her eyes darkened. "Always before his letters came. But this summer, not a word. Perhaps he's only forgetful of me." She clasped her hands and lifted them to her lips. She stared beyond the room. "I believe myself foolish, yet I picture some dreadful thing."

"That's natural, but certainly you're wrong. The posts must be irregular and not reliable from such a distance."

"I know you're right in what you say," said Jenavere.

"Or perhaps he's travelled elsewhere, and your letters haven't yet caught him up."

"Or that," Jenavere agreed. They sat in silence. Then she said, "The fearfulness of it is that I can do nothing. I can only bide and see. And I can't bear it—yet it must be borne."

There was nothing to be said. Laura gazed mutely and Jenavere eloquently. At last Jenavere spoke again. "I think the winter will be harsh. It was harsh last winter. Do you know, sitting at my window, I saw a wolf out on the pasture. Only one, poor thing, walking in the snow."

"Wolves are rare in these parts," said Laura.

"So they are. It was the cold brought it down. I didn't tell Marsall. He would have been out to hunt it. Where can it have gone to, I wonder," said Jenavere. "It took none of the sheep. The winter was hard on it. And this one will be worse. Strength is needed to get through. I'm not sure I shall outlive this winter."

"Oh," said Laura. "Oh . . ."

"Or perhaps I'm mistaken. Perhaps I'll last. The sickly are often the most tenacious. If only," Jenavere said, "if only Daniel would write to me."

Laura sighed. Jenavere was telling her that she died for his letter. There was nothing to be done. One of the cats came and jumped on Laura's lap, and she stroked its purring silken length.

Jenavere stirred the red fire with the poker. She made an effort. "I hear that you have a suitor, Laura?"

Laura said, "It's most *un*suitable."

"Because he isn't a village man? Would you prefer that?"

"The village men are unappealing," said Laura. She realized Jenavere must have heard of her plight through the gossiping of her two housemaids—though probably not Rosamunde Ax. This far the story had spread. "My family have fastened on Mr Worth like vampires, and he allows it. All for the value of walks he takes with me, for there's nothing else."

"Maybe he's content," said Jenavere. "He's mercurial and does as he wants, not as the rest do. He's to buy the farm from Marsall. Twice, when I met him, he was very civil."

"But I shouldn't encourage him, Jenavere," said Laura, using the gift of her patron's name severely. "Only harm can come to me. Already I'm the talk of the county."

"So you are," agreed Jenavere, and suddenly she gave a little laugh. "But the talk is of your unassailable virtue, all at his expense. You've turned the tables on philandering, Laura."

A blundering entry sounded below, and clump of boots. Marsall had come home early in the autumn afternoon, as now he frequently did, leaving the overseeing to his lieutenants.

A shout sounded, Marsall calling on Rosamunde. It had in it every unseemliness possible to man.

"My son," said Jenavere, with a curl of her lip. She sat like a queen. It was obvious that Marsall, though her flesh and blood, was never hers. Presently she passed Laura the book, and Laura read aloud.

When the session ended, and Laura, paid, took her leave, her heart was heavy for the other woman. It seemed to Laura her troubles were small compared to Jenavere's overmastering one.

In the kitchen, Marsall was at his ale. He gave Laura no attention. She was too slim and altogether too fine to stir his senses; he preferred grosser stuff. Rosamunde as usual did not grant her a word.

* * *

There was a harvest dance at the village. Laura would normally have avoided it, but her mother insisted the two younger girls could not go without her, and they carped and whined, and her mother chid her for an uppity uncharitable ingrate. Eventually she gave in.

At the dance then, while the fiddler sawed, and the other couples bounced, Laura sat in a corner, not allowing herself to be lugged about. Elfie and Alice were, however, lugged about all they liked, and vowed to stay until the last chord.

After perhaps an hour, the door opened and Hyperion Worth entered.

There was a hush, although the fiddler played on, his blackberry eyes squinting over the bow. But Hyperion breasted the gaping room without a glance, smiling not haughty, and singled Laura out for a spin. Evidently he knew himself the talk of the neighbourhood, and did not mind it.

Laura was at first incensed, and then, finding that he would not, now, take No as an answer, and that he danced very nicely, she felt a reluctant pleasure. For where else in the village, or the county, might be come on so handsome and easy a man?

After this they danced every dance the fiddler gave out, and the girls watched with green eyes and the men muttered, but gradually a sort of good-humour came on. Hyperion Worth did not lord it among them, neither did he ape their own manners. He was distinct, natural and shining, and one by one they warmed to him. That he courted Laura was obvious, and did it openly, too, to his credit. The rural morality was less strict than that of the city. It was Laura who viewed yielding as a fall, not necessarily they.

And Laura danced and was happy, a blithe thing that had found its match.

When the dance ended, Hyperion Worth escorted all the Wheelwright daughters to their home.

He lingered outside with Laura.

"You shouldn't have come tonight," she said, a lie against all her instincts.

"I'm sorry. But if you hadn't been there I should have made off again."

Laura thought of going in to the smirking mother and the bed of sisters. She acknowledged that she loathed her family. How much she preferred Hyperion's company, that gave her only flowers and energies. She too was disposed to linger, and therefore bade him a sudden goodnight.

"The winter's coming," said Hyperion. "The bird will hide its head under its wing, icicles drip, and wolves come down from the woods perhaps, like last year."

"I heard of a winter wolf," said Laura unguardedly. "But they hadn't been seen in these parts for a decade."

"Be careful as you travel," said Hyperion.

"Oh, wolves do no harm, except sometimes to the sheep."

"Nevertheless," said Hyperion, "I wish I had the power to forbid your journeying far in the winter."

"When the snow comes, the snow will forbid me."

Both he and she glimpsed before them the long winter white, when possibly the roads and lanes would be impassable, and they should not see each other at all.

"I dream of you often, Laura," said Hyperion.

"Good-night, Mr Worth," said Laura again, and went inside.

* * *

Winter came. It came with flamboyant flaming leaves and berries that shrivelled in a night. Winds roared across the land, the trees bent and some were torn out. Rain fell and storms raged. There came the vast quiet of a freezing cold. The ground was hard as iron. Then the freezing opened and from the umber sky the snow dropped down. The snow settled and the freezing door closed again upon it; and, on the face of this bitter white world, the chimneys and the cow-byres steamed and the sheep crept grey as cinders, and now and then a man or woman passed like the last man or woman on earth.

The night of the snow Laura had gone up to the Vehmund farm. Her mother had earnestly packed her off, with the words, "There may be snow and then you must stay there, and probably you'll get some good from it." For the Vehmunds were thought still to be wealthy, especially since they were selling out.

Laura was glad enough to go, and Jenavere's request, which had come this time by a tinker, made her think that Jenavere too, conceivably, wished to maroon her at the farm for a few days. Jenavere's loneliness was awesome.

When Laura arrived, the sky was like green mud and flakes were already drifting downwards.

In Jenavere's room there was an atmosphere of cosiness debatably introduced for Laura's benefit. A dish of scarlet winter apples, the winter curtains of red, the fire bright, the patchwork of multihued cats upon the bed, and Jenavere in a brown dress.

They sat by the fire awhile and spoke of the weather.

"I'm sorry you may be snowed up here. Will you mind?"

"I'm glad to be free of my folk," said Laura.

"Daniel's room is ready to be slept in. Janet has put on sheets and laid the hearth."

After a time, Laura read from the book, until she saw that, like a comforted child, Jenavere had slipped asleep in her chair.

Despite her gown, the woman was now like a ghost. Pale and painfully thin, and on her hair no lustre.

She's fading without him, Laura thought. *Inch by inch and minute by minute. Her Daniel.*

And it came to Laura to wonder what love must be like, love like that. It was a fearful thing, to love.

In the evening, she had supper with Jenavere in the fastness of her room, and soon after moonrise (a frigid globe, whiter even than the snow that seemed to have fallen from it) she went to bed in the selected chamber, for the bedtime of the farm was early.

Although very tired, Laura examined Daniel's room with curiosity. She looked for some trace of him, but there was nothing. He had passed from the house, himself, like a ghost. And she lay awake, afraid that Jenavere's premonition was correct, that he had perished, and finally news must come of it, which would surely kill Jenavere too.

In the night, Laura dreamed of wolves howling eerily across the desert of snow. She saw them running, and something dark and low ran after them, far darker and far different than they. It seemed they fled it, but she could not see what it was, and even in sleep she was glad of that.

For two days the snow and freezing held the land in marble, then there came a day of lights. Like any lively creature pent up, Laura could not resist. She told Jenavere that she must walk about a little on the hard and icy lanes and paths.

Laura set out about ten in the morning, but as soon as she was in the orchard, she saw two of Marsall's men sitting their horses on the pasture. These men were not above taking an interest in her, and so she turned her track away from them, towards the hills and the forest's edge.

The sun shone cold as a grey opal, and the whiteness of the scenery caused her eyes to ache, but she kept on, stretching her limbs in movement, shaking off the sleep of her days indoors.

The paths were ungiving as steel, and slippery, but as she came up into the tree-line, Laura heard the musical dripping of a thousand points of ice touched by the faint sun.

After a time, she lost sight of the farm below among the big trees, all of which were clothed in white, and glittering like jewels. Under the trees, the tented oaks and glacial ash, the fir trees like bears, frozen fern displayed itself like crochet-work.

Laura reached the wide stream. It was frozen fast in its banks, long milky drifts and greenish cores, with here and there a frozen boulder rising like a coign of glass.

As Laura stood there on the rim, the sun slid behind a pane of cloud and all the light went out. It was like an eclipse, a twilight of short black shadows.

In this uncanny murk, Laura's sight altered, to see things she had not seen before.

She stood transfixed, staring.

About halfway down the still glassy vein of the stream, one boulder jutted that was bigger than the rest.

Inside the ice of it was a stone of a peculiar shape.

Laura began to walk upstream, her eyes fixed on the

boulder, disbelieving. Yet as she came nearer, its extraordinary aspect grew more obvious, until at last she faced it over the glass water, and there could be no doubt.

Inside a mound of ice larger than herself, ice in parts opaque and in others transparent as crystal, an animal had been caught. It was a wolf. Stone grey, its body crouched there, as motionless as stone. But the head was raised, the eyes and the mouth open, as if to protest in terror and anger at what had befallen it.

Laura glared into the glare of the iced-over eyes, pale yellow as parchment, unglowing and dead. Fixed forever, the ghastly miracle of the frozen wolf confronted her, and she felt the primitive panic wake in her that waits in wild places.

Then the light darkened even further, as if the sun had died.

Laura heard an insane rushing in her ears; the scene before her flickered and flared.

It seemed the stream had come unlocked and now poured down at her from its heights, bringing huge rocks and broken trees, and swarming with a cargo of death. Over the waters were swept the skeletons of beasts, cows and sheep, and after these, lifted by some tidal out-boiling of the earth, the bones of ancient monsters: dinosaurs and dragons and great bat-like birds. Through the dark tunnel of the air they dashed towards her, and Laura, with a scream of utter fear, turned from their way, unable to defend herself against their lawless panoply.

She ran through the hall of the trees, over the treacherous snow, to be suddenly crushed to death or life on a human breast.

"Laura—Laura? Here I am. What is it?"

Hearing so unexpectedly the voice of Hyperion Worth, Laura opened her eyes.

The sun was out again, the landscape white. The stream, the petrified wolf, and all the rushing bones, were left behind.

"I saw—" said Laura. "I saw—"

"What did you see? Has one of those louts dared to affront you?"

"No," she said. "But there was a wolf frozen in a great bubble of ice."

He did not tell her this was not so. He held her to him until she became Laura again, and drew away. Then he said, "I came to sort some business with Vehmund, but he's in his cups already. Excuse me that I followed you. These paths aren't safe."

Laura acquiesced.

He was encouraged by her meekness, and that she had lain against him.

"My carriage is on the road below the farm. Let me take you to my house."

Laura was about to protest, but her denial would be mechanical. She did not want the snow any longer, nor the snow-woman Jenavere with her sorrow and her talk of wolves. Without quite knowing what she said, she answered, "Yes."

Hyperion Worth conducted her down the hill in his arm, and at the farmhouse a message was left with the maid Janet, to the effect that Laura had been called away home.

Laura felt a pang at abandoning Jenavere Vehmund. But she could not withstand her own wishes. She had put them off so long that now they had power over her.

The carriage indeed waited on the road, a dangerous enterprise, but typical enough of Hyperion. The horses stood on the deadly surface like beetles on china, and when they started off they went with care at scarcely more than a walk, one of the coachmen walking along-side.

Higher up, the road had been cleared in areas, and their progress was more sprightly.

Laura sat in the carriage as aloofly as she was able with Hyperion's arm about her and her hands warming in his. Tall rocks passed, cliffs of snow. She had been deeply shocked by something perhaps only imagined, and this had robbed her of her courage to say No.

There was slight conversation during the drive.

At last, after hours or days, during which Laura had dozed fitfully, the carriage turned in at a pair of gateposts and rumbled along a broad cleared drive hemmed by snowy lindens. A plate of ice went by—the lake. Turning in a half circle, the carriage halted.

Hyperion got out and helped Laura down.

"Now just look. Isn't it worth seeing?"

And she gazed up at the mansion in the snow. Its walls were of a white the snow had changed nearly to blue, and its myriad windows were like dark beryls, save here and there some shone with golden light. Snow outlined the multitude of points, turrets and galleries, the pinnacles and weathervanes; and on the terrace before it were white snow people, statues that the snow had carefully remade.

They mounted the steps and went in at a cavernous door, into a cave of hall so enormous Laura felt at once lost to everything, herself included.

On a table by the colossal fire—like a burning city— was champagne standing appropriately in ice. Hyperion pressed on Laura a glass of this.

Happenings became vague, simple, and surrounded by a rosy aureole.

She was conducted to a beautiful room and, in a pear-shaped bath before the fire, Laura washed herself in a soap of cream and roses. Then came underthings of a luxuriance that was ridiculous, and next a dress of sapphire silk: a dress for the evening, cut low at the neck. A woman came, as smart as polish, and did up Laura's hair into a sort of diadem, putting white flowers in it. And where could flowers come from—out of the snow?

Like a princess in a fairy tale, Laura went down the staircase of the mansion, and Hyperion, handsome as a prince, led her into a parlour that shone like gold from burnished things in firelight. Here they dined.

All this while Laura knew herself in a dream, and that she must wake from it or, if not, *bring* herself awake. But the shadow of the morning's terror had cast her up into this brightness. She stayed one corner of herself, and let the rest do as it would.

Hyperion was matchless. He assisted her in the most light-hearted fashion when she was uncertain about the nature of the eating utensils; he spoke to her frivolously of the season, the house, herself. He praised her, but if anything rather less than he had ever done. His eyes said what his lips did not.

When the meal was finished and cleared, the long windows showed only black sky and the white surreal earth of the snow. The drapes were let down across this view, and it was banished. They sat by the parlour fireplace, she on a velvet chair and he at her feet, and drank a sweet white wine with the smell of fruit. He did not, had not, spoken of her going.

Despite the wine, the fire, the blissful heavy silence of a mansion which ran like a perfect clock from the ministrations of its servants, Laura began to awake.

"What a wonderful day you've given me," she said.

"You'd been badly frightened, and deserved a wonderful day."

"I did see it. A wolf in ice."

"I believe you, Laura. I'd never doubt you. It's very strange, but then so many things are."

"I feel," Laura said, still under the influence of the wine and not fully woken, "as if an oracle had been uttered. My life can't be the same."

"Oh, Laura," said Hyperion Worth, setting aside his glass and taking up her hand, "let that be true."

Laura woke. She did not remove her hand, but she said, "You're too good a man, sir, to make me pay for my enjoyment."

"Yes, Laura, yes. I'd never want to ask you for payment. It wasn't done for that. But to see you—as you are now. Like a blue orchid, a rowan tree at dusk."

"Your words are always pretty. But I daren't heed them."

"Heed them, Laura. Oh, Laura, I've waited so long."

"I never told you to wait. To wait implies that what you desire will be yours in the end."

"Be mine then, Laura."

"Now it's said," murmured Laura, taking back her hand. "At long last. You want to disgrace me."

"No. I want to possess you. My Athene can be Aphrodite."

"No," said Laura.

"Yes."

"Unthinking pleasure to you, and the wreck of me," said Laura, and thought how prim her untamed voice now sounded.

"I love you, Laura. I desire and want you. I've held myself in check through most of a year. Don't torture me more."

"I don't mean to torture. But I must defend myself."

"If you knew only half the pain you've cost me. The sleepless nights and black days. How can I bear it?"

"Find another," said Laura, "more willing, less proud."

Hyperion groaned. He laid his head in her lap and gently but decidedly he grasped her with his hand, her lower belly, the mound of her femininity, through the blue gown.

"You don't know what it is to me," he said. "You put me on the rack."

Laura rose to her feet and his hand fell away.

Hyperion flung his arms about her legs and, burying his face in her dress, he wept.

Nonplussed she stood above him.

Does it mean so much that he must cry like a child?

She felt an abrupt and total weariness. She was sick of him, of his pursuit, and now of his entreaty. She was exhausted by the world, with its portents and omens, its snows and imprisoned wolves and imprisoned women, its fairy tales. She did not have the strength to beat him off. What did it matter? To fall from grace—what grace? Let him have his way. Let them be done with it, and then he would leave her in peace.

"Have me then," she said coldly. "Do what you must."

He raised his face. He was flushed and glorious, his eyes holy. "Do you mean it? You permit me?"

"Yes."

"Laura, my goddess."

"You needn't flatter any more. I grant it. Now get on."

She looked for something violent and mad; so the stories had primed her.

Instead Hyperion rose, and taking her into his embrace he kissed her. He kissed her in a way of which she had never heard, which she found, by stages, surprising, disgusting, comforting, curious, fascinating, exhilarating. This continued for a long while, and when it ended she found they were both trembling.

Then he led her from the room, across the hall and up the stairway, along corridors, to a bedchamber. So well-trained were the servants of the perfect house that they were hiding in their burrows, not one other did Laura see on their journey, only him.

The bedroom was furnished in blue, like her dress, but soon he had divested her of that, and thrust off his own clothes like something breaking from a cocoon.

She was not distressed at her own nudity, or his. They were a comely couple: he athletic and slim and she slenderly voluptuous. But from his manhood she looked away; she knew (from the stories) that this weapon would be used on her.

On the great four-poster bed they dallied. She came to want his brutality, to be taken, subdued. At the same time she was afraid, and also of herself, for she seemed now not to *be* herself. She had meant to give, and so to have done with it. But this was different.

When he broke into her, she was hurt, rent, and all her astonished joy withered. She thought, cynically: *Of course. Well, I have allowed it.* In other words, *It is my fault.*

Hyperion cried aloud with the transports of his delight, and through her hurt she regarded him stoically. She felt, as before, an affectionate contempt; the loss of her virginity had, oddly, given it back to her.

When it was over, she got up from under him, and wrapped herself quickly in a cover. The flowers had dropped from her hair.

"What are you doing?" he asked.

"I should like my own clothes, and then to go home."

"It's so late," he said. "Will you make my poor horses travel by night on the snow?"

"Very well," she said. "Let me go back to the other room to sleep. And in the morning let me go."

He sat up and looked at her. He had been ravished, as well as, or more than, she.

"Very well, Laura. I'll do whatever you want."

2

From a colourless sky the birds came down like a black rain or wind. They settled on the bones below.

They were feeding, somehow, on these bald bones. It was a graveyard of things unburied. The skeletons of flocks and herds were there, but also the ivory of great forgotten beasts. Through the middle of it ran the stream, a frozen road, and sometimes the crows landed there in preference, next strutting up the bank to seize and devour.

A raven rose in the air, tangled in a ribcage. For a moment the ribcage flew with black wings, and long vertebrae hung down, a tail of plates rattling on the ice. Then it gave way, was shattered, and the bird flew free, straight forward into his brain.

A woman exclaimed. And then spoke words in an unknown language.

He saw her sitting across a sunlit room, a window behind a fretted screen . . . She got up and made gestures at him to lie still.

He lay still.

The woman hastened out of the room.

Daniel looked about him. The chamber was bare, like

the cell of some religious; only the bed, the chair, one small table with some jars and bottles on it, the window strewing beads of light through the screen on to a polished floor. Behind him on the wall an outflung Christ on a crucifix, touched with gold.

The door opened again and an elderly and white-faced man came in, beaming. His grey hair was long, and tied at his neck with ribbon. He spoke in French.

"My dear guest. How glad I am to see you revived."

"Where do I find myself?" said Daniel softly.

"In my house, the house of Leon Bernardin." The man turned to the old woman who had been watching Daniel's coma or sleep. "Maria, fetch the soup. My guest will be hungry."

She went out again. Leon Bernardin sat down in the chair. "You were found in the village," he said calmly. "I had them bring you here, where we can best care for you. There have been dangers. But we'll speak of that another time."

Daniel sat up in the bed. He wore a clean nightshirt. He felt no weakness; rather he was refreshed, and hungry. He remembered in a surge the ship wallowing on the rocks, his swim, the walking inland and up to the high place. And there—he could not recollect what had gone on there. The dim shadow of a man appeared, and in his hand a flaming glimmering jewel. And then there had been pain, a long while lying under a hard sky, and the rain falling, and drinking from the cup of a stone that had collected the water. But all that might have been a dream, like the dream of the crows which had picked his bones and the bones of dinosaurs.

In any case, why had he been on the ship? Where had he been going?

"You've lain here for some while," said Leon Bernardin. "Do you remember how you came here?"

"No," said Daniel.

"Do you remember your name?"

"My name is Daniel Vehmund."

"That's good. You know yourself. We thought at first the beast had mouthed you, but you had no wounds."

"What beast?" said Daniel. He found himself tense, strung like an instrument for some horrible note.

"Should I speak of it? Some thing has begun to haunt the village. It preys by night. For two nights in succession men died. Tomasio the woodcutter, Seliq the tavern boy. A woman reported seeing a creature like a large dog. When you were found beside the fountain, they feared you'd been set on, but you carried no mark and were alive. The others . . . torn in pieces. But there have been no further attacks. Two nights have passed. Perhaps it's gone."

Daniel saw in his mind's eye a tall thin man, and behind him a white word was written on a wall. There came a blast of fire.

"I shouldn't have taxed you with it," said the elderly Bernardin.

"Where does the beast come from?" Daniel asked.

"The village fears something supernatural. They say it came down from the ruined castle on the hill. The castle is accursed. Evil men practised infamies there under the cloaks of Christian knights."

The door was opened and the woman, Maria, came in with the soup and bread.

"When you've eaten, you must rest again. I shall return this evening."

Bernardin got up with the help of his cane.

Ravenous, Daniel barely saw him go. He was eating, yes, like a wolf.

Daniel lay on his back, watching the light alter through the screen.

He thought of the beast—he could not visualize its shape—slinking down from the Crusader castle to the village on the plain.

He had no memories, nothing to account for the woodcutter, or the Arab boy from the inn.

Had someone shot him? It seemed probable. He had given the diamond, sold the diamond, to a man in the ruins, and the man's servant had fired at him and taken back the money very likely. (It was a large sum, would Bernardin not have mentioned it otherwise?) And they had left him for dead. But he had not died. He had lain in limbo, there in the yard of the castle, scarcely aware, days, a month, drinking the rain when it fell. And then. And then the moon had grown round, and the alteration had come, and somehow it had made nothing of the wound or the ball of lead lodged in him. (For certainly the men on the ship had fired at the beast, and the beast had made nothing of *their* shot.) As a beast he had come here and done the things recounted—a large dog, the woman had said . . . And then, when the change left him, he lay there by their fountain, and finally they found him and brought him to the house of this charitable and unwise old man. And he slept—two nights, was it? And grew strong and well.

I become a beast.

In the aftermath of the carnage of the *Cos* it had not seemed real to him. But now it seemed real. It was a fact.

He had sold the diamond to be rid of it, of *it*, since the diamond had begun it. But to be rid of the diamond was not the answer, evidently, for the change had come to him anyway. He recalled how he had drunk the urak with the diamond in the cup. The robber of tombs had said to him in the hovel, "It is yours. Take it, for the love of God."

The stone belonged to him, the beast belonged to him. In some incoherent way he knew why but, strain after the logic of it as he would, he could not find the sense. Only the terror.

Daniel watched the light alter. He was serene, as if terror did not matter. A brassy sheen was on the floor now. Afternoon was ending over the orange orchards of the plain.

But tonight he was only a man. It was the moon which truly ruled him. The diamond had given him to the moon. It had no power except for the two or three nights of its fullness. And then must he be vital, too, or he could not metamorphose for all three of those nights? These were lessons he learnt and would have to learn.

A beast. He became a beast.

And he could not die.

Out in the courtyard a long table had been laid beautifully with elegant things. Crimson candles burned in narrow sconces and crystal glass waited like tears for the red, red wine. A vine grew up the wall, and above were the stars and the roofs of the house. Somewhere a guitar was played softly. Insects came to the lights and burned.

The old man, Bernardin, lived alone but for his woman servant and the boy who attended to the more mechanical needs of the house. There had been a donkey, but it grew ancient and died. There had been a clever bird, too, which talked. But the cage was left open—the boy was careless—and the bird escaped. All these events Bernardin told Daniel over the dishes of minced spiced meat and lemon rice. He spoke also of the village, its little life. Between his words other knowledge protruded ready to be plucked. Bernardin was rich, respected, lonely. He had taken to Daniel as to a beautiful child discovered wandering in the valley. Bernardin suspected Daniel of nothing, and wished to extract his own story simply in order to know him better.

Daniel found that lying, now, came easily and comfortably, for had he not lived a year and more of lies? Besides, the truth was beyond him, beyond all of them. He listened to himself with mild interest as he told how men had set on him, Julinus' men of course, and robbed him. That he had wandered to the village and collapsed there. In his former days he had been a clerk; he did not mention where. He did not mention the shipwreck, only that he was making for the nearest port. That part of the tale was also dreamlike, for was it of any validity where he went? He was now surely one of the properly homeless, an exile, outcast, under an evil spell. Yet all the while he thought and felt this, he was not unquiet. What had happened to him? Could something so fundamental as shock have thieved all humanity from him? Yes, for it had happened before. It had happened on the day he left the farm, walking away over the tracks in the twilight, his father's body left behind across the road's beginning. He had not been himself since that hour. And the man he had been before that hour he could not at last remember.

Old Bernardin was dismayed at the false story, and commiserated. It apparently did not occur to him to doubt a word of what Daniel said. Daniel was golden in the candlelight, dressed in old-fashioned garments of the house, a youth from the youth of Bernardin.

"What has befallen you is a dreadful thing," said Bernardin. "Whatever I can, you must let me do to recompense you."

"You're already too kind."

"Not at all. It's my pleasure."

So it was. Bernardin had an old man's boredom. He was tired of his fine house, its monkish yet superb accessories, his books, his servants, the villagers.

He asked Daniel eager questions regarding his plans.

"I'd hoped to get home," Daniel said. But the phrase was currently actually laughable to him—and he did laugh.

"There," said Bernardin, "the very idea of your own country lifts your spirits. We must see what can be done."

He will, Daniel thought, *propose to loan me the money to get back to England. But not yet. He isn't finished playing with me, yet.*

And indeed Bernardin made no promises of any sort, but kept Daniel in conversation of a low, meandering, unfruitful kind, until Maria appeared on the edge of the court with a candle in her hand.

"Ah, my Maria has come to warn me to bed. I'm an old man. I must keep strict hours, like an infant." But he beamed upon Daniel again and went away with the candle, placidly.

Maria cleared the table. The guitar had stopped playing and somewhere a dog howled.

Maria said something that Daniel took to mean the dog which howled had been Tomasio's.

And I killed him. No, not I. But a part of me.

The lesser moon had not showed over the courtyard of Leon Bernardin. The night had grown colder.

The woman muttered something. Then she said in rough French, "My master's taken with you."

"He's too good," said Daniel.

She said nothing else and went away, leaving the table bare but for the candles, the glasses and the wine.

Daniel drank some more, and tried to press himself mentally against the howling of the dog, that revelation of what he had been, and done. But he could feel nothing, although he believed it had happened.

If I go to England, it will happen there also.

He tried again to picture what he became. He looked into the shadows all around the court. Something like that?

Bernardin conducted Daniel on slow sedate walks about the village. There were fields, and close-by the oranges were cultivated. Shade trees grew beside low white walls.

In the village plaza there was the church, with its tower and vessels of gold and silver. They climbed up, Bernardin hobbling, to look at the bell, on which words of the scriptures were incised in church Latin. On the plaza too was the tavern, and here they rested. Leon Bernardin was treated like a don. Fruit and wine were brought to him and to his guest. An Arab girl waited on them, the sister of Seliq who had been torn apart. The blue rims of her black eyes showed no sorrow, only acceptance. Already the terrible event had become a history, it was past. For some reason they did not realize that with the full moon the creature of death would return.

Leon Bernardin had begun to teach Daniel the language and dialects of the region, but at night he had Daniel read to him from French novels. Also, they played chess, but Daniel was impatient with this game and not a clever player.

Rather than interrogate him on his days as a clerk, Bernardin asked questions about England. Daniel lied. He had been brought up in the city by an aunt; his par-

ents were deceased. Sometimes it would niggle him that
he had relegated his mother also to the realms of the
dead. It seemed an unlucky thing to do. He wondered if
her letters had continued to go to the French Inn, awaiting him there in vain.

Daniel should insist now that he travel on. Perhaps
Bernardin would fund him, or not. At least he had a
smattering of the language at last, to help where French
could not.

But he did not posit his departure either to Bernardin
or properly to himself. It was as if he used the fine house
to wait in. And, that being so, there was only one thing he
could be waiting for. Yet if he believed that, then surely
he should be gone, should find some wild tract of land
where the moon might work on him without harm to any
other.

He did not fear it. He regarded the return of the
change to himself with an equanimity that was in no form
aided by doubt. He could not fathom his own mood. It
seemed he was at peace with the unacceptable, the unspeakable.

"You're tired with our game," said Bernardin, as they
sat over the chessboard.

Above, the sky was radiant with stars. Half a moon
hung over the fields, hidden from view by the walls of the
house.

"I was only thinking," said Daniel, "of your great kindness to me, and how it's all given on trust."

"Holy scripture instructs us to succour the needy and
assist the traveller," said Bernardin.

"And this you've amply done. But here you have me in
your home. And what do you know of me?"

"You've told me of yourself."

"Perhaps I've told you lies."

Bernardin regarded Daniel with a steadfast, very nearly tender smile.

"Only consider," said Daniel, pleased with the curiousness of what he had set in motion, "I was found, brought here, without money, without documents. I might be anyone. Some bandit perhaps, now ensconced in your house. Or worse. I might be much worse."

"Come, come," said Bernardin, "you must allow some intelligence to my years. I have judged your character and find nothing amiss with it."

"Perhaps I'm cunning. Perhaps I have misled you."

"Never."

"Have you ever heard of the shape-changer?"

Bernardin's face fell a little. He frowned and stared at Daniel.

"What do you mean?"

Daniel, cat-like, skipped ably back a short way:

"What do I mean? That like some plant I may set myself to appear brightly, only in order to attract my prey."

Bernardin's frown melted. "Would you then tell me of it?"

"Oh, yes. In order to disarm you further."

"You're saying I must not trust you, Daniel?"

"I'm surprised, Señor, that you do."

Bernardin nodded. He got up stiffly, leaning on his cane, which was carved with tiny figures and the heads of animals.

"Come, Daniel. Come with me. I'll show you something."

Daniel pushed back his chair and followed Bernardin over the courtyard and back into the house.

They traversed a central corridor, then turned aside and went down a stair into a dark place lit only by a lantern hooked up on the wall. This lamp Bernardin removed. Leaning his cane on the wall and reaching into his breast, he produced a large key. Across the dark lobby was a door which he accordingly unlocked.

The rays of the lamp fell into a sunken chamber rimmed by broken pillars.

"An old Roman bath was here," said Bernardin, "which I caused to be incorporated into my house. We must go down again." And, so saying, he climbed down some steps of stone into the basin, the floor of which was covered by some ten or twelve flickering inches of water.

Surprised, Daniel went after him. The country boots that they had worn for their evening's walk kept the feet of both men dry as the water washed over them.

Bernardin stooped awkwardly, and with a peculiar chuckle pulled up a stone from the floor of the bath.

"Do you see?"

Something shone under the stone. Even in the flirting light there could be no question. It was gold, a heap of yellow shining coins.

Bernardin dropped the stone back with a splash, lifted another, and now Daniel beheld silver money.

Other stones were raised. Beneath them all the glitter, grey or yellow, came up through the water.

"My hoard," said Bernardin. "A quaint idea, is it not?"

He went stiffly to the side of the bath, and the lantern showed up a wine-rack there with huge unwieldy bottles. Bernardin drew one out and held it up to the light, revealing the big winged notes folded close inside.

"Very quaint," said Daniel.

Bernardin said, "Now you know my secret. A thief might break in and search my coffers uselessly. And what is here—an ancient bath in ruins and some old wine."

Daniel did not speak.

"You see how I fear you," said Bernardin.

In the sharp flare of the lantern his face had become a caricature, grinning as if in horror or panic.

"You overwhelm me," Daniel said. He wondered if Bernardin would offer him now his passage home. But there was no need, for Bernardin had shown him the treasure-house and how the treasure was to be taken. He would only have to subtract the key from over Bernardin's heart.

They were in a weird compact, the old man and himself. Daniel could not be sure what was meant by it. Had he been set the test of *not* stealing from the hoard, or had Bernardin demonstrated the way to the hoard so that he might be spared from some obscure violence? Did Bernardin, in a manner hidden even to himself, know he stood in the presence of something damned?

Daniel felt a deep depression. He would kill Bernardin and take all his gold, his silver and his banknotes. It was so simple. And since he could feel no compunction, no dread of his own foul act, he stepped aside into a type of sorrow, a malaise.

"Your secret's safe in my hands," he said.

"Of course."

Daniel noticed his first clumsiness late in the month, as the moon began to round. He knocked over a wine glass. But there were other lesser instances, an awkwardness in buttoning his coat, removing and donning clothes generally. His sense of taste was also less, the spicy meats, the sweet oranges pale on his palate. Sometimes the landscape blurred for a moment. All these were preparatory things.

In the village they had concluded Leon Bernardin had

adopted the handsome and charming foreigner. It amused them, or in some instances irritated.

They were picking the oranges. Daniel walked through viridian tunnels lit by amber fruit, and the amber arms of girls, young men. *Which will die?*

He was strong now, and *it* would be strong. It would have three whole nights under the roaring moon.

Daniel sat above the groves and looked away to the distant hill where the brown bones of the castle were just visible. When the workers passed him, he spoke to them gently, in a friendly fashion, wondering if this one or this one would be rent in pieces.

What has become of me? he thought. But no thrill of pain or fear went through him. *I'm coming to like it.* It was as if he carried a godlike power within him, invisible to all, potent as thunder.

Perhaps something else could be tried. Since he could not make himself go away. But this would mean speaking honestly to Bernardin. For if he admitted the truth to the villagers and they credited him, they would burn him alive. He did not think Bernardin would behave in such a way; he would not become confused or frightened. The old man had a library full of books of learning; he knew of many matters, had an esoteric side to him. Was he here in order to work some countering magic? Was such a thing conceivable?

Bernardin was in his priestly study, where he sometimes retired in the evenings if he could bear to drag himself away from the company of Daniel. This was the room lined by books, having one polished desk of a myriad drawers, two carved chairs, and a footstool of red velvet. On one wall was a plain crucifix, on another a religious painting: disciples on the road to Jerusalem, done in a clear cool style against a setting sun that matched the stool.

The old man seemed glad that Daniel had come to find him. He asked him to sit and read out to him several passages from a volume of essays, asking for Daniel's opinion on the meaning, and correcting small faults in his understanding of both language and syntax.

When this was over, Daniel stood up again.

The window, behind one of the fretted screens, was deepening itself towards sunfall. Tonight was the last night before the full moon.

"Señor," said Daniel, "nine days ago we had a slight discussion of my worth, probably you recall. I said you were unwise to trust me, and you did me the great honour of trusting me yet further."

Leon Bernardin bowed in solemn acknowledgement.

"I remain convinced of your virtue, Daniel."

"For that I thank you. However, since I still enjoy your hospitality, I'm afraid I must now warn you, gravely, of a fact concerning me."

Leon Bernardin raised his eyebrows, almost playfully.

"What terrible thing is this?"

"I'm subject to a disease. It affects me at the full moon. For three nights I become a creature without reason. Dangerous and brimmed by fury."

"You joke with me."

"No, I tell you the frankest truth. I should have told you sooner. But the thing itself may seem unlikely to you, seeing me as I am. I put it off, but now I can't delay any longer. Tomorrow night I will be a peril to you and your household, and to your village at large."

"You mean that *lunacy* affects you——"

"Much more dreadful than madness. If I describe to

you the fact, you'll suppose I'm mistaken, or already crazed."

Bernardin's old white face was like a crushed paper. Fear was already written there, but fear had as yet no name.

"If I'm to hear you out," he said, "you must be exact with me."

"I change into a beast," said Daniel. "The monster which killed Tomasio and the boy—that was myself, as I become."

Bernardin stood up, but held to the desk.

"You speak the truth?"

"I do. I assure you, tomorrow night, before moonrise, you must bind me, chain me, and lock me in."

"I have read of such things," said Bernardin.

"Good. Then you'll have some preparation."

"You'll give yourself over to me?"

"*I* will. But the beast, when it comes, is masterless."

Bernardin drew a deep breath. "God masters all things."

Daniel had long since ceased to accept notions of God. "How can God, if He exists, allow such a creature to be?"

"To make trial of us."

Daniel went away smiling, leaving Bernardin to whatever ritual readyings, maybe prayers.

I have told him. He is forewarned.

How could Bernardin do anything of any effect against what came? Daniel laughed, as he had done when he considered England.

The boy entered Daniel's chamber the next afternoon, with Leon Bernardin. They brought cord ropes. Bernardin had sworn the boy to secrecy, on the Bible; the foreign gentleman was subject to fits, and must be bound to prevent his hurting himself.

Daniel had been feverish all day, not wanting to eat or drink. He lay on the bed and permitted them to tie him up tightly.

"Will there be a rod for the mouth," asked the boy, "to stop him biting his tongue?"

But Bernardin sent the boy away.

"Forgive me, Daniel. I wasn't strong enough to tie the ropes alone, and be sure of them."

Daniel smiled. "I can scarcely move a finger."

"You yourself were insistent on that."

"So I was." Daniel added, "Well before moonrise, you must go out and lock the door."

"I shall lock the door, but I'll remain with you."

"No," said Daniel, "don't do that."

"You must allow it. I'm a scientific man, Daniel. I want to see what occurs. I shall keep sacred articles with me."

"You think it will be stayed by a cross?"

"I believe it isn't more potent than God."

"You're only a man, Leon Bernardin. And this—is a beast of the Devil."

Bernardin shuddered. "Nevertheless."

A ghastly curiosity burned in his eyes. He was like the child that begs for ghost stories, which thereafter terrify it for a year.

"Let me persuade you not to stay," said Daniel, "but to go to your own room and lock and bar the door."

Bernardin said, didactically, "As you are, you know me and strive for my good. If this thing evolves from you, some part of you must linger inside it. That part may be appealed to."

"No. I don't think it to be so. It isn't me. Or it's some portion of me that my humanity keeps buried."

"From the dark half of the soul," said Bernardin. "The shadow inside the heart."

"Just so. The Devil in me."

"Christ sweeps out the Devil."

"You aren't the Christ."

"My faith is sound."

"Be warned. Remember Tomasio."

Bernardin crossed himself, and went from the room.

In the dusk, Leon Bernardin came back, shut and locked the door, set down a heavy book on the table and seated himself in the chair.

Daniel was apparently asleep, muttering softly to himself now and then, in fragments of his native speech.

Bernardin payed no heed to this. He laid a little cross of ebony and silver on the pages of the Bible, which stood open at Revelations, the passages which read: 'And the beast which I saw was like unto a leopard, and his feet were as the feet of a bear, and his mouth as the mouth of a lion . . . Who is like unto the beast? Who is able to make war with him? . . . And I saw as it were a sea of glass mingled with fire: and them that had gotten the victory over the beast.'

The old man had taken some of the precautions of a magus. He had bathed himself and anointed himself with various tinctures, and even dressed in a certain order. On his chest hung a tiny cross of gold set with seed-pearls, and on his hand was a ring which a cardinal had blessed.

So implicit was Bernardin's faith in God that he was not afraid; at least, he did not think that he was. That his hands trembled he ascribed to excitement, for perhaps he was about to witness something stupendous.

At the same time he had a genuine wish to watch over Daniel, whom he loved as he loved all attractive benign things, the sunset behind the plain, the leather of a beautiful book of fascinating stories. He did not want Daniel to leave him, for Bernardin had had few loves and no sons. Nor did he truly desire that Daniel be transformed into a monster. Should this happen, and he was partially convinced that it might, Bernardin would set himself and the omnipotence of God against the bane. If he could, he would free Daniel of its tyranny.

What Bernardin actually expected to see was something in the form of an event he had already been told of, years ago. A stranger passing through the village had dined with Bernardin and, among other marvels, had recounted the sighting of one possessed. When the demon came on him the young man had first frothed at the lips, then fallen down. After this a frightful cracking of his joints was heard and the boy commenced to run about on all fours. From his body and face tough hair sprouted, and his eyes were bloodshot to a startling scarlet. When the fit went off, ousted by the holy water of the priest, the hair had dropped out of the body, and with rest the joints and bones resettled to their proper affinity, so he was able once more to stand upright. Interviewing the fellow, he seemed to have no recollection of how he was when the possession was on him, but his surpassing energy and strength had been vouched for. It was said he had run up the side of a house like a lizard.

Therefore Bernardin was steeled for phenomena of sorts.

He sat quietly, whispering prayers that he felt were suitable to the occasion, one hand on his golden cross and the other on the Bible.

When the moon rose, he was not aware of it; it had for him no noise, and was not to be seen in the room.

Daniel however began to twist and turn, as best he could in his ties.

Suddenly he uttered a succession of horrible cries, screams of agony.

Bernardin got up. He felt a qualm despite himself. "It comes," he said, under his breath.

He had sent the old woman Maria to her room, and advised her that she should lock her door and stay inside, despite anything she might hear, for the Englishman was ill and had admitted he might turn violent. The boy, Bernardin had sent away.

There was no other near.

Bernardin watched as Daniel struggled and plunged, shrieking, in his bonds. His eyes were fast shut. His tortured hands seemed reaching after some rung in chaos.

Then the alteration began.

At first Bernardin was not sure, wondering if his strained eyes were tricking him. A quivering and flittering of Daniel's flesh seemed to be taking place. Bernardin stole up to the bed. It was not the fault of Bernardin's eyesight. The flesh—*moved*. The flesh *crawled* on Daniel's bones.

With a grunt of loathing, Bernardin retreated, back against the wall, and snatched up the second crucifix from the Bible.

Huge waves were running now over Daniel's body. He seemed to be dissolving in flame which did not destroy or blacken. And even as the old man watched, appalled, the movement of the flesh infected the clothing of the body so it too started to shiver and pulse, and next the very ropes which bound Daniel to the bed took on a mad life, as if they were thick with worms and beetles, shifting over and along each other ceaselessly.

Daniel's outcry had ended. He was oblivious now to

this blasphemy. No man could stay conscious undergoing it. Could a man stay sane who only watched?

Bernardin held the larger crucifix to his lips. He mumbled prayers now, unlawful prayers that had to do with protection from the forces of Hell.

The thing on the bed was a seething welter, a quag of tissues. Through it veins and arteries appeared, momentarily, what might be an eye, a bone, a skein of hair. There was no visible blood. The writhing mass wallowed, and darkened. Into it were sucked the shirt and breeches, the underlinen, and all the coiling ropes. It was a cauldron, a stew of stuffs, all melted down to one.

Bernardin sobbed. He spoke aloud in a quavering voice, words antique as the castle of the height, to do with the halting of hellishness.

And the mass on the bed curdled in together and became a long thick bolster of darkness. Out of which, as if with the screech of irons, four muscular bestial limbs were abruptly cast, and finally an unformed stodge of head, which gradually and meticulously put on a shape.

Bernardin crept away around the sides of the room, and reaching the door, he fumbled the key into the lock.

From the bed, unbound, since the cords had become a piece of it, the black thing stared with cold black eyes. Ears had grown and lay flat to the head. It was shaggy, the hair oozing out of it, so that still its surface wriggled and shivered. But the eyes were motionless and intent. Bernardin had inadvertently looked into them, and there he saw nothing, absolutely *no* thing, neither age nor infancy, nothing remotely human, nothing that was animal, not wickedness or thought, not even instinct. Whatever had come there merely was. But it *was*.

The key turned and the door opened, and, as it did so,

the creature Daniel Vehmund had become slipped easily from the bed.

Bernardin dropped the crucifix and fled around the door, which he slammed shut and locked with the key in a hand of ice.

"Sweet Jesu——"

In the corridor the familiar few lamps burned. The doors were there, polished, known. Nothing looked as it should, as if everything had been warped.

As Bernardin stood there at a loss, he heard the splintering scrape as the four claws, like hooks of metal, ripped down the door.

He was not astonished. It was a creature of all possibility.

He turned and saw the door dismembered. It was done without any waste, not even quickly, only thoroughly.

And when the shards fell away, the beast stepped out, like a shadow from a wood.

Bernardin spoke pitifully in a low and humble voice. "Daniel. Know me, Daniel. I am your friend."

But Daniel was not there. Daniel had been taken apart and reassembled as this.

"Daniel . . ." said Bernardin softly.

The old man backed away down the corridor in the distorted lamplight. Without his cane he moved ungainly, like a sort of crab, and he was very slow. The beast pursued him as slowly. They moved like figments of a dream, soundless now.

When Bernardin reached the door of his chamber, he turned the knob and entered, backwards, not bothering to secure the barrier against what came.

And what came, came on—and went in after Bernardin, out of the light.

* * *

Maria had heard the cries of the young man, Daniel, and set herself to pray for her master. She did this piously, but without much fear, for she had great respect for Leon Bernardin.

When silence succeeded the noise, Maria was content, and climbed into her early bed.

Some while later she heard further gruesome cries, from another area of the house which she rightly interpreted as her master's bedchamber.

Maria was brave, or stupid. She put on her shawl and picked up a candlestick for assistance. Coming up into the corridor, she presently saw the ruined door of Daniel's room, and felt a chill of alarm. She turned then resolutely for Bernardin's chamber. The door was open, and inside was darkness. Maria did not reach the darkness. Instead the dark came out into the corridor to meet her.

Maria's bravery was not equal to this.

She thought it was a bear, a kind of bear, and while it stood immobile and looked at her, she spun about screaming. And then in a moment it had reached her and smashed her skull with one blow.

In the night a drunken man passed below the house of Leon Bernardin and, looking up, he saw a shape on the flat roof in the moonlight. He took it for a lion and ran away to his home. But no one believed him, seeing how much he had consumed. In the morning he did not believe himself.

Sunlight lay about like Bernardin's coins, when Daniel woke.

He was in the bedroom he had been given, on the floor. At first he noted nothing amiss, but then saw the broken door. *He* had done that, or what he had become had done it.

Daniel sat up with care, but this time he did not feel ill or much debilitated, only rather tired, with a tremor in his limbs as if after hectic unaccustomed exercise. His body was becoming compliant. He was growing used to metamorphosis.

When he went into the corridor he beheld the old woman's body. She had not been eviscerated or even cut; a single blow had brought her down and killed her.

In Bernardin's chamber the body of Bernardin was as Daniel recollected from the ship. It did not shock him. He had looked for nothing else.

As he was breakfasting in the kitchen, Bernardin's boy came in.

"Your master says you may take a holiday for the next two days."

Daniel pondered idly if he had a compulsion to save the boy, sending him off again. But it was expedient he should not see the bodies.

The boy anyway was pleased and not amazed, for Bernardin had always treated him benevolently. He congratulated Daniel on his recovery from the fit.

At the door he offered, "Luis said last night there was a lion on the roof."

"So there was," said Daniel. "I myself saw it."

The boy stared at him round-eyed, then, bit by bit, gave in to amusement. He went out laughing.

During the day Daniel rested on his bed, now and then reading Leon Bernardin's books. He was sorry for the old man in a wry, uninvolved way. He regretted the woman too. Perhaps she would have been safe if she had stayed in her room. But then probably the creature would have sensed and sought her.

Sunlight went through the house in a brilliant tide, and then a sunset came, and after that the evening.

Daniel dreaded only the agony of transference. Would that too grow less? It had seemed perhaps a little less, but it was terrible for all that.

He would know when it was due, for he would hear the howl of the moon on the rim of the earth.

He lugged the woman's corpse into Bernardin's chamber, an impropriety, and shut the door on them.

What would happen on the second night?

On the second morning, after the second night, two men were found by the fountain in the plaza. Both had been torn open and disembowelled. The attack was apparently too swift for screams. Odd pad-marks were shown in the blood and matter, leading across the square towards the church; but here the blood was blotted by the dry dusty earth and all trace vanished.

Something had prowled the village in the night, the same thing which had come there before. Children had had ill dreams, women had lain sleepless. Strangely the tethered goats and the fowl of the village had not been harmed, though they were frisky and nervous.

Now the connection of the lunar disc occurred to them.

It was a beast, dormant at other times, driven by the full moon to kill.

While the village rumbled with its terrors, Daniel was busy in the house of Leon Bernardin. He was disturbed only once by the return of the boy, garrulous with the horrors of the night before. Daniel sent him off again, explaining that Bernardin was at his studies and Maria elsewhere in the house. The boy was disappointed in Daniel, who had shown little interest in the awful story of the slaughter. "They say it is . . . a *werewolf*." "Yes," said Daniel absently. "You know, Señor: one who is a man, but changes at full moon into a *wolf*." Daniel shrugged. He said, "Wolves aren't so savage." "Yes, yes," insisted the boy. "Wolves are fearsome. They lust to kill." It was plain he knew nothing of wolves beyond tales around a flagon at night.

Daniel wondered if the boy had told anyone about the tying up. But he had been sworn, and it seemed not.

When the boy was dismissed, Daniel resumed his labour in the house. Once or twice he thought of the village, wondering what they would do to protect themselves on the third night. He felt neither fear nor apprehension, no check at all.

The moon rose in a turquoise sky, and the village lay like a toy, no motion beyond the dip of trees and bushes to the night wind, every door and window closed. Even the tavern had shut its doors; few had ventured there and at sunset these made off.

The carpenter was anxious for his donkey; he had wanted to bring her into the house but his wife refused. The stable was flimsy; anyone could break in, let alone the powerful beast which ripped men apart. The carpenter's wife was a bold woman. She oversaw the locking of the doors, the closing of the shutters, then served the evening meal as usual. Aside from the crucifix placed on the table, there was no special protection. "We're safe enough in here," she said. "Poor Rosa," said the carpenter, speaking of the donkey outside in her unsafe shed.

On the streets and alleys of the village there was silence. Now and then some scrap of rubbish blew by, crisping and rustling. A lizard which had basked too long on a wall scurried to its cranny under a clay jar. No

warmth or glow from open doors or through the grills of
windows, which had been shut up. A goat uneasy in its
stall, trampling. A flight of moths searching for a lamp.
No more than this.

There was one door left ajar. It was the door to the
house of Leon Bernardin.

The night was darker now. Wan stars attended the
moon. White glare spaced out the streets and houses
mathematically, and drew black shadow where the moon
did not pry. It was an eerie, antipathetic light, like that of
some alien planet, but it was only moonlight, and the
moon was only the earth's. The moon was a dead thing,
the slave of the world, its luminescence that of the hidden sun, distorted. Yet the moon was not like a slave. It
was a force, bending the darkness, singing like the sea in
the ear.

Shadow came from the house of Leon Bernardin and
walked the village. When it reached the plaza it raised its
head, and the eyes of the shadow were white and flat as
two cold coins.

The beast climbed the pedestal of the fountain. It
looked into the water, where the moon reflected. The
beast licked at the water, lapping up the white moon,
which fell back from its tongue and was whole again.

All about the square were the houses of the village,
their courtyards with little trees. The tavern bulked long
and low, unlit tonight. And into the sky soared the church
tower with its bell.

The beast, the shadow, took up its walk again. It
passed by the closed houses, sometimes declining its
head as if to snuff under the doors.

"What's that scratching?"

Perhaps it heard the voices from inside. It scraped delicately at the door, leaving long marks on it, and passed on while the household froze like statues.

On two or three doors it scratched, and went away, leaving the inhabitants stricken like stone.

Then it went up over a courtyard wall and slid down into the dark the other side. And there was a door through which it drove its talons, and cut the wood into strips. There came a dim shrieking from the room. A man rushed out and fired a blast from a gun, but the beast moved through the fire and settled on him, and so his shouts were stopped; and instead the listeners heard the noises of flesh pulled off from bone, the wet noise of blood.

In the neighbouring houses others heard the screaming, the crash of the gun, further, more dreadful cries . . . and then nothing, only a soundlessness.

Furniture was pushed up against doors. Before crucifixes men and women went on their knees. Children wept.

But it was gone, gone away elsewhere, to a house where it flowed up the wall and got in through a high window, pushing between the bars of the grill so they cracked and fell out on the floor. And there it went down and came among a family of ten persons, as swift as smoke. And in that place there was a sort of whirlwind and, like broken dolls in an explosion, portions of human things were flung about.

From this carnage it came out glistening, fireflies of moonlit blood on its coat of hair.

Shining shadow, it moved up the street and climbed up to a house top, and only sat there.

"Something is on the roof!"

In the room below they crossed themselves and prayed to the Mother of God.

But the beast only sat on the house roof, staring at the moon and shining.

The places it had ravaged were selected for some random suggestion of entry apparent only to itself. Elsewhere it had scored the doors, but passed over like the Angel of Death. It had no reasoning ability, perhaps a cunning of some sort. It communed with the moon, but how and in what way, this thing, this monster of the shadow-soul, the darkness of the heart, this beast of the *id* made manifest?

It was not Daniel. As it had not been Daniel who had killed. It was not Daniel, descending like a coil of rope, who went down again and visited again the houses to the melody of screams and prayers and the wild claps of guns. Guns were nothing to it, nor bullets, knives. It was impervious, it was like a creature made of mud, receiving strikes, absorbing them, and closing over the spots, healing like a swamp.

It slew women quickly, almost as an afterthought. But men it savaged. It was primarily a despoiler of men.

Over and over, under the arch of the moon, it killed, doors and bars not withstanding it. Where the houses were joined, it burst through the baked wall. So when one group stood in silent horror hearing the cries of close neighbours, *it* had come through to them like a black machine. And the man who listened with his ear to the wall . . . the claws had gone through his very head, pinning him there while the beast burst outwards all around him.

And in the end it was as if a war had run over the village, and in the houses which stood untouched a stifled crying and imprecation went on, like a boiling of the earth. And the stink of blood and offal was carried by the wind.

But the moon was going down, and the creature now followed it, back to the house of Leon Bernardin, and there, moved presumably by some positive instinct after all, it brushed a way inside.

After the moon had gone, there was a dusk, and now a fearful new quiet sumped the village.

Nothing moved. No sound came, for half the prayers and tears had struck on stony ground; the other half were worn out.

Suddenly in the east the sky opened wide like an enormous window. The rescue of dawn.

At midmorning a crowd marched through the village.

Since sunrise they had been out, those that had survived the night. They had found the dead. They had wailed and lamented. The bell in the church had been rung.

Then the men had gathered at the tavern.

Then there had been talk of coincidence, the coming of the unknown foreigner who lodged at Leon Bernardin's house, and the acts of the beast.

The boy was brought forward. He told how he had been fobbed off from the house by the foreigner, last seen tied by cords, now talking so indolently, his hair so thick, like a pelt, and his eyes gleaming a peculiar yellow.

They marched to the house of Leon Bernardin, with the priest holding up a cross and with all the useless guns, with sticks and stone. They found the door shut, so, when no one answered their shouts, they broke it down.

In the house they found the rooms empty, but for the buzzing bedroom where the two bodies lay: Maria like a white old icon, and Bernardin in a tarn of blood which the flies played on.

The boy ran down some stairs, calling.

He showed them an antique bathhouse of the Romans, with all the paving heaved up and smashed bottles all over the ground. Bernardin had kept his money here, and it was gone.

Rosa the donkey was also gone, led from her stable after moonset in the dusk, when the carpenter and his wife shook beneath their table.

Of the foreigner there was no other sign.

3

A thaw in the week before Christmas melted the long snow and turned the ways to sludge. Then came another freezing, and changed the earth again to iron. Icicles overhung the roof of the ivy cottage, and the hard trees held back a low sky. Jason Wheelwright did not venture far from home. His wife was at her Christmas baking, which is to say that cool Laura, whining Alice and Elfie were, under her directions.

Laura's mood was dark and still, like that of a pool which has been disturbed then left to resume its surface quietness.

There had been no unwanted outcome from her seduction. To the world she was yet herself. She was glad that she had given in to the entreaties of Hyperion Worth, and that now he left her—as she wished—alone.

The family, when they spoke of him, spoke intimately and expectantly, for they did not realize the good time was now over. They believed it was the snow which had kept him away from Laura's orbit, and they had high hopes of the spring. This would prove tedious, but there was little to be done.

An increasing annoyance at her family, however, bubbled under Laura's smooth upper layer. Their ways of going on had come to prick at her like sharpened pins. She began to dream that perhaps in springtime, when they saw their loss and became truly unbearable, she would be off. She would make her way somehow to the town, or the city, take on servant's work, and so be rid of the Wheelwrights altogether. With such amorphous plans she stayed herself through the Christmas week.

On Christmas Day there was the usual trouble. The previous night, blithe with ale, Mr and Mrs Wheelwright had vowed they would go to church in the morning. The morning found them too weary, and then they moped and mooned in their chairs. The dinner was late in beginning, and later in eating, and not very tasty, for it had not had proper attention. The Christmas brandy, though, revived Jason and his wife; and Alice and Elfie were made quite stupid by it.

"What an old glum she is," said Mrs Wheelwright of calm, sober Laura. "No wonder that man hasn't bothered to visit."

"He'll come, he'll come," said Jason heartily. "You'll see."

Laura said, "Perhaps he's done with me."

"What talk is that?" asked her mother. "You've no business to let him be done with you."

"A horse he promised me," said Jason. "I'll have my horse, miss, before you pack him off."

Laura sighed, and began to clear the plates.

She had heard grim things of the city, but could anything be worse than this?

As she was putting the plates into the tub, the sound of a horse's hoofs rang out on the iron ground above.

The family sat up like a kennel of dogs, alert and

ready, and only Laura at the tub knew quite well that
whoever approached, it would not be Hyperion Worth.

Presently the door was knocked on.

Jason rolled to open it, already vociferous with welcome.

"Come in, sir. Come in. Only just a moment ago we
were drinking your health."

Oddly Jason's welcome did not falter, and in through
the door from the steely afternoon stepped the visitor. It
was Hyperion.

Laura felt a flood of rage, painful as a blush.

She had thought to be rid of him, but he had come
back for more.

Mr Worth had brought a hamper of Christmas sweetmeats with him which far outshone the dainties of the
table. The family, though newly stuffed, set to with a will.

Hyperion came to Laura as she resolutely scrubbed the
dishes. The general hubbub of the Wheelwrights allowed
them to speak as they would.

"Have I angered you?"

"Yes."

"You're angry at my conduct when last we were together."

"Not at all. It was very natural and honest. I rewarded
it."

"So you did, Laura."

"But that was in the hope of ending *this.*"

"Unfortunately," said Hyperion humbly, "you had the
opposite effect. Only the roads have kept me away so
long."

Laura had the urge to break the plates. She subdued it.

"You'll find no further kindness in me," she said.

"I don't believe you so cruel."

Laura stared from the greasy water to her family. With

less grace than pigs, they foraged in the hamper. Then, their snouts coming up for air, Elfie and Alice looked at her and giggled.

"A drop of brandy, Mr Worth," suggested Jason from the table.

"Not just yet, Mr Wheelwright."

"Best haste, sir. It won't last long."

"I could do with it for courage," said Hyperion Worth to Laura. "But I'll make on without."

"How can you fear me," said Laura with scorn. "I'm your victim."

"I deny it. I'm *yours.*"

Laura's hand, before she knew it, flew from the tub to strike him—Hyperion caught her hand like a precious egg and, holding it still, dropped to one knee beside the table. Arrested, the pigs looked up from their feast.

"Laura," said Hyperion clearly, "I know I don't deserve you, but will you do me the honour of becoming my wife?"

It was so quiet in the room that the fall of light hurt the ears.

Mr Wheelwright was a picture, with open mouth and starting eyes. Mrs Wheelwright held a handkerchief to her mouth as if afraid of shouting. The two daughters had gone as red as cherries.

But Laura was ice. She stared on Hyperion as he knelt in his glamour before her. She had heard of such a thing only in stories of the least realistic kind—fairy tales—and through her mind went the idea that he mocked her or had gone mad. Yet his face, composed and clear, told her neither of these states applied. Hyperion Worth, a handsome gentleman of great means, was kneeling at her feet as if indeed he had just fitted the glass slipper on to one of them. He meant all he had said, and before witnesses.

Then Laura felt a different rage. Not that she was being toyed with, but that the situation was itself absurd. How dared he kneel here in this sty, with these creatures looking, using her as his focus?

She parted her lips to deride, to refuse and condemn him. And in that second remembered all: the snowy statues, the beryl windows and the lake of ice, the caves of rooms, the parlour, the bedchamber, the flowers come from the snow. And she remembered how he had cried to have her, and there was no need of this, since he had done so.

Before her inner eye there passed the image of a smoky city and the backbreaking work of some scullery-maid, and, too, the picture of her life spent here, among her kin.

"Mr Worth," said Laura, "I accept."

With an elegance amounting to dignity, Hyperion rose, and kissed her damp and greasy hand, and then her cheek.

"And now, Mr Wheelwright, I take it you've no objection?"

Jason could only gobble like a turkey-cock. His wife burst into a storm of tears, bemusement, or jealousy. Alice and Elfie were white as leached washing.

Laura thought perhaps she herself had taken leave of her senses. She wondered if she had imagined everything that had just taken place. Perhaps something else of moment had happened.

But Hyperion led her to the table and sat down with her. "We must discuss," he said, "the wedding arrangements."

The wedding was to be at a church two miles from Hyperion's mansion. Presently he drove Laura out there in the trap, to see the place where she should arrive as a bride.

The country was wild, not drilled into fields and ditches or long pastures, but rough and rocky, running away to the woods. The church itself lay up a hill, a Saxon church of stone, guarded by great old yew trees and cypresses bent to the wind.

When they arrived no one was about, and in solemn silence they viewed the simple interior of the church, soon to be hung with roses from the Worth hothouse.

Coming out again under the tower, they saw the priest below, plodding up the slope with an empty basket on his arm.

The land behind him was desolate, ancient-looking, still patched with obdurate scales of snow, and the black smoulder of the woods beyond.

"There, Father," said Hyperion, as the priest walked up to the gate, "have you been out feeding the needy?"

"Just so," said the priest. "You've come at the right time to see my parishioners at dinner." He glanced at Laura. "I trust the lady won't be frightened."

"Laura's a country girl, as you know."

She stood with Hyperion and the priest and looked down the length of the hill. Below, among some bushes, she had seen laid out on the ground what must be food from the priest's basket. And now there was a movement from the wood. Three dark forms detached themselves from the trees, and came loping out across the empty vista.

"Wolves," said Laura. "You feed the wolves?"

"Poor things, the winter's hard on them."

"Here is a man," said Hyperion, "who believes the Christian teaching applies to all things."

The three wolves were lean and grey, shaggy in their

winter coats. They ran straight up to the food, apparently knowing the time and place of the delivery, and having watched for it.

"Some offal and half a chicken," said the priest, "but there's also part of an apple pie. They'll eat that too."

With only an occasional glance about, to be sure no one approached, the slender wolves ate with a heartiness that was both fierce and touching. They did not squabble over the food, but shared it equally. Once one raised its head and stared up the slope at them with lemon-green eyes full of sensitive thought.

"They look at you as a man does," said Hyperion. "An innocent and intelligent man."

When the wolves had finished their meal, they abruptly played together, rolling over on the panes of snow.

Laura made an involuntary movement, and instantly all three sprang up and trotted away.

"They never let me near," said the priest. "Formalities must always be observed. I tried waiting for them lower down, and they wouldn't come."

The wolves gained the tree-line and went in one by one, like thin grey clouds were gone.

"There is an old story," said the priest, "that my predecessor would feed the wolves and let them sleep in the church. One was come on curled up in the font."

They went down to the priest's house and took tea.

"It was a wolf which brought us together," Hyperion remarked to Laura.

"I think now that I must have imagined it."

"Don't discredit yourself."

"I've never dared," she said, "to go back and look."

"The thaw will have released your wolf from the ice," he said, "or at least sent it down the stream, to some river perhaps, and the sea."

Laura thought of Jenavere Vehmund, locked in the ice of her room, and was speechless, until she must ably answer questions to do with her marriage, which the priest put to her.

After dark, Jenavere would listen to the drunken sounds of her son and his fellows in the kitchen. The nights were long. The kitchen was lighted, she knew, by a lamp on the mantel, another on the table, and by the blazing hearth. In her corner crouched Rosamunde Ax, ready to wait on these superior men. Their rowdiness did not disturb her, and when they sent her away she went, if not with regret, then with a sort of complacency.

Long after the drunken growling had died out, and the stumbling heavy steps of Marsall came up the stairs towards his bed, Jenavere lay awake. She lay in the black icicle of the winter night, and thought of her second son. She saw him in mysterious Eastern places, dead in an alley, shovelled into some markerless grave. Or she saw him revelling too, forgetting her.

She wanted him to be alive. She wanted him to have forgotten her, if it meant that he lived.

Then, again, she pictured her own death. Why was it so aloof? She had thought the winter would kill her, not so much its cold, for her room was kept warm, but its barrenness, its clutch upon all things frail.

She had nothing to live for, yet she lived. How strange.

That evening, the drunken steps of Marsall did not bypass her door. He knocked, and she went in her dressing-gown to open it.

He used his exaggerated voice for her, slurred with ale.

"The farm's not ours now, Mother. It's Worth's. And I'm the hired man. What would my father have thought?"

Jenavere said nothing.

Marsall smiled. He held a candle which tilted danger-ously.

"He'd never have done it. Never sold. Not he. Do you think," said Marsall, "that lily of yours will ever come back to complain? Your Daniel?"

"No, Marsall."

"No, I don't think he will. Sold into bondage some-where. His fair skin and pretty hair will have caught the eye of some old bugger. Yes, Mother, Daniel will be a catamite by now."

Jenavere drew in her breath, but still no words came out.

Marsall grinned. "What else was he good for?"

"You hated him," said Jenavere bitterly. "You hate him still, and so you say these things."

"Hate? No. I wouldn't waste it on him. Pretty Daniel. What do you think he did at his *school*? Those places are hotbeds of it. And he knew, you can be sure, how to use his silky arse."

Jenavere turned away.

"Go to bed," she said to Marsall.

Marsall lumbered forward. He caught her by the arm and swung her round.

"Don't you order me about. You live here on my bounty, and don't you forget it. I could throw you out. Let's see how you'd do then."

Jenavere stared at her son. He was like a *thing* to her, scarcely human, hideous and deformed, some jest.

"Don't you look at me like that," he said, for his drunkard's perception had made out what his bleary eyes could not. "You bitch. You watch your step with me."

And he swung his hand and slapped her across the face.

The blow almost brought her down.

She staggered back into her chair.

She thought: *It has begun again.*

More than terror she felt a searing anger and despair.

"Yes," he said, pleased at what he had done, this echo of his father, "you be careful, old woman. I'm still the master here."

Then he stumbled out and left her alone.

And, for the first time then, she considered that she herself might put an end to her life. It came to her as a crystal revelation, pure and solid; gleaming.

It was a winter wedding, but a fine day for all that.

The church on the wild upland was the colour of honey in the sunlight. Crows cawed about the woods.

Laura wore a dress of white silk and a lace veil dotted by blue forget-me-nots of beadwork.

Half the village came to see her, but on Hyperion's side there was no one to come—and perhaps as well.

Throughout the ceremony Laura's mother cried noisily, as if to show herself for what she was to the bride. Jason was already jolly. The two sisters, who were not asked to be maids to the bride, sat sullen in their new frocks. Although Laura's family was therefore entirely present, she barely acknowledged them. For her this was the casting off.

The breakfast was held in the big house. There was great merrymaking, hogsheads of ciders, urns of beer, pale champagne. And at the day's end the rejoicing went unsteadily away along the lane, and bride and groom were left to their canopied bed.

He did not come to her as if now he had a right to do so, but modestly and urgently, as at the first.

She admitted him with a truly divine indifference.

She was stunned, almost literally, by all the glories that had been unleashed for her. Her escape into this glittering adventure. But of sex she now anticipated nothing, and received it only with kindness. He had made her a lady with fifty rooms at her disposal, a park, a lake, and so many thousands a year. He was, besides, handsome and amusing. The least she could do was succumb gracefully. Gracefully she succumbed.

And as he travelled upon her, finding out in her new continents and secret seas of sweetness, Laura went over in her mind an itinerary of what her life might now be.

"We shall go to the city. I'll show you off there," he told her during their repose.

She thought how she would have seen the city from its rank underside, and now would see it from aloft, flying in winged carriages along the widest streets, and out between snowy pillars into golden rooms.

She must try to be for him what he required. She must be beautiful and happy. He had earned that much.

She liked him now. It would not be so hard. And what she needed to know he would teach her, of his class, of the world, and of his own wants.

Hyperion took her to the city.

It was extraordinary, another planet. As she was borne across the peaks of stone bridges, she glimpsed the subways below, the alleys of yellow rubbish declining like the road to Hell. There was a broad river decked by boats, but it had muddy banks where fires of refuse burned by night. Lamps lit the streets after dark in necklaces of pale green pearls. There was a cathedral with a dome like a glistening onion. There were galleries of art and music, the theatre and the opera house. Hyperion took her to every point of the city's compass, its icing-sugar heights, gowned in charm from his riches. But she was always aware of the other, darker side, the shadows under the bridge. They lured her in a strange unanswered manner. There, but for Hyperion, she too might have gone.

The life he was providing her was like skating on a lake. He gave to beggars in columned porches, and bought lovely purple violets from hags to ring Laura's white throat.

She said nothing to him of the squalor, the shadow. And he did not speak of it to her. She felt no fear, almost an attraction, as if she might go down into Hell protected now by what her husband had made her.

They walked in a museum of ancient things, old gods of blue stone, ivory amulets and silver eyes. Here there was a faint reverberation of the dark outside. It had always been. She saw, as they came from the theatre in their spangles, to the carriage, beings without legs on the pavements.

One night the howling of dogs woke her, as the carts and drunkenness of the city nights had failed to do. It was a country sound, a wild sound. They had been looking that day at a statue on the river bank: a man with a dog's head. It seemed she had dreamed something of the sort. She did not wake Hyperion Worth. She lay and thought of the wolves at the parish church, feeding on pies in the bushes. There were no wolves in the city.

On their fifteenth night, they went to a private house, to a famous salon there.

The host and hostess were vague dummy figures in expensive clothes, who accepted Laura at once as what she was not, as she had come to expect.

In the huge drawing-room, girdled by exotic bird-drawn wallpaper, a crowd milled with champagne in its hands.

"What a crush," said Hyperion. "But there's to be a magician. I thought you'd enjoy that."

"A magician. What do you mean?"

"Oh, not some penny conjuror. A bizarre foreigner. He's dazzled a great many people. I thought we might see for ourselves."

Each thing he offered her like an exquisite sweet on a painted dish. It would be churlish not to applaud. Laura applauded, and for the first was dismayed at this continuous display her new life entailed. But it was little enough to be in accord with his enthusiasms. Like sex, one could pretend to be pleased.

Finally one end of the large room was cleared, chairs brought, and the crowd sat down in a semicircle. Hyperion contrived that he and Laura be at the front, although to one side.

A man entered, and after him two assistants, carrying things.

The moment Laura saw him she felt misgiving.

He was very tall, abnormally so, thin and straight, with grey hair and strongly marked brows. He wore evening clothes, and was actually as well dressed as the best in the room. But it was none of these things which alerted her. There was to him something very real in the false atmosphere of the salon and the city—like the howl of the dogs she had heard by night. However he might mask it, this man was like a hermit of the woods, of a mountain. Why he had come here was a mystery to her, for social fame and money were surely immaterial to what he was. Then she thought that perhaps to act in this way was a sort of game to him, and this obscurely frightened her. She wished she were not at the front of the crowd.

The two assistants, uncouth-looking men, but also well-dressed and self-effacing, had put down a chair, a small table, and on this latter a lamp. Without a word to his audience, the man proceeded to light the lamp on the table, while his assistants drew back to one side. It was a perfectly ordinary lamp, or looked so. Along the walls of the room the candles flamed; it was scarcely necessary.

A hush had fallen on the audience. Without being requested, they were attentive, and receptive.

The man drew himself up to his notable height. He spoke without an accent of any kind, yet rather oddly.

"That you may know me, I am Julinus. What I will show you now are not marvels, but a mere scientific rehearsal of matter. Whether you will regard what you see as wonders, I do not predict. But I must ask that you remember there is no danger, whatever may occur. No harm will come to you."

There was a little flutter, especially from the women in the room. Julinus allowed it to come and go.

Then he spoke a phrase to the lamp, probably in Latin.

The flame in the lamp rose up through the chimney and bloomed out like a flower at the top. This flower twisted and elongated. A snake uncoiled into the air. It was exactly shaped and formed of flame. It lengthened, attached itself to the magician's arm, and curled itself around and around. At last its head reached to his lips. Opening his mouth, Julinus permitted the serpent to enter. It flowed away into him and was gone. The lamp went out.

There was a slight rustling and whispering.

Julinus leaned to the lamp. He blew into it and the flame came from his mouth, and lit the lamp again.

There was a burst of clapping, out of place, quickly falling silent.

Julinus turned his attention to the chair. He pointed at

it. On the chair appeared the ghostly image of a seated woman.

Although transparent she was quite evident to all the onlookers, some of whom craned to see. She wore the clothes of three centuries earlier, a great comb in her hair, flounced sleeves, and this was clearly to be seen though the room showed through her. She got up from the chair almost as soon as she was made visible. She walked across the chamber, and coming to the wall, went through it, vanishing.

Julinus pointed again, and three men in stockings and high collars walked out of the wall where the woman had gone, and coming to the lamp table stood there for a moment talking, soundlessly, before all three winked out.

There followed five more ghosts, a child playing with a ball, two young women arm in arm, a running boy who flashed through the room to the accompaniment of startled cries, and one man—the last—who appeared walking upside-down on the ceiling.

This brought some laughter and another burst of irrepressible applause.

"Now," said Julinus, "I must ask the assistance of a lady. I repeat, there is nothing to fear. Whoever entrusts herself to my art will be completely secure."

There was some speculation in the audience, and, while it went on, Julinus' dark eyes, oddly remote and dull, passed slowly along the rows of people. To her discomfort, these eyes paused upon Laura, but she averted her gaze at once. She had no intention of becoming the magician's dupe.

There were however fashionable women only too ready to enter his lawless game. Two of these, laughing and pretending abashment, presented themselves before Julinus.

Julinus did not smile or offer any pleasantry. He selected the elder of the two women, and sent the other politely and at once away; she went with an annoyed fluff of her fan.

The elder woman Julinus seated in the chair. She was perhaps in her fortieth year, with beautiful shoulders and a lined throat fettered by small rubies. She seemed both gratified and nervous at her choice.

"You will have heard," Julinus said to the room, "the theory of reincarnation, that each one has lived many lives. Now I propose to demonstrate the lives which, perhaps, my medium here has lived. You have only to watch her closely."

Then he bowed to the woman's ear and said something to her. Her face underwent a sudden change. She paled, her jaw stiffened and her eyes drooped. Her hands, which had been uneasily clasping at each other, fell loose into her lap.

Laura stared at her, almost afraid to look away. And all at once a wave of heat or steam seemed to blur the outline of the woman. There in the chair, then, was an oriental dowager, her black hair hard as lacquer on her head, her robe dripping with crimson and pearl.

The chamber made its exclamation. But in a moment the blurring interruption came again, and Julinus' subject had changed once more, into an ancient stick, crunched together in the chair, dressed in garments of some mediaeval period, with huge keys at her belt.

A second or so, and this vision too was gone, and in the chair sat a black woman in some outlandish dress, perhaps some native of a distant isle, with green feathers in her ears and bones round her neck.

This change brought a clamour, but it also was gone in an instant; and there instead was a fresh apple-blossom girl, in the corseted garments of the English Renascence. She carried a spice-orange in a golden cage, and glanced this way and that imperiously.

There followed the most curious image of all. The girl rose from the chair and, turning round, revealed her back. She had none. Before them was an old man, clad in a flowing robe that seemed of the same silk as the girl's lush gown. His head was hooded with an opaque material grown out of the samite of her little veil, but he was long bearded, gnarled, with eyes like hoar-frost, and carrying in his hand a wintry staff.

Slowly this apparition turned and turned about. From one side it was a girl only, and from the other only an old man. Revolving, it was for an instant both, two sets of features on one skull, two bodies on one stem.

The room did not know what to make of it, and there began to be quick unnerved sounds, not least perhaps from the woman's companion.

Julinus took the lamp from the table and raised it high.

The dual figure, male crone and female youth, began to turn faster, to spin on the spot like some mechanical device. The colours and construction of it merged. To Laura it then seemed a mermaid appeared, and a man in armour. Then these were gone. The woman with the rubies again stood below the lamp, pale still but bright-eyed, coming to herself as if from a deep sleep.

Julinus laid his hand on her arm and she laughed abruptly, unsuitably. She blushed, and moved a step towards the audience, unsteady as if drunk, and her companion hastened out to reclaim her.

When she had gone, Julinus set down the lamp again.

He spoke. "Last, in this pantomime of matter, I will show you how inanimate things are more malleable than is thought. I beg you not to be alarmed. Remember, nothing can harm you."

And, before the audience was quite ready, Julinus raised his arms.

The chair which his assistants had brought on, and in which the changeable woman had sat, began itself to twist and crumple. It screwed itself into a knot, then, in a series of snapping spasms, opened out again. It was no longer a chair but a lion with a coal-black mane. Its eyes too were black. It stared about the room, and there was some noise, but Julinus was seen to hold the lion by a leash. He jerked it and the lion sat submissively. The table with the lamp next contorted. It consumed the lamp, curled inward and around, and widened out again into a slender deer. This, going to the lion, nuzzled it. The lion opened its jaws; it began to swallow the deer, yet in turn the deer was swallowing the lion. They folded into each other and went to nothing.

There were the sounds of a jungle.

Looking up, Laura saw the fronds of the wallpaper swaying, and the birds enamelled there flaring their wings. Pelicans passed across the ceiling.

Gradually the light of the room sank low. A night was coming over the salon, which had been full of the day of candles. One by one these sticks of wax went blank.

The audience, flustered, cried out and fell dubiously quiet.

The ceiling was a sky of night, sprinkled with stars. The moon appeared there with an angel's face. The room of people sat gazing up at it in astonishment. The angelic moon went over and was gone, and now across the upper space there tore the arrow of a meteor, lighting everything like fire. A woman shrieked. And the candles of the room came up again.

Everything was ordinary. The salon was as it had been. The table and the chair . . . the lamp, which now the magician was blowing out. Order was restored, with some embarrassment.

"Are you so calm, Laura?" Hyperion asked. "I'll admit, I'm shaken. I saw a gigantic snake in a thicket—and that last firework was something. Did you see the birds flying off the wallpaper?"

"Perhaps," said Laura.

"The man's decidedly a master illusionist. Or I'll bet," Hyperion added, "the whole room has been rigged."

In just such a way, the audience was now resettling itself. Doors were opening to admit more champagne, and the hostess was at Julinus' elbow.

"And where now for supper?" Hyperion said to Laura.

She said, "Anywhere but here."

As they sat in their hotel parlour on the following morning, Julinus came to call on them.

He was shown in as a gentleman. Obviously Hyperion was entertained, though he put on his stern face. Laura had never known him capable of anger, and only of *one* of the great passions.

"What do you want?"

"I hope you'll forgive my troubling you, but I was told you were something of a connoisseur. And of your marriage."

"The devil you were," said Hyperion, mildly.

"Your wife's face shone from the crowd," said Julinus. He was only cold, exact. "I have in my possession a jewel which would becomingly decorate your wife."

"No," Laura said.

Julinus looked at her. "You are his," he said, urbane. "If he chooses to adorn you with it, you must."

"Look here," said Hyperion, "I liked your act, but I'm not in the market for common hucksters."

"Nor I. This gem is very rare. It comes from the near East. Although I found it elsewhere. It's a crime to keep it in a box. It should be displayed, and on a woman."

Julinus went to the table beside Hyperion's chair. He removed from his coat a box of plain wood, and opened it. Inside, on black velvet, lay something like a vast tear, coruscating white.

"You must be quite mad," said Hyperion after an interval, "to walk about with that in your pocket."

"I credit destiny," said Julinus. "If one would take it from me, he must try. But no one has."

"In God's name, where did you get it?"

"In darkness."

"You stole it."

"No. This jewel selected me as its guardian. It comes and it goes. Now it returns. It must go to you."

"I don't think so," said Hyperion. "I don't care to afford it."

"I haven't yet quoted to you a price."

Laura got up. "I'll go into the other room."

Hyperion, surprised, looked at her. "As you like, darling."

She went away quickly, and shut herself into the bedroom. She did not want to see or hear what would take place.

The jewel. It reminded her of icy things. She recalled the stream, the frozen rock of ice with the flaw of the wolf inside it, and she was filled by an awful loneliness, as if she were in a desert of snow without help.

Then she stepped to listen at the door, and she heard Julinus saying, "You see, the mark there. Almost like an animal. It is a magical stone."

Laura walked to the window and watched the carriages driving in the park below.

She thought of Jenavere Vehmund, to whom she had written of her marriage. She thought of the green-white flame of the diamond at Jenavere's throat. Something curious had struck Laura. *Return*, he had said, the magician; *Now it must go to you.* As if it had been hers before, or had belonged to her family, some distant branch she had never known.

When at long last she heard the outer door close, and Hyperion knocked on the inner one, she saw him enter with distaste. He seemed elated, tickled, as she had known he would.

"I'll get someone to look into the affair," he said. "But who'd think it? Waltzing about the city with that diamond on him like a humbug."

"You'll have it then," she said.

"Should you like me to?"

"An unlucky stone," she said, softly.

"He told me it had belonged to princes. But, then, he would. God knows what it's worth."

"You'll buy it and make me wear it," she said.

"Make you? You'd be the envy of the county. How lovely it would look on you, Laura. Between your white breasts."

She felt something move about them in the conventional room. It was a power which had already drawn her to him, as if in mockery, and made her what now she was, a mannequin for diamonds. She felt a dart of fear, and then a strange sensation, as if she stood in a high place, the wind whirling about her . . . and below the cities of the plain before judgement fell on them.

Hyperion came to her with the familiar excitement and hunger.

This was her bondage. Not the drudgery of servitude in rags, but this lace enslavement. She had made her bargain. She gave in.

All day she was haunted by the image of the diamond. It hung before her like a gleaming eye. She thought she would dream of it, but only dreamed of darkness, stars, an empty place. And the next morning she told herself she was foolish, for it was only a jewel, like the emeralds Hyperion had already given her to wear.

PART THREE

PART THREE

1

 In a shaft of spring sunlight through the door, dark Rosamunde Ax was scrubbing the kitchen table. She did this with a sort of cruelty, unaware and silent. And, all about, the farm was quiet but for the occasional cry of a lamb from the hills.

When a shadow fell across the table Rosamunde believed Marsall must have arrived early, as he often did now, from the duties Mr Worth had kept him for. But there was an oddity in this. For Marsall would have made a noise, indeed, had his own especial noise: heavy boots and loud breath, and perhaps a whistle thinking of the ale to come.

Rosamunde turned. And there in the doorway was the tall silhouette of a man, with about his head an aureole of flaming gold, like a saint's halo in a painting. It was unusual enough to make her start, in a constricted, weasel-like way she had.

"Yes?" she said, her voice a threat, and into her little hand she took a knife that was lying on the dresser.

Not so wild, maybe. Had there not been a murder here?

Then the man shifted an inch or so. She saw he carried

a bag over his back like some pedlar, but also the daylight picked out the features of his face. It seemed to her she knew him—and then that he was a stranger. And then she saw it was Daniel Vehmund, the dead master's second son.

"So, Rosamunde, you recognize me now."

But she did not recognize him. He was very changed. She identified him only as you might tell a man from having seen the child he had once been. Daniel had been slim and clean and different. He had learned the foppish ways of a scholar, and she had despised him. A youth, fey, a weakling.

This man was not like that. So soon, instantly, she saw, she *scented* strength like a fire, and a powerful sheathed maleness like a sword in velvet.

Daniel *then* had had little to do with her, had barely seen her. But Daniel *now* saw her intently, as if he stared down on her from a colossal height, the way a hawk scans the earth for prey, and anything that moves is of interest to it.

Rosamunde felt this gaze bending her like reluctant metal.

She said sourly, "It's Master Daniel."

"Home from far places," he added. "And a long walk."

He had come, it seemed, over the land on foot, bearing the bag; strong, indifferent, yet fascinated too by everything. She thought of him walking so, looking about at the things which moved and those which stood still. And at last down through the orchard, across the garden, to the door, without a sound.

"Mistress is sleeping," said Rosamunde. It was instinctive malice, to keep Jenavere from her son as long as possible.

"And Marsall, where's he?"

"Out with the hired men. The farm's gone now."

"To a man called Worth. Yes, I heard talk of it at the inn."

Rosamunde was sorry he had heard already. But he did not seem vexed. What came from him was a sort of amusement. Perhaps that was what it was.

To show him he did not matter, she put down the knife and resumed her scrubbing of the table.

Daniel came into the room and went past her, and a heat shone off him, or some electricity. The old woman shivered, but did not any more pause. She felt but did not see as he passed through the door and on to the stair, and then she heard the faintest note of his boots on the treads, ascending, as if he *let* her hear.

He was going up to the woman. To that fool Jenavere. The shock might kill her.

Rosamunde scrubbed now with a slow rhythm, listening to the room overhead, but made out only the door knocked on softly, and then opened; no footsteps overhead, for the ceiling was a solid one. And she might not have heard him anyway, for he had come to the kitchen like a vapour.

Rosamunde scrubbed slowly, alert for Jenavere's cry, and there was none.

Then she heard the phantom fall of footsteps descending again.

He was just inside the kitchen. He said, "I'll want my room."

"The girls are off to the village," said Rosamunde.

"Then you see to it."

Rosamunde straightened up. "I tend to the things of Master Marsall."

Something happened then which took her by surprise. He was suddenly before her, as if he had sprung right across the kitchen—yet she had scarcely seen him move. He stood over her, close, as if he meant to touch her. Such power came off him she shrank and her face screwed up, her eyes clenched as if at a bright light. She wanted to push him away, but she did not dare. Daniel had never frightened her before.

"You'll do as I say," he said.

"Yes," she said, "Master Daniel."

And then he had gone by her and was sitting in a chair by the hearth, a place where his father had been used to sit, and where Marsall sat when not drinking at the table. Daniel sat there as if it had been made ready for him, and the lump of the bag lay on the floor by his foot.

Rosamunde looked at him, trying to work out what had happened. He was very brown. His hair was thick as a lion's mane. There was something peculiar about his eyes, but she had noticed that at once.

She dried her hands and went out to see to his room, to put new linen on the bed and lay the fire. That girl had slept there last, the harlot who had seduced the land-owner and gone up so high she never bothered with Jenavere any more.

Rosamunde saw to the room punctiliously, but when she had made the bed, she spat into it. Then she drew off in a vague dread. It was as if he could know what she had done and, down in the kitchen, he was considering it.

She hoped Marsall would come soon. He was usually in by now, careless of his bought duties to Worth's land. What would happen when Marsall arrived?

She went down and he, Daniel, was sitting as before. He had not moved. She thought of an animal which waits in one position, on a rock.

Before she had got across the kitchen, she heard the horse on the slope, and then Marsall's heavy-booted feet.

Marsall shouldered in at the door.

The day was less bright than it had been, the sun further over, yet his slanted shadow fell across the room. He brought the normal smell of muddy fields, horses, his own big body.

"Eh?" said Marsall, standing there in the doorway. And then, "Who's this?"

Rosamunde only attended, in the shadow by the wall.

After a while, Daniel spoke.

"Don't you know me?"

"You've made yourself comfortable," said Marsall resentfully.

"Why not?"

"I say again, who are you?"

"Your brother," Daniel said.

Marsall swore. He rubbed his trousered thigh with one great paw, as if cleaning a weapon, in case.

"Daniel," said Marsall.

He moved into the kitchen cautiously, as though it were not familiar to him, then catching up a chair from the table, placed it the other side of the hearth. He sat down facing Daniel, or the stranger who had said he was Daniel, who it was just possible to see might be Daniel, very changed.

Marsall called to Rosamunde. "Get ale."

She obeyed him at once.

Marsall sat, squinting at Daniel.

"You're back then."

"As you see."

Marsall smiled, friendly and welcoming, crafty, obvious.

"We thought you were gone for good, eh?"

"No."

"Didn't make your fortune then? Things failed you, there."

"In fact," said Daniel, "the reverse."

"Eh?"

"I made my fortune. I'm rich, Marsall. My bag's full of gold."

"Get on." Marsall laughed, and as the ale came, he gulped it.

"I met a wealthy man who left me all his money when he died," said Daniel. He was cool; he did not touch the ale.

"Did he, now? Why was that?"

"He had no heirs."

"But he liked you, eh?"

"He feared me."

"Yes." Marsall laughed heartily, "A man would be afraid of you, Daniel."

"You sold the farm," said Daniel.

"So I did."

"I could buy it back. That's how much gold there is. And to spare."

"You'll get me all hot and bothered over this gold. I might get jealous."

"That would be a shame. You'll have to stew."

Marsall laughed again. "Bravely said. And to think, all those beatings I gave you when we were children."

"I haven't forgotten."

Marsall looked up. His little eyes glanced into Daniel's face. Westering sunlight struck across the kitchen. It gave a weird luminescence to the eyes of Daniel. He had been away and got too clever.

"Well," said Marsall, "we'll see. The house is mine now."

"Did they ever catch him?" said Daniel. "The murderer?"

Marsall grunted. "The tinker that did for our dad."

"That one, yes."

"He was off," said Marsall. "Off with the money."

"Murderer and thief," said Daniel gently. He seemed entertained, by the words, by Marsall hunching on the chair and Rosamunde crouched like a scrawny imp to fill Marsall's cup. By death, old and new. "Did you grieve?"

"He was my dad. A good dad. The best."

"Strange he couldn't defend himself," said Daniel.

"Yes. But the villain came at him from behind."

"Indeed."

Marsall said, "He'd never have sold the farm. But there. Money from that too. I've got plans for the money."

"Have you."

"We'll see." Marsall grinned into his ale. Was he at all aware that his muttering produced the picture of an ungainly toad squatting atop a heap of coins? What would he do with the money? He did not have enough imagination. Like the father, he would store it up in a dark cramped place . . .

He was already deep into the ale, and the copper condensing of the kitchen's light paraphrased the confine of his drink-bleared thoughts. He was not scared of Daniel, for Daniel it was, and Daniel was nothing to fear. Daniel was a lily, and only the light had made his eyes so curious, so like a beast's eyes shining in the shade.

Rosamunde had begun to make the supper, and odours of fried meats and black gravy began to fill the room.

Daniel rose. He lifted up the big bag that had lain

patiently by him like his dog. Marsall's eyes followed it, not careful now, openly considering.

"Yes," Daniel said, "full of gold. If you like, later I'll show you some. But for now I'll take it to my room."

"Does the old woman know you're back?" Marsall asked.

Daniel paused, looked at him.

"I mean," said Marsall, helpfully, "our mother."

"Yes," said Daniel softly. He turned and was gone. The darkness made him seem to vanish magically at the doorway.

Marsall listened to hear him climb the stair, and heard nothing.

"Light the bloody lamps," said Marsall to Rosamunde Ax.

And for Daniel above, as he turned along the passage, the light bloomed out below, casting his own shadow faintly before him. But he did not study his shadow, as he no longer studied his face and body for any signs, portents, or his mind for anything at all.

Daniel reached the door to the bedroom for the second time, and knocked again lightly, too light for them to catch it beneath. But Jenavere spoke behind the door.

He had left the shortest of letters lying under her lax, sleeping hand. *I am home.* She had looked, as she slept, not so much old as ruined. She had looked destroyed, like a torn white paper. He was prepared to go in and see her ghost, and that was irrelevant, for, though a husk, it was the remains of *her*.

But when he opened the door she stood by her fireplace, upright, in a red gown. She was shining from the fire, with a high colour in her cheeks.

He entered and shut the door, and waited there.

They looked at each other.

"You were sleeping when I came before. I didn't want to wake you."

"I woke up and found it. I thought Marsall had played a trick on me. And then I knew your writing. He's too stupid to be so cunning. I look ill when I sleep," she said. "Don't judge me by that. I'm well now. I'm alive."

But when he went to her and put his arms around her, she lay against him and she thought, *Now I can die. Now it is safe.* As if she could trust everything to him, even existence itself, snuffing out into the peace of nothingness, now he had come home.

The climb up to the graveyard was effortful; the blond man in the smart coat of a slightly foreign cut, the woman in grey who leaned on his arm, they made their way quite slowly.

On the ashy green plateau the graves ran black and white, most tilting. Here and there a thorn tree hovered like a witch. The old church was a ruin. A priest must come from the village to make a burial.

The man and woman stopped at the edge, looking across the yard of death.

"I was afraid you could never come back," Jenavere said. "But now that you're here, I know it doesn't matter in the least. How can he harm you now?"

Daniel did not reply, and after a moment they walked down the pale green lanes among the slabs of graves.

Vehmund's pit was a little to one side, out on the flank of the hill. It was a wind-scoured spot, and the mound, overgrown now and with the stone already leaning, had the same neglected look as all the rest. The dead were forgotten on this upland.

A raven lifted from the eyeless tower of the church and flew away.

Daniel stared down in silence.

"That's all I left of him," he said at last.

"Less than you left," said Jenavere.

"I would have put him in an open place," said Daniel, "like certain sects of the East. Let the vultures have him."

Jenavere, too, looked down at the grave.

"It's over now," she said. "He kept you away so long."

They glanced from the grave and off about the landscape, the undulating hills, the woods in their first transparent scarf of green.

Jenavere was fragile and thin, but her spirit held her together so she seemed unflagging and nearly young. As Daniel looked across the hills, she watched his face. She saw the changes in him, the strengths that were like the new bark of a growing tree. Distance and time had filled him up. He was to her flawless. She wanted only to be with him, to hear his voice, and sense the passage of his thoughts.

"I don't know what I shall do here," he said. Then, "Or I do know. We shall live very quietly, you and I, and let Marsall blunder about in his own way. He's nothing to us. Perhaps the money he's made will itch him and he'll take himself off somewhere."

"Yes," she said.

"We'll stay at home in our burrow," he said, "and let the dark things go about their business. You must trust me," he said.

"Who else is there?" she said simply. "I made you go, and winter came. I'm glad you're here."

"Odd things may happen," he said. "You mustn't pay them any attention."

"As long as you're safe, and with me."

"I shall be, Mother. I'll never leave you again."

She held to him tightly, like a young girl, not anxiously saying that other dreams might interpose, that there might come a season when after all he would have to leave her again. She believed him.

"Tell me about those foreign parts," she said, like a child, asking for a story.

So he told her again of the golden East, the dust and spice, the amber days, the palm trees and camels.

As he spoke, they drifted away from the grave of the husband father.

While they went down the slope again, and he recounted the sights of a tiger in a cage and the manticore on the door of Surim Bey, she remembered how the cats would no longer come to her bedroom. They had slunk off, and kept thereafter to the outer environs of the farm, as they had been used to do in the time of the tyrant.

But now Daniel was with her, and the warm solace of the cats was not necessary. Probably they only felt the spring.

This morning there had been something curious. Rosamunde Ax had come to the bedchamber door, bringing primroses in a little vase. She had put these flowers on Jenavere's dressing-table without a word, and gone away.

Daniel came soundlessly to the door of his room, and stood watching Marsall, as he kneeled over the open bag. A few bright coins had scattered on the carpet. One Marsall held in his hand, trying to decipher it. Daniel stayed there, observing, motionless. Marsall remained unaware, putting down the coin, taking up and trying another.

"Some foreign currency I left unchanged," Daniel said at last.

Marsall dropped the coin, turned, and lumbered to his feet.

"You never locked your door," blustered Marsall. "The bag was lying there."

"I knew you'd come to see."

Marsall frowned. "What if I did?"

"Nothing at all. Are you pleased to find me well-off?"

"If it's real——"

"It's real. Gold and silver and common bronze. The money of this country and elsewhere. Some of the coins are quite ancient, and worth more."

"Where did you get it?"

"I told you. It was left to me."

Marsall looked uneasily sly. "Or you stole it."

Daniel said quietly, carelessly, "I was shown where it was, and no one objected when I helped myself."

"A trick," said Marsall. He had had some ale, and without a challenge he was good-humoured and threatening, not sure yet if he had the upper hand, yet sure he had not been bested.

"Picture the house where the money was," said Daniel, "it was peaceful as a grave."

Marsall checked, sensing a play of words that eluded him.

"Well, you've got it now," he said. "What will you do with it?"

"Oh, sit on my hoard, as you do, and Father did."

"Won't you share with me?" said Marsall, frowning.

"Perhaps later we can agree on something," Daniel said lightly.

Marsall came and stood next to Daniel in the doorway.

"Or I can take it."

"No," said Daniel, simply.

Marsall glowered. He felt himself levered backward by

Daniel's gleaming eyes. They had grown very yellow in the East, very clear. Marsall retreated into himself, with an idea he was not ready yet to smash Daniel down. The time would come; it was not now.

Below in the kitchen Rosamunde had made tea as well as setting out the ale. Two pairs of boots had been cleaned, one Daniel's.

"There's late lambing," Marsall said to Rosamunde. "There's one they think'll breach. Can you still use your hands?"

"If they send me word, I'll go," said Rosamunde.

"Sleep in the barn up the hill," said Marsall. He let her fill his cup with ale, and looked on as she poured the tea for Daniel. "You've learned to be a fine gentleman."

Daniel drank. He said, "Rosamunde, have you taken tea up to my mother?"

"Yes, Master Daniel."

"Her," said Marsall. "Is she having tea now?"

"Why not?"

"She idles up there in the bedchamber. I've a mind to that room myself. She's no need of it now Father's gone."

"Leave her alone, Marsall," said Daniel.

"It's a waste."

"We all waste something."

Marsall parted his lips to answer, and hesitated. A horse was coming down from the orchard.

"Go and see who that is," said Marsall to the old woman.

Rosamunde looked from the window.

"Mr Worth."

"Stinking eggs," said Marsall. "That one. Another fine gentleman. What's he want? Isn't his fancy slut of a wife enough to take up his time?"

A few minutes later Hyperion Worth entered the kitchen with his easy tread.

To Daniel's eyes this man was very young, untouched as a spring leaf. He abounded in grace, and doffed his hat to Rosamunde, who went away into her corner unflattered and ungratified.

"Mr Vehmund," said Worth to Marsall, "I'd hoped to find you out on the pasture."

"It does well enough," said Marsall Vehmund.

"Yes. But you're employed to overlook it."

"So I do," said Marsall, and consumed some ale. "Have a drink."

"I'll take some tea," said Hyperion, and looked at Daniel.

"Rosamunde," said Daniel, "pour Mr Worth some tea."

And Rosamunde came out like a black ant and did as she was bid.

Hyperion Worth sat down at the table. He said, "Since Mr Vehmund doesn't see fit to introduce us, I am Hyperion Worth, the present owner of the farm. And you, sir?"

"Daniel Vehmund."

"Ah, the prodigal son. Forgive me—why should I call you prodigal? But at any rate you've come back from distant climes."

"He's come back rich," said Marsall in his slurring, intrusive way.

Hyperion smiled. "Then congratulations are in order."

"Got hold of a fortune," persisted Marsall. "Won't say how."

"None of us like to talk intimately of our money," said Hyperion fastidiously. "We prefer to discuss its works."

Marsall grunted.

Hyperion looked Daniel over with great interest. As with Jenavere, who had clearly once been a beauty, Daniel was a marvel to find in this place. Plainly he would take after the mother, as the other one had not.

"It's always pleasant," Hyperion therefore added, "to make good for oneself abroad. My funds were very commonly got. How did you find foreign travel, Mr Vehmund?"

Daniel spoke briefly, colourfully, a kind of paraphrase of his conversation with Jenavere.

Hyperion Worth seemed captivated.

Marsall sat there drinking, and ignored.

"And this man with a manticore, was he a magician?"

"Not at all. A prosperous merchant."

"But you met with magicians?" said Hyperion seriously.

"One perhaps. But he passed from my life very quickly."

"In a salon of the city my wife and I watched a very strange magical act. I've never seen anything like it. The fellow was rumoured to have travelled in the Orient."

Daniel said, "Not everyone comes back from the East tainted with glamours."

As he said this, everything about him belied it. He was a creature of dark and pale gold, as ill-suited to the Vehmund kitchen as the manticore itself. As Hyperion was to say to Laura afterwards, "Flying carpets and dancing snakes might have risen from under his hands."

"We're to have a supper at the house," Hyperion said in his rich man's artless way. "To introduce my beautiful wife to the county. Will you honour us by accepting an invitation?" Daniel did not at once respond. Marsall gave out a noise, mockery and disgust combined. Hyperion said, "Laura will be drowned in boredom, I'm truly afraid of it. One guest who shines may outweigh the rest, and she'll forgive me."

"My aim is to live quietly," said Daniel.

"The supper will be overly quiet."

"How can I refuse you politely."

"There is no way." Hyperion leaned forward and took Daniel's hand, held it, shook it as an afterthought. "The house is worthy of a look. And so, believe me, is Laura."

Marsall said something to the effect that Laura had been a peasant girl of the muddy lanes, a milkmaid with red hands.

"Which reminds me," said Hyperion, turning on him with exquisite hauteur, "the ewes need more attention, Mr Vehmund, and they don't get it from you. I'll ask that you mend your ways."

"The farm's yours now, Mr Worth. I'm only your man."

"I expect my men to earn their wages."

Marsall uttered a type of laugh. Hyperion looked at him and then dusted him, as it were, off the corner of vision. To Daniel he said, "I'll send word to you." Then he drained his tea and, with a bow to stony Rosamunde, went out.

"He's fallen in love with you, too," said Marsall to Daniel. "He likes pretty things."

"And you'll lose your work if you cross him," said Daniel.

"I'll lose it then. What do I care? Let the ninny bleat over his sheep as he wants. They're nothing to me now."

She held fast to the elixir of his return, and had the patience to see nothing else. After all, what else was there to see? Daniel had come back. He was taller, perhaps altered, but only as a boy alters to become a man.

Jenavere was exalted, and strength flowed like wine into her body. She could, would, examine nothing else. Even monstrous Marsall was powerless against this new Daniel —as the old monster had ultimately become.

The attentions Rosamunde sifted upon her, these too were the fruit of Daniel's return; for Rosamunde, the vicious slave, had found Daniel also to be her master. She cowered before him, polishing his boots where she had only cleansed Marsall's, making him dainties unlike the normal coarse fare of the house. To Jenavere, Rosamunde brought flowers and little cakes. One day, in her mirror, Jenavere saw Rosamunde creeping about her room, setting things to rights—in the red firelight a wicked fairy tamed.

Jenavere thought of the grave they had visited, she and her son. The walk had tired her, but it had been their triumph. How foolish she had been, thinking he must not come to the house, must stay far off, as if the dead thing could rise from its pit to accuse him. Daniel's gold was too pure for such dead dross to spoil it.

He had done it all for her. And he had come back to her.

She floated on the balm of this novel era, and paid no heed to any shadow.

For now and then he had said something to her that might have summoned shadows. That she might find him changed—she had, and did not mind it; that he might sometimes be absent and she must not fear. He had brought with him some treasure of the East, she was sure of it, although of this he did not speak. Had he entered into a compact with mages? She would believe in anything he told her. If he told her nothing of it, that did not weigh with her. He was a miracle. Daniel.

She had become again, subtly, a queen in the house, as

she had been briefly when first she came to it with that beast, her husband. He had beaten and shocked her royalty from her, but Daniel had made it over again.

She thought only of him, all day, in the darkness before she slept. She dreamed of him, ordinary things, how he stood and walked about, his voice, how he told her stories.

Although once she dreamed that they were on a high tower. The moon was above, near, an enormous bud of whiteness, and he pointed up to the moon and said, *Let's fly there.* And perhaps they had.

Another time she dreamed two dogs were fighting in the orchard, tearing each other, but in the house Daniel sat by the fire, turning a bright knife in his hands. And the dog fight ceased to concern her.

One night, too, Jenavere dreamed of Laura, who had married Hyperion Worth. She was being driven in a huge silver carriage, but she wore a darned frock and there was a dead lamb in her lap.

None of the cats came to Jenavere's room. The kittens did not come to be presented. She missed them, for all she did not need them now. Perhaps it was the visitation of Rosamunde Ax which had driven them away.

On some evenings Jenavere and Daniel would sit in the bedroom and play cards, or Daniel would read to her; and below they heard Marsall dimly stirring like a pig thick in its midden. Jenavere would recall how Marsall had struck her, but she said nothing of it. That blow had been like a presage of this joy. The last hard frost before the spring.

A moon three-quarters full shone through the casement and mingled with the candlelight on Laura, as she brushed her red storm of hair, which crackled like a fire.

Hyperion, in his satin dressing-gown, sat watching.

"How beautiful you are."

Laura continued the long strokes of the brush, and hair sprayed up like smoke and sparks. She was used to her own beauty, and Hyperion's constant references to it made her slightly uncomfortable. Besides, his compliments were always the prelude to desire. Since she did not share the hunger of his lust, sometimes she wished that she might be excused it. She was too honourable, however, to evade.

"Thank you, Hyperion."

"Don't thank me. Thank God, who made you."

"Do you think so?" she asked.

"Yes, I see Him like a master sculptor, forming you of clouds and sunsets. It can't, can it, have been your parents?"

Hyperion, of his generosity, had installed Mr and Mrs Wheelwright, Elfie and Alice, in a small pleasant house, allotted them a servant woman, and a sum of money per annum. There they might laze and sulk and drink themselves to death.

Laura said nothing, nor did she think of her former family. The cold glisten of the moon drew her to the window.

"It will be, I think," said Hyperion, "a late moonrise, the night of our supper. But, in any case, secondary to your own. Do you like your dress?"

"Of course," she said. And then, "A white dress like a bride's."

"Like the spring moon," said Hyperion, and came up to her back to slip his hands around her waist. "And as bright."

"You want me to wear the diamond," she said.

"Naturally. Now it's been set. It will become you incredibly well."

"It's too exotic for me. Won't they all talk? It's bad enough already."

"Is Laura afraid?"

"It's you that should fear."

"What?" he said, aghast, for he had never, in his adult life, and seldom in his childhood, had to fear anything.

"I don't know," said Laura. "But you tempt fate with me—you know you do. You should have wed some woman of your own class."

"You're my wife. They'll see it and bow down to your glory."

"I don't suppose so," she said. She was faintly irritated by his romantic optimism. She herself had no fears exactly, yet was a little embarrassed at being shown off and vaunted.

But Hyperion's hands had already risen to her breasts and were caressing her eagerly.

Laura had a sense of frustration. Then her own ingratitude repelled her. She had been given so much and rescued so swiftly, how dared she quibble? She turned to him with a vital pretence of pleasure.

Having been invited to the Worth mansion, the county came. The opulent who were aristocratic, the opulent who were not, combined with, perforce, displays of deference and courtesy in the wide Worth ballroom, beneath its chandeliers like bouquets of burning crystal flowers.

Hyperion mustered his guests with guileless aplomb. His well-trained servants moved among them. Glasses, like bulbs of rain chased with decorations of fine mist, were borne about, and the champagne effervesced. In the supper room beyond were glimpses of icicled silver, and three silver salmon on banks of asphodel.

Hyperion voiced regret his wife was not yet down. A fault had been found with her dress—such things were regular in these fallen days. It was a lie. A huge and curving marble staircase led into the ballroom. At seven o'clock Laura was to descend. He had planned this theatricality with glee, like her genius, as if she were some famous actress whose entrance must be spectacular. Anyone of wit who had seen the stair and met Hyperion would know the lie for what it was. But how many persons of wit would be present? Hyperion, remembering, trusted Daniel Vehmund would be. Daniel surely could be relied on to enjoy both the lie and its excuse.

Hyperion would be putting his own man in on the Vehmund land, and letting the elder brother go. But Daniel he would like to cultivate, and perhaps the fragile platinum mother. They would be fit people to entertain, fit companions for Laura, attractive and strange.

Mr Worth passed from group to group of the drinking nobility and yeomanry of his corner of the world. He delighted in their cumbersome being, for they could so easily be shaken off. First, however, he meant them to be dazzled.

A lord, who Hyperion had gifted privately with the title of *"Cabbage"*, held Hyperion in talk. "My daughter says, what a capital space for a dance."

"I believe the ballroom was designed for that very purpose."

Lord Cabbage considered this. Eventually he said, "I'm glad to see that fool Ossiter isn't here. Goes after moths with a net. All he can talk about."

"I've never heard of Ossiter."

"Mounts the damn things on pins. Chases them by

night over the fields, scaring country lovers in the hay. Not a man's sport. Do you ride to hounds, by the by?"

"Suffer the little foxes," said Hyperion.

"Oh, they don't suffer, the blighters," said Lord Cabbage. "They live damned well. I've heard wolves were seen in the snow. A wolf hunt, now that would be a thing."

"The Romans recommended it," said Hyperion, "but there was an abundance of wolves, then." He saw Daniel Vehmund across the room, standing alone like an island. Hyperion was surprised. It came to him that, after all, he had not thought Daniel would appear.

Hyperion detached himself from Lord Cabbage.

Daniel's glass was full, nearly untouched, unless it had been refurbished many times. He was properly dressed as a clerk, but in clothes that did not exactly fit: some old dinner suit of the farmhouse kept for jaunts, maybe his father's. His handsomeness arose from his garments like light out of darkness, but on his face was a strained, ironic expression.

"Here you are," said Hyperion.

"I'm accustomed to accepting summonses," said Daniel. "You sent your carriage."

"Not to coerce," said Hyperion. "A hopeful gesture."

Daniel raised his wine. The movement was abrupt and oddly clumsy (for one did not expect clumsiness of Daniel), and a drop of the butterfly liquid spotted his coat. Daniel's eyes were slow, almost sleepy. He looked not as he had been before, but like a dangerous animal half drugged, yet never by wine. Hyperion was intrigued.

"It seemed wise to pluck you from your environment, your brother's blight."

"You'll be rid of him," said Daniel.

"Certainly. But let's not speak of that. I trust our acquaintance can transcend such bounds."

"Where's your famous wife?" asked Daniel, nearly brutishly.

"Laura is to come down that stair on the stroke of seven. Your vigil will be rewarded."

"That's good. Had it been much later, I'd be gone."

"But you'll sup with us?"

"No," said Daniel. "Before eight o'clock I must be off."

"Some urgent business."

"The most urgent."

"The carriage stays at your disposal," said Hyperion.

"I shan't need your carriage."

"A walk," said Hyperion, "across land lit by the full moon. Doubtless she and I will long for that in the crowd of our guests."

"Stay indoors, Mr Worth," said Daniel. "Trust the old instinct and avoid the dark."

"Still talk of wolves?" said Hyperion. "They're harmless now; the spring sees to it they get plenty to eat."

"Not wolves," said Daniel. "There are other things to dread."

"You are tinted by your Eastern experience, Mr Vehmund. I'm delighted. What demons do you detect in our rural landscape? Did you bring one home with you?"

"In a bottle," said Daniel. He seemed amused.

"And all we can offer you is wine."

Both men looked across the pond of people. Women's gowns of various shades were woven together like flowers, the sparkle of jewelry on bare flesh either young and fair or aging as stretched petals. And these punctuated by the fully-clad uniform shapes of the men in their armour

of black and white. It was as gaudy, in its own way, as the
sukh, but it was not of the sukh that Daniel thought.

Beside the lightness and ebullience of Hyperion's notions, Daniel's brain perceived through a shadow-lens the
festive images, which on this night, always on such a
night, were dreamlike and hollow. He had come to Hyperion's gingerbread house out of malevolence, to be the
ghoul at their feast. He had not meant to come at all, and
the appearance of the carriage had for a moment discon-
certed him, for he was already half stupefied with the
approach of his own personal night, his nemesis, the descent into unknown delirium. The carriage was not a
threat, but it was an interruption. He had already made
his plans. He had intended to leave the farm and go up
into the wood, and there lose himself to what he would
become. But then he visualized this other place, the acre-
age about the mansion, its wild spots and uplands. He
knew from experience the thing which claimed him made
nothing of distance, and would probably tend homeward
as the day returned towards the earth. The idea of monstrousness at large in so much dark, so many miles, be-
guiled him, had even been worth his father's clothes. And
the danger, that too. For the moon, full and bone white,
would rise soon after eight o'clock. He could enter the
brink of the banquet and must then fly it. He believed he
experienced some essence of the self he would come to
be, out in the depths of the moonlight; and so in that way
now he saw the lighted house there at the nub of grounds
and trees, the figures coming and going in innocent
unknowledge.

And how many of these dressed fleshly dolls would
stray into the rivers of the moon, where he should find
them?

A clock in the ballroom, ornate and raised up like an idol, struck seven times.

Daniel felt an intense quickening, and wondered at it. The rich fellow's wife, a girl of the fields, was about to come down in some confectionery robe, and what did that mean?

The guests were looking up. Something had drawn their attention to the head of the stair. A figure was there. It moved out on to the staircase.

A dullness, a darkness, seemed to fill in the air of the well-lit room. Only the stairway gleamed, and the pale figure descending.

The dress was like the moon, but not the young moon; a moon rather which sunk, an old dense white, so that the long gloves on her arms were whiter, and her skin another white again. Her red hair was combered up, but for two long ringlets that fell to her bare shoulders like coils of spun copper. She looked, as Hyperion had intended, like a creature in a fairy tale, where milkmaids became princesses with no bother.

All this Daniel saw, far off, and was slightly pleased by. And then it was as if the woman called Laura flamed up and burnt through his eyes to his mind. She became alive and real, the only real thing beside himself, more than himself, for at this stage he was losing his identity. On the whiteness of her skin the glint of golden filigree. In the low scoop of the gown, between her white breasts, a star. It flashed and fluttered green, then whiter than anything in the room.

Hyperion had gone forward. He met Laura on the lower steps. He kissed her hand before them all. Then led her down into the chamber. The guests closed over them like waters.

Daniel moved with them, Hyperion and Laura, distant

yet parallel, along the ballroom. Glimpses came between
the many-coloured dresses, the penguin evening-dress of
the men, between arms and faces, fans and glass. Laura's
whiteness and her two fires.

Daniel lost track of Hyperion. Hyperion did not matter. It was Laura he followed, Laura clothed in the diamond.

They moved together as one, gliding, halting, going on.
And suddenly both came around a grove of people and
were face to face: Daniel, and Laura on the arm of her
husband.

"Daniel Vehmund, this is my wife."

Hyperion was scarcely there. It was to Daniel as if he
saw her through the diamond, caught inside the jewel.

Her face looked beautiful, and unsoft as adamant. She
was held in glittering ice.

Daniel did not bow to Laura or embrace her hand. He
stared down at her, and the tension of his look was such
that all the colour left her skin. For Laura, also, the rest
of the room and its people faded away, Hyperion with
them. She stood alone with Daniel on some peak by
night, and from his eyes came such a force she felt she
would be taken and torn, rent apart by it, but she was
powerless to cry for help. Never in her life had she felt
such a thing, never dreamed it could exist.

Hyperion said lightly, firmly, "Come, Mr Vehmund. I
don't expect this of you."

Daniel raised his eyes and looked at Hyperion. Hyperion started, checked himself, and laughed. "It was wrong
of me to subject you to so much beauty. I myself am
stunned by it."

"No, Hyperion," murmured Laura. And abruptly she
coloured like red wine running into crystal. She removed
her eyes from Daniel's and gazed away into thin air.

Daniel said, "You're right." He said, still to Hyperion, "Only the jewel does her justice."

"My own thought. Pretty, isn't it?"

"I have seen it before," said Daniel. "In the East it was briefly in my possession. Then later I gave it up."

"Surely not. You're joking, Daniel Vehmund."

"Of course," said Daniel. "But it's called the Wolf, isn't it? For a little flaw at its heart like a wolf running."

"I believe so. Obviously tales of this stone have gone ahead of its viewing."

"Where did you come by it?" Daniel asked.

"I hope you're enjoying the champagne," said Hyperion.

"The diamond only counts," Daniel said, "where it is this minute. Lying over the heart of your wife."

Astonished, Laura looked at him again. She put her white gloved hand up over the white satin curve of her flesh, to where the diamond scorched.

"I don't mean to frighten you," Daniel said to her.

She said softly, "But you do."

"Then you must excuse me. The full moon affects me. Others have remarked it. I act differently at full moon."

"If the diamond was yours——" she said.

"It doesn't belong to me now. I let someone take it, and perhaps he brought it to you. I would have brought it to you if I could have foreseen . . ." He broke off, and Laura felt a burning finger pass from his eyes into the jewel and so into her breast. She seemed tied to him by cords of electricity and, in an effort to break free, she sought Hyperion.

"How hot the room is. Won't they open the doors?"

"It shall be done," said Hyperion. "We'll see to it ourselves, and leave Mr Vehmund to his reverie on gems."

Daniel now stayed in one spot and watched them move

away from him among the guests again. As if borne
through a senseless wood, Laura turned once and looked
back.

Daniel felt the clothes of his hated father stirring on
his back, too stupid to taunt him. And miles off there
rose a slim low sound that no one else would hear, the
note of the moon as it came up towards the rim of the
earth.

Laura was like the diamond now; it shone through her
transparently, and through her bleeding hair. All over the
ballroom she blazed. And between her breasts the jewel
was green as ice, losing its whiteness to hers.

Hyperion had made it clear what he thought.

Hyperion was only another of the shadowy dolls of the
feast.

The servants were opening the french doors at one end
of the ballroom. A cool scented waft of darkness came in
on the overheated chamber.

Out there were the lawns and trees, water, the woods
and rocky hills, trickled by starlight. This was where he
must now go.

He would leave them to the fortress of their lighted
house, that one small glow against all the torrent of the
night and the scream of the risen moon.

Already fierce pains swept through his body, twisting
with a strange deep ache.

Daniel walked across the ballroom, between groups
who glanced aside from him with little affronted noises.

Laura in heaven, set in the moon.

At the threshold of the night he dropped the precious
champagne glass so it broke on the ballroom floor. In the
din, few noticed.

Then he sprang out into the dark, and ran, heavily,

forgetting everything, stumbling and bounding, to meet the coming of madness.

Hyperion's supper had turned out a success. Laura was so lovely, and already her husband had trained her so well, just as she had been educated by her surroundings and all he had shown her. She was like a figurine that perfectly mechanically moved. Everything she did was correct. She spoke little, but when she did so there was nothing to betray her. She must have been a changeling, some aristocratic baby left to the Wheelwrights by mistake. They became, the gathering, comfortable with the idea that Laura was after all acceptable in her position as lady. The men looked with fresh respect at Hyperion, the sorcerer who had invented her.

There was the supper then: the great fishes and the vast roasts, the puddings of alabaster webbed with glassy sugar. Plants appeared to grow up through the table: little palm trees and orange trees with enamel fruits.

Then the candles burned down and the light was riper, more mature. The evening had grown cold, and all the doors and windows were shut. There came to be a group about the salon fire, with Laura enthroned as its head, in a wide armchair, and some of the merchants and lordlings even sitting at her feet on cushions, and Hyperion, the king of this impromptu court, circling pleasantly about to himself refill the empty glasses and offer the marzipan sweets to flushed young women with tight-boned waists and crenelated sheeny hair.

The company told stories. They spoke of damsels in high towers, headless horsemen, broken promises, and fortunes found in attics.

Lord Cabbage called on Laura for a tale. She looked at him as she had been looking at all of them, with deep

dark eyes like the blackest lights. She was so calm they
had marvelled, and were now entranced. They did not
know it was the calm of shock.

She had dreaded this evening, but in the end none of it
had meant anything. She had wandered in a trance
through all of its proceedings, perfect and exact because
she was barely there. All she had thought about was
Jenavere's son. Daniel, who had come back from other
places like a young man in one of these stories, come
back and stared at her so she could hide nothing from
him. He had seen all of her—more than if he had seen
her naked. He had beheld her psyche, touched it. That
was all she could think of.

Misunderstanding her hesitation, Hyperion interposed.

"My wife is the queen of her court, sir. She may summon stories, but needn't fashion any."

"No, no," said Lord Cabbage, "it's her turn, I say."

Laura said, "I'll tell you about the king's ship."

It was a history she had heard in the village school,
where the children had sat wide-eyed at it, and later all
but Laura forgot. While she had been a child at the village, Daniel had been a child at the Vehmund farm. They
had never met, and yet how close they were, a few miles
of distance, an hour or two of time.

"The ship," said Laura, "was the most beautiful. It was
painted blue with saffron masts and sails of gold. At the
prow was carved a huge fish, and in its eyes were set two
topazes, and in its crest was a sapphire. Those that rode
in the ship had dressed for her in azure and yellow of
many shades, and they too had their sapphires and topazes, their lapis, turquoise and citrine. The king's son
was among them, in a coat like the sea, and he was blond.
Many of the king's friends or their children were also on
the ship. It was thought a great honour to be there. It was

a fair fine day, and the oarsmen rowed the painted oars, and the gold sails opened to the wind. Off went the ship like a greyhound, and those on shore cheered her away, and the musicians played a lively tune. At sunset she was to return, when the sky matched her."

The fire cracked and Laura paused. Her face was thoughtful and remote, yet in her throat her heart beat quickly. And on her breast the fabulous diamond, which several had discussed, none but Daniel mentioned, quivered. The group by the fire was hanging on Laura's words. She seemed not to see them. Nor Hyperion, standing to one side with a bright decanter in his hands.

"And, at sunset, they gathered on the shore, looking for the ship coming back. But all the blue and gold they saw was in heaven, and the clouds took on the shape of ships, but no ship was to be seen. They looked for her sails, and listened for the sound of her horn. But the sea was empty, a vast mystery. When the dark came, the king ordered out half his fleet, to search the water for the painted ship. And all night under the clear and mocking moon, they searched the ocean up and down. But finding nothing, they returned to the king at daybreak. Then the king sent them out again, and the other half of the fleet with them. A month they searched, under the moon and under the sun, and they saw nothing of the painted ship, not a spar, not an oar, no sign of her, as if the waves had swallowed her entire."

Laura sat now in a long silence, her hands gathered in her lap, and her audience by the fire waited. The diamond leapt with light.

She said, "The king grieved, and his courtiers with him. There was not a person there but had had someone dear to them on the painted ship."

One of the young ladies in the group let out a sigh. Then laughed at herself. No one else stirred.

Hyperion said, almost sharply, "Come, you can't leave it there."

Laura did not look at him. She said, "The months passed, and next the years passed. Three years to the day, an old sailor was brought before the king. 'Fear nothing,' said the king to him. 'Only speak what you have spoken before.' Then the sailor told his tale. That once, at sea, fishing by night on the open water, he saw pass below him in the depths far down, a painted ship of blue and brilliant gold that burned and shone as if the sun were on her in the dead of night. And on her decks was a host in blue and yellow, and yellow and blue jewels. And they laughed and gestured and drank from jewelled cups, there in the sea. And all were skeletons. And on the rowers' benches the skeleton rowers worked the oars. And in the look-out on the mast a skeleton stared with his sockets away through the sea. And so the ship passed by and was gone. After the old sailor had told this, the king rewarded him and sent him on his way. 'Tell your story wherever you are able. But add that it was the king's ship you saw, and his son numbered among the dead. And that truly the powers of this world have no mercy.' "

"A good yarn," said Lord Cabbage inappropriately in the stillness. And to his daughter, "What do you say, Ada?"

"I don't see the point," said Ada, who liked to dance. "I don't see the point of a king's son who becomes a skeleton."

"Perhaps," said a merchant at the fireside, "his father sent him off on the ship and deliberately had the vessel sunk. Perhaps he feared his son."

"That would be the worst crime in the world," said one of the ladies.

"The worst crime is for a son to kill his father."

"Perhaps he had planned it," said the merchant, "and his father dealt with him the first."

Hyperion said, "My wife's unmoved."

Laura sat like a statue. She was thinking of Daniel the king's son, going to the bottom of the sea, his blond hair coiled with the blue murks of the deep, the fish swimming about his body. She had killed him. She had changed him into a spectre.

"Laura," said Hyperion briskly, "you must give account of yourself."

Despite everything, he was challenging her—not her ally but her foe. Yet she was beyond him, and his party, and did not care.

"It's only a story," she said.

She shifted a little, and the diamond shot again a blazing ray, like a meteor.

The women stared, maybe with envy, and the men with a debased approval, for this was how a lovely woman should be hung with her husband's trophies. Only Hyperion had averted his eyes, and was offering the marzipan to Ada.

None of them looked at Laura as Daniel had looked. He had walked away into the night, lawlessly, without decorum.

She turned her head to glance at the long, curtained windows.

From far off, up on the hills of the world, a sound unfolded down the night.

It was inimical, so much so that none of those who heard it could comprehend it. Yet their hair stood on end. It was a terrible cry, having nothing to do with anything living. Unfocused as the voice of the wind, yet animal, *sentient*.

"What the devil was that?"

One of the women, released, gave a faint scream.

"A fox. They make the foulest noises, like souls in torment."

"That wasn't any fox."

Lord Cabbage strode to a long window, thrust back the curtain and looked out.

"Nothing to be seen. And the moon's up. It's clear as day."

Men crowded to the windows of the salon. Lord Cabbage opened his. The women pressed back. "Don't—don't—something's out there."

And suddenly it came again, that cry, thin and strong, relentless, floating down like the bugle note of death, hunting, hungry and alone. They could hear in it now all that was evil; they hung on it until it stopped, and one of the women became faint.

"Close the window, there's nothing to see. It's some animal. Perhaps a wolf."

"A wolf howl's bad enough, but that—that was like the voice of the damned."

The window was shut, the fainting woman seen to.

Laura sat with the firelight painting her white face. Hyperion did not go to her to console her. She said nothing. But she held the diamond in her hand against her breasts and it sparkled through her fingers, live, like a white-green coal.

"You hear these noises in the country."

"The nights out here are noisier than in town."

"Damned if I know what it was."

They stoked the fire, not waiting for the servants. They drew back to the firelight. Here in their candlelit cave they felt the weight and size of night leaning on every wall.

Laura thought: *It's the crowing of fate. It's my downfall howling on the hills.*

Out in the night the moonlit dark dropped from the air.

Long copes and coves of shadow, every angle tuned silver.

The fox and the ferret ran across the open stoles of light, and were away into the surf of shade.

On trees, bristled with spring, the moon dripped like white water.

There was a humming, buzzing of nocturnal life.

That would suddenly fall quiet.

Blackness passed, a blot, a voiceless thunder. The grass parted and sprang back. At the edges of the woods darknesses were linked, unravelled.

An owl in an elm top sat mute, gargoyle of feathers. Underfoot mice froze like stones.

The blackness passed over and rolled away downhill, and the night took back its breath, the leaves breathed, the grasses unwove, the stones wriggled under the ferns, and the owl hooted.

So it came and went, black silence, like a ball of primeval stuff, too old, too galvanized to rest. Opening the doors of the moonlight to go through, without a sound.

The man who hunted moths was out with his net and his killing jar, prancing along the hillsides of the umber world. The moon lit the way like a torch. Already he had seen uncommon prey: the small black moth *Carbo,* with the crimson specks on its wings, only grey in the moonlight.

Ossiter, the hunter, had no time for men and women.

He was rich, and treated servants and acquaintances alike, with unconcealed anathema. His earth was a room full of winged things on pins. These delighted him. And, in the nights of spring and summer, he roamed about the uplands, crept up on the trees where the papery life gathered in the dark. He liked to catch and hold, saw no beauty in flight, wanted to possess in stasis, the wings stretched unresting, to display their design and colour.

In his head, as he galloped along the slopes after Carbo, was a vague unnecessary image of some supper party he had heard of, some man displaying his wingless living wife, and a diamond there had been talk of. But Carbo was more interesting than a diamond. Where was Carbo flying so fast?

Pursuing the black moth, Ossiter travelled down the wild meadows, and came into an outskirt of the wood.

The trees were not dense, but interfering, they clotted in the way, and he was afraid of losing the moth.

The moth was intent on something. Suddenly Ossiter thought he saw a light. It was phosphorus perhaps on the brim of some muddy pool, or the moon striking on a reflective surface. The moth was attracted to this light, whatever it was. Ossiter hastened after. Already he beheld Carbo, burning black and sparked with red upon the pin, safely his for ever. For Ossiter encircled himself with walls of moths.

There was a second light, surely, next to the first. And then both went out, and only the harsh flare of the moon was sliced between the trees to guide him.

Carbo had settled on something. Perhaps the stump of a tree. The wings flitted closed.

Ossiter thumped through the wood with the net outstretched, and brought it down with a graceless accuracy over the moth and the dark lump whereon it rested.

The darkness burst. It was like a shower of coals. Ossiter felt his net disintegrate as a thing long and black came up through it. He could not think what it was, or what had happened. He glimpsed the moth, flying up and away from him, escaping——

Two moons opened under Ossiter's hand. They astonished him. He gazed at them in utter ignorance. Then his hand and arm were swallowed up in darkness.

There was a fearful pain, as if he had been burnt by a hundred points of fire.

Ossiter screamed and tried to pull away, and the dark came up his arm, ingesting flesh and bone as it came.

The hunter of moths saw the ultimate hunter, its carven face that put out the moon, the black void of throat full of his own body. Then the huge jaws flapped like a trap door, and closed.

The broken net, the killing jar, fell in the moon-watered fern. The moon watched, uninclined to look away.

Rosamunde Ax was in the Vehmund kitchen kneading dough, the oven heating behind her.

The pale yellow of the early sunlight, now disturbed, coalesced into the hair and eyes of Daniel entering through the door.

As she had done earlier, Rosamunde straightened up.

There was to Daniel, inside the aura of gold, a density of darkness. His gait, as he came in, was almost ungainly, yet there was a peculiar animal fluidity to his movements, as though two natures coexisted in him, despite each other.

"Rosamunde," he said, and his voice seemed to come from some depth, laughingly, like water.

"Master Daniel."

"Why do you stare?" he said. "You've seen me be-fore."

Rosamunde lowered her eyes. "Shall I make tea?"

"No. I'm not in the mood for tea. I've been out all night, on the land. Under the moon. I've travelled a long way. Slept in a hedgerow."

Rosamunde did not answer. She had thought he had slept in a white bed at the mansion; came back in a car-riage left on the road.

He did not look dishevelled. He looked complete and whole. Unshaven, the hair on his jaw had grown so quickly and so thickly it was almost a beard. He walked forward to the table. He exuded a scent of grass and rocks, bark, darkness still. He looked at Rosamunde, and her old knees shook. She wanted to kneel down. "Bak-ing?" he asked.

"I must be up at the lambing later."

"Rosamunde among the sheep," he said. "Do you have any pity on the poor beasts?"

"Dumb creatures," she said.

He was like some elemental thing, lightning; the kitchen could hardly hold him. He touched the back of her floury hand and it was like a shock.

"You see harmony in the universe," said Daniel Vehmund. "Beasts are the servants of man, there for his convenience."

Rosamunde found that she stared at him again.

"There is a beast," said Daniel softly, "that doesn't serve mankind. More ravening than the most desperate wolf. It goes by night over the lean hills, following the moon. Lock your door, Rosamunde Ax, and hide under your bed."

Rosamunde shook all over now, and did not properly

know why. She wanted to lie down on the floor and clasp his boots in her hands. She did not feel old.

Daniel drew away from her. He said, "You'll take tea up to my mother when she wakes."

"Yes, Master Daniel."

"I suppose my brother's in a drunken stupor."

Daniel crossed the room towards the stairs. Rosamunde pursued him with her eyes. Under her hands the dough felt like wet flesh.

Daniel flicked through the door like a leaf turning, and was gone.

Day broadened on the farmhouse, bright in the fresh foliage of the sheltered orchard, mellowing the stone, painting the new shoots on the vine. Windows gleamed and faded as the sun passed over. Now and then a brindled cat arrowed through the tall grasses, avoiding the house. On the hills round about, the shadows of clouds revolved like wheels in the sky.

In the afternoon, the twig figure of Rosamunde Ax came out of the building and went away along the track towards the upper pastures. Later still the two housemaids emerged, going off for their monthly jaunt to the village, where they would stay the night with their ample village parents. Miles high a dog barked. Birds swarmed. Bees were gathering in the slender flowers of the herb garden.

The sun roved westward.

A frog, seated on the water-butt near the kitchen door, leaped away in a glide of green. Three white chickens pecked.

A strange expectancy was on the valley. Not peace, as the slowly quartering light and soft stillness made believe.

In the house, the three quiescences that were human

things had begun to stir. Jenavere restless in her room, pacing, sitting, while the clock ticked. Marsall, roused from his coma, ducking his heavy small head in a basin of water. Daniel lying on his back, his golden eyes on the swarthy sunshine which slipped from the ceiling.

They suspected, in varying degrees, a thread drawing them together, a triangle of beings in the house which cats now would not enter.

The sun went down in red smoke.

Marsall kicked some article across his room, barged out and tramped along the passage. He banged on the door of Jenavere's chamber. No response. Marsall banged again, and shouted for good measure. "I know you're in there, woman."

Then he opened the door.

The room was dipped in thin red, for the whole sky, even the east, glowed. Jenavere sat in her chair, her feet on the footstool. Rosamunde had lit her a fire, and there were yellow flowers in a jar.

Marsall did not like the aspect of Jenavere since Daniel's return. She had straightened up like a plant getting sudden sunlight. Her face was proud and serene, as if she looked down at him from a battlement.

"I didn't bid you enter," she said.

"No. But I came in any way. You can't deny your door to me. I'd break it down if I had to."

"Yes, I believe that."

"Good, good. You believe it, Mother."

"What do you want?" she said.

Marsall looked about him. His head was thick, but it would clear when he got to his ale. He had been thinking meanwhile. It was time to make himself plain.

"I want this room," he said. "It's the master's bedchamber. It's mine by rights. Now my father's gone, you'll pass it on to me. I've let you nestle here too long."

"This room has always been mine," she said.

"No. Never yours. *His.* I'll take it."

Jenavere did not move from her chair.

"I won't give it up," she said.

"Yes. Tomorrow. The old bat can shift your things."

"I'm accustomed to this room."

"The bed's too big for you. The room's too big. You rattle about like a pip in a pod. Resign yourself. You'll have the other."

"I shan't go," she said.

"*Won't* you."

"Daniel will defend me," she said, naming her champion as Marsall had known she would.

"That baby? Let him try. I'll thrash him for you."

Trouble chased across her face like clouds, then faded. "Why must you reduce everything to violence, Marsall?"

"Must I? I'm only after my rights. This room's mine. I'll have no more of your whining, old lady. Expect to move."

Marsall swung out. He was eager for his drink.

After he had gone, leaving the door wide, Jenavere got up from her chair. She stood in the middle of the room, as the rose light melted into greyness. Then, gathering herself, she went to the lamp on the mantelpiece and lit it.

Outside the window the orchards glowed dully, disembodied in the spring dusk. The chickens had gone to their house. The hills were bundles of smooth blackness. Jenavere felt her hemming-in by silent landscape and by Marsall's unholy will. Could Daniel help her? At the brink she hesitated. She remembered all at once savage contests in the childhood of her two sons. They had

fought, and Daniel had been defeated, often horribly.
Now Daniel was changed. She had blossomed at his
power, but if it were to be tested, what then?

Yet she had no other recourse. Marsall wanted to snuff
her out. To make her elderly and invalid, to squeeze her
away by degrees. It was his poison which had harmed her,
as sure as if he had dropped some tincture into her food.

She moved along the corridor to Daniel's room, now in
the dark. As she raised her hand to the panels of the
door, it was gently opened.

There was no light in Daniel's room. All the shadow
seemed gathered into him.

"What is it, Mother?"

"I've had a visit from your brother. He means to take
my bedroom." And she thought, *How petty it is.*

Daniel said, his voice low, "He shan't. Your room's
pleasant and faces east. The proper room for you to
have."

"What can I do?"

"I'll talk to him," Daniel said.

She thought how almost supernatural his voice was, so
certain in the dark. She breathed deeply, as if taking oxy-
gen from his nearness.

"I was helpless until you came back."

"I'm here," he said. He leaned forward and kissed her
forehead, and the press of his lips, dry and warm, lit like
a star there so she expected a flame to light up the passage. "Go in now," he said. "I'll deal with it."

He could see in the dark, and watched her go hesi-
tantly away to her room, the sacred room of her queen-
ship which should not be wrested from her. Daniel had a
feeling like suppressed laughter. He had had it before at
this time. The night outside seemed to call to him in
silken voices. The touch of his own garments on his skin

was both an irritant and an exhilaration. In a little more than an hour, the moon would rise above the hills. He could sense the pull of it, like a huge tide turning in his blood. He was in here, but also he was elsewhere.

He went down the stairs to the kitchen.

The two lamps were alight and Marsall, with tonight no Rosamunde to wait on him, no cronies to make up to him, sat by the low fire, drinking deep.

"Ah, dear Daniel," said Marsall. "Have some ale. It'll do you good."

"I'm not here to be done good. Let our mother alone."

"Let our mother alone," Marsall repeated, in his exaggerated voice now already slurred and muddied by drink. "What have I done to her?"

"Let her keep her room."

"Oh, that. No, I don't think so. I need it. Maybe I'll bring home a bride to the farm. One of us must carry on the Vehmund name. And since only one of us is capable . . . I'll need the big bed. And my wife'll be mistress. Not that worn-out old bitch."

"Don't call her names."

"Who'll stop me?"

"I'll stop you, if I must."

Daniel had moved across the kitchen to the door. He opened it and stared out into the night. He was only partly in the kitchen, and he had sounded remote. Most of him was on the hill. The moon pulsed under the ground, under his heart.

Marsall stood up. He swaggered brutishly by the fire.

"You'll stop me, eh? Come on, then."

Daniel said with an insane sweet courtesy, "I must be going out."

"*Out* is it? Running off. Such a brave fellow. You go then. You go. I'll persuade the old woman, never fear. I'll bring her round. Father could do that. Father never let her say no. He had a way with him, our dad."

Daniel half looked back into the kitchen. The fire caught his eyes. They were awesome as planets, only Marsall was too sottish to see.

"How do you mean, you'll persuade her?"

"A man's strength. She's had a taste before. It brought her round."

"You struck her."

"A tap. I can slap her and have enough left for you. When you get back from your fine friends."

Daniel stood between the shining firelight and the glittering dark. *"I won't go then."*

"Not go? Go if you want."

"No. I'll stay here with you."

Daniel smiled. He closed the door carefully, shot the bolts.

Marsall grunted and put down his empty cup.

He went lurching forward at Daniel, who stepped away from him. Marsall reached out, ruffled Daniel's linen shirt.

"Scared of me, aren't you, daisy flower? Scared of your big brother."

Daniel moved backward. He was in the doorway under the stairs. He was still smiling, his eyes were limpid, almost sightless, hypnotized.

"I'll deal with you," said Marsall. He aimed a blow at Daniel, who danced back, and was on the stair. Marsall came after him. "Spoil your prettiness for you. Then the rich gentlemen won't want you at their dinners."

Daniel was halfway up the stair. His eyes looked totally blind. The smile had gone and his face contorted as though with pain. Marsall's second blow took him in the chest. Daniel rocked but did not go over. He stretched

out and caught Marsall, hauling him upwards. They
gained the stairs' top. Daniel spat in Marsall's face, and
Marsall roared. Daniel was away and Marsall surged after him. They were in darkness.

"You can't hear it," said Daniel. "The moon——"

Marsall snatched at Daniel, swung him. Daniel
groaned. For an instant they seemed to struggle, Marsall
with Daniel, Daniel with some preoccupying other thing.
Then Marsall pushed Daniel below him on the stair.
Marsall shoved, and cast Daniel off into space, down the
flight.

Daniel fell without a sound towards the kitchen below,
jointlessly. There was a loose and pallid impact. Weightless. Marsall peered after.

Where the rich light came through from the kitchen
door there was nothing. Daniel had fallen in the dark
under the stair. A moment went by.

Then, Daniel screamed. The noise was unspeakable.
After the first cry, a second, worse.

"Christ. I've killed him."

Marsall leaned on the wall. It came to him in a turgid
flash he could say Daniel had toppled down the stair by
himself. No one could blame Marsall; there were no witnesses.

As the awful screaming started up again, Marsall heard
the door of Jenavere's disputed room flung wide. She
came upon him like a frightened bird in the shadow, and
the soft distorted glow followed from her chamber lamp.

"What have you done?"

She did not touch him but something of her beat
against him.

"He fell. The idiot."

"Daniel——" she said, and tried to thrust a way past
him, and Marsall held her in the passage.

"You can't help him," Marsall shouted above Daniel's screams. "He's got his just deserts."

Jenavere too uttered a mad hoarse shriek.

Marsall lifted up his heavy fist to hammer her into silence—and halted.

The fearsome screams had ceased below.

Marsall let the woman go. She did not move. They stood together in the black angle between the two distant lamps.

"He's dead," said Marsall.

Jenavere made a tiny cry, wordless, beyond words.

"Yes, he's bloody dead. That's your Daniel."

There came the mildest noise, quiet, like a coal or stick falling on the kitchen hearth.

Marsall did not heed it. He primed himself now to descend and interview the body of his brother.

Before he had taken a step, another noise began which arrested him.

It was so deep, it was like a bubbling of black lava under the boards of the house, like the respiration of a swamp. Something growled below, there in the darkness.

Marsall was startled. Not considering what he did, he took a pace backward, but the action was not cerebral. He was telling himself that what he heard were the last choking breaths of a dying man.

Then the shadow moved under the stair. It hunched upward, and the wooden treads creaked. Something was coming up. Very slowly, very completely. Each stair cracked at the impact.

Two dots of brilliance gleamed scarlet in the air.

Marsall shouted. "Get back! I'll do for you——"

Beneath the two round fires another line of flame was formed, a palisade.

It was Daniel. Somehow his eyes and teeth caught the

vagrant light of Jenavere's lamp. He came on all fours, too injured to stand upright.

Marsall forced himself on to the stair. He would kick Daniel down again. For it must be Daniel. Only Daniel had been there, and Marsall had beaten him. Marsall began to descend.

There was a sudden incredible splintering. Marsall saw the treads shattering up like spray, and through them reared a black limb. It clashed against his leg and great hooks of white agony sank into his calf. Screaming now in turn, Marsall was pulled headlong. He crashed along the staircase and rolled to the door of the kitchen. Something thudded against him, and poked him through.

Marsall lay on his back in a storm of hurt, in the cavern of that lamplit, firelit place; so familiar, his den of maleness, where he drank and women waited on him; where his father had sat like a lord, where his father had died.

He had an awareness of the ridiculous, lying there, for someone had thrown him down. But now he would get up and fix all that.

Through the door flowed the dark.

Marsall lay on the floor, and looked. His eyes bulged and he began to scream again, just as Daniel had. The dark had a shape, the shape of some animal, maybe like a boar, a huge black pig. But the head was enormous and the eyes were dark now, glimmering, and the vast teeth, row by row, stared.

In a frenzy, Marsall tried to kick out his booted feet, the damaged leg and the whole one. And the vast teeth snapped like a scythe.

Marsall screamed for God. He screamed for his father. The black pig with the head of death tore through his abdomen and coils of life spilled out. The blood fountained to the walls and hissed into the fire. Still Marsall screamed, and then the face of the animal came down over his, and it tore away the last of him, with his voice.

There was no sound now but for the flutter of the wicks in the two lamps. Then there came the rhythm of a woman's breathing.

The beast raised its head. It looked and seemed to see. Jenavere stood in the doorway, her arms relaxed at her sides. Like a Madonna of butchery she had watched it all. The blood had even splashed her a little, bright red drops on the grey colour of her skirt, dainty like beadwork.

Her face was expressionless, her eyes unclouded.

She held out her hand.

The beast moved like a black ribbon, as if floating.

"There," she said. "There."

It went to her and she touched its bristling hair where blood clung like garnets. She stroked its great forehead where the ears lay back like folded leaves. It had no genitals, she had noticed; under its belly was only empty flesh. It was not a creature of regeneration.

It leaned on her body. It was hot as a furnace. She did not fear it. She was sick only with joy.

After a few minutes the woman crossed the kitchen to undo the door. Moonlight entered the room.

The beast which had disembowelled Marsall went by Jenavere and out into the night.

She shut the door on it and moved back through the blood-stained kitchen, past Marsall's corpse. She went up the broken stair like one half asleep, and going in to her room, closed herself away.

An hour after sunrise, Rosamunde Ax returned to the farm from the hills. She had been walking since before first light. In her arms, wrapped in a piece of blanket, was a lamb sloughed from a dead mother. Finding the door undone, Rosamunde came straight in.

The kitchen was painted in new dyes and on the floor lay the body of Marsall, its guts out on the ground and one leg separated from it.

Rosamunde crouched forward like a crow.

From the chair by the hearth Daniel Vehmund spoke to her.

"You'll clean it all up, Rosamunde."

Her fingers, scrubbed of the birth blood of sheep, twitched. She bowed her head and felt the power of him astride her, merciless. The lamb bleated.

"Yes," she said. "Yes, Master."

2

Seen in the spring dusk, the fairy-tale mansion of Hyperion Worth palely darkened, its pinnacles etched into the chill sky, its terrace crowded with white statues dabbed by gold as windows came alight. The long lawns swept to the liquid mirror of the lake. The young leaves were thickening on the trees of the linden walk, where through the afternoon a thrush had sung, silent now. Silence crept up on the house like waters. Oblivious, apparently, the rich man and his wife carried out their evening, dining on the inside of the glass and brick at a beaming table of candles and wines, then at cards in the parlour. The flawless servants waited on them and vanished when not in use. Outside, the moon rose. Her hard disc reflected in the lake. The rich man's wife made excuses, and went up the staircase, alone, to her apartment.

Laura locked her door, and moved about the bedroom in belated wonderment. All this was hers.

The satin wallpaper. The blue and green tapestries from France. The columned bed. Laura undid her jewel-box. She took out the pearls, the emerald necklace and earrings, the bracelets of gold. She drew out the diamond Hyperion had bought from the magician Julinus. It seemed dull tonight, clouded and mysterious, the tiny flaw a blot having no shape.

Without calling for the assistance of her maid, Laura drew off her sumptuous gown, her shoes with rosettes of silver, the silk stockings, garters, the froth of petticoats, the beribboned cage of stays. She stood in her white skin and let down her hair.

This was how witches had worked their spells, and danced for the Devil, alone and naked in huts and halls. Laura pointed her feet one after the other. Only her hands had been ruined. They would never be a lady's. Yet they were whiter now, and wore marriage rings.

Laura poised before her glass and put the sulky diamond about her neck. The jewel fell between the white moons of her breasts.

She thought of Daniel. Not as she had seen him two nights ago, in the ballroom of the house. But here with her, locked inside this room. Daniel staring at the diamond, this time on her nakedness. Her naked body.

Laura plucked a rose from a vase. She held it between her breasts against the diamond, then against the red brush between her thighs.

Suppose he returned to the house. Suppose he was in the gardens of the house even now.

She went to the window and, before she had considered, pressed herself against the glass. It was cold and a shudder ran over her body. But she did not draw back. She thought of Daniel, in the night of the park, looking up at her.

The moon was on the lake. The grass seemed blue, and the shadows of trees cut like chasms.

Something moved in the darkness. She saw it, low and black, pouring from one shadow to the next.

Laura rubbed her flesh against the glass. The diamond

scraped. And out in the dark two eyes ignited, and were gone.

It was some beast which was out there, looking at her. Some beast, not Daniel.

The tingling left her body and she was suffused by sudden self-consciousness and shame. She drew away and snatched up her dressing-gown. She took off the diamond and shut it in the box.

She sat by the fire, thinking of wandering in the wood, and Daniel appearing between the trees. Of sitting in the parlour of the house, and Daniel coming in through the door.

Someone had been found dead up on the meadows; she had heard two of the servants, usually invisible and inaudible, talking of it in low voices. The corpse was torn apart and wolves were blamed. She thought of standing by the upland church where she had been married, and the wolves feeding below and Daniel walking along the path, towards her.

In the morning, Laura joined her husband at breakfast, as frequently now she failed to do. He regarded her across the carven ham, the dish of eggs, and hot bread.

"I was sorry not to say good-night to you, Laura."

By this he meant sorry not to have made love to her. Laura felt a familiar annoyance. Since the night of the supper she had kept herself from him, retiring early, locking her door.

"I was so tired."

"Of course."

He had given her everything, she thought, and she did not keep her part of their bargain. She had been more generous when free, awarding him her body without hope of gain. But he could not have enough of her. Usu-

ally when he came to her bed, every night if she allowed
it, he would seek her body two or three times, waking her
gently in the dark, always courteous. But his eagerness
grated on her, and the pretence she must make, having
made it at the beginning. She could not very well yearn
for her former bedroom with the ratty Elfie and Alice
lying by, but she yearned instead for the very privacy he
had given her, the wide chamber and canopied couch she
wished to enjoy alone . . . Or was it so simple? When
she had consented to Hyperion, she had not known of
Jenavere's son.

She remembered how she had slept those nights at the
farm in Daniel's bed. She had thought he had died. She
had fled from Jenavere's pain.

"Hyperion, will it suit you if I take the carriage? I want
to go and see Mrs Vehmund."

He looked surprised a moment, as if he saw into her
mind and had not suspected. Yet surely he had suspected,
and certainly he could not read her brain.

"The carriage? Yes, Laura. The drive will do you
good." He added, "She must be in better spirits, with her
son home." And then, "What did you think of him?"

Laura said steadily, "He isn't like her."

"Really? I thought him very like. Except in his manners, which were rougher than I'd expected."

Laura said, "There was some gossip at your party my
maid told me of. That he'd made a fortune in foreign
places."

"Very probably. Well good luck to him. Did you note
his eyes?"

"His eyes," repeated Laura. Was Hyperion testing her?

"They mesmerized me," said Hyperion, rather as a
woman would have done. "Feral. Like a pagan god from
the wood come in to laugh at our civilized festivity."

"How fanciful you are."

Hyperion drank his tea without thirst.

"You must give him my respects, at the farm."

"Oh, I doubt he'll be there."

"Avoid the other one: Marsall."

"I always have," she said.

She watched him recall her former days as a milkmaid, when she had gone to the Vehmund farm as Jenavere's paid companion. No possessiveness coloured his expression, no glint of ownership. He was a fair man, honourable and translucent, and all at once a great pity for him tore through her, making her hands tremble so she set down her cup.

"You must come back for dinner," he said. "I miss you, my Laura."

"Naturally I will."

How much better she spoke, since she had been with him. She heard herself with resignation. Suppose she had been a milkmaid still, and gone back to the farm for Jenavere, and Daniel had been there, home from his travels—this young wolf-god of the woods Hyperion had magnified before her.

"And Laura," Hyperion said, "if you return after sunset, don't get out of the carriage before you reach the drive. There have been some incidents."

"The man who hunted moths. I heard the servants talking."

"They've no business to discuss such things where you can hear. But yes, that man. And a shepherd. His sheep were all unharmed, but he—well, he was dead."

"Wolves aren't usually so savage," she said, not attending. Already she was on her way, rattling between the uplands and the rocky heights where the trees clung, towards the pastures of the farm, and the wood above, from which she had once run away.

"It may be a lunatic," said Hyperion. "A man—not a poor wolf. I want you safe."

She smiled and thanked him. He got up from the table leaving his food unfinished and his tea undrunk, and went away into his house.

The journey was filled by an acid alertness. She might have been travelling through a strange new country. She looked at everything as if it were alien, perhaps threatening, and was aware of a tense sharp excitement. Guilt overlay all these feelings. Yet why should she be guilty? She had neglected Jenavere Vehmund, and meant to put that right. Daniel would surely not be there, for certainly he had some business or other that took him away.

It was past noon when the carriage was halted on the road. Laura walked up alone, over the hill, and descended into the valley of the farm. The beeches were a clear and tawny green, and the blossom was gone from the leafy orchard. Laura paused a moment on the track, looking down at the stone house between the trees. She could tell nothing from looking. Smoke rose from chimneys, the chickens picked about the yard. No other signs.

When she came to it, the kitchen door was shut. As a lady, probably Laura should have gone to the other entrance. Laura raised her hand in its pearly glove, its silver bracelet, and knocked.

She expected one of the maids or Rosamunde Ax to open it, and indeed it was Rosamunde who did so.

"Yes?" Rosamunde said. She glared at Laura with utter contempt, but it was the scorn of unknowing. Evidently she did not recognize, in this gloved and feathered being, the girl who had come to read.

"I'm here to see your mistress."

Besides her lack of recognition, and more importantly, Rosamunde was also changed. Or, rather, reduced to essence. Her ancient Pictish origins had never been more obvious, her brownness and darkness, her harsh, hard, crinkled littleness, like a bitter nut. Out of her face the unfriendly animal eyes regarded Laura viciously yet distantly. As if she were listening to some high-pitched song of the fairie people that Laura could not detect.

"Mistress is sick," said Rosamunde.

"I'm sorry to hear it," Laura answered briskly, not to be put off. "I've brought her some things to do her good." In the basket were hot-house peaches and other ambitious fruit. Rosamunde glanced at these. Suddenly she seemed to see Laura after all.

"Go up then," she said, as she would have done to a dairy-maid, coarse and indifferent.

"You had better go first and announce me."

Rosamunde hunched there. She eyed the great kitchen which had seen murder, a proprietary scan. She might have been saying that only the kitchen mattered. But then she turned and went out and up the stair.

Laura, despite her words, followed directly after her.

In the vague light on the stairway she saw a startling damage.

"What's happened here?"

"Master Marsall," said Rosamunde.

"What, did he fall?"

"No," said Rosamunde. Nothing else.

Laura side-stepped the broken treads from which dagger-like splinters protruded. In one of his drunken flounderings, Marsall Vehmund had managed this. Where was he now? Hyperion had mentioned Marsall no longer performed his paid duties on the land.

Rosamunde had reached Jenavere's door. She rapped, and went in, shutting the door behind her.

Laura stood in the corridor. Her hands trembled, and slowly the fine hair rose on her neck. Nothing moved. She could hear only the singing of birds.

Rosamunde came out. "You're to go in."

Laura brushed past her, and herself pushed shut the door on Rosamunde Ax.

Laura remembered Jenavere, like a painting, sitting upright in her chair with a striped cat on her knees. It had been winter and the wall of the cold had pressed against the window, and Laura had longed for the tinsel air outside. Now everything was altered, as if a page had been turned in a book. *That* Jenavere was gone. Today's spring Jenavere lay in bed, on a bank of pillows, the patchwork quilt the only colour. She looked not old, but like a skin which has been emptied. Her hair was in a long and slender plait, childish. Her face was childish too, so cleansed and devoid of anything but the remote shy pair of eyes. As if to augment the symbol, a lamb rested in a shawl against her side. She was holding in her fingers a small teapot of milk, and the lamb was sucking at the spout.

Jenavere gazed at Laura, as always, from far off, but now how much farther.

"Oh, Laura, how lovely you look. How your new life suits you."

And Jenavere's generosity had the effect of irritating Laura, who wanted to shake her and say, *But what of you? Why don't you complain?*

"I do well enough," said Laura. "I'm sorry to see you ill."

"Yes," said Jenavere.

"I'd hoped that your . . ." Laura faltered; "that your son—his return—would make you well."

"It did," said Jenavere. Her eyes were nearly tranced now, a nacreous glaze hung over them. "Something happened then. I was glad. I rejoiced. Too much gladness, Laura. I find it's brought me down like a blow. Isn't it curious? To endure so long on crusts and water, and the wine kills you."

Laura's heart had started up as if in fright. Its beating made her aware of the heavy warm drop which lay beside it, under her clothes.

"*What* happened, Jenavere?"

Jenavere blinked. She lowered her eyes to the lamb which was butting at her for more milk. She dipped her fingers in the milk and let it suck at those.

"Happened? Oh, a dream, Laura. An angry dream come true. Something in the depths of me, rising up." Mystified, obscurely alarmed, Laura watched her. "But it was too much. I couldn't bear it. Perhaps that's just."

"You must rest. You'll recover with the fine weather." Laura spoke like a silly country girl.

"I doubt it. I felt something break inside me, like a thin glass. What could it be? It's done now."

"You mustn't talk like that. You must set yourself to getting well."

"Why?" said Jenavere, calmly.

"For—his sake," Laura said.

Jenavere seemed to see all of her for the first time. Not the carapace of plumes and velvet, but some inner display. Jenavere regarded it with a faint, removed hostility, which suddenly vanished back into her look of trance. "He's beyond me now."

"What do you mean?"

"You saw him, Laura. You saw my son."

Laura became nervous. The blood rose in her face. She put it down and fiddled with the basket of fruit.

"These are for you. From Hyperion's magical hot-house. Yes, I saw Daniel Vehmund. But only for a moment."

"He learned secrets in the East."

"What secrets? What are you saying?"

"I don't know, Laura. It doesn't matter. Forgive me. I tire easily . . ."

Laura put the fruit on a table. The lamb sucked ceaselessly. It was very small but its movements were fierce and predatory. It seemed to be drawing the life from Jenavere, out of her fingers. She had suckled two sons at her breasts.

Laura blushed again. She longed, as before, to escape from Jenavere, so sick and seeing so much.

"I mustn't weary you. But I'll call later in the spring——"

"This room will be vacant then."

"Jenavere!" Laura had become too refined not to be shocked.

"Stay a while longer now," said Jenavere, feeding the vampiric lamb. "You've come such a way. And Daniel will be here in a moment."

Rather than redden, Laura now felt herself go white.

"I thought he would be out on the land. It must come hard—that Marsall sold it. And Marsall——"

"Marsall has disappeared," said Jenavere softly. Her face was smooth as snow, without a line. Her eyes had darkened. "Some of his companions came to ask after him. We, of course, thought he had gone off with them, but apparently not. He went in the afternoon and failed to return."

Laura clutched at this. She feigned concern. "Has a search been made?"

"His friends are searching. We've had no word."

Laura recalled Jenavere's slight comments, her expressions regarding Marsall. She thought of Jenavere's terror and despair when Daniel had been lost.

"Did he go out armed?" asked Laura. She added carefully, "There have been deaths from wolves. But Marsall is very strong."

"We've heard of the wolf deaths," said Jenavere. She looked content and sleepy. "No, Marsall was unarmed."

She supposes him slaughtered and is pleased. Laura's original nature received this idea without dismay. Marsall was a monster.

"Perhaps you'll have news soon," said Laura. She recollected what Jenavere had said, that Daniel would be coming to the room. Laura began to gather herself together, as if to leave. Her heart drummed, and in that instant a light knock sounded on the door.

Jenavere called to her son to enter. Her eyes lit with a sourceless triumph as they passed across Laura. Then Daniel Vehmund was in the room.

He was only a man. Laura's sinews loosened and she knew disappointment of a sort so elusive she did not grasp what she felt. Young and handsome and golden, he stood within the chamber, and then he turned his eyes on Laura. He did not seem surprised that she was there. She imagined some politeness would now go back and forth between them, and she was composed.

But then the reality of him reached her, like sound coming after light.

At once he was like flame, tall as the room, burning on her, terrible.

She began to tremble quite violently, and between her

breasts the diamond she had put on for him leapt as if alive.

She must look away. She averted her eyes, as though disdainfully, and fixed them on the window.

"How kind of the wife of Hyperion Worth," said Daniel Vehmund, "to visit my mother."

"Not kind," said Laura, squeezing out her voice. "A belated courtesy. Once I would come and read for Mrs Vehmund."

"But you were a daughter of the cottages then."

Jenavere said nothing, did not intervene. The lamb was nestled close and had stopped its feeding to sleep.

Laura was afraid. She seemed near to panic. What should she do? She should never have come here.

"My husband," she said, "means me to forget my origins."

"That's easily done."

"I imagine I should thank you for the compliment. But I'm not ashamed of my humble birth."

"No, I meant," he said, "you don't look earthly at all. A beautiful lady from another planet, perhaps."

And Laura felt beautiful. Felt it as never in her life, like a garment covering her.

She stared at him in a kind of desperate wonderment.

But Daniel crossed to the bed where his mother lay. He lifted her hand and held it.

"How are you doing?"

Laura was touched by his tenderness. Then a wave of jealousy surged through her.

"I must sleep now," Jenavere said to Daniel. "Take Laura to the parlour and have Rosamunde make tea."

Laura recalled how, formerly, Rosamunde had never been prevailed on for such acts.

Daniel lightly replaced Jenavere's hand on the cover,

like a flower. The sleeping lamb did not stir. Jenavere's eyes were stony and unkind, and her mouth was sad. Then she smiled at Laura forgivingly. Her lids slipped down.

Daniel opened the door and Laura passed through it in a heaviness of relief, a light quickening of fear.

At the back of the house, the parlour was a closed box hinting at dampness and cold, unaired and the fire un-laid. Visitors had not been shown into it for years and, though the maids had dusted there, the curtains were thick with cobwebs.

"Will you sit down? Shall I send for tea?" he asked her, casually and ironically.

"No thank you." Laura could not have swallowed tea. She stood in the midst of the room and he stood facing her, across a table with a shawl upon it and a dish of wax fruit.

The ridiculousness of their situation was borne in on both of them. He responded with apparent yet hidden mirth, she almost with terror. Jenavere had sent them to this, and they had come as if they must.

"I'm sorry to see Mrs Vehmund so sick. Can nothing be done?"

Daniel said harshly, dismissively, "Nothing."

"Her system received some shock," Laura said.

He said, "So it seems."

"And now your brother has gone missing."

"Marsall? Yes. Dead drunk in some ditch, no doubt."

And abruptly he laughed. Laura started at it. It was as if some strong drink had gone down into her stomach.

"Aren't you concerned, Mr Vehmund?"

"Not at all. I'd like to see him dead."

"You bear a grudge——"

"No grudge. Pure malice. Laura"—he turned on her the blazing vigour of his look—"if I may call you so? Why not? I see. I haven't known you long enough. But then, for me, you can't be rich Mrs Worth. You only have one name. I was going to say, that I didn't want to lie to you. That I wanted to be truthful. I hated my father, too. When I learned of his death I was mad with delight. But I don't shock you. That's good."

"You do shock me very much. Is that your purpose?"

"I have no purpose. This is something I learnt on my travels. Simply to be. I exist, Laura. I've sensed, if not met, my own soul. A dreadful marvel."

"I'm too naive to understand your Eastern mysteries."

"And yet," he said, "you have the diamond."

Laura flinched. Like a tear of fire, the jewel shone inward on her breast. Could he see it through her gown?

"Hyperion gave me the diamond."

"Hyperion, the instrument. One night in a hovel, in a cup of liquor, the diamond struck against my mouth. It was found in a tomb, in the bowel of a king. An intimate gem. Where is it now?"

"In my jewel-box," she said.

"Didn't you wear it for me?" he said.

She took a step away. "For you? Of course not."

"Don't you know," he said, "I can feel its presence. Like the daytime moon. Did you realize, the moon roars, Laura? It calls out as it pulls on the chains of the tides. And the diamond's like the moon."

She said, "I must go. I must leave."

"After you came so far."

"To see Jenavere."

He moved around the table and the whole room went to a dull, colourless mist. She watched him approach her, and she waited.

"Here you are," he said.

He slid one arm around her waist and in his other hand he caught her throat. She felt the breath ebb out of her and gave herself up. His eyes burned and became a bar of yellow water, under which she sank.

She was scarcely conscious of the nature of the kiss, plains of flesh which pressed and savaged each other, only of a union in which she was lost. Her body was bent like a bow. She could not feel the floor and hung in space. She was in darkness. It was night, a wood, and he devoured her, and she gave herself to his devouring.

Laura tried to free herself; she wrenched her head away. He let her go.

She stood gasping in a place without form, and void but for him.

He said nothing, and the hunger in his face nearly threw her back against his body.

She seemed to have been drowned. Some of her hair had come loose, her clothes felt torn and weighty with water. She struggled to the door of the unused room and went out, and moved through the house without seeing it, and meeting with no one, and so into the sunlight of the garden and the orchard. Where was she? How had she come there? She could not run for her skirts and corsets, the plumes of her hat, her leaden feet, the boulder hung about her neck. She walked as quickly as she could up the hill towards the road beneath.

When the sun set, Rosamunde Ax came to Jenavere's room. She saw to the fire, building it up in castles of wood, and drawing the fading flowers from their jar, replaced them with a cushion of anemones. As she reached towards the mantel, Jenavere's soft voice stayed her. "Don't light the lamp. The fire's enough."

Rosamunde's shadow passed across the window. The first star was visible above the hills.

"Shall I fetch tea?"

"No, thank you, Rosamunde."

"I've made a soup for your supper."

"I'm grateful. Will you bring a little more milk then, for the lamb?"

"It's coming around," said Rosamunde. "It'll live."

Jenavere did not reply. The lamb slept, pressed into her side. She was restful to it, for she had no strength, and hardly ever moved to disturb it.

Rosamunde stood at the foot of the bed. The firelight was red behind her; she was like a spirit of darkness, and Jenavere regarded her with equanimity. For some moments they remained in this way, as though a conversation went on between them, but neither woman said a word. Then Rosamunde bobbed her head and went about the room and out of the door.

A few minutes later, Daniel came in.

He kissed Jenavere, and she was like a shell, so weightless, nearly floating there.

"Don't you want a lamp?"

"This is kinder for my eyes."

"A peaceful light," he said, "an English light."

He sat on the bed beside her.

Presently she said, "How quiet it is now."

"Yes."

"He can't make a noise any more."

"Marsall," he said.

"Marsall."

They sat in silence for some while, and the fire crackled, searing up through the burning castles of the wood.

She said at last, very softly, "You mustn't think that I mind it, now. It isn't pain that's brought me to this."

"I know, Mother."

"It was my victory. A champion out of the night. It was as if it came from the dark of me. My will."

He said, "What did you see? Can you tell me?"

"A beast," she said. "A beast from the dark."

"What—sort of beast? Was it like a wolf?"

"No. It was really like nothing animal."

"I thought so."

"It was a creature that had been coiled at the base of the heart and the spirit."

"It was *me,* myself, Mother."

"All of us," she said. "If we could."

"I don't remember anything of it. But it knew you."

"I wasn't afraid. It was my glory. I bore Marsall and he was my son, and I rejoiced. I wonder," she said, "when they'll find his body? The pieces of him."

"Any day."

"Across his father's grave," she said. "You flung it there, as you told me you would?"

"Yes."

"They'll think he fell down drunk there and was attacked."

"Unless Rosamunde speaks to anyone."

"Rosamunde is your slave. She was his, but she turned from him. You could do anything, and Rosamunde wouldn't speak."

"How strange this house is now," he said. "A demon tended by two faithful women."

"There is another," she said.

He glanced at her and away. "I told you about the diamond. Laura has it."

"Laura is meant for you," she said. She was cold, and the fire glittered in her eyes. "My time is done."

"Don't say that."

"I shall die shortly. At any hour I expect it."

"No——" he said, as strengthless in that instant as she.

"There's no choice," she said. She took his hand. "Laura will be yours."

"She has a husband. The rich Mr Worth."

"What does that matter? You're beyond their laws."

"I am," he said. "It doesn't matter, as you say."

After a minute she said slowly, "Don't think me patient and resigned. I'm like you. I have the Devil in me. But I never gave it life. And now there's no chance. I must go away. Live for me, Daniel. Be cruel and terrible, and a lord. Rule inside this little space as I never could."

"It makes me powerful," he said, "but I serve the beast. Not a lord—more a slave than Rosamunde."

"Who knows," she said.

"I know."

"Would you change it?"

"Too late," he said, but he laughed low, under the murmur of the fire.

Jenavere frowned. "My future's empty," she said, "but I'm not afraid. Something's there, beyond this. I see that now. How could this be everything?"

"I should never have left you."

"Now I shall leave you."

He looked at her intently, and she in turn watched him. She was searching intuitively for a massive sadness, thinking perhaps how he had wept as a child at going from her, and how, the last time, after the murder of the first monster (her husband), Daniel's eyes had burned full of tears. But his eyes were only bright now, focused and compassionate. He was beyond grief. Had moved past it into that future she could not persist to see.

* * *

Marsall's body was found on a fine morning. It lay across the upland grave in pieces and was decomposed. Small creatures had been busy with it.

An inquest was held in the village. The man who presided came from the town; he had come to oversee other inquests: the shepherd, and Mr Ossiter. The verdict was the same too, and the result the same. A wolf hunt got up, which yielded no results at all. No wolves were discovered.

Marsall was buried quickly, as if in embarrassment. Daniel attended the rite, as the inquest; also a few hands from the farm. Marsall's drinking companions did not appear.

There were no more killings and, as the month went on, the wolf deaths lost their vitality of fear.

Laura stood on top of a green hill with her husband.

They had walked up there in the pale golden afternoon, and now Hyperion's park lay spread around them, its smooth lawns and glossy groves haunted by statues, the oases of trees, the huge lake starred by white ducks, the summerhouse and the folly. In the distance hung the mansion itself, like a model, refracting windows.

Laura was working hard at her role of happiness and content. She had almost fooled herself. Hyperion also strove to meet her advance. They had conversed and chattered. Nothing escaped them: the lines of the park, the flight of birds. They did not speak of the night of the supper party, when from just such a hill an extraordinary cry had sounded down the dark.

"I've been thinking of a balloon," said Hyperion.

"A balloon?" she asked vivaciously.

Hyperion gazed at the tree-tops of his kingdom.

Soaked in riches, he treated these things as wholesome toys.

"A hot-air balloon. Imagine it drifting down on the lawn before the house. Coloured like a butterfly. How picturesque."

"And should you fly in it?"

"Yes—you and I, both of us. Up to heaven and back."

"Surely, if it was heaven, there's no return except a fall." She saw at once she had said the wrong thing, for he looked startled into distress.

He said, "If we find heaven, we should stay, Laura."

"Of course," she said. "Who would want to leave?"

He smiled at her, seriously. "There's always bound to be a snake in Eden. The trick is to avoid it."

"Or to tread on it," she said fiercely, "to beat it to death."

"Too strong, Laura. Once there's a death in Paradise, it's no longer Paradise."

"It's hopeless then," she said. She looked at him sullenly. "If you won't fight."

"I won't fight for what's already lost," he said.

"Who can say if it is."

"Is it?" he said. "Laura?"

She lowered her eyes to the green ground where the flowers were springing. A blackbird sang in a tree, and ten minutes ago they would have remarked on it as if no blackbird ever before had been known to sing.

"I can't find what to say," she murmured. "I'm your wife. You gave me that."

"And what," he said, "will Daniel Vehmund give you?"

"Nothing," she said, "that I'll take."

"Maybe you yourself are taken, and haven't any choice."

"Why do you tempt me?" she said. "Can't you see, I'm

determined to be honourable? Do you think me such a slut?"

He said, "I think a net has been thrown over you. You struggle and resist, but the net isn't broken."

"Then help me break it."

"If you want me to. What must I do?"

"Don't talk about snakes in heaven. This isn't heaven."

"Oh, yes. For me."

She sighed. "You give me too much power."

"I only acknowledge your power."

"Make me a little less," she said. "I'm just Laura."

"What are you," he said, "to him?"

"God knows. Nothing. Something—the diamond—you made me wear it, and the spell started there."

"This is a fairy tale, then," he said, "and the nice part of it is over."

"Listen to the blackbird," she said.

But he gave her his arm, and they went down through the park in silence.

As the days went by, greener and lengthening, the bubbles of fire lingered on Jenavere's hearth, the mark of her need, that spring had nothing to do with her—or the summer to come.

She lay and watched the fire.

At intervals she fed the lamb. The lamb symbolized the season of her decline, as the cats had signified her loneliness.

Gradually the room grew dimmer. The lights melted from the walls, and only the hearth was left, like a warm heart.

Jenavere saw into this fiery heart, how it cracked and darkness smoked out of it.

Daniel would come soon to sit with her. But he was not

Daniel any more, not her son. A glowing demon had returned to her in Daniel's place. She was glad. The serene world, which had been indifferent to their suffering, should pay now in coins of blood. Her own malignancy did not frighten her. She was not afraid.

The fire was smaller, darker, and farther off. Daniel would not be in time. She did not care. Everything was so simple after all. The fire was miles below, in the hollow of a hill, faint as a breath of rosy mist. As she ascended from it she heard a door opening in another dimension. There came a flicker in her of loss. But then it was gone, and she was away.

Daniel crossed the room and stood looking down at his mother. He had been going to read her another chapter of the book, but she would never hear it now. The lamb slept in her arm, not noticing yet that she grew cold.

As though in the distance, Daniel felt the hurt of severance. Some part of him urgently strove to bring it closer. But his humanity was altered. He could only be sorry.

He wondered where she had gone to, for clearly she was no longer present on the bed. This was the first of many deaths he had beheld in calmness and in human shape. He waited for its meaning to grow evident. But it had no meaning at all. Death, and parting, had somehow become immaterial.

Then the lamb, sensing its second desertion, woke and bleated shrilly.

Out into the night was not where she would have chosen to go, Laura's maid.

However, her duties called her back to the house. Laura would probably require her for assistance with her dinner dress, although Laura, not being by birth a lady, often sent her away.

The maid had been trysting with a groom in the stable. Hyperion's horses had stamped and breathed at their antics, and, after, the maidservant had brushed the hay off her skirt and put up her hair. The groom was socially beneath her, but his shiny eyes, broad back, and the smell of horses had brought her down into the straw.

She stood by the stable door.

"I don't care for the dark. Who's to know what's out there?"

"The *beast* is out there," said the groom partly in fun, for, beyond their sexual play, they had little liking for each other.

"Don't you tell me about a beast! That's a story."

"It's all the talk from here to the town. It wasn't a wolf did for old Ossiter."

"Get on with you."

"You pick up your petticoats and run, girl. Or the old beastie'll get you."

She flounced out into the courtyard and walked with dignity across the cobblestones. Coming between the walls, she saw the slopes of the park lying black under a mahogany sky. Up amid the trees, what might not conceal itself? Wolves surely would not venture so near the house, although she had been told of severe winters when they had done so. Chat of the wolf deaths had ebbed, yet it seemed to her she was not the only one wary of darkness.

Around the corner of the house, the long lighted windows of the parlour shone above the terrace. One stood ajar. Probably no one was there, and it was too soon indeed for Mr Worth and his wife to come down. She might risk going in that way, which would save her a tramp in blackness to the pantry door.

She ran up the steps, along the terrace, under the pagan statues modest only with ivy. Was violent death a punishment for sin, and had she sinned sufficiently to earn it?

Something moved in the darkness. It was like a filament of the black air. The servant girl jumped to a halt under the upraised hand of a Grecian god.

She did not scream, because an innate sense of her own worth prevented her believing in the truth of her own death.

Down the steps from the terrace—what was it? A thing which might have been a man, but moved so fast it was like a slide of water.

The girl stared, trembling, out into the shadow—and ahead of her the safe light.

She could no longer see anything that was in motion, only groups of trees rippling as a wave of wind slipped over the black sheen of the lake.

She must go on now, hurry to the window and get in.

As she started forward a weird unearthly cry oozed up, out of the stones at her feet.

Now she shrieked, pushed beyond unconscious reason.

The window of the parlour was opened wide and the flower of lamplight burst on to the terrace. There stood Hypcrion's steward in his black and white.

"What's all this noise?"

Laura's maid did not have her voice. She pointed at the edge of the wall beneath the window.

The butler looked down, and exclaimed.

"A *lamb*."

The lamb gazed up at him with gemmy eyes. It bleated again. It had been carried for miles in a whirlwind of physical movement, through darkness, and left here alone in a basket. It was too weak to wander away. It stayed, sinister in its pitiableness, to be taken in.

* * *

The day of the funeral was very hot. Green sweat trickled
down the limbs of the trees, and the sweat of flesh was on
the faces of the mourners, above their close black garments. Jenavere Vehmund was not to be buried in the
wild upland graveyard, but in a village plot, behind
the church. Some comment had been made on this, that
the wife and mother did not lie down properly beside her
husband and her elder son. It was thought the remaining
son, a stranger now in his ways, had judged the traditional place too bleak, and tinted besides by the torn
body of his brother found there. Maybe Jenavere had
died from the shock of that. The village turned out to see
her down into the earth. She too had been an alien, a
lady from another sphere. She would be the first
Vehmund in the village yard.

So the village packed the church with its black and its
sweat. They stared at Daniel, the stranger who had been
away.

They agreed he was foreign, might have come from the
tents of some desert tribe, or the gaudy bazaars. Though
he had dressed soberly, he did not have the village style,
crammed into stays and collars, laced and buttoned up to
the chin. There was a pliancy to him, an animal graceful-
ness. His face was composed as a stone, yet there was no
tragedy or even common regret in it. Of all things it was
nearest to utter calm, and the straight line of the lips
somehow half suggested a smile. The eyes made the face
cruel. None of them looked at him unmoved; all were
flurried, grew instinctively anxious and resentful. So that
by the time they came out of the church and followed the
coffin to its pit, there was not one of them that was not in
some way allergic to Daniel Vehmund, that would not
have liked to best or belittle him, and would dare neither.

The priest hovered over the hole in the ground, the ripe dark earth that also perspired, moist as a mouth.

"Thou knowest, Lord, the secrets of our hearts."

The coffin was down in the pit. Daniel Vehmund threw soil upon it.

". . . Who shall change our vile body . . ."

Jenavere was not in the box. She had gone back into the cosmic chaos that unlocked the threads of her personality, and that had no name for her. She was spread out like the sky, and tiny as a mote of dust. Jenavere was no more.

Daniel glanced about him and rows of glass gazes above tight collars fell away. The fox in the poultry yard, he eyed these black chickens. He would pluck them and wring their necks. He would tear out their buttoned-down souls and send them off to chaos and namelessness.

He felt nothing for Jenavere but an area of emptiness, like a room inside his mind where the furnishings had crumbled in a night.

The congregation spoke the Lord's Prayer.

Daniel did not speak it.

And, as they recited the words, the villagers watched his unmoving lips that nearly smiled. In the blister of light and heat he did not sweat. They saw this with further disapproval. The colour of his hair was the colour of gold from the East.

A few feet away from him was the woman from the Vehmund farm, dark like an imp, Rosamunde Ax. What did she know?

"Hasten Thy kingdom, that we, and all those of our brethren, departed in the true faith of Thy name, may have our perfect consummation and bliss."

A carriage came rattling down the village road, the brown horses springing to the churchyard gate.

The watchers turned to see a new sight.

And they beheld the carriage door opened by a coach-man, and a lady get out and walk in through the gateway. She stopped among the graves beneath the green trees. She wore a dress of black silk, and under her plumed black hat a furnace of hair lay coiled. In her arm was something white, like a sheaf of flowers.

They knew enough to give her her title. The whisper ran that Mrs Worth had come to pay her last respects, rather late.

Nor did she advance to the grave. She stood in the distance, like the shadow of something. The flowers on her arm moved. It was a live thing she carried.

"Amen," said the priest, and the mourners echoed him.

Having nothing to say to Daniel, or to Rosamunde, they curved away from the pit of death, and went off over the churchyard. Those that came near Laura divided like a river and flowed by, though a proportion noticed her dress was silk, and that a lamb lay on her arm like a lap-dog.

Only the priest and Daniel poised now over the pit— and Rosamunde Ax at the pit's corner.

"The headstone is to be marble?" said the priest.

"A pretty grave," said Daniel.

The priest took him literally. "Indeed, it will be a credit to you."

"And on the Final Day, all the bodies will rise up," said Daniel.

"Scripture says so."

Daniel laughed. It was a terrible laugh, so easy and so mild. The priest shivered at it. He opened his mouth to say that faith was everything and impiety a blunder, but Daniel was no longer paying him attention, only looking away at the young woman in black who stood among the trees.

The priest took his leave. As he passed her, Rosamunde Ax muttered, the old witch, but he did not catch what she said.

Daniel followed the villagers' path across the graveyard, but when he came to Laura, he halted. She faced him with her head up and her eyes wide.

"Why are you here?" he said.

"I received your messenger."

"The lamb," he said. "I see it prospers."

"Why did you ride so far to the house and not come in? Hyperion wouldn't turn you away."

"I didn't ride to your mansion. I ran. So many miles. I can do that, now."

"And why," she said, "did you bring the lamb to me?"

"I thought you would rear it, now my mother's not able to."

"I'll rear the lamb, for Jenavere's sake," she said. "But you must understand, Mr Vehmund, there can be nothing between us."

He said, "Where's the diamond?"

"I'll send you the diamond. You shall have it."

"No, it has me. Keep it. I like the idea of it in your keeping. On your breast."

"I'll never wear it again."

"Wear it," he said, "the nights of the full moon."

"The moon obsesses you," she said.

"Yes. The moon and the diamond, and you."

"I mustn't obsess you," she said. They stood six feet apart, and all around the trees held them in a slim green glass.

"Poor Laura," he said, "the jungle's all about you and you won't see it. In five more nights," he said, "the moon will be full. What happens then? Madness comes out of the ground and leaps over all the graves."

"Don't try to frighten me again."

"I know the church you were married in," he said. "They say the priest there feeds the wolves in winter and they sleep in the font."

"Marriage is a bargain," said Laura.

"Your marriage wasn't made in heaven," he said. "You should have waited, milkmaid."

She turned her back on him and walked to her carriage, with the lamb lying docile in her arm. She felt its weight now. It was heavy with words.

Daniel remained under the trees, and perhaps he watched her driven away, but she could not be sure. She was sure of nothing.

Hyperion Worth perused his study slowly. It was an opulent and rather useless room. For Hyperion studied nothing and did not often come here to be alone. An array of a few suitable masculine things, remnants of an earlier tradition, intrigued and vaguely amused him. The case of guns, which he would never dream of using; the sabre on the wall from some ancient war whose ethic he would have frowned on. There were books, some of which he had read, or partly read. On the desk, under the imposing inkstand, was a pencil drawing of a hot-air balloon.

The balloon was consoling. He remembered seeing one as a child, passing over the city sky. He was in a carriage with an aunt. "What is that?" "Don't be vulgar. Pay no attention." For months therefore he had been in ignorance of the nature of the magical beauteous sky-passing thing. At last he confided in a servant, the coachman, and the truth of the balloon was explained to him.

Servants had sometimes been intrusive in Hyperion's

childhood, and so, in the mansion of his adult years he had encouraged their invisibility. Odd then that now their presence was becoming felt, their murmurs and rumours overheard.

They talked about Laura; that had already somehow infiltrated through the doors and walls and reached him. Her excursions in the carriage. Her waiting in a green graveyard with Daniel Vehmund. The whispers were not censorious but peculiarly affrighted.

The other whispering had to do with the full moon. It was dark and murky, superstitious and unreasoning, and it ran now through a sort of unseen gutter along the whole length of the house. He could not make it out, and had he been less aware, he would probably have missed it altogether. There was some fear of the moon. Some element of closing doors and windows fast, drawing the drapes, not allowing the moon to reflect on anything. Of not listening.

He thought of the strange cry which had sounded down through the park on the night of the supper. He had dreamed of it, he believed, standing alone on a hill in the dark and hearing the cry again, knowing an awful danger was near him, and powerless; but what had happened thereafter he could not recall. Even so the cry, in some way dreams of the cry, had mingled in the murmur-gutter of smothered talk.

Only Laura seemed oblivious to it, or indifferent. She was like an illustration, so clear her white and red, she might have been drawn purposely to show the blurring of everything else.

She had made it plain, delicately plain, that tonight he would be welcome in her bed.

And he had hesitated; he had come here to delay.

He did not consider why. There was a subterranean

drift within his mind, like the gutter of darkness in the house, which suggested to him it would be wrong to go to her now. But, like the rumours of the house, he tried to ignore and dismiss this signal. So he left the study and went up through the building towards the vast blue and green room he had given her, with its French tapestries of unicorns and arbours, its priestess-prettiness.

At his knock she gathered him in, soft-voiced.

The chamber had the petal glow of the pink alabaster lamp. Laura lay back on her pillows, her whiteness sheathed in edges of lace.

He looked at her in wonder, and without desire. As in the fairy story, he had come to the bower of the princess. But she was under a spell and it was not due to him to break it. His skull also would decorate the hedge of thorns, before the *true* prince entered at the appointed hour.

But she held out her smooth arms.

She said she was glad he had come to her.

Her black eyes, that had always before seemed so warm, proud and flirtatious by turns, honest always, now had a look of deep sunken darkness. It would repel her to give herself, yet she would do it.

This made him angry, and the anger brought on a type of lust. So he took off his clothes and went into the bed with her.

As he put his hand on her shoulder, something rustled on the pillow.

The orphan lamb nestled there, creamy like the linen, and watching him.

"So you bring that animal into your bed?"

"It has no mother."

"It will disapprove. For a lamb, it's very prudish."

But he meant that the lamb was a spy. Through its eyes looked others, seeing all they did.

Hyperion possessed Laura. She was his; she belonged to him.

She had always acted a passion for him. He knew something of women, enough to understand this, and to hope that one day the reality of what she pretended might sweep through her. But now, of course, it could not. His was not the kiss to wake her.

The spasm that should be triumph was only inevitable. A black despair settled on him at once, and, that she should not see it, he left her quickly.

The glittering eyes of the lamb followed him out.

In the corridor of his house he felt a sudden mad terror. He braced himself against it, and it rushed by and was gone.

But as he stood alone there, he sensed the whispering of the mansion, the shadows, the speaking silence. Astonished he glanced about, looking for some source, a way to be rid of all this. But like the presage of winter, there was no means to avoid the coming thing. It ran towards him lightly over the flowery fields, under the starry sky.

Like the child he had once been, he wept for half a minute. Then he let go of Laura like a rose, and observed her fall into the dark, and left her there, with the whispers.

About the Saxon church the old yews and cypresses had lifted their heads. The old land was green, and the woods were green, looking thicker and older still, as if Romans might march out of them, or painted people ride in chariots.

Laura sent the carriage away. Summer was coming,

and she would walk back to the house. She had been
used to walking. It would do her good.

She tried the church. It was shut against her. She considered the priest's cottage below; she would not trouble
him.

She stepped down to where she had seen the wolves
feeding.

The bushes had budded; the filled trees encroached
upon the slope. Bluebells had come and gone, and now
white parsley flowers clouded the rocky earth. She
thought of her wedding veil, marvelling, for that had
been another Laura, the Laura who had been wed in the
church.

Even the church diminished as she went down into the
wolf wood.

The forest was jade, pierced by sprays of light. The
earth was black with mud, for there had been rain in the
night, and flowers lay like garlands, and the great ferns,
primordial, sprang in fountains upward. The woodland
sweated with scent, and crystals of moisture dripped from
leaf to leaf. One fell on her cheek like a tear. She remembered Jenavere, buried in black under green. Death finished everything. But death was far off.

Laura shook herself. She felt her life, her body. She
was so young. Everything else was nonsense.

She took off her hat and let it drop into the flowers.
She plucked the pins out of her hair, and let that go like
water from a wild spring.

She wished she was a child again, before any responsi-
bility had come to her. Running through the cool stream,
along the paths of summer—not knowing this other
Laura lay before her, to bar her way.

But the woods were antique. They were full of elder

gods, of sprites and nymphs and demons. Here she was free.

Laura pushed off her shoes and stood in the mud in her fine stockings.

Daniel Vehmund walked out between the trees.

She saw him without surprise.

Of course, he had mentioned this place, the church, and the wolves. As if to invite her. Had he come here daily, awaiting her?

She seemed no longer to see him clearly. It was not sight she wanted, but sensation.

He walked up, and directly took her hand.

"Mr Worth's wife."

She left her hand in his and said nothing.

"How is your husband?" he said.

"He's well."

"Oh, good. Well, but not here."

She said: "I brought you the diamond."

"Yes?"

"Since you think the diamond is yours."

"Where is it?" he said.

She put her hand to her throat, and drew up the golden chain, slowly, until the hard gleam of light came out above her collar. He let go of her hand and caught at the jewel. "Warm," he said.

She stood there and felt the power of his possession wash up the chain of the diamond, as though he held her now by a fetter.

"Take it," she said.

As in the graveyard, the vitreous bottle of the trees enclosed them. But it was easy to believe they were in a jungle now. Steam and sunlight rose from the ground.

Daniel's hands pulled open the buttons of her bodice, gently and swiftly. They gave in acquiescence. One broke

and span away. The diamond fell back on to her flesh. It
burnt. More roughly, he pulled at the armour of lace and
struts that covered her body. Bones snapped. Ruination.
He had her against him. Where she touched him, the
length of her, she ached and flamed. She had never felt
true arousal before. She tore at his shirt, not knowing
what she did, to come at the skin beneath.

They knelt in the flowers. Stalks brushed her throat as
she lay folded across his arm. His mouth and hand moved
over her naked breasts, and the diamond moved over
them. Her hair felt wet and heavy. She felt the muscles of
his back, the edges of his ribcage. Then she lay flat on the
earth, her spine against its teeming smoking green, and
Daniel pinned her there with the weight of his body.

They were no longer gentle, exploratory. They grasped
each other and the ground, their hands full of flesh, grass,
the soft ripe mud. They kissed like eaters, drawing on
each other's tongues as if dying of thirst, biting at each
other's lips, then detaching themselves to stare at each
other, before coming together again in a kind of rage.

There in the streaming green sunlight under the trees
as if in water, where the wolves had come and gone, he
fought through the white petticoats to come at the hot
coal of the centre of her.

As they joined, each gave a smothered cry of relief as
if, before, they had been broken apart, and now mended.

Then they wrestled like enemies, rolling in the black
mud, with the flowers crushed between them.

All the wood seemed moving with them, as if they had
disturbed it into utmost life. Bubbles of air burst and
leaves were shaken loose on them.

The roots of trees were in her back, pushing at her, the
upper surface of her body was clamped to his, and in her
hands he writhed, burying inside her, deeper and more

deep, his strength and will. Under her elbow was the skeleton of a stoat, threshed out of its grave by their fury. The mud smelled of death and life, of rivers and time, and broken flowers covered her eyes.

She struggled upward into delirium, beating and clawing at him, her partner in this. At her screams, silver insects rose from the bushes and in the high tops of trees birds flashed away.

As she opened her eyes she saw above her the face of a blind golden beast, and felt the shuddering surge as his journey ended, with a low agonised cry. Then his eyes opened too on her.

They had created a great silence.

Beneath its orb, they looked at each other. They did not speak. No longer one flesh, they drew apart, and were separate.

The world seemed in stasis. The sun did not move.

Then the diamond slid across her breast, cool now, hard and whole.

She sat up. The mud was all over her. Her clothes were stained and a little torn. Stems in her hair.

Daniel was sitting on a stone.

"I've spoilt your appearance," he said. "Come to the farm."

"It's miles away," she said.

"Yes, I forgot. Too far for you to go without your carriage."

She got to her feet and shook out her skirts. She pulled up the broken corset and the lace and began to do up her bodice.

"I've marked you for the woods," he said.

She held the diamond in her hand, the chain still about her neck. He watched her. Secretively, she put the jewel down again, inside her clothes.

He said, "When will you come to me?"

"I can't," she said. "It's impossible." The words were meaningless and she listened to them as she spoke, indifferent.

"Then I must come to you."

"You must leave me alone."

He rose. She had ripped his shirt and he, too, was covered in mud, the green blood of the grass. They were both like the victims of some terrible accident, escaped just barely with their lives.

Up in the heights of the trees, birds began to chirrup. The silence was over.

Laura turned from Daniel. She found her shoes, left her hat. She went back through the wood. She thought of the priest emerging and seeing her, or of meeting someone on the road. She thought of the invisible servants of the house, who now had started to be seen, seeing her also as she was. She must say she fell. Something startled her, some animal, and she fell down.

Daniel followed her from the wood. He walked slowly behind her, and she wondered if he would pursue her through the country to Hyperion's mansion. How things looked, their state, did not concern him. He had noted it only in order to detain her.

She should have given him the diamond. But she had kept the diamond. She should not think of his face above her, or his cry.

A little past the church, Daniel stopped following Laura, and presently, when she glanced back, he had vanished.

Would it be conceivable to pretend nothing at all had happened?

3

Flesh met flesh in the half dark. Garment rubbed eagerly against garment.

"Don't be rough. I shouldn't be here," she said.

"But you are. And you like my strength."

He was already forcing her, but she was very ready and force was only a symbol. She fell back, pulling on him.

"You flouncy bitch," he said. He thought of riding her down and letting go the flood inside her, but better not risk it; there would be hell to answer if he got her in the family way, and her the mistress's bitsy maid. But it would pay her out, dancing in here with her airs, as if she did him the favour and her not able to get enough of him.

Under her back the straw rustled, and behind their partitions the five horses breathed calmly, accustomed now to this human action. The low-burning lantern gave a heavy glow.

Outside, beyond the enclosures of the house, the round pale yellow moon of early summer had risen on the slopes and trees, the breaks of water, the wild meadows.

The girl who was Laura's maid sensed the moon. In the middle of her desperate rush on the straw, a weird

half-dream overtook her. Inside her closed lids she saw
her own self running through the woodland where, civilized creature that she was, she had never gone. And, as
she ran, the moon glimpsed out and blinked away behind
the trees, as if it played a game with her. But something
else came after. Dark and low to the ground——

She opened her eyes, finding the man, the groom,
grunting on her. She had lost the thread of their dialogue.

"Stop," she said.

"No," said he and lunged into her more vigorously, to
teach her not to tease.

Rocked by his energy, herself stilled, she glanced about
at every shadow, childish in the midst of this adult act.
And as she did so, the calm horses altered, began to
shake their heads and shift their feet, moving back
against the farther wall.

"Wait——" she whispered, digging her fingers into his
insensate flesh. But he was occupied.

The door swung a little.

A slice of dark sky appeared above. And, beneath, another darkness.

She could not see properly, for the thrusting mass of
body which lay on hers, holding her down.

"No," she said, "no—no——"

The beast was in the stable. The beast that the
rumours had kept alive all month. It was here.

She could not see it, only the black shape merging in
and out of the shadows. It was formless, silent.

And then it came up above her lover's back and she
saw it all, the vast shoulders and the nightmare head.

She choked and let out a shrill wavering shriek.

"You scream, girl," the groom mumbled, mistaking.

But the sinewy limb reached over and the great black

paw flared above him. It tore off the top of his head, scalped him. And before he could cry out, he had been lifted entirely away. There was a shower of blood.

The terrified horses trampled in their stalls.

Covered in red rain, the girl tried to right herself, but the dark flowed back for her. She was felled by a blow as she crawled across the straw. Face down and dead, it did not matter to her now that her hair was loose, and her skirts rucked up.

Hyperion's butler had seen that the parlour window had been left undone. It seemed to him that it was Mr Worth's wife who did this habitually, letting in the warm air, in her peasant's way.

Like an effigy he poised on the carpeted floor, the silver tray on his hand, the decanter of rubicund spirit, the dainty goblets.

He did not know he poised so between life and death.

When he walked to the window, left arm outstretched to draw in the pane of glass and close it against the night, no special thoughts at all were in his head.

As he reached the glass, the night came in instead, a long piece of it, thick with hair and pierced by incredible claws. It scooped him out into the dark. And as he went, the carpet was folded, a chair fell, and he cried, but the cry changed to other strangled sounds. The tray crashed on the terrace and the goblets shattered. By some fluke the decanter fell down without its stopper to rest upon his outflung palm. The decanter became filled and coloured by blood.

Presently the body was come on, with the decanter of scarlet blood lighted up by the parlour lights, and the head below the steps, and other portions scattered over the lawn.

* * *

Hyperion rose as Laura entered the room.

He was startled by her appearance. She wore a green gown, and the diamond he had bought for her dazzled on her breast. The atmosphere of the house was not suited to this. Unconsciously he had expected her to dress soberly. Not for form's sake, but out of sensibility.

He said at once, "There will have to be an inquest."

"These terrible deaths."

She spoke, as if in a time of plague, of dreadful things that could not be helped and were of no real consequence for her.

"God knows," he said, and could find nothing applicable to go on with.

She seated herself before the fire.

He thought of the house, which seethed. He looked at Laura, garbed without the help of her dead maid.

"How beautiful you look," he said. It was a criticism.

"Thank you."

"As if nothing at all had happened."

"Do you hold me responsible, then?" she asked.

"Oh, Laura."

"Because perhaps I am."

He said slowly, "What do you mean?"

"You brought me here. Everything was different. Through that chink, perhaps, evil stole in."

"You said, I recall, the diamond . . ."

"Was unlucky?" she said. "Of course it is. Shall I throw it in the fire?"

"A stone impervious to flames."

"You'd prefer," she said, "I wore sackcloth and dusted my head with ashes."

"The servants will leave me," he said. "They came to me in a body, as if the house were under a curse."

"It is."

"Is it? Why?"

"I've brought you low, Hyperion. I've made you vulnerable to darkness and what lives in the dark."

"You speak as if you knew what it was——"

"I do know."

He stared at her. Under the blush of the fire, her face was set and pale.

"What then?" he said.

"Any one of them," she said, "would tell you."

"But they won't. They talk about—a beast. Do they mean a wolf? No, it seems not. Nor a madman."

"A beast," she said softly, looking into the fire. "I don't know——"

"You said that you did."

"Oh," she said, "something we've conjured. A demon."

"*I've* conjured? How?"

"No, not you. Fear. Hope." She raised her head. "Abandon," she said.

"This is a ridiculous conversation," he said. "There's some simple, ghastly explanation."

"Yes."

"Demons don't exist, Laura."

She touched the diamond. A dot of light came out of it, like a bullet.

"I believe in them," she said. "Now."

Hyperion glanced at the door. No one would come to announce dinner. The parlour was shut up.

"The whole county's rife with stories," he said. "There's been trouble over at the farm since the death of Marsall Vehmund. Perhaps I should ride over there. Have a word with the men." Laura said nothing. "Call in on Daniel."

Laura sighed. She gazed into the fire as if at a distant land.

"You must do what you think best," she said.

"What I think best . . . is to do nothing. I'm lazy."

"Perhaps that would be the wisest course."

Overhead, the moon gnawed at the roof. Every window, every door, was fast. No one ventured out after sunset.

No sounds came from the park or from the hills.

Tomorrow morning five of the servants, having announced this, would go away.

"How is your lamb?" he said to Laura.

"Much stronger. It walks about."

"We'll never know who left it there."

"No," she said.

He pictured the horses, trembling and spattered with blood, unscathed in the stable. And the decanter shining red on the terrace.

"The wolf shall also dwell with the lamb," Hyperion said.

Terror was dreary, and he could not shake it off.

The farm kitchen was circling with the earth towards sunfall. A low fire burned in the grate, mostly for the purposes of the kettle suspended above. Soft hazel bloom came in at the window. The brown witch Rosamunde was sewing between the two areas of light, working on a torn shirt with close, clever stitches. She was almost alone in the house, for the two maids had been dismissed at Jenavere's death. When the door from the stairs opened, she did not look up. Daniel Vehmund came into the kitchen, and took his father's seat at the side of the hearth.

"Shall I make tea?" Rosamunde asked.

"No tea," he said. He seemed to have a slight difficulty in enunciating his words; as formerly Marsall had, when drunk. Rosamunde sewed on. Daniel said, "Soon it will get dark. Full moon again. The third night."

Rosamunde did not speak. She had been up to the sheep-washing, and they had turned her away. The excuse had been that she was not needed, but in the past, when the farm had been Marsall's, they had always included her, like the bad fairy at the christening, fearful to leave her out. Now there had come a stronger aversion. They talked of the farmhouse and of Daniel, when Rosamunde was not near. She did not hear, or heed, what was said. She knew, herself, at night the master went out. He went out into the orchard and away up the hills. She never saw him return, though often before first light she was awake.

"How long have you served here?" Daniel said.

"Since I was a girl, Master."

What had she been then? Thin and little and crabbed, with her black hair knotted back, turning the milk sour in the pails of neighbours.

"And you've had no other life," he said.

"None." She spoke with stony pride.

"And what a paragon you are," he said. "Even the butchering of Marsall—you've kept it to yourself."

"His day was done," she said.

"Oh, yes? And my day come?" She did not reply. Daniel said, "But it was a wild beast, a wolf, saw to Marsall."

Rosamunde's eyes came up with a black low flash. And went down again to the needle. The shirt itself might have been rent by wolves in the woods.

"A beast," said Rosamunde. "That's what they speak of."

"What do they say?"

"That it lives at full moon, after dark. Is then, and does then. And is gone."

"How wise they are. And what do *you* think?"

"It's not for me."

"Don't you fear it?"

"It's risen to its victory," she said.

"Risen," he said, "from Hell. But do you lock your door?"

"No, Master."

"Sensible, Rosamunde. It could break down a door. Perhaps it will be close tonight. Where will you go?"

Rosamunde's black eyes moved up again. They fixed on Daniel, greedy of purchase.

"Where could I go?"

"Somewhere. Some house in the village."

"No one would take me."

"You must try."

The gleam in the black eyes was fierce and bright.

"I'll abide here."

"Better not, Rosamunde."

"I'll abide here. Like the mistress did."

"The mistress was safe."

"Who's safe?" said Rosamunde. "It will come."

"But in such a way?" he said. There was a sort of pity, or only scorn, in his congested voice. On the backs of his hands the firelight caught the bristle of the golden hair.

"I've seen many kinds of death."

"I killed Marsall," he said. "You know that. When I was the beast." She sewed. He said, "But I killed my father, too. No tinker, no thief. It was Daniel."

"You were different then."

"But the beast must have been in me, even so."

"Yes."

"And do you think it will spare you, Rosamunde Ax?"

She sewed on at the shirt the wolves had torn in the wood, the two wolves in the mud, under the green trees. He was rich supposedly, and could buy twenty shirts if he chose. But her needle frisked in and out. She did not say she would hide herself.

Through the window now the light was the colour of pink powder in a box.

"Shall I make supper?" said Rosamunde.

"No supper."

All around, the gathering of evening cast its impression on the land. On the hills the sheep bleated. Soon they would be shorn. The heat of summer would swell, and bake the grass and scald the leaves of the trees. But in every month the moon would grow round as a wheel, hanging in the broad sky. The pallid moon was over; now came the mature yellow moon of summer, and there would come the amber moon of autumn, and last the white winter moon that seemed to have no back.

All natural illumination went from the kitchen, and Rosamunde's needle glinted in the firelight before she put down her work.

"I'll be off," said Daniel. He stood up awkwardly and paced to the yard door. Outside dusk stole through the orchard. The smell of herbs rose from the garden.

When he had gone, Rosamunde too went to the door, and opening it stepped out. She moved around among the plants, bending and snatching in the twilight. Then crossing to the yard, she shut the chickens in their house. She looked about her, but the hills now were soft and dim, and veils of darkness covered the sky.

She went in again, and lighting the two lamps she got to work upon the kitchen. She scrubbed the table and the floor. She put her herbs in bunches and hung them up like garlands. She rubbed the pans, and took the kettle from the fire. In the lamplight she finished mending the shirt Daniel had left her, and folded it, laying it on the big chair, where he would find it. All this while the door to the yard and the garden stood wide, and night's blackness gradually filled it up. To this the old woman paid no attention, nor, on leaving the kitchen, did she shut either of the doors.

Her room was at the highest point of the house, a long, low attic ideally suited to her shortness. Here she performed her own business, whatever it was. By the compacted bed, narrow as a stick, a Bible lay on a stool. Rosamunde could not read, but she had been taught in infancy the names of all the books of the Bible, and nightly, like a prayer, she would say them through, following them on the page with her finger.

Rosamunde Ax took off her clothes and, using the ewer of cold water, washed herself. Naked, it was curiously possible to see she was a woman still, and not an imp. Next she drew on her nightgown, and then she undid her hair. It had remained sable, and fell below her waist. She combed it with an old wooden comb. Then she took the crown she had made and borne up here in her skirt, the wreath of fennel and rosemary and other stuff from the garden, and put it on her head.

She sat on her bed in her white robe and green diadem like an elderly maiden at the dawn of her wedding day. Rosamunde Ax had never wed, and never had she been coaxed or tumbled. She was a virgin bride, little, gnarled, and ancient as the apple trees.

On her lap she placed the Bible and opened it, and said aloud the names as she followed with her finger.

"Genesis, Exodus, Leviticus, Numbers. Deuteronomy, Joshua, Judges, Ruth."

Through a tiny window the black night looked. The

moon had risen and its blaze arched up on the ceiling. Something slid and shone—a falling star.

"Samuel One, Samuel Two, Kings One, Kings Two, Chronicles One, Chronicles Two," said Rosamunde Ax. "Ezra, Nehemiah, Esther, Job."

It seemed to her the door below, the door to the kitchen, had moved slightly, brushed by something. Rosamunde spoke more quickly.

"Psalms, Proverbs, Ecclesiastes, The Song of Solomon, Isaiah, Jeremiah, Lamentations."

On the inner stairs, where the damage was, the broken place, a kind of sound . . . Not sure, perhaps imagined.

"Ezekiel," said Rosamunde.

She remembered being a tiny child, and the priest's rod striking her knuckles. She had forgotten, then.

Up the stairs, something was advancing. She felt it like a warmth and flicker, a torch drawing near.

"Daniel," she said, "Hosea, Joel, Amos. Obadiah, Jonah, Micah, Nahum, Habbukkuk."

It was past the first floor now, seeking the back stair. She listened. She heard a faint singing in her ears, like far-off bells.

"Zephaniah," she said, "Haggai, Zechariah, Malachi."

Beyond her door the stairwell was darkness, and now the beast surfaced from the dark. It entered the attic. She saw it.

Rosamunde looked a long while, sitting with the Bible on her lap. The beast too was still, its flat black eyes on hers. The snout wrinkled. Its head was ebony. Its legs were like pillars of iron.

Slowly, Rosamunde slid the book aside. She got down on her knees.

The beast watched. Then it came close.

She felt heat from it, like a fire. It had no smell.

Rosamunde lay down on her face on the attic floor.

The beast's forelimb surged like black lightning. Rosamunde's body jerked and quivered. Her spine had been snapped. Like a wrecked snake she writhed there, staring.

The beast walked in front of her again. Her eyes were bulging and spit ran from her mouth. She tried to speak.

"Master," said Rosamunde Ax.

The taloned paw swept across her face and crushed it, crushed out the spark in her eyes.

Above and below, the Vehmund farmhouse rested in equilibrium: the roof, the beams, the floors and walls and stays.

In the kitchen the lamps died by degrees. In the attic the candle burned into its socket and went out. A low wind came from the south to rush the fruit trees, and a scarf of clouds swam across the moon.

The night was all the moon. That great countenance, implacable as a clock, stood over the world, telling some unbelievable time. And, in the orchard, darkness sat looking at it, with murder slipped away like water. The soulless eyes reflected the moon, so it was set like jewelry twice in the long black muzzle. The black tongue ticked against the fangs like daggers. Into the grasses an unborn apple fell before its hour.

PART FOUR

Coming up in the world, if so they had, did not improve the Wheelwrights. The large house which Hyperion Worth had bought for them, near the edges of the town, was equipped with several rooms, both kitchen and pleasure gardens, a horse and a servant. And here, with nothing much now to pretend to occupy their time, they festered. With the house had come an annual benefice, and thus no bread-winning was required. The white-haired buxom servant woman took care of their domestic work, which left Mrs Wheelwright, Elfie and Alice free as toads, if without a toad's inherent charmingness. All day long the three females slopped about indoors or in their garden, eating and playing cards, and yawning themselves asleep. A natural doughiness in their figures had rounded into fatness, their dress was fine, but their hair done like nests, for by now laziness had bred an utter lack of energy. They were dollops.

Jason meanwhile had stayed active, still going about the fairs and markets, buying up rubbish, getting drunk, and buying more. The house was by midsummer another junk-shop, with bits of machines in its back corridors, ugly pictures in horrible frames stacked behind its sofas,

and hobby-horses peering through its bannisters. The live
horse, too, was often at large on the road, being carelessly stabled. At least once a week it wandered into gardens along the lane and ate of things not intended as
snacks for horses. As a result war existed between the
Wheelwrights and their near neighbours.

To their own and their external contaminations the
Wheelwrights were oblivious, or indifferent. As they
spoke of Laura, the fount of their luck, with alternate
blind boasting or affronted contempt, prickly she did not
visit, but mostly forgetting her, just so they judged everything, taking it for granted, amnesiac at its true value,
irritated by its very being when at variance to their own.
And in this way they had gained the hatred of their allotted servant, Bess Mubby.

Bess, unlike the floating Wheelwrights, was a woman
of extremes. Had she laboured in a household of any
niceness, one which appreciated her skills, she would
have given it loyalty and goodwill out of all proportion.
But she found herself treated like a ghost—her sterling
deeds were overlooked, the gleaming mirrors and sumptuous pies, as if they came from magic, her every slight
human noise was complained of, and on meeting her
about the house they brushed her aside. Bess Mubby at
first had tried the harder to delight. But when no notice
was taken, she began to look at the family sharply. To
Bess it seemed a ghastly mishap that she had landed
among such creatures. Hers was a simple, dedicated
mind. She redrew the Wheelwrights as devils.

The servant woman cleared the table of their mess,
and it was as though she cleared the trough of evil pigs.
That they did not compliment or thank her now came as
no surprise. Trying to dust and polish in the house, and
constantly impeded by the drunkard's bought junk, Bess

curbed her warrior soul. Washing the linen of the slothful daughters, Bess remembered her own sisters singing at their red-handed toil. The Wheelwrights were not human. They were funguses grown in muck. Useless. A blight. And she served them.

As the summer rose to its golden arch and turned over into its brassy ending, Bess made her plan to go away. She had rover's blood inside her frame, and knew quite well how to be off and lost if she had to. First, a final cleaning was in order, a scouring and scraping of rubbish. For Bess was neat of spirit, not one to leave the dirt in corners, or the cobweb attached to the beam.

The Wheelwrights were sitting down to their afternoon dinner, a pie of livers, kidneys, beef and mushrooms, under a crust of beautiful architecture, all of which they accepted with barely a glance.

The daughters were fractious today, and the mother had devised some reason for it.

"It's a bad sister our Laur is to Alice and Elfie," she said.

"Laur?" asked Jason, as if he really had forgotten his eldest daughter.

"Yes, indeed. Her now with her fancy house and husband, going about in society, and hasn't sent for the girls, to introduce them. Why shouldn't they catch rich men too?"

"Well there's that," agreed Jason.

"Certainly there is. It's pure selfishness. She always was an awkward girl."

"But a queen," said Jason. "Give her her due. She took his eye."

"But does she think her duty's ended there, the wretch? Why, if it wasn't for all my words and advice, she'd never have got the man. She owes him to me. But she's too high for us now."

"That was always her way. Too proud. Too proud by half."

"Where would she be but for us?"

"Unborn," observed Jason, with reason on his side.

"Truly," said Mrs Wheelwright, "and she can thank me too for my agony, for she was a difficult birth."

Jason drank some wine, for the family had graduated to this drink. "I've heard about some odd goings-on that way. A pack of mad wolves out killing. Two or three times a month."

"You can be sure *they're* safe enough, Laur and her spouse."

"Perhaps we should write to her," Jason suggested. By which he meant they should pay a scribe to do so, for their penmanship was strictly limited.

"Write? Beg charity? She should come hurrying to our door. She should be on her knees in gratitude."

They had by now carved the pie and begun to eat it. The taste was delicious, but they did not mention this, even when Bess Mubby came with extra vegetables.

The servant woman saw to her task in silence. When all the mouths were full, she spoke.

"I was out early to gather these mushrooms."

Mrs Wheelwright gazed at her in perplexity, as at a ghost which spoke. The husband did not look up. Elfie and Alice also seemed not to hear, eyes and mouths lowered to their plates.

"Yes," said the Wheelwright servant, "the dew was on them."

Then she stood by the wall and watched the family eat.

Mrs Wheelwright parted her lips.

"Go on," she said. "We have what we need."

"Yes, don't skulk there," said Alice, who was learning to echo.

Bess departed from the room, and going to her kitchen, which was glorious from her attention, she sat down at the table, to wait.

The Wheelwrights ate all the pie, and most of the vegetables. Quite a quantity of wine was also consumed. The talk of Laura had ebbed. Jason had begun to recount his genius at picking up an old rusted mangle at the fair. Mrs Wheelwright still offered now and then the picture of Alice and Elfie deprived of suppers, dances and suitors. Alice and Elfie in person had begun on some apples, hopeful that, by magic, a custard or pudding might appear on the table.

But the ghost did not come from the kitchen with any further dishes. No, the ghost sat there with her bag packed at her feet, listening for the church bell in the distance which would sound the hour.

The bell sounded.

"How hot I am," said Jason. "I'll take a turn about the yard."

In their chairs Mrs Wheelwright and the daughters dozed. Elfie was snoring.

Jason went out into the lovely garden with its rose trees now outpouring to the ground from lack of care, the beds of flowers wild, and he trod the path where the moss was making a rug. As he perambulated there, reflecting without recrimination that he had taken a touch too much wine, Bess Mubby came from the back door and went around the fence.

He saw her go with slight astonishment. This uncredited drudge of his, to where was she wending? Perhaps some relative was at hand and Mrs Wheelwright had granted leave. In the grasp of his slave, Jason saw the bag.

"Ho——" called Jason, and recollecting, ". . . Bess."

Bess turned and gave to him a look such as a mouse gives to a cheese.

"Yes, sir?"

"Where are you off to?"

"The hills," said Bess, who had rover's blood in her.

"What hills are those?"

"Why, sir, where the fairies come from."

"Well, you say. Be back by supper-time."

Bess smirked. And for a moment, to Mr Wheelwright, who had drunk deep and eaten three helpings of the pie, it seemed Bess Mubby had a pair of heads, and both were shaken at him in a kindly, knowing way.

He let her go, not realizing she had brushed him down from the beam and out of the corner—Mrs Wheelwright, Elfie and Alice with him.

Up in her ivory tower, which was already ringed with thorny briars, Laura was sitting. About her was the luxury of her bedroom, and in her lap lay the emerald necklace Hyperion had given her at their marriage. She looked at it, but instead she saw the emerald summer days she had spent with him.

How handsome Hyperion was, how gentlemanly, light-hearted and generous. She reviewed his every dealing with her, and could find fault with nothing. But then, she did not want to fault him.

Months had passed, four and more, since she had lain with Daniel Vehmund in the wolves' wood.

Through the summer, many of the servants had gone from the Worth mansion. There were the terrible murders of the girl who was her maid, the groom, the

man who was Hyperion's butler. And after these, like
crows, the black stories of awful things that could not be,
of hunts which found no quarry, and bodies come on at
dawn. In the crystal globe of her world, Laura did not
listen to whispers. She did not need to. In her heart she
knew that Daniel was the source of all darkness, without
understanding or explanation. He came to her at night in
dreams, and would not be put off. She tried to set Hyperion in his place, but Daniel was infinite, like God—as
God had been to her in childhood. He saw all and was
everything. Useless to deny.

Yet Hyperion was her husband. And the mansion was
her fortress. If Daniel would claim her, why had he not
done so? It had been a momentary thing, then, for him.
He had had her now. Unlike Hyperion, Daniel was satisfied . . . Only the diamond in its box recalled some
awesome spell binding them, and she had locked it away.

Surely she had only to stay faithful, surely all else was
lie and dream, myth, fancy, hallucination. As the wolf
which had been inside the ice, and the tale she had told
of drowning.

But this speculation was unhelpful. All summer she
had wrestled with the Angel of Destruction. Daniel
stayed like her shadow. Hyperion, the good and easy husband, had no weight and scarcely any substance. *He* was
the dream from which, at some uncertain time, she would
awake.

Laura looked across the room. Beneath the windows
stood the lamb, now grown bigger. It was snow-white
from its indoor life, and though it went out each day to
sample the lawn, it had hit on the habit of cropping the
carpet, which turned bald in parts. From this occupation
it now glanced up at her with sombre eyes.

Laura rose, and going to the lamb, she fastened around its neck the precious emeralds.

A symbol of the ridiculousness, and the lost fight, there was nothing really absurd in the image of such an animal decorated in such a way. Rather there was something barbaric and ominous in the sight, memorable of strange gods hung with gems above desert altars. Laura saw this instinctively, and with a sudden pang.

And on the door came a rapid knock. It must be the soft-footed maid, now often seen, who took the place of the dead. Laura bade her come in. In she came, and stood there with a face of fear.

"Oh, madam."

"What is it?" said Laura, and her heart sank in a painful beat.

"A man's come. Mr Worth says you're to please go down to the parlour at once."

Laura thought, *She knows nothing, yet is afraid of it.*

"Then, yes," said Laura, "I'll go at once."

He did not come for me himself. He does not want to spare me. I too am afraid, not knowing.

She went down the stair carefully, as if she were giddy or very old.

In the parlour, from which the close stigma of death had now been thrust away, roses in bowls and blue flames of iris before the hearth, Hyperion approached her and took her hands.

"I'm sorry, Laura. You must prepare yourself for a great shock." She stared at him blankly. The great shocks had already been, the nights of murder, and dreaming. "Your family, unfortunately . . ." Hyperion paused to gather himself. A year ago he would have been unfitted by this news, too bright and buoyant to deliver it. But things had happened to chasten him and dull his sunlight. He was grave and suitable now.

He told her quietly, as the man sat by in a chair, that Mr and Mrs Wheelwright, and their younger daughters, had died together in an afternoon, poisoned by a pie where deadly fungus had been cooked in error as mushrooms. Remnants of this meal supplied the clue. While the servant who had concocted it had evidently fled, on seeing what her ignorance had done, nor had she been found since.

So much Hyperion told Laura, while the messenger sat restive in the chair. Hyperion did not relate how Jason had been discovered contorted in his garden, about a tree, his extraordinary posture having drawn the attention of a passing carter. Nor of the twisted paroxysmal limbs of the two girls and the wife, who must have flung themselves about the room in a sort of dance of death.

When the mitigated events had been offered, Hyperion drew Laura on to a sofa.

She sat stunned with horror at her lack of grief. Her family had been a trial to her, yet how could it be she owed them nothing? Could she not even shiver or weep out of common pity?

And from mere numbness she said, "I must go there."

"If you wish, Laura. Of course I'll go with you."

"No," she said, at a loss, "let me go alone." It seemed to her she must walk to the spot barefoot, she must offer *something* for their sake. She did not want Hyperion to witness her coldness at their grave. He might try to comfort her.

The man got up from the chair and bowed to Laura fawningly. He said the Wheelwrights had been characters in the neighbourhood, popular people who would be missed. Laura stared through him, knowing him for a fool.

Then the man had gone away, and Hyperion sat beside her, holding her hand. "What shall I do?" he said, "how can I help you?"

"To bear my loss?" she said.

"I can't imagine what you feel," he said. "I was an orphan."

She looked down into herself to study her feelings, which did not exist. And then at last she wept from misery and shame.

Herald of autumn, a storm rode over the land. The carriage raced under the swords of lightnings which glared on it and changed it to a phantom. Then it dashed through the streaming rain, and from the sluices of the road huge explosions of water showered its windows. Laura kept her place at the centre of this maelstrom, her thoughts scattered and fragmentary.

So they came to the house that had been her family's, where she had never visited. In the torrent it seemed melted and shapeless. Under the umbrella of the coachman, Laura hastened to the door.

A man in black admitted her solemnly, and she was conducted into a room where four open coffins took up the space. She was left alone with them.

This was her penance. She fulfilled it.

She went to each coffin and stood gazing in.

Jason was the first. They had been at pains with him. His ruddy face was smoothed out and touched up with colour. How peaceful he looked, smug almost. They had had to break some of his bones to get him to lie tidily in his best coat and waistcoat, but this did not show. He might have been supposed to have died simply and in good cheer. Just so Mrs Wheelwright lay immaculate in her lace-trimmed cap; and Alice appeared better than in life, her cheeks blossomed with paint and her hair attended to. Only with Elfie the poison had left an eradicable mark, twisting up her lip to one side, and they had not been able to straighten it, so it seemed she leered.

Laura was heavy with their deaths, these four unloved strangers. She considered their wasted lives, the ungarnered youth of her sisters. She felt she should speak to them, but could not.

Thunder and lightning crashed simultaneously, turning the window to a livid mirror and making the four faces lurch with spurious life. At least the sky cried for them.

Laura went to the door and opened it.

Outside, she stood in the passage. From an adjacent chamber came a murmur of sound above the splashing rain. Laura entered the doorway, and hesitated.

The undertakers were positioned in their black. Up the room from them was a table covered in a red baize cloth, where another black-clad man made passes with three dun cups. He moved the vessels rhythmically about over the table, circling each other.

When the cups stopped moving, the undertakers murmured again.

"There," said one, and pointed to the second cup.

"Here?" The cup was raised on emptiness.

The group remonstrated. Something had been expected to be under the second cup. The man lifted each of the other cups in turn, to show only the tablecloth.

"Where is it then?" demanded the man who had let Laura in.

The man with the cups touched his breast. Something shining came up into his fingers. It was a silver coin.

"What are you doing?" said Laura firmly.

The funeral men looked about, embarrassed. Their leader said challengingly to Laura, "This fellow wishes to clear the house of anything unwanted."

Laura stared through the fluttering ethyl reflection of the rain, which seemed to shake the room like shattered glass. She saw the man with the cups and the coin had pockmarked cheeks, which she had not noticed before. He was Julinus, the magician.

She was suffused by abject terror. It was as if she had reached the end of the world.

Julinus spoke to the men, and to a dog-like figure reminding her also of the entertainment in the salon, whom he addressed as Aaron, and in perplexity Laura watched them withdraw. This was some nightmare.

And then, just as in a dream, Julinus' tongue slid out of his mouth like that of a gargoyle. For a moment she glimpsed a fearful join across it, like a strike of the lightning healed over.

They were at one of the windows. Laura beheld the diamond rain falling. It was the deluge. There was no hope.

"You are deeply affected by the death of your parents," Julinus announced.

Laura did not reply. Then she cried out: "That scar across your tongue——"

"The mark of a wound. I have several."

"Why did you display it to me?"

"Did I? Perhaps by accident."

"Why are you here?" she said. "What's your purpose?"

"I buy what isn't wanted, and sell it elsewhere."

"But that can't be. In the city . . ." she said, and halted.

"Ah, you believe you've seen me before. Are you certain?"

She gazed into his face. She was sure. But Julinus only smiled. He said, "We strive after meaning in our lives. We try to make patterns. Everything must have a goal. Sometimes this isn't so. Some things merely are. They come to be, they run their course, and are done with."

"The diamond," she said, "do you remember it?"

"A fabulous jewel made out of common elements of the earth. A piece of dirt transformed by a miracle into ice and light."

A million profligate diamonds flashed as they hit the roadway. The carriage was there, dim through the rain as if made of smoke.

"You became another man," said Laura. "Yet you were in wait here, for me. You think you have some business with me. What is it?"

"I will tell you something," said Julinus, "about Daniel Vehmund." Julinus looked into the rain. His pockmarks gave him a face of battered silver. He spoke in French, and Laura did not understand.

"What?"

"I said that I watched him out of interest—Daniel. He slept on a hillside, in a ruin. My man Aaron wrote on the wall the word *Terepha*. That is 'Unfit'—something rent and unusable. Later, Aaron shot Daniel Vehmund, point-blank through the heart, with a pistol."

"Obviously not," said Laura.

"Oh, yes. Daniel is indestructible now. He could not be killed. Why, the very transformation he undergoes with each full moon, that alone is enough to kill him, but does not. He's like the diamond now. The common clay has become something miraculous, invulnerable."

"By transformation," she said, "what do you mean?"

"Don't you already know? Haven't you tasted of it?"

Laura gripped her hands together. She was trapped, but how and why? The men were outside. And the dead in their boxes waiting for burial. But somehow Julinus knew of the wolves' wood.

"I must go out now," said Laura.

"Daniel becomes a beast," Julinus said.

"Which beast?"

"The beast which murders and tears. The beast which can't be killed by anything on or of the earth. Not steel, not wood, bullet, acid, poison, fire. Nothing. Earth refashioned Daniel. *Is* Daniel. Can't strike against itself."

"Yes," said Laura. "All right. Now you must let me go."

"Go," said Julinus. "Tell yourself it was a dream."

Laura turned and ran towards the door. There she stopped. She said quickly, "Don't take anything from the house. My husband will deal with all that."

Julinus did not answer. Perhaps he had vanished from the room.

She did not look back to see, but got out into the passage, and went to the place where the men and the dead bodies attended on her arrival.

Autumn dissolved in rain. The rushing water which had lashed Laura in her black, and dashed into the four Wheelwright graves, played too upon a mound between the orchard and the garden of the Vehmund farm, and wild plants came up and hid it, nourishing themselves on rain and on the corpse of Rosamunde Ax below.

The rain rained the wet sallow leaves from the trees. The streams and rivers rose in their banks. The sheep were led to shelter over the hills.

Under the mansion of Hyperion Worth, the lake

flooded the lower lawns. The statues stood slick as fish in the sea. Old blood was washed away.

Mr Worth and his wife grew steadily apart as if the rain warped them to it.

The rainy moon was hidden in the cloud. The full moon came and towered in the storm.

In a village, a malcontent, left overnight in a type of iron cage, was found torn to shreds, the iron bars twisted and snapped from their sockets. A sleepless woman half a mile off had seen something pass along the road beneath the spasmodic moonlight. It was not a dog or wolf, but some new animal. In the rain its coat of heavy hair had seemed to writhe. She had been afraid it would break in, despite the locks and bolts, but it only went by without looking, its head raised—a streaming, pointing, huge, unwieldy head presented to the moon.

Hyperion's servants had mostly left him. He let them go. One night the carriage and horses were stolen by a drunken groom. This fellow let the other horses loose, and they too disappeared in the watery wilderness of the country. Hyperion and his wife seemed alone in the mansion now, like shipwrecks on a desert island, surrounded by the ocean of the rain.

2

A falling star. *Quick, make a wish.* But there were so many muddled desires they could not be sorted in time, and the star was gone, then another and another. Another and another, gone.

The red-headed girl watched the strangeness of the skies. It had continued three nights, this fall of stars. It seemed foreboding, like the descent of outlawed angels, not quaint things to be wished on.

Behind her, the elderly maid, the only woman left in the house beside Laura herself, creaked about the room. She was setting out the dinner dress which Laura would wear to the simple meal cooked by the old man, the only other man besides Hyperion.

The rain had ended and a great ring of frost come down on the countryside. By the lake the reeds were brittle as sugar in the frozen flooded mud, and the ducks had flown away. They had never been known to do so before. It seemed they had fled the cold frost that would shut their wings and turn them into stones. The statues on the terrace glimmered with ice. The stars were like drops of hard frost that fell.

Laura put on the dress, and the elderly maid assisted

her as best she could. Laura twisted up her own hair, and
the maid hovered by her, lifting up her hands ineffectu-
ally above Laura's head. On the bed, the lamb sat watching in its emeralds Laura had never taken off.

When she was ready, Laura went down, leaving the
maid to tidy the bedroom as she was able, and the lamb
to study her.

They were to dine in the parlour. Here she had been
told of her family's collective death, and from here the
butler had been dragged out to savagery. The curtains
were thick across the long windows. No flowers had come
from the garden or the hothouse to the table. Here, too,
she had been first seduced. Here she had acquiesced.

Hyperion stood by the fire, and Laura looked at him
with a detached surprise. He was a human man, with
head and torso and limbs. He was actual, and she had
been made his.

"It's dismal, isn't it?" he said at once. "And slightly
macabre. Being here, like this."

"Yes," she said.

"I was thinking. We could go away for the winter. I'm
afraid it will mean a stiff walk to the nearest village—I
can go and fetch back some transport. Then we'll be off."

"Where?"

"The city, the ends of the earth—anywhere that's
cheerful."

She gazed at him. The room was full of shadows, the
candles did not burn well. It was as if he spoke of leaving
a besieged city; it was not realistic that they could go. But
was it only that she did not want to? Here she was alone
with him, but other nuances were also here.

"Whatever you think," she said.

"It's a blow. I rather relished sitting out a snow with

you. It's possible to skate on the lake . . . But the house won't run properly; it will be inconvenient and dreary."

He had never bemoaned the flight of the groom with all the horses and the carriage, nor the defection of his servants. He regretted such things as if they were in the natural order, like winter itself. He did not chafe at her either, did not question or press her. They had moved to a distance from each other, and subtleties would be lost across such miles.

The door opened, and the old man, clad in black, as Laura was still required to be, entered and brought a big china dish to the table.

Hyperion greeted man and dish graciously. He took off the cover. Some sort of stew or ragout steamed in the bowl. The old man helped them to portions of this, and then went out.

They ate in silence.

Laura thought of how the butler had been dragged on to the terrace outside, and what had become of him there. She could not feel anything beyond depression, oddly tempered by a faint bleak excitement. Daniel Vehmund . . . with each full moon . . . the transformation . . . the *beast*——

"Yes, we should go away," Laura said. "How soon will it be?"

"Tomorrow, if you like. There must be a carriage somewhere."

"A cart would do," she said.

Hyperion laughed, and she caught a glimpse of the man he had been, but only for a moment.

"We shall take your little sheep with us," he said. "What will they make of it in the hotel? Mrs Worth's funny dog with an emerald collar."

Then something scratched harshly at the windows.

They sat still, he and she, their eyes on each other.

The scratching came again.

They waited. Silence. Hyperion put down his glass and Laura laid down her knife and fork.

"What can it be?" he said, mockingly.

"There's no moon," she said.

"Ah, yes. All the stories. No moon, and no full moon for twenty days. No monster then. Let's see."

He got up, and going to a window pulled wide the drapes. Nothing was visible but blackness, and over it the lighter black of the sky, along which there slipped a single stitch of thin silver, a shooting star above the park.

Hyperion went to a cabinet and took out a pistol. He tried it in his hand. "Supposedly no good against anything supernatural," he said.

"Not any use at all," she said.

"But who knows, this may be real." He plucked one of the candlestands off the table. "Are you brave enough to open the window for me? Shut it behind me when I'm outside."

She did as he asked and Hyperion stepped through into the night. Laura shut the window, but stayed pressed at the pane, a slender subdivision of darkness on the golden room.

Hyperion crossed the terrace, holding up the light. There was no wind, the air so cold it was like a dense substance that must be breasted. Stars glittered sparsely, but below, the lake water had a half invisible glow, like the surface of a polished table. A shape passed between this and the candlelight.

"Who's there?" Hyperion shouted.

The night shape wavered and enlarged. Suddenly a man with yellow hair swung forward into the candlelight. He stood looking up at Hyperion on the terrace.

"Mr Vehmund."

"Mr Worth." Daniel gestured fluently. "Won't you come down? There's nothing to fear. I've something to show you."

Hyperion glanced back at the silhouette of his exquisite wife impaled upon the pane. Then, holding the pistol still and the candelabra, he went down the steps to the lawn.

Daniel met him graciously, as if leading him into a salon.

"What is it?" Hyperion said.

Daniel's face was smiling, vivid and wild, the picture of a combed, couth, shaven satyr. Then it was gone. He had blown out the candles.

"Look," said Daniel's voice from the blackness. "The night. I wanted to show you only that."

Hyperion stayed immobile. Perhaps he looked about, or tried to; he was still dazzled by the flames.

"My night vision," said Daniel, "is remarkable. Everything's as clear as day. But not for you, perhaps? A shame. You miss so much."

Hyperion's sight adjusted to darkness. Yet the landscape was deeply black, long folds, and curving forms that might be trees, the distanced shimmer of lake. Above, in the bluish slab of sky, the stars were bold now as brooches.

Yet the gaze was drawn irresistibly back to the gold oblong of light resting in the black air, the candlelit window of the room where Laura stood, like the pupil of an eye.

"The stars," Daniel said, "already perished and gone out, but their lies still burning. Fossils. But there is the moon," said Daniel, "up on the terrace."

"Why are you here?" said Hyperion.

"Aren't I welcome? I've come to visit you. You and the lady in the moon."

"Did you come on foot?"

"Of course."

"Then I can't turn you away."

"Should you like to?" said Daniel. "Do it."

"But it would make no difference," Hyperion said. "Have you become an animal, Mr Vehmund? I mean," he added, "these manoeuvres by night. The scratching on the window. All your talk of seeing in the dark."

And in the dark, Daniel poised, as if considering. He said, "I don't know what I am. There are names for it but they're inadequate. I hesitate to give myself a title or status. You own the Vehmund land. Did you know, your men won't come near the farmhouse? I've lived alone there some while, and haven't seen a soul. Such foolish idle superstition. You should scotch it, Mr Worth."

Hyperion Worth began to see something of Daniel's face. In the dark it was fine as a mask, yet alive, vibrantly so; a life that sizzled between the sky and the earth.

They both looked then towards the light of the window.

Hyperion said, "I was sorry to hear of the death of your mother."

"Well," Daniel said. That was all. There was no grief or anger, neither resignation. It was not indifference. Hyperion saw in a perceptive flash, painful and demoralizing, what had absorbed the icon of Jenavere—not eclipsing but evolving out of it. Jenavere was not dead. She had translated, into Laura. A Laura who was both queen and slave, creatrix and object of metamorphosis.

The wolf stood by him in the darkness, its golden eyes on the golden window.

Laura too was to be a wolf, or the maiden who tends on wolves, Beauty with the Beast.

"She isn't yours," Hyperion said lightly.

"Oh, yes."

"Then what am I?"

"The impediment."

"How you do astound me, Daniel Vehmund. Should you be so frank on such a matter?"

"There's no choice. I like you," said Daniel. "We should have been friends if nothing extraordinary had happened."

"Then I must protect her from you."

"Try by all means."

"And you'll try on your own account," said Hyperion.

"Night is on my side."

"Maybe." Hyperion closed his eyes a moment, black within black. "You assume Laura has no will or wishes of her own."

Daniel said nothing.

In a kind of fear, Hyperion looked out again, at total darkness. Laura, as if she had heard it all, had gone back from the window and drawn the curtain over.

Daniel was a few feet away, under the terrace wall.

Hyperion glanced about. The nightscape had grown clearer and more definite. He saw the shining lake, the flock of trees grouped under the sky, the hills above the house. He heard a peculiar vibration, and thought it was in his ear, the physical presage of dismay.

"I shall go in, to my wife," Hyperion said. "You, obviously, will come in as you want."

"I could climb the walls of your house," said Daniel. "But not now."

"How many have you killed?" said Hyperion coldly. "How do you manage it? Oh, I forgot. You turn into a creature of darkness. Are you truly mad, Mr Vehmund, taking the acts of a maniac for your own?"

Daniel went up on to the steps. He ascended. He said nothing.

The noise in Hyperion's ear was louder. It seemed to come from behind him, and above. Involuntarily, he looked upward. The stars were trembling, as if through tears.

Daniel was on the terrace, where Hyperion had been. He stood by the balustrade, looking away. "Listen."

"You hear it too," Hyperion said.

"In the East, they would say that God passed behind the sky."

The two of them stayed motionless. But the night was now full of a sort of rushing, like dry rain. The sound had grown. It was raw and tearing, echoing off the roof of heaven and the sides of the hills, until it seemed to come from everywhere at once.

Far away, from hidden cots and sheds, dogs had begun to howl.

Abruptly a burn appeared in the surface of the sky. It was seared and red hot. It spread with an appalling swiftness.

The night was no longer black, but scarlet. Hyperion saw the façade of his house, the statues, Daniel himself, steeped in blood and fire, leap out. The lake woke like a sheet of lava, and the horizons of hills and trees caught as if alight, bright as noon.

From all sides birds burst into a fiendish fluttering and screeching at the advent of this dawn of a day in Hell. Elsewhere the world was petrified and without dimension. A howl mightier than those of all the dogs came from above. The sky split on a seam of boiling whiteness.

In the house the window was thrust wide, pale as ashes in the uproar of lights.

"Go back!" Hyperion shouted.

His voice was lost in tumult.

Something passed over. It was like the Angel of Death, in Exodus; just so that must have been, Egypt's night engulfed in fire and the colossal shriek of wings.

Hyperion fell to the grass as if a giant hand had swept him there.

Hearing seemed poured away down an enormous drain, and the redness and fire with it.

The night darkened. Then, over the hills, there was a gust of white.

In rapid succession the sky there went crimson, molten pink, and faded instantly to purple. An explosion shook the ground. The walls of darkness and air shook. The stars shook, but did not come loose.

The tremor melted from the land, and Hyperion rose to his feet. He saw the house unscathed; and, held in the rim of the hills behind, a soft blush, flame or smoke, gently made its pillar.

After all, one star had fallen to the earth.

He had read of such things, and in his mind he rehearsed the facts of what he had seen. It had been a godstone, a thunderbolt. A meteorite.

In the trees the birds flapped and hopped, twittering in terror. In the circle of night the dogs were barking now, and miles off a church bell might be heard ringing.

Daniel was on the terrace, like one of the statues, impervious. Laura leaned by the opened window, both her hands gripped at her throat. In the room beyond, the two old servants stood like two waxwork dummies, their withered faces raised and still.

In the ancient world it would have been an omen, and

men would, inevitably have wound the forces of space
and nature on to their own lives. The crash of stellar
debris on to the world: what could it portend but the
collapse of some towering edifice?

Hyperion stared at the terrace, his wife, the man, the
antique black chorus of his retainers.

Could so vast a thing spell only the descent and shattering of *his* tiny empire, his miniature tumble into the
abyss?

Fire had fallen from heaven. In the night the snow came.
It was early in the season. From the coverts of the land
they named it another prodigy.

By her window Laura watched the snow as it filled up
the platter of the earth.

She thought of the Christmas Hyperion had promised
her, the boughs of holly, the logs on the hearth, the tall
tree decked with flowers of gilt paper and rosy ribbons,
the carol singers who trooped to the door, the feast. It
had been immaterial to her then and now was not to be.

Daniel had come into the house. He had sat in the
parlour, and he and Hyperion had drunk brandy. Hyperion had talked of the meteor, and Daniel had gazed into
the ordinary fire. At Laura, Daniel had only glanced. The
mansion seemed to be his, Hyperion his lodger, Laura
some facet of the furnishings, expected to be there, un-
questioned.

She was horribly shaken. The thing which had gone
over the house to bury itself among the hills, that did not
frighten her more than Daniel's advent. Indeed it seemed
to evidence his appearance, like an arrow shot to mark a
place.

Laura bore with Daniel's presence, and the desultory
lecture Hyperion was giving on the meteor, for one quar-

ter of an hour. Then she absented herself. She sought her
room and locked the door. This was mere bluff. Nothing
could be kept out.

The maid did not come to the room, and Laura undid
her dress and put on instead her dressing-gown. The
lamb had got down from the bed, and lay by the bedroom
fire, the emeralds winking serpent-green about its neck.
It did not behave, and no longer looked, properly for or
of its kind. It was a new animal, a sort of hybrid, symbolic
of something or other. If the passage of the meteor had
disturbed it was not apparent. Probably it had forgotten.

Something terrible would happen. It was only a question of time.

A poignant rage stirred through Laura. She was powerless. Besides, she did not know what to do.

The snow fluttered down. The park was white now,
lurid against the sky.

The bolt from space would be burning in the snow,
Hyperion had said. People would go to look at it. It was
no more than two or three miles off.

Somewhere in the house Daniel must be sleeping, unless Hyperion and he remained in the parlour, drinking,
Hyperion talking.

In the black and white hours of morning, Laura fell
asleep. She dreamed of the wolves running by a frozen
sea. Each wave lay on the shore in a lap of quartz, and
from their grey bodies, as they ran, the wolves cast cold
black shadows. A frozen ship lay in the frozen sea, and a
wolf was on its deck, locked in the ice. But the shadows
were more important than the wolves. They broke away,
and rolled inland. The sky turned bright and there was a
crack of sound. Laura woke.

Grey as the wolves, the light was in the room and on
the park.

From her window Laura saw two dark figures picking their way slowly and carefully across the cake-icing of the lawns. One held the other's arm and carried a basket. She realized it was the old man and woman, Hyperion's last servants, departing over the snow.

The meteor had moved like a fiery wind, a scythe of bitumen, on the last mile of its journey. It had carved the tops from trees, then flattened them, cutting its avenue to the earth. A scene of devastation led to it, which the snow had sheeted but not hidden in the sombre afternoon. The full stop to its flight had been a hillside. The hill was riven. Huge boulders and chunks of rock had exploded out and gushed away down the slope. Everywhere the white snow was pocked by the smouldering craters of the meteor's own disintegration. Yet the bulk of it had stayed entire, lodged in the hill like a fist slammed into yielding mud. What was visible of it was the size of a small carriage, in shape like a crushed globe. It was greyish black, but at its heart, against the hill, seethed a magenta core from which thin yellow smoke went up. The ruby flicker played on the white snow, turning it red, and it flushed the faces of adjacent heights, paling and rising with the momentum of a forge. Off from the top of the meteor hill the snow had melted at once; it was savagely green. And, roused by the prompting heat, snow-drops had put out their delicate spears, mistaking carnage for spring.

With midday, the sightseers came. Some lingered, and as the afternoon went on, others arrived. There were traps with restless horses troubled by the curious metallic smell of the fallen star. Ladies and gentlemen had brought flasks of wine and boxes of food, to enjoy the spectacle at leisure. There were men and women of the villages, too, who had driven up on wagons or ramshackle carts, and a few who had walked there.

The lord who did not know himself to have been nicknamed 'Cabbage', had brought his daughter, the ringleted Ada. They stood on the snow, regarding this ball which had dived from space, this fragment perhaps of some other planet.

"How ugly it is," said Ada, and rubbed together her lavender gloves. It had been necessary, she felt, that she witness it. But it did not thrill her. What was the point of it?

"You're spoilt," said Lord Cabbage. "I'll be damned if you aren't. You'd have taken notice if it had landed in the orangery." Ada tossed her head. Lord Cabbage looked down the slope. "There's Worth come to see. And that farming fellow."

Ada observed with some tempered interest. Hyperion Worth was nothing to her, for he had married, and Daniel Vehmund was beneath her, yet she had heard of him. She had heard a piece of bizarre local gossip, that he was thought to be a werewolf, capable of changing into a ravening wolf-man at every waxing of the moon. Such an idea, while ridiculous, might have its source in something. Certainly he was very handsome, in a saffron way. Ada thought him more intriguing than the meteor. She had not noted him at Hyperion's supper.

At that moment Hyperion Worth raised his head. Lord Cabbage saluted him, and strode down the slope. Ada stepped after.

It seemed to her that Mr Worth was white and pinched. Daniel Vehmund stood beside him, and perhaps this notorious person had gained some hold over Mr Worth. Ada could think of no other reason for one man being in another's thrall.

"So, you've come to look at the firework," said Lord Cabbage.

"Yes indeed," said Hyperion. "May I present my companion?" He presented him, and introduced Lord Cabbage by his proper name. Ada too was offered. Daniel barely looked at either the lord or his daughter, although he nodded politely and smiled.

"I didn't see your carriage," said Lord Cabbage.

"I have none. My servants have run away."

"The devil they have? These country scares, no doubt. Can I be of help?"

"Not at all, thank you," said Hyperion. He stared at the throbbing magenta heart of the meteor. "I'm destined to my insolation. There's no escape, it seems."

"Escape?" Lord Cabbage gazed askance.

"I view it in the Roman way. Something falls towards me. Such a surprise—I'm a light character, as you know."

"What talk. Can't I persuade you to come to our ramble of a house? Beastly cold in winter, but at least the amenities. Shall I send my carriage?"

"You're too kind," said Hyperion. "Send nothing."

"But why——"

"My wife," said Hyperion. "I doubt if she would go with me." He was strange, jaunty and abstruse, as if caught up in a whirl of noises and colours no other could hear or see.

"Well, it's as you wish, of course."

"I'll treasure your generosity," said Hyperion.

"We must understand," interposed Ada, in an acid little voice, "Mr Worth can't leave his guest."

Daniel favoured her with one brief glance. It was not human but animal, though amused. Ada did not like it, yet she was too sensible to be unnerved. She thought, *He's a villain.* She was irritated that she seemed to have made no impression. Perhaps he was mentally dull, as the elder Vehmund brother had been reported to be. Legend said Daniel had killed this brother, as a beast. Some truth there, maybe? Was Daniel Vehmund insane?

Lord Cabbage said, "Mr Vehmund has his own home to go to."

"Not at all," said Hyperion with a pallid blitheness. "That place is as bleak and untended as my mansion."

"Well, I don't know," said Lord Cabbage. Plainly he was thinking better of his invitation. "However, we must be off. My regards to Mrs Worth."

"And tell her to be wary of wolves," said Ada. "There have been some nasty stories." But Daniel did not glance at her again.

As the man and his daughter went away along the snow, Daniel spoke.

"You should accept his hospitality."

"And leave Laura to you."

"If necessary. Really, you'd do better to go."

Throughout their walk to this spot, they had discussed unamazing things, as if they had been friendly acquaintances. Though, now and then, Hyperion had turned his back to Daniel, or trodden ahead of him, as if giving an opportunity to be struck from behind. At one of these junctures, Daniel had laughed. Nothing else had occurred.

Hyperion, too, had suggested the trek to see the meteor, as if Daniel were a general visitor, and nothing was on their minds but natural curiosity. Laura had kept to her room. She had said she would make supper in the kitchen from which the cook and all the maids of service, and the last old man, had fled.

Hyperion looked gracefully upon Daniel.

"You'll have to kill me to get rid of me."

"Why make it needful?"

"So you admit, murder's on your mind."

"Murder's in the air, without doubt. But the choice is yours. You have nineteen days."

Hyperion said, "You truly claim it, do you? Some monstrousness at full moon. *You* have done all these terrible things."

"You must decide if you believe so."

"Of course not. There has to be some reason, some logic in the universe."

Daniel pointed at the meteor in the hill.

"Does that have logic, and reason?"

A pair of men had appeared, working their way up and around the fractured hillside. They were too far off to be seen in any detail. One carried a shining pick.

"Have you observed enough of it?" Hyperion asked graciously. "Do you want to climb up and try for a trophy?"

"No," said Daniel. He indicated the distant carriage of Lord Cabbage, and the man and girl hesitating before it. "If you hurry, you can catch him up."

"Let's turn back," Hyperion said, "before the sun sets. I mustn't expose you to the possible dangers of the night road."

Ada descended through the broken wood in the twilight, the coachman clumping behind her. It had taken her some while to persuade her father to allow her to go, accompanied by the escort, down to the caravan she had sighted among the trees. Ada did not believe in monsters or see a purpose in drowned ships, but she was venturous, and conventionally superstitious. The meteor had made her peevish, and the meeting with Hyperion Worth, who was wed, and Daniel Vehmund, who had not noticed

her, had had a fraught effect, unsettling. The caravan
denoted gypsies. She would have her fortune told. She
had spurned such an act six months before, when at a
dancing party an old gypsy woman had been in the be-
low-stairs, and one by one the girls went out to her to
learn their fate, returning pleased, frightened and gig-
gling. Ada, desiring to be unique, had refused, then.

The snow piled high about the caravan, which was
ramshackle, with no horse in evidence. It would seem the
vehicle had been here before the meteor fell.

On the door the coachman knocked loudly.

The door moved. It was open.

"Is anyone there?" Ada exclaimed.

There was no answer.

"Best to leave it," said the coachman.

Ada brushed him aside. "Wait for me here," she said,
and got up into the caravan.

She had no more compunction at entering than she
would have done on breaching the room of one of her
servants. These people and things were there for her use.
She had been taught this. Yet the inside of the caravan
was not as might have been anticipated. It was very dark,
and full of levels, like the inside of a cupboard. Through
one small window came the faint glaring intermittent
glow the meteor was making in the blackening sky. Then
a yellow light flared up at her feet.

Ada started. Not only was the caravan occupied, but
she had found herself surrounded by an audience of eyes.

"Please be careful," she said tartly. "My father's man is
outside."

A male voice said from behind the lamp: "You need
fear no violence."

"I don't fear it," snapped Ada. "Do you tell fortunes?"

"If you wish."

Ada's eyes had adjusted to the light. It came from a lamp burning on a low table. Behind it sat a picturesque figure, but not clad in proper gypsy costume. It was a man in a leaden robe, his head wrapped in a faded cloth, like an illustration from some book of oriental tales. All about were suitable esoteric objects, old books and rolls of parchment, and, perched on heights and in crannies of the room, peculiar doll-like cats with glittering eyes. Nothing else watched her but these, and having examined them, Ada dismissed them all.

"I have a few pence," said Ada, who was also thrifty. "Will that do?"

"Payment is superfluous. But come nearer, and sit down."

Boldly, or stupidly, Ada complied. She went up and sat before the lamp on a cushion, facing the oriental gypsy.

She thought him, as she had thought the stellar ball, 'ugly'. That was the sum of her feeling. She held out her hand, and he took it. As he put down his head he made a weird motion with his neck, like a snake's. That would not have given her pause, but something did, for she caught a glimpse of a hideous scar across his throat, revealed a moment by the neck of the robe, then hidden again

"There is no necessity for nervousness," said the turbaned man, the light catching like sequins in the moon craters of his cheeks. "Your hand shows a calm and sanguine life. You will never want. You will never suffer any serious illness or misfortune. You will marry where you wish and where it is auspicious. You will have one child, a boy, easily and without peril. You will live into a long and comfortable old age." He released her hand and, rather astonishing her, it dropped down limp and cold. "You will," he said, "be very unhappy."

Ada tried to find her voice, but she could not.

With a sense of outrage she got up and moved back through the caravan, between the rows of gleaming glass eyes. All the while she attempted to summon some stern or cutting reply; all the while something struggled wildly inside her and she crammed it down.

Reaching the door, words and audibility came to her.

"You should be thankful I don't see you punished for your impertinence."

Behind the light he bowed. And then the lamp went out.

In a frenzy Ada would afterwards remember to have been annoyance, she scrabbled for the door and jumped out into the snow.

The coachman stood by a shattered tree, smoking his pipe. In that ruined landscape she saw his face; it was that of an enemy. And for an instant the whole world was naked and horrible before her. But she put down at once the veil.

"Come along. My father's waiting."

By the time she reached the carriage, she was herself again, or the self she consented to be. She had forgotten the words in the caravan as nonsense, a proof that such things were silly.

On the night hill two men had climbed up and were chipping at the dark side of the meteor. The other sightseers were gone, or going away. There was no sign of Mr Worth or his villainous companion.

She got into the conveyance and it started off. Just for a second the face of her father, too, was that of a stranger, but this also passed. That evening she would write in her diary that she had beheld a meteorite, but it was not such a marvel, and that a gypsy had told her fortune, saying all the expected things, and that she doubted there would ever be a ball at the Worth mansion now, for Mr Worth looked ill and strained and nothing much might be hoped of him.

Mr Worth and Mr Vehmund dined that night alone. The fare was homely but pleasant, concocted by Laura in the deserted kitchen. She had left the meal for them, like a spirit. They did not see her.

After the meal, host and guest strolled through the mansion, Hyperion with a candlebranch which he held up to illumine particular paintings, tapestries, pieces of sculpture, groins in the ceiling.

They discussed art, and Daniel spoke of the artistry of foreign climes.

"I'm very fond of this house," Hyperion said. "You can see why I won't be ousted. Why I'll stand to defend my place here with a drawn sword."

"It will do you no good."

"But I can't help myself."

They parted to sleep, or not to sleep, in their allotted grottoes of silk and linen.

Night winged slowly over the roof.

In the white snow morning, Laura came to Hyperion's chamber. He was up, wearing his dressing-gown and seated in a chair. The room was cold.

"I must lay you a fire," she said.

"No, you're not my servant. I'll see to it myself."

She said, "He doesn't come near me, and my door is locked." Hyperion said nothing. Laura said, "You spoke to me before of going away."

"Yes . . ." he said. "We could go. But the house——"

"Let him have the house if he wants," she said, "let him wander about in it till it bores him."

"I don't think the house means anything to him," said Hyperion. "There's the tale of the money he's said to have accumulated. He does nothing with that. I think the house to him is just another tract of land. Yet he's possessed it. He'd open all the doors and let the snow blow through. The wolves would come down and make lairs in the parlour and the ballroom."

"In the spring, you can come back with men, and clear him out."

"The spring," Hyperion said.

"We must get away from him," she said.

"He believes he turns into a beast. He'd come after us. God knows what he'd do."

"All the more reason to be gone."

"You'll be safe," Hyperion said. "Obviously, there's a part for you in the myth."

"I wished him dead the moment I met him," she said. "I drowned him in a story. Don't you remember?"

"Oh, was that it?" Hyperion looked into the sky beyond the window. "Do you know, I do credit that he can't be killed. The pistol would be useless." Laura made a little sound of indrawn breath. "He's easily the finest company. We went to the meteor along the old lane; it runs almost all the way. Our dialogue never flagged. And when we came to it, the star, the light of it shone on him. A creature of rarity."

"Won't you take me away," she said.

"It's too late, my love."

"Why?"

"We can only walk. He'd come after us and walk with us. Somehow we should all come back. It would be the same with a carriage."

"He's bewitched you," Laura said.

"Laura has such faith in spells."

"I shall stay in my room," she said.

"Yes, it might be best to do that. Until you no longer can."

Days passed, and nights. Hyperion sat in his study, reading old letters from his childhood, making idle drawings out of books. Then he would rise and seek Daniel, and find him somewhere in the mansion, and they would patrol the corridors and discuss the hounds and nymphs in the paintings. Laura would go unseen, by back ways, to the kitchen. Great cupboards full of provisions and the cold pantry, like the arctic now, supplied the phantom suppers in the parlour. In her room, under the alabaster lamp, Laura unpicked her dresses and sewed them up differently. Each morning on waking she felt a fear of the day, she was afraid of meeting Daniel in the house, and went about more and more often, thinking she saw him behind pillars, at the corners of passageways, watching her.

More snow fell and now changed the appearance of everything, so from the windows the landscape was unrecognizable but for the lake of black ice. Nothing moved on the earth. There were no birds. All life seemed gone but theirs.

During the afternoon, Hyperion had seen the lamb on the terrace in its sparkling green collar. The snow had seemed to surprise it and soon it went in, vanishing from sight. He did not know what Laura fed the lamb, perhaps cakes and wine. It had an odd look, not ovine, yet not properly dog-like either. Probably its alien existence was turning it into a new animal.

Hyperion set and lit the parlour fire. He sat at a small table playing card games he had invented as a child.

Later he went up to dress for dining, because it was his custom. He had lent Daniel suitable clothes that he too might honour the ritual, and Daniel did indeed honour it, coming to the table always exactly dressed, far better than on the night of the festivity long ago.

They were two gentlemen, served by an invisible housekeeper. Hyperion no longer saw Laura. He did not know if Daniel did. It did not matter, like the going away.

When Hyperion returned to the parlour, Daniel was there. He still acted as a guest, and waited for his host, his hands empty.

"Once one of these decanters was full of blood," said Hyperion.

Daniel accepted his drink. He stood in the light of the candles and the fire, while on the table a covered dish steamed.

"You forget," said Daniel, "such murders are committed by a thing without memory."

"How convenient."

"Yes, it is. The liberty of lawlessness without the guilt."

"Are you impervious?" said Hyperion.

"To what? To conscience? To bullets?"

"Both," said Hyperion.

Daniel said, "Both."

"There it is," Hyperion said. "I've been thinking of my childhood. It was like a path, leading somewhere. But it led here."

"You should have gone off in that man's carriage."

"And miss such revelations? I want to see."

"To see what?" said Daniel.

"What you become. If you become—anything."

"I become myself."

"A self you refuse all knowledge and memory of."

"Am *refused.*"

The fire glittered on the backs of Daniel's hands. There was a brazen bloom there. And on his jaw. And in his eyes.

"Teach me," said Hyperion.

"I can't. Besides, it isn't in you."

"Perdition? It is."

"No, you belong with the angels, Mr Worth."

"And Laura," Hyperion said.

"In Hell," Daniel answered, "with me."

Hyperion frowned. "Why?"

"Laura rules herself. Which is a sin."

"Why?" Hyperion said again. His pale shadowed face was fascinated, the eyes stretched on pain.

"It isn't permitted us, Mr Worth, to rule. We must yield. To God or the Devil."

Hyperion said, humbly, "I find it difficult to believe in either."

"Belief isn't necessary. You yourself may attract the attention of heaven or the pit."

"I prefer the old gods."

"Cling to them then," Daniel said.

He moved to the table and hesitated above the steaming dish.

Hyperion joined him. They stood together.

The dish smelled of nothing. Of steam, but no other thing.

Hyperion lifted off the lid.

In the dish were round stones and snapped twigs, bathed in hot black water. Laura, the phantom housekeeper, had suddenly supplied a dinner in keeping with dark conversation, shadows, isolation, metaphysics, and snow.

Daniel turned to Hyperion. He took Hyperion's head, a skull covered by flesh, features and fawn hair, between his hands. Daniel kissed Hyperion on the lips. Then Daniel left Hyperion. He walked out of the room, and away up the staircase.

Hyperion crossed the chamber, and filled his glass from the decanter.

Her door was locked, as he had known it would be. He leaned against it, and thrust with one arm, and the door gave.

Inside, the room was red with firelight, as he had seen his mother's room in sunset, if he recollected it.

Before the fire was the lamb, with the wet green gems about its throat. It turned its head, and looked at him, but it did not run away.

Laura was at the black window, in a long robe that caught the colour of the fire, as her hair took the fire into itself. She too turned, slowly, and gazed at Daniel. Apart from fire, she was as white as the snow, her eyes black as the night.

He went to her without a word, and unspeaking, unprotesting, she received him. Her face was stern, the Athene face Hyperion had once spoken of.

Human thought came to Daniel in bursts, and now he thought of Marjannah in her red dress alight with spangles, and her long black hair pouring down. Marjannah might have had this role, if the diamond had been hung on her, if her wildness had been like Laura's. But Marjannah was a child of veils and golden screens, a slave girl. She would have died. She had been lucky.

For a moment it was bizarre to him, the journey he had taken. He saw it as if through a tunnel of light. Then there was only the strength of power, the simplicity of all things.

He pulled down the glowing robe. Her white body

shone out at him. She was not wearing the diamond, perhaps had hidden it. Yet the diamond was in her skin, had impregnated her; it was a symbol, perhaps no longer integral, only the first chord of the song.

With his hands he described the stem of her, the flowering breasts. Her face changed, as he had seen it do in the wood. She was avid and cruel. Her hand sprang out and raked at him, but he eluded the blow, took her hand and opened it with his kiss.

He mouthed her breasts, her body, kneeling down before her. Reaching the mound of her sex, he penetrated her with his tongue, softly eating her alive as she leaned back, whispering and sighing on the black window.

When he stood again, she had given herself. He picked her up and placed her on the wide bed. He threw his clothes down on the floor. Firelight ran like liquid copper over their bodies.

Almost as soon as he had entered her she twisted into the living death of orgasm. A long stammering scream extended from her lips like smoke, and coiled away through the hollows of the emptied mansion. In whatever room he occupied, Hyperion could not fail to hear it.

Daniel did not want or need to expend himself. Instead he leaned above her, looking at her beauty, which itself seemed to feed him. As he did so, he appeared to smoulder and burn, the fire catching on a fine gilding of hair which covered his entire skin.

The moon was rising, three-quarters full and snow white, as if winter had fallen on it also. The earth was like the moon, so pale, so black. And the house rested on the moon's surface, and he and she in it. Soon they would be alone, held in the white hand of the waste. Silence would come down, and vast stillness, like the frozen heart of the diamond.

* * *

Hyperion was writing a letter to one of his dead aunts.
He had not liked her—liked her the least, in fact—and so
he felt free to recount everything, although he employed
euphemisms and conventional clichés, so as not to shock
her too directly. Already he had covered many pages.

'Today, I found the glass doors of the salon left wide open.
The snow had drifted in, and ice hung on the chandeliers in
the ballroom beyond. This is Laura's manner of telling me
that things are anyway coming to pass as I predicted. That I
must be gone. Although, of course, I have not seen her, or
him, since their conjunction.

'Obviously, there is no way for me to go now, even if I
would. Perhaps Laura recalls that a lane behind the park
(the route we took to the meteor) is sheltered and therefore
still perhaps passable. But I would need to get much further
than that.

'I do believe he will change. I've seen him changing.
Through his eyes something looked at me. Is that conceivable or am I only another victim of the delusion?

'I shall, naturally, discover. In two more nights, the moon
is full.

'I found an old book, God knows how it came here, on
werewolves. It shows a man covered in pelt tearing apart a
sheep. I can kill him with a silver bullet, apparently. I don't
accept this. I sense he has been attacked before, and nothing prevailed. It seems he believes in God, so why should
God, or the idea of God, or purity, or silver, hold sway over
him? I wish he had spoken to me in detail about it. I should
have been intrigued—or would I have argued? But then
probably he doesn't, himself, completely know.

'What will happen to Laura? Will she lead him over the
grounds by a crimson leash?

'A supper of cold pigeon and bread. An exquisite wine.
There are several more bottles. These will be useful. What
other weapon do I have?

'Her cries of joy echo about the rooms. Or do I only hear
again the first one?

'Laura too has metamorphosed. She has become a soul-
creature. This is her essence, which I was unable to release.

'My house feels like a cathedral of snow. I don't know it
after all. It will become a lair of beasts, a haunt of owls.'

She had descended from the high tower into the gutters
of the wood. She thought of herself as a savage, free of
all constraint. But that was not so, she was not like that.

Daniel slept through the day. She examined him.
Asleep, his personality dispersed, she might suppose he
had no hold on her, and wonder what she was doing.

But it was easy to wake him. And he would turn to her
like a bright wave, rolling up over her.

Laura had risen and dressed, in black. She was restless
at confinement. Already she had been about the mansion, using it for exercise, meeting no one. At night she
went to the kitchen and took food, uncooked things that
might be eaten like a picnic. Smoke rose from the chimney of Hyperion's study. He had not gone away. She
wished he would attempt it, and, without pity, visualized
him fallen miles off in the snow, disabled. She was angry
with him. He had done nothing right. He should have left
her alone.

Finally she unlocked the drawer, took out the box, and
unlocked this in turn.

She held the diamond suspended above Daniel's sleeping body.

The jewel hung, like a lodestone. But he did not wake,
or respond.

She snatched the diamond away into her hands.

She went down through the house. The lamb followed her, leaping along the stairs, taking the awkwardness of its unnatural environment for granted.

Outside, the vast chamber of the cold rang with white silence.

The snow was frozen solidly, and Laura walked across it with slow, determined care. The lamb came to the edge of the terrace, no further. Laura glanced back at it. It was like her peculiar child, a demon child to which she did not speak.

She began to go down along the white lawn under the china sky, conspicuous in her black cloak. Despite the heavy garments she had put on, the coldness seemed to sting her bones. The snow was like a Biblical calamity, some huge drought or blasting by fire, or obliterating deluge. She felt herself very small, visible to something that watched from above.

She walked for a long time, placing her feet cautiously. At last she came to the black border of the frozen lake.

Branches, smashed by the snow's weight, had dropped about the lake from the shapeless mounds of trees. She searched, and found what she wanted.

With frightened stealth Laura stepped out on to the slate of black ice. Her heart was beating with iron strokes. She was afraid of the ice, on which Hyperion had told her it was possible to skate. And it was more than this.

She reached a part where the ice showed more thinly, long weed caught in it like the tinsel hair of a dead naiad.

Laura moved back, and from this distance thrust at the thinner ice with her chosen stick. A sound bounced up from the blow and seemed to hit the walls and ceiling of sky. A terrible enormity was in this flat note. Laura listened. Then she turned and gazed back towards the house. There was a man's figure on the terrace steps.

Laura renewed her grip upon the pointed branch, and struck again at the frozen table of the lake, with all her might.

The noise of the blow was different. A sudden crack appeared. She leaned towards it and stabbed down with the stick once more. She staggered, and for an instant felt the ice shift beneath her, bearing her into the black horror of water beneath. Then the motion stopped. She was kneeling on the lake, the branch spun away. A little hole had appeared, filled with black ink.

Laura drew the diamond out of her cloak.

She cupped it in her hand. It was like winter itself, the cause of the snow. Within it, the faint flaw, the wolf in the ice. Did she dare?

She turned again, and the man was coming swiftly over the white lawn, as if he trod on air. Gold touched him in the bloodless light. It was Daniel.

She stooped forward and let the diamond slip evasively into the hole in the lake, like a smooth fish. It went without a ruffle, with one pale flicker of greenish fire.

The black water was blank. Already cold was healing the crack, and soon new ice would form across the broken place.

Laura stood up, and moved inch by inch off the lake's surface, back on to the whiteness of the shore.

There she stood, and waited.

Daniel came down the slope, drew level with her, and halted. He wore only the shirt and breeches in which he had slept. It did not seem he felt the cold at all. His eyes shone, moving over her, going to the black lake.

"I threw the diamond in," she said. "The water's quite deep."

"Under the ice," he said.

"Under the ice."

He looked at the lake with his shining eyes.

"You expected me to crawl about there and scrabble for it. Or did you think the beast would do it, scratching at the ice and howling, while the wolves in the woods hid their eyes?" Laura did not speak. "It will change nothing," he said.

"But it brought you to me," she said, "and I've thrown it away."

"It's served its purpose. It was only a present Hyperion gave you that you've thrown away. Lie down in the snow," he said. "I want you now."

She had thought herself a savage, so she did what he said. Bitter as fire the cold met her back. Fearful, the cold burnt her breasts, but next the flame of his mouth ran over them. Freezing and heat dashed her. She climbed through stages of oblivion towards the forge's heart. Above, the dead sky wheeled. And his face was covered with a gold-leaf of hair. He was the beast and the demon, coupling with her.

She heard herself screaming as her body convulsed. *This is what he has made me.* The sky engorged with her cries, which plunged to earth far away. She seemed to lie in the atmosphere, expelled from her own flesh.

Then she was pulled down again, and Daniel lay on her, and the cold burnt. She made out the thin bleating of the lamb on the terrace, and she wanted to go to it, her child.

'Tonight is the first night of the full moon. Tonight it will happen. Here, therefore, I must end.'

In the hothouse, its heat unmaintained, the fruit and flowers were dying. The chalcedony grapevine had turned black, its beads mummified raisins. Hyperion filled his arms with cold-burned roses.

In the salon, he spread the long table with a scalloped white cloth, and laid it scrupulously, as he had watched the housemaids lay tables, when a child. He set fourteen places, and the place at the table's head. He arranged candles to either side down the table's length, and put the roses into two great blanched bowls. On a stand he built the withering oranges and bright ruined apples into a mountain. He had seen such arrangements made often, and their result more often still. His skill amused him. From his cellar he had brought out a kingly champagne, and from early morning, when he began, he had been drinking it.

He had lighted the fire in the large fireplace, and the cut wood stood ready. Gradually the snow melted from the floor, but not completely, for Hyperion had left the long window ajar. There the snow lay crisp and, beyond, the acres of snow and the white sky, which, with afternoon, turgidly thickened.

Despite the fire the room was obdurately cold. The beautiful champagne kept this from him. He loved the champagne and went to it trustingly. It did not fail him. He reached the gentle first fine plateau of drunkenness, from which it is possible to view the fall of worlds philosophically. The wine was good enough that, with care, it would lift him and hold him high above what came. He saluted it with glasses of perfect crystal.

In his study he had arranged things, and tidied his papers. He finished his letter to his dead aunt as the light began to go.

'And so I draw away from land. What a foolish and meaningless life it has been, and yet I enjoyed it. I still have my

chance, to run out into the snow. But I don't want to take that way, which in any case I think would be pointless. The drifts are impassable. He would find me, after moonrise. And I belong here. This is mine. This is all I have. How far away Laura is now, as if she had become a star. I mistook her. Who is she?

'But well, dear aunt, the day is sinking down. I must dress for my champagne dinner and take my seat in the banquet hall.

'I do not believe this will reach you. I do not believe, although I am going where you have gone, that I will meet you there.'

The red fire crackled on the hearth.

There the armchairs and the cushions had once been grouped, and Laura sat, queen of the little court, telling her story. All gone now.

The fire cast rouged shadows about the room. The only other light came from the candles at the upper end of the table. The banqueter had not lit them all. Their flames were cool and still, for no wind moved on the landscape outside or came in at the open window. And only the fire made sound, with now and then the small quiet clink of the bottle on the crystal.

On Hyperion's elegant plate, the peelings of an apple he had slowly eaten. The sculpted silver knife, alone of all the cutlery to be used, rested on the plate's rim.

Hyperion drank, at intervals. His face was young and calm. A slight smile drew up his mouth, let it go, presently drew it up again. He ·sat facing the open window across the room, waiting for the night to step in over the sill.

Half an hour ago, moonrise.

Would there be time to uncork another bottle? Yes,

surely. He separated the glass neck from the cork deftly; it scarcely made a noise. The glittering foam of drink splashed into the goblet.

"Light," Hyperion said aloud, "that's what it is. Wine, and light." He drank. "How wonderful to have both."

Through the window the black was solid above the glimmer of the snow.

Nothing moved. No sound.

"On such a night," said Hyperion. He drank the champagne. He saw the room from a distance, and felt his face smile again. "There never was such a night." Miles away, a dog barked, in another country. Hyperion listened, amazed. Beyond the tall transparent walls that stretched from earth to heaven, other lives existed and would continue. "Blessed are the dead," said Hyperion, "for they are dead." The dog stopped barking. Hyperion paused, and then he drank. The dog did not bark again.

In the window, the sheen of the snow intensified. The full moon was reaching it, bringing it alive.

Hyperion watched. Never had he beheld the action of the moon so evident. But there had never before been a moon like this one. Partly he had the urge to get up and go out, to see. To see this gargantuan and staring moon, enormous, brushing the tops of the hills. But he did not leave his chair at the table's head. He might be interrupted. There would be no sense in that.

Most of the bottle was gone. Might there be time——

The fire hissed and danced. A shower of damp soot had spattered into it.

In fascination, Hyperion turned his head to look instead at the hearth.

The fire steadied. Then came a gush, a rush, like gravel; the flames folded sideways and smoke unravelled into the room.

"Something wicked," said Hyperion.

He filled the goblet briskly, up to the brim, the last of the wine.

Blackness crashed on to the fire. The blaze did not go out, but flared up again in jets, and the room was rocked to a jumping torchlight.

A long black form, like a stick of burnished stone, slid from the chimney down into the incendiary plain.

This stick was not like anything, had no reference. Then the long tendons flexed in it. It was a limb. It had a black pad, and huge claws spread in the bed of the fire.

The chimney gave birth.

A second darkness followed the forelimb out.

A head protruded down into the hearth. The head of night. Two gleaming jewels were in it. They moved. The muzzle wrinkled. It was alive.

The rest came out in a black bolt. There was chaos, and then creation stood up, in the fire, which licked it hungrily.

Hyperion Worth saw the shape which was not like that he had read of, that was like a pig or a bear, that was not like a wolf. The back and haunches and the articulated posts of the legs, the ruffed thunder of the head hanging there with the snout crinkling off and the bladed teeth and the black tongue. The eyes had no intelligence. They were like the eyes of something clockwork.

Hyperion addressed them. "Welcome." He raised his glass.

The werewolf bounded from the hearth. It sprang up on to the table. It was on fire, outlined by darting buds of flame, and it burned, and did not burn. Yet, as it passed, the unlit candles ignited with a sizzle, one by one; they leapt alight, beginning at once to melt, the wicks curling out of them.

It trod on porcelain plates, over the silver service of the table. The white and pink roses with their brown patina brushed against its ugly flawless burning body. A rose burst into flame, and cinders drifted to the cloth.

It came to the mound of fruits. It seemed to look down at them. Untouched, oranges rolled from the platter and off on to the floor.

"Your good health."

Hyperion drained the glass, and let it drop. It shattered. The beast turned. Hyperion began to laugh.

The beast looked back at him. It launched itself like an engine. It struck Hyperion in the breast and bore him over. Hyperion fell, laughing. He lay under the beast, laughing, and it tore him wide open; but he was on the height, the pain lay in the valley, and only there the blood burst. He beheld his own viscera ripped away, and night crouched on him, its hide wriggling with blood and fire. "Love your enemy," said Hyperion. The claws sheared through his neck, the spinal cord. His eyes were still glowing and full of laughter. Hyperion's lips said, without sound, "I love you." The silken champagne bubbled from his severed belly; his eyes set. His mouth set in its smile.

A bird's nest tumbled into the fire from the rifled chimney.

The candleflames bent and straightened.

She had performed her penance, and how simple it had been. The dead faces in the coffins, embalmed for her perusal. Only one mouth a little twisted. And now. What was there to fear? Fairy tales? They were meaningless, and did she not know better?

How terrible the moon, not white at all but almond pink in the dark blue sky. And the lunar country of the snow.

In some part of her she knew it all, as if she had been told. But Laura rose above knowledge as she had risen above ignorance.

She moved about her chamber, and she pondered if she should stay there. It was only night, after all. Another night. Daniel had left her, but of course he would leave her sometimes. And the moon was full, but it was simply the moon.

The lamb sat by the fire, with its front feet tucked under. The emeralds were now inseparable from it. It had shown no signs of unease.

Nor had there been any outcry or alarm.

Laura hesitated before her mirror. She wore one of the black dresses, but her hair lay loose. She remembered her mother's admonition, *"It looks its best unbound"*—the contrivance to catch Hyperion Worth.

She went to the lamb and touched its head.

"What shall mamma do?"

And heard her own words, startled. For she now addressed the lamb as she had heard old women do their lap-dogs, as if she could never have any child but this one.

Laura went out of the room and shut the door. She carried a lighted oil-lamp with her, for the passageways were dark, save where the moon burned through. She was aware of the gothic element of this, as if from a novel: the lone woman with her light passing along the sombre funnels of a house wildly striped with moonshine.

She came to Hyperion's study. It was cold and empty; he might have been gone a week.

Methodically she went down the wide stairway, into the cavern of the hall, which had become a wintry cave indeed. How loud her footsteps on the floor. She turned aside to the parlour, but it too was vacant, with a stale neglected air.

So she made her way to the ballroom.

It was, after all, like a scene from a story. The moon came in at every one of the glass doors, and the space was white and void and stark as if stripped by a merciless sun of ice. Into it the crystallized chandeliers depended like snowflakes in a microscope.

Through this waste of white, a pencil line of brownish colour showed. The salon door was ajar. The brownness faded, and pulsed up. A fire was burning in the salon.

She moved towards it, reached the door and opened it, and went through. "Hyperion . . ."

Two or three candles were alight on the table. Others had melted down into grotesque shapes. Flowers and spilled fruit. The window gaped. It was freezing.

There was a horrible stench. A girl of the farms, as she had been, she knew it in a moment. And so she attained a pinnacle of terror in a few seconds, before she even saw. But then her lamp picked out what lay beyond the table: all that was left of the man she had married, unbeliev-able.

Under the pink-white moon, over the lunar slopes, the woman walked now with her lamp, following the walls of the house.

Never mind the cold.

Laura did not know how she had come there. But she had a purpose in her walking. She was walking away from the terror in the room. Yet the terror had come with her.

Soon I'll be there.

But she did not know where she went.

She came around the house, and stood below the ter-

race. Behind her all the windows were in darkness. The
house was only a rock.

Below, the white lawns ran to the grey lake.

At the edge of the lake, on the ice, something was. It
was black, and had a form. To Laura it was like a wolf. A
type of wolf with a huge unwieldy head raised up.

She stood on the snow with her burning light. The
beast on the lake could come at her in an instant. But she
was not afraid of it. She was only afraid.

Just then, it turned. The awful mass of head swung
about. It looked at her. It must be looking at her, high-
lighted on the whiteness with her lamp. But it had no
plan to attack her, so much was obvious. She was an
adjunct to it, some component that was acceptable.

Her blood ran with the ice.

Yet the thing on the lake looked away from her again.
It raised its muzzle. It was staring at the moon as if at any
minute it could lift away into the sky, sucked up into the
disc.

Laura was hypnotized. She was changing to glass or a
pillar of salt. She must force herself. Her feet were
rooted to the spot.

On the lake the beast gazed up at the moon.

Laura pried her feet loose from the earth, one after
the other.

Beneath the wall of the park, the ancient lane dipped
deep as the bed of a river. Trees overhung it, a canopy,
and the snow which had not fallen thickly into it was
frozen hard as stone. Footsteps were visible, memories of
a life which the snow's endurance had driven under-
ground, and aloft; but no longer were there the footprints
of two men who had gone out this way, and later returned to the house above.

Laura was clad sensibly for a journey, in the opulent clothes her husband, torn in pieces, eviscerated and beheaded, had given her against the winter. She was alone. She had fed the lamb and shut it in her room of tapestries. It was in no more danger than she herself had been. She would come back for it, this toy child. She would come back with village men, and with a priest, with soldiers if she could, with every appurtenance of violence. She would be credited, because she must. It would be by day, in safety. She would lead them to him. And if they could not kill him, he must be confined, inside some cell of steel he could not break, under the ground or in the sea. She said a prayer as she picked along the lane, but it was remote to her. Daniel, not God, was omnipresent.

Sometimes there would be a little sound, snow dislodged by its own weight, wood cracking in the cold. But she would expect the thing from the lake to leap down to her, to bar her way. And what would she do if that happened? But it did not happen.

She did not think of omnipresent Daniel. She had been shown the *reason* for Daniel. What had brought her to him, what had bound her, it was *that*—that thing which had stared upward at the moon. She had betrayed Hyperion, her true friend.

She went quite fast, for she was strong and had a natural quality of balance, and all her determination. Terror had slendered to a tiny mote at the bottom of her brain. She kept it there firmly, and trudged on.

Once she slipped and fell against a leaning branch, which saved her. Then she pictured Hyperion's fall, as she had postulated it, out in the desert of snow with no one to help him. "God forgive me," she said aloud. That was her subsequent prayer, more vital than the first.

The night was awesome, so big, so frigid, so utterly in league with darkness. But Laura held it off.

She did not know where the lane led, save that it went by the area where the thunderbolt, the meteor, had come down. Beyond she would come on some village or house. She would appeal to them, mildly at first; she would say Daniel was mad, and describe what he had done. Either in their minds or in their psyches they would realize what this meant, as in her own way she had understood the substance of her lover.

The dark became opaque. The moon was setting somewhere over the high banks of the lane.

Laura was not tired. A dreadful elation keyed her up. Hours had gone by, but other hours would be dispensed with.

Suddenly the lane went very black. The moon had gone.

Laura stopped, and in the distance she heard a bird singing, out of the night.

The lane rose towards this music. She climbed up in the blackness and the song ebbed away. But instead a vague glow began to come. She thought it was the sunrise; and an instinctive gladness made her go more quickly, as if to meet with it.

A glacial hillside drew the lane up from its riverbed. On either side of the path the roots of trees struck from the snow, and Laura caught them to assist herself. The last yards, in her ornate cloak, she crawled and scrambled like an animal, and so emerged on the top of the slide, into a nightmarish upland.

An avenue of broken and felled trees led across a jagged plain, which in places smoked, to a hill which burned.

In all other directions the snow piled between colossal

stones. There showed, too, what might have been a track, which was now a coil of blackest ice, choked soon enough by great drifts of white. Other hill crests, quilted white, hemmed in the vista.

Laura stared. This was a terminus. It would not be possible to go much farther across such terrain.

Along the slope, in the wrecked wood, grimly touched off and on by the flame from a hill, a ramshackle caravan was canted.

Laura approached it with misgiving. In such a hovel she had not thought to seek for assistance. But no smoulder came from the chimney pipe of the dwelling, and when, with difficulty, she had gained the door, she found it swinging open. Inside the caravan was nothing, nothing at all; it was a shell, and snow had carpeted the floor.

Laura looked away, between the riven trees, towards the fiery hill. For a second, this was a view in Hell. But it was only that here the meteor had hit the earth, the burning only the insistent heat not yet gone out.

And then the bird sang again, over the hill top, sweet and harsh, a rose upon a thorn.

Real light was beginning in the sky, the milk of dawn; it was not only her fancy.

Laura went between the trees, her energy leaving her, to be replaced by a fey ecstatic fixity.

The sun came up under a hill, and woke the crowns of the land. The hill above the red coal of the meteor was a long green apron, purpled over by violets, and gold with daffodils in splashing sheets. Hares were feeding there, and in the rising heaven a knot of birds flew back and forth, as if over a flowering island in the ocean.

Tears welled from Laura's eyes. She covered her face with her hands and wept.

But the bird was singing to her again. It was a robin on

a torn black branch. Beyond, along the avenue, something gleamed like the daffodils.

She went to it, and saw a heap of golden coins laid out exactly in a circle. They were a poor man's dream, the kind of treasure trove Jason Wheelwright had been fond of hankering after, riches spread out on the ground. But now they seemed to serve the purpose of a marker. For at their centre a black shard was standing up in the snow.

The shard was smoothed at its upper end, and it was unlike anything, anything ever seen or visible, except for the greater body above which had plunged into the hill. Seeing the shard, you could not miss that it had been chipped off from its parent the meteor, chipped and burnished, and sunk point downwards in the cooling snow of earth.

A word was scratched clearly into it, filled in with some white deposit. *Terumah.*

Laura lent down and drew the shard out of the snow. She observed the word exactly. What did it mean?

The point was sharp. Thin and long, like a tooth.

The robin flew away to the green hill.

Laura wiped her eyes, and turned, to look back the way she had come, holding the shard of the meteor in her hand.

3

 The ship of the air, the balloon, had floated
for miles above the land of snow and ice.
She had herself all the lustre of the winter,
a gaseous melon of silver and white, with
only her little round basket below to reveal she had any
purpose other than simply to *be,* up in the vanilla sky.
Her name was on the basket, too, in silver lettering:
Duchess of Palmaria. Ethereally she seemed to drift, but
she had a goal, to which her sailor-captain was gradually
guiding her. His attention was given mostly to this, but in
the intervals, he watched the ground. Such a winter! The
country white from end to end, its rivers frozen. Here
and there the leaden dead eye of a pond, or the dark
steaming hutches of a village under its lids of snow. Once
a flight of black rooks arose, which circled the *Duchess*
round, shouting to each other, but the kiss of her furnace
breath frightened them away.

Unlike his vessel, the balloonist was a meaty, ruddy
man, in greatcoat and cap, his face partitioned by a thick
moustache. His pleasure in the journey had nothing
dreamlike to it. There had been a sum of money, and
there was to be more. That summer he had entertained
at fairs. A horse in harness strapped to the balloon was

taken up, he riding on its back in the air, like a prince of the Arabian Nights. But the horse, more often than not frightened, had defecated on the heads of the crowd below. With the cold came the promise of this job, easy and lucrative, and if eccentric, no more so than flying horses.

A consultation with his map confirmed for the balloonist that he was nearing his destination. He made adjustments to the gores. The range of hills was sweeping down into a valley, and there below, sure enough, was the house as it had been described, a dainty palace with peaks and turrets, balconies and spires, all heavily iced over. He must set down upon the lawn above that black mirror of lake. Not simple, perhaps, for one who did not know the *Duchess*, but he knew her, and on this still day was quite confident.

He steered her in above the trees and let go her anchor.

The carpet of world bloomed up, taking on an extra dimension. The hills rounded and swayed behind. The pretty anchor scratched the polish of the lake of ice.

Like a feather, the balloon alighted on the snow.

The balloonist busied himself with the furnace, and the gores. He left the balloon inflated, for she was to be ogled. But when he looked again at the rich man's mansion, he felt his first anxiety. For the whole household had been due to come out and give him welcome, so Mr Worth had vowed. And no one at all was there.

And then, a glass window opened, and out on to the terrace stepped a female in a black dress, like the rooks. *Someone's died.* The thought assailed him bleakly. Then he lowered the short silver ladder, and got out of the *Duchess of Palmaria*, and went to learn.

The way over the snow-lawn was not nice, and when he came to the bastion of the terrace, he plodded along it to the steps, which seemed mostly a slide of ice. He looked up.

She was a very beautiful woman, on the terrace, in a lady's mourning gown, with her roan-red hair loose like a minx's. Beside her stood a dog. But no, it was a sort of lamb, almost grown up into a sheep, its barbaric coat brushed like gossamer, and a choker of shining green stones round its neck.

"Good-day, madam. Can I inquire for Mr Worth?"

She looked at him with midnight eyes, blacker than her clothes.

"Did he invite you here?" she said.

"Indeed he did. A show. To please his wife."

"I," she said, "am his wife." She blinked. She said, "His widow."

As I thought then. "Pray accept my condolences, madam. What a dreadful thing. He was young."

"And kind, and good," she said. Her midnight eyes were dry. Certainly, they were hotter than her hair. He gazed at her in unease. "You mustn't remain," she said.

"Well, Mrs Worth. What can I say? I've been put to some trouble to fulfil your husband's request. I was to expect . . . remuneration."

"I'm sorry," she said.

Was she mad? Something so gorgeous and so feral, her tide of hair unpinned, her narrow waist snapped in. He had seen an actress look like this, in a city play, as she went to murder her foe.

"Do you notice the balloon? The *Duchess of Palmaria*. Brought to your estate at Mr Worth's request. And my own expense."

"Yes?" From her height she stared down on him. The young sheep in the necklace stared too.

"It's difficult," he said. "I regret troubling you at such a time."

"You want money?" she said.

"I'm forced to say that I do. The voyage, you understand."

She looked away towards the balloon. Silver and niveum, it rested on the white lawn, heavenly and pragmatic, a mirage made usable. A tear that could fall up instead of down.

"Come on to the terrace," she said.

Slipping and slithering, clinging to the stone banister, he fought his way over the steps and dropped to his knees inadvertently before the lamb. It moved delicately aside.

"Follow me," she said, "into the house."

They went into a pleasant, undusted parlour. Her skirt swept snow into the room, and he brought it in on his boots. No one minded, apparently.

She led him on into a large hall with an unlit fireplace. The house was cold as the grounds outside. Not a single servant displayed himself. The little sheep pattered at the woman's side.

He had a sudden dramatic confused idea she had walled herself up in the mansion and meant to freeze to death, like some primal queen at the demise of her husband. And he had interrupted.

They crossed the hall. She drew him through a corridor and an anteroom, and flung wide the white doors of a ballroom, also white—with snow.

The balloonist gaped. It was a scene from a drama about a polar princess. Strands of snow had come from a doorway and crept along the floor. The chandeliers were stalactites of ice. A long stair led into the room, made for entrances. There was a complex clock which had stopped.

He did not say anything. He kept his own counsel.

The red-haired woman paused before the door of the adjoining chamber. She raised her pale and perfect face, composed.

"There is," she said, "a madman in this house. At the full moon, and of course it is the full moon, incredible power and brutality encompass him. During the day he sleeps. He sleeps now, until moonrise. This madman killed my husband. You must see for yourself."

She moved into the room, an elegant salon. He went after her with feelings of dislike.

Windows ran to the floor and they stood open, and it was here the snow had got in; it lay on the carpet in islands.

The table was encased by frost. It had been laid for some dinner party, with fine china and silver, goblets and candles. Crumpled, blackened flowers crowded in bowls. The candles had burned; some had poured from their sconces. A plate or two had been disrupted.

Fringes of ice were on the drapes. Beyond the windows whiteness shrieked at the sky. He had anticipated coloured clothes, hot wine with spices, flashing fires. The bitter day, unassuaged, increased its sadism.

"Look around you," the woman said.

"At what, madam, would you have me look?"

She did not reply.

The balloonist, lord of the sky chariot, stamped his feet against the indoor frost and snow. He turned his head unwillingly.

He saw a cluster of dull red glass on a wall. It was odd. He peered about and saw more of it. Something had sprayed up, and frozen. There was a fallen chair.

He did not accept what he saw, and moved intuitively into the room to observe more closely. And found he must accept it, in fact. On the floor lay a corpse, pre-

served by winter. But more than that. A body cloven and
its machinery pulled out and twisted round the furniture.
The objects were pallid now or dark, tripe and iron in the
stony cold. On a battlefield, once, he had seen such a
sight. He had been younger then, and harder.

There was a human head by the fireplace. The face was
all shrunken and swollen and out of shape, and preserv-
ing winter had glazed the eyes like bonbons. The head
smiled, but he had seen that too, in that other arena of
death. Impossible to tell anything about this carved being, save it had been youthful, and a man. And, a rich
man, actually, for the coat was very fine under its glacier
claret lace of blood.

The balloonist lifted his eyes and looked back at the
doorway, to find out what the woman did.

She stood there, that was all, impassive, black and red
and white.

The balloonist straightened, macabrely conscious of
himself as a figure of fun.

"Is it—is this—this is your husband?"

"Yes it is. What the madman has left of him."

"You said—the villain's asleep?"

"He is. But you must go away quickly."

"To fetch some help."

"If you like."

"Yet you——"

"You see he hasn't harmed me." Yes, he could see
that. "But you he'll kill." A sudden wave of sheer terror
burst over him. Instinctively again, he moved, this time
towards the open windows.

On the floor, between the islands of the snow, the
sneer of dead laughter pursued him. And over there the
woman stood immune, with the lamb-creature at her
skirt.

"You must hurry away," she said.

"The country's impassable," he said, "on foot. I've seen. The balloon will take a while to prepare. The furnace, you see, must be built up high to make enough heat, and so get pressure——"

"Don't delay," said the woman implacably.

He had no thought of speaking again of money, no want for hospitality. He had reached the windows. He put out one foot and sank into a drift of white quicksand. A cry broke from him, and so he learned how unnerved he had become, he who had ridden horses in the sky.

"The nearest village . . ." he said. "I'll do what I can. It will depend on how she sails. The ability to steer such a craft . . ." He was outside now. The cold pierced him and he recalled the blaze of the furnace up under the quivering gores, the soul of the balloon. "You should come with me, Mrs Worth."

She glanced at him. With relief he acknowledged she had refused.

As he trod back around the picturesque grisly house, he shook and muttered, his brain churning on its own way, trying to be clear. It was all insanity, all she had said. Had she killed the man herself? She looked capable of it. But such strength——

He longed to run, probably tumbling and breaking an ankle. His blood boiled to rush into the cover of the trees, up the hills. Somehow he sensed this would be futile, that somehow the madman would catch up to him, like the giant in a legend, *Fee-fi-fo-fum.*

Did eyes watch from the blind windows?

He must return to the *Duchess;* that grand lady would stick by him. Sling the coke into her furnace, stretch the gores, throw out the ballast, cut the anchor—no matter where she went, so long as it was far from here. "Don't panic. Be a man." But he was trotting now, around the walls of eyes, towards the lake.

Up in the air the raven flew, over the chalky sky. It was a bird of bone, black, carrying a scroll in its beak.

"Do not delay now," said Surim Bey. "Go elsewhere." He wore his spotless house robes, and brilliant rings. "There was a sultan who fed books of learning to the birds, that they might be wise."

Coins glittered in the pool at his feet and the shadow of the bone bird passed over. It dropped the scroll, which, when it struck the ground, turned into a yellow veil.

"Kill me," said Marjannah.

"No, I'll leave you. You'll be safe."

Daniel saw the tapestry, sapphire and viridian, on the wall, the unicorn and maidens. He lay on Laura's pillared bed, its covers still quick with the cream and russet scent of Laura's body.

He thought of his mother, Jenavere, teaching him how to pray. Then her image faded, and he sat up.

Mauveine winter dusk was in the window. Soon, it would be time.

It was as if his mind was before him, saying *Shall I think now?* And he assented quietly. For it was not necessary to think, had not been so for a vast while. How unimportant everything had become. For three nights of each month he *was*. He did not remember, but just as Surim Bey had craved for his drugs and his sex, so Daniel craved for his true life, the life that came with the full moon.

And now he thought about it, gently. And wonderingly he went over, in his thoughts, the events that lay between. Was this house now his? Yes, for he had killed the other man. The man and the house were really immaterial. But Laura was his lust, the immutable balance of flesh that complemented the moon-lust of the spirit, the life-urge that was the reverse of the face of murder and destruction. Laura, who had thrown the diamond into the lake. Would he fish for it in the spring? What bait should he use?

Daniel lay down again. His body was, as usual, heavy and feverish, tingling and aching, readying itself to leap, expand, turn inside-out, releasing the embryo at its core.

Thinking did not merit attention. He had done enough.

He shut his eyes, and just then the door opened. And with his preternatural hearing he discerned the entry of the lamb into the room. After this, the swish of Laura's skirts.

Lazily, Daniel lifted his eyelids and watched her. She came and sat down on the bed, drawing the lamb up on to her lap. Laura began to undo the front of her dress. She peeled away its black casements and slipped down the top of her under-bodice. Her breasts, whiter than the white silk ribbons, glowed like two moons, with jasmine flowers of rose. She coaxed the head of the lamb, kindly, tenderly. She gave it her breast, and like a baby it sucked.

"I'll never have a child," she said.

Daniel watched her. Then he reached out to describe her other moon breast with his fingers.

"What a child it would be," he said, "if you could."

Carefully she disengaged the lamb, and set it on the floor. It walked towards the fire and, bowing its head, chewed at the carpet there.

Laura turned to Daniel. She sank against his body, and lay over him. She stared into his eyes.

"All this while," she said, "you were asleep with it under you. I believed you'd find it out. But you haven't. I searched in Hyperion's books and I discovered the word. What it meant. *That which is raised up. The Sacrifice.*" She slid her hand around his head and among the pillows, and got something out, which was black as the bird of bone.

Daniel watched her. She arched up and sat back. And then she raised the blackness up above her, over her head in both her hands.

Kill me, Marjannah said.

Laura's arms, her entire upper torso, came whirling down, and Daniel felt a blow against his chest like the roar of a mighty gong.

Some ceaseless movement within him *stopped.*

Amazed, he opened his eyes wide. Scalding liquid was running over him, and in his body a fount had erupted, blocking and stifling him. He could not speak. But in his eyes she saw the dazzle of other memory, another blow, a bullet in his heart, the change beneath the moon, the healing. There was no death.

"He told me," Laura said, kneeling over him, her hands loose and empty. "Nothing can hurt you. Nothing of the earth."

The shard of the meteor, the fallen star, protruded from his breast like a black bone.

Laura eased herself from the bed. She went away across the chamber. The fire lit her like a painted statue.

"You'll alter," she said, "but *that* can't. It will stay in you, lodged in you. And in what you become. It will kill you. *Kill it.* Was meant and made to."

A strangeness went through his eyes then. Even over the room she saw it. There was no name for what it was. And the eyes closed.

Laura left the bedroom swiftly, the lamb at her heels.

She went to Hyperion's study, where she had set another fire, and where the books lay all across the desk, and she had found the drawing of the hot-air balloon. She was not afraid. She did not fear a beast. She was past fear, and past all things. She took the lamb into her lap, and rocked it in the firelight.

There they sat, and it grew dark.

Later, the sky changed, and the moon rose, and she heard something go by the door, something sluggish and dragging, the scrape of claws like a burden. Or she imagined that she did.

"Hush," she said to the lamb. "Go to sleep, my love."

The sailor-captain of the flying ship had brought her back to readiness. Her furnace gushed and palpitated, throwing a fierce light upward, and away along the levels of the snow. The ballast was out, the anchor shorn. Now he could only wait for her to lift, and she took her time, with the waywardness of the Duchess she was. Only one more breath it would seem was needed. He attended on it, in the basket; and as he did, his terror enlarged and clung and roped him like a weed.

And then, from the pile of that foul, uncanny, snowed-over mansion up the lawn, something came out.

It was black and low. A shadow that was real. It was a dog. A huge dog.

As this happened, the moon arrived on the roofs of the house, and all the snow flared up. The balloonist of the *Duchess of Palmaria* saw the huge black dog begin to come towards him over the flaming sheet of white, and behind it there ran out a trail, like a jet satin scarf.

In God's glory, what was it? It seemed to crawl, and yet the power of it, the fearsome strength . . . and it came back to the man in the basket, what he had seen lying on the salon floor. And for no reason, without reason, he knew the crawling, creeping, dog-like thing must not get near to him. And all at once the awful impulse to run overcame him, as it almost had before, and now irresistibly. And pushing himself from the basket of his craft, the man thumped over into the snow, and prized himself free, and turned and staggered away, in silence, in the noiseless terror of nightmare and night.

The beast lurched on, slow, and never more like an engine, but one which failed. Its burlesque head drooped, its muzzle was in the snow. Its eyes were buttons. Only the moon pushed it, and the blood rivered behind it from the staring shard in its guts, which had remained.

After a long while, it reached the glimmering tear-drop of the balloon, and here it gazed around itself, mindless, motivated. And presently it put up its terrible limbs on the frame of the basket, and so hauled itself up, and over, and dropped inside.

The *Duchess of Palmaria* shuddered. And took her last hot breath.

Like a bubble, so weightless and so fair, she wafted off into the air, she flew into the height of the enormous sky.

She was half a world above the earth, and the moonlight drenched her. Like a wonderful silver seed she hung in heaven, but the moon was the fruit of the tree. And the monster in her belly swung itself against her side and its head went up, went up to see, to see. Never so close, never so intimate, the light, the lesser of the two great lights that had been made to rule the night. With the blade deep inside its darkness, eating it alive, killing it as promised, what it was, what it had been when a man, the beast held up its head as the balloon floated. The beast stared with the fathomless discs of its eyes, and was borne higher and higher, away and away. Lost in the moon.

*An exciting preview
of the new gothic
horror novel*

PERSONAL DARKNESS

by

Tanith Lee

Coming from Dell in July 1994

Chapter One

The girl in the rain:

He had been watching her for about twenty minutes.

Timothy's plan had been to clean his car, but the rain had beaten him to it. He had gone to the window of the room his mother called the living room, and his father, obstinately, the lounge, and was looking out at the water sluicing the street. He did not wonder if it was raining at the country hotel where his parents were spending the weekend. The only second thought he gave them was one of pleasure in their absence.

The Mini Metro shone like blue tinfoil in the downpour. And across the road, between the green cascades of the raining trees, was this girl.

She looked tall, though he thought actually she was not, very. It was her slimness which created the impression. She had a marvelous figure, in her tight-belted raincoat. And plastered all over her was a thick soaked spillage of jet-black hair. Her face was pale: her eyes were black with makeup and her lips scarlet. She was just amazing. And wet. She was certainly that, simply standing there under the gushing tap of the rain, staring across at the house.

Timothy assumed she could not see him through the net curtain. And yet he had the notion she was waiting for him to make some signal.

Finally, after twenty-five minutes, he made it.

He lifted the curtain and waved at her.

He might have been a ghost. She did not react.

"Fucking blind," said Timothy. It was nice to say something like this in the living room, without his mother going up the wall. He had to be careful at work, too, where Mr. Cummings would come scuttling along the rows of computers like a poisonous wood louse. "Got those figures yet, Timothy? Mr. Andrews is waiting." And, breathing his halitosis briskly over Timothy's shoulder, "You should wash your mouth out. I don't want that kind of language."

Timothy forgot his mother and Mr. Cummings. The terrific girl was crossing the street, toward him.

She was past his car, up on the pavement, coming through the gateposts. She had great legs, and weird shoes. Then she was on the steps.

Timothy turned round and stood in the big room with its pallid mother-chosen satin-finish walls and parent-selected furniture and objects. He, now, waited.

The doorbell buzzed.

Timothy had one curious moment. He felt faintly affronted, assailed. Threatened? Then that went, it was childish, and he told himself that maybe he could be onto something good here.

When he opened the door, he grinned at once, to let her see he liked the look of her. She was sensational, even though her eye makeup was running in the wet, which he wished it had not been. Her clothes were pretty odd, too. The raincoat looked as if it had come out of a dustbin. His grin sagged a little.

"Hi," said Timothy, defensively.

The girl said, "Mrs. Watt?"

"No, sorry." Was he relieved?

"Yes," said the girl. Her voice was clear and quite flat, like a soft musical chime wrongly played. "Mrs. Watt lives here."

"She doesn't. Never heard of her."

"This is the house," said the girl. She paused. She said, "She lives with her daughter, Liz. Liz and Brian."

Something plucked at Timothy's memory. Had the people Dad bought the house from last year been called Liz and Brian? Everyone had got quite matey when the deal was struck.

"I think—they've moved. The people before us."

The girl stared into his face. Her eyes were not only made up black, they *were* black. Black as black paint. He had never seen a white woman with eyes as dark as that, maybe not a black woman either.

"She's gone," said the girl. There was a note of something after all. Was it regret?

"I'm afraid so." It was fairly obvious no possessive, well-heeled mother had packed the girl off on such a journey. Frankly, she looked as if she had been living rough. Her ankle boots, a glance had told him, were broken, and newspaper protruded soggily from the cracks. She had a split plastic shoulder bag.

"What'll you do?" asked Timothy.

The girl stood and looked at him, and behind her the rain poured as if forever.

And behind *him* was the pale yellow house, with all its rooms at his disposal, open as a hand to Saturday afternoon and Saturday night and all Sunday until ten in the evening, when they would be back.

"Why don't you come in a minute," said Timothy. "You must be wet."

She did not hesitate, neither did she thank him. She walked straight into the hall, where the big mirror reflected her darkly above the wilting flowers his fussy weekending mother had forgotten to throw out.

He thought of things in horror movies that had to be invited over the threshold. But only for a second. At once she took off her raincoat. She wore a scruffy, skimpy black skirt into which was tucked a gray T-shirt with holes. The rain had got through the topcoat easily and she was damp. Everything clung. She was slender as a bone, with big perfect breasts that had little wicked points. Her hair hung to her bottom in black stripes and water drops ran off it. The presage of excitement was fulfilled. He was aroused.

"You'd better have a towel," said Timothy.

He left her in the hall and started up the stairs. At the linen cupboard, out of her sight, he made a joyful gesture to himself. Then hurried back with the big fluffy towel.

Better not to leave her alone too long, just in case.

First of all he made tea in the kitchen. As he was doing this she said she was hungry. So he grudgingly put some bread in the toaster. She sat on one of the stools at the breakfast bar, with her hair up in the towel. The eye makeup was in unwiped trickles down her face, but her red lips were pristine even after she ate the toast, very quickly, as if she were starving. So he had to offer to make some more. She accepted.

If she had been living rough, he realized, she was

probably dirty. She did not smell. The rain must have cleaned her somewhat, but it would not be enough.

"Would you like a bath? You must be cold."

"All right," she said.

He ran the hot water for her into the avocado-colored bath, and put in some of his mother's expensive bath foam. He had always liked the scent of this, although recently not on his mother. She was too old for that sort of perfume, though he still felt he had to give it to her at Christmas.

The girl went into the bathroom with a T-shirt of his own Timothy had sportingly offered her. He hoped she had clean underclothes in her nasty plastic bag. He could hardly give her his mother's, that would be going too far.

He wanted to see his protégée improved. Know she was cleaned up. If she looked all right, he might take her out to dinner at the Italian.

When she came back, she looked wonderful. She had washed her hair and dried it, bathed, and redone her makeup. Her hair, dry, was like frayed black silk, and the new black T-shirt, though it clung rather less, still emphasized her breasts. God knew what he would do about shoes, though. She was now barefoot. Her feet were good, not ugly like so many girls' feet. She must have trimmed her toenails, as she had trimmed the long nails on her fingers, and both sets were now bloodred.

"That's great," said Timothy. "You did look a bit— well. What happened? You ran away from home?"

"Yes," said the girl, without faltering.

"You'll have to go back," he said. At twenty-two, he was more responsible than she. Besides, he would have to unload her before Sunday night.

"I can't," said the girl. She had not told him her name, although he had revealed his as Tim.

"Of course you can. Parents are bloody awful, I know, but they do have their uses."

She regarded him carefully. Her eyes were even more fascinating now the shadow and mascara had been realigned. She looked like a singer. He wished Rob could get a look at her. For a moment he basked in the future enjoyment of telling Rob all about her. Then he and she went into the lounge–living room and had gin and tonics.

"No, you're going to have to go back. You can phone them, if you like. Tell them you're with a girl-friend, or something. You can stay here tonight. Plenty of room." He thought of rolling with her in his narrow bed, squeezed together. Thank God he had kept stocked up. Like Rob said, you never knew your luck.

The girl sat on the sofa, her long legs—even though she was not tall, she had the right proportions —visible almost to the tops of her thighs. No unwanted hair. No tights. Perhaps no pants?

"I can't go back," she said again.

"Come on. Don't be dramatic. Why not?"

"My father," she said. She drank her gin slowly and steadily, like lemonade on a hot afternoon. "My father abused me."

Timothy put down his glass. He was shocked.

"You mean he—you mean he—what do you mean?"

"I mean he slept with me."

"Jesus," said Timothy. "That's fucking disgusting."

"Yes."

Timothy took both their glasses and poured generous gin and tonics. He would have to remember to get replacements from Viney's.

When he handed the girl her drink she was demure and still, as if she had told him nothing very much.

"Does your mother know?" he asked. Under the shock was a dim prurience, curiosity. She had been broken into, and in unacceptable circumstances. This made her less attractive. And more.

"Yes, my mother knew. And my grandmother."

"Didn't they try to stop it?"

"Oh no."

She was matter-of-fact. Suddenly she said, as if awarding him a favor, "My name's Ruth."

"Yeah," said Timothy, and drank his gin.

Could he still chance her in the Italian, where he was? He would have to. He was not going to cook, and already she had had two rounds of toast, a packet of biscuits, and three apples from the fruit stand. Her legs . . . He would have to loan her some jeans. And she could wear his old trainers, the ones he had had when he was thirteen. He had small feet for a man.

Maybe she was lying about her dad.

She was only seventeen. Girls had fantasies. Remember Jean, who said she had slept with David Bowie?

Later, two or three gins later, when he was wondering if perhaps he need not wait until after the Italian dinner, she sidetracked him. She asked, politely, if she could see the house. The drinks had seemed to make no impression on her.

Showing her the house bored him. He was not

proud of it, none of it was his, not even his own room, really.

But then, this Mrs. Watt person who had presumably been her only friend, and not much of one at that, had lived here.

Ruth had already seen the kitchen with its dishwasher, computerized washing machine, ranks of polished knives and utensils, fanged juicers, and endless other gadgets. And the lounge–living room, with china in cupboards, fat TV, *Home and Gardens* on the coffee table, and the music center. Ruth had actually investigated that. But his mother's seldom played highlights from *Swan Lake*, Beethoven, and Dvořák had not held her interest.

The dining room was small, and superfluously glistened from the cleaner's superfluous attentions.

Upstairs, Timothy showed Ruth the bedrooms, and his father's study, quickly. The house had been extended at some time, and there were rooms of various sizes, some now lying fallow. Timothy's was the big room with the inclusive bathroom. Here Ruth paused, looking round at his posters briefly, showing less interest even than before in his music center and discs of *Level 42*. This room too had been recently decorated, but it was not Timothy's taste. He had let his mother choose, not really knowing what his taste in rooms was.

Ruth did look down from here onto the garden, and she remarked, nearly incongruously, "There's the cedar tree."

Apparently Mrs. Watt had mentioned this tree.

Nothing else was said.

They descended again, and Timothy wondered if Ruth would like to see his car, but she would be seeing it anyway when they went out. That should be soon. He was anxious by now with desire, but also hungry. An early dinner, and they could make a long night of it. Bring back some wine. And a video. Something she would like.

Somehow, she struck him after all as slightly child-ish.

He leant her the jeans and trainers, and offered her a spray of the scent that went with the bath foam. In his parents' bedroom he felt a touch savage, and put on Ruth's milk-white ears a pair of large gold earrings. But Ruth, with a peculiar expression, re-moved these.

Another instant of unease then. She had come to him as a gypsy, but what had she been before? Had the possibly fantasized, abusing father been very rich and cultured, hanging on the ears of his courtesan daughter orient jade and priceless pearl?

The blue-for-a-boy car took them neatly down to the *Monte Doro*, which happily opened at six on Sat-urdays.

The tables were robed in russet and apple green, and from the ceiling hung a chandelier of ice-green Perrier bottles. It was not crowded yet, and the man-ager came rustling out and lit their candle hastily.

Timothy was glad he had brought his Visa card. Ruth had a starter of tomato salad with mozzarella and mushrooms, and went on to chicken wrapped in ham with a cream and brandy sauce, new potatoes, broccoli, and carrots. She wanted dessert too, a trifle topped by nuts and cherries, and then some goat cheese and biscuits. Timothy was used to girls who had to watch their weight. Obviously Ruth did not, or else she was making up for time lost in the wilds.

They had a bottle of Frascati with their meal, and Timothy bought another bottle, with the help of his card, to take away with them.

He drove back carefully. He knew he was over the limit but it was not very far, and he reckoned he was a good driver: the drink had not affected him. Besides, he had had only one glass of wine in the restaurant.

The video he had picked up was *Dragonslayer*. He thought Ruth would like this, although he supposed it was fairly absurd. The photography, landscapes, and animation had not pleased him, but he believed the love scene might do something for Ruth. She was young, and female.

To his surprise, the dragon seemed to concern her most.

He had slipped his arm around her as they watched on the sofa before the big screen of the TV.

She grew tense. She did not like it when the hero attacked the dragon. She said, low and harsh, "He's hurt it," and then, "Shake him *off*. Kill him." She did not mean the dragon should die.

And when it did she was hard, like iron, under Timothy's supporting, barely caressive arm.

He had attempted to kiss her before, at the moment of the kiss in the film, and she resisted. He did not press her.

When the film was over he said, "You liked the dragon best."

"It was beautiful," she said.

"How'd you like to be sacrificed to it? Burned up?"

Ruth said primly, "I'd have talked to it. The magician knew how, but he didn't. All the people were stupid. Horrible."

Timothy opened the new bottle of Frascati. To his dismay, Ruth asked if she could eat an orange. He was afraid she had an alcohol hunger and might be sick. But she ate the orange, and another, and nothing else happened.

"You know," said Timothy, settling beside her again, "you're gorgeous. You are. And your hair . . ."

She let him stroke her hair, and next her shoulder, but when he brought his lips near hers again she said, "No, thank you."

Timothy sat up.

"I'm not your father. You have to get over that."

"No I don't."

"Oh, Ruth——"

A car growled out in the street, a lion returning to its lair. He knew its voice, but this was not feasible. No. He heard the car draw to a standstill behind the Mini Metro.

They could not— They had meant to be gone all weekend. *No.*

Intuitively, Timothy's eyes darted about the room. The strewn gin glasses, the wine, the orange peel not quite on the plate, the video box—and Ruth. Smelling of his mother's perfume, barefoot, red in lip and nail. Black as night of eye.

"Oh Christ. Oh fucking shit—"

Feet on the steps.

A rumble of voices.

The key in the lock.

"Timothy?"

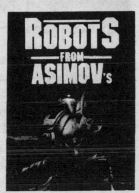